DAW titles by
JENNIFER ROBERSON

THE SWORD-DANCER SAGA
SWORD-DANCER   SWORD-BORN
SWORD-SINGER   SWORD-SWORN
SWORD-MAKER   SWORD-BOUND*
SWORD-BREAKER   SWORD-BEARER*

(THE SWORD-DANCER SAGA is also available in the
NOVELS OF TIGER AND DEL omnibus editions)

CHRONICLES OF THE CHEYSULI
SHAPECHANGERS   A PRIDE OF PRINCES
THE SONG OF HOMANA   DAUGHTER OF THE LION
LEGACY OF THE SWORD   FLIGHT OF THE RAVEN
TRACK OF THE WHITE WOLF   A TAPESTRY OF LIONS

CHEYSULI OMNIBUS EDITIONS
SHAPECHANGER'S SONG   CHILDREN OF THE LION
(Books One and Two)   (Books Five and Six)
LEGACY OF THE WOLF   THE LION THRONE
(Books Three and Four)   (Books Seven and Eight)

THE KARAVANS UNIVERSE
KARAVANS   THE WILD ROAD
DEEPWOOD   DRAGON MOON*

THE GOLDEN KEY
(with Melanie Rawn and Kate Elliott)

ANTHOLOGIES
(as editor)
RETURN TO AVALON
HIGHWAYMEN: ROBBERS AND ROGUES

*Coming soon from DAW Books

JENNIFER ROBERSON

THE WILD ROAD

Book Three of *Karavans*

DAW BOOKS, INC.

DONALD A. WOLLHEIM, FOUNDER

375 Hudson Street, New York, NY 10014

ELIZABETH R. WOLLHEIM

SHEILA E. GILBERT

PUBLISHERS

www.dawbooks.com

For Brian Gross and Frances Robertson Gross,
Tom Watson and Linda Watson,
For help above and beyond at just the right time!

THE
WILD ROAD

Prologue

*F*OR BRODHI, WAITING was well-nigh impossible in such circumstances as these.

He paced because he must. His hands were bound before him, but that did not interfere with his pacing. His body would not resort to stillness even when he wished it. Nor would his mind. It was afire with thoughts, sparking with anger, and altogether unwilling to wait a single moment. But he was trained to anticipate tests, to comprehend that at no time was he completely free of evaluation. And *here* it was far worse than in the human world. This was his own world. Alisanos ran in his blood. Alisanos wreathed his bones. It was, all at once, enemy, parent, lover.

It was even his savior—or possibly his death, depending on the tests.

Brodhi swore viciously. Ruined, all of it. So many human years spent in the human world, accepting the journey, enduring the tests, and yet he was back in Alisanos well before time. He had transgressed. The primaries had the right to declare his journey ended, all the tests failed, and to pronounce sentence upon him. Death was possible but not likely. Worse, yes; worse than death was entirely possible.

He might be castrated.

Declared a neuter.

Karadath's son.

Nausea threatened. To deflect it, Brodhi looked around the large chamber, purposely marking details that ordinarily meant nothing to him. It was starkly beautiful, abloom with candlelight. Woven carpets beneath his booted feet were thick and comfortable. Spiraling iron candleracks pleased the eye with their grace and elegance. The massive candles were hand-etched with care and bore gilt geometric designs echoing those chiseled into friezes at floor and ceiling.

The hide curtain, should he touch it, would warm silkily to his hand, answering his blood. Pieced together from hides of glossy bronze and deep, rich russet, it was otherwise plain; its adornment lay in the splendid network of scales, running with gold, ruddy with light, as if the curtain were wet.

Everything in the Kiba, the large round pit at the center of Alisanos, was made or maintained by neuters.

Rage rose up within him. It heated his skin, deepened its hue; dropped the ruddy scrim over his eyes. Hair tingled on the back of his neck, on his forearms, at his genitals. He would not be made into a neuter. It was not in him to serve. He was *dioscuri*, and he would be served. He would one day be a primary, and thus a god.

A rich, musky scent permeated the room. There were no chairs, no stools, no benches. He was not to sit. He was, merely, to wait.

Brodhi spun around as he heard the steps at the chamber doorway. His anger burned so that he could not keep silent though he had sworn to himself to do so. Rhuan affected him that way much of the time. But these circumstances were significantly more provocative than any before. "This is *your* doing. This—"

He would have said more, but he broke off as Karadath stepped through the entryway behind Rhuan. Brodhi had had no time to reacquaint himself with his sire's personal power, the sense of incandescent *presence* that lived in every primary. But in the years of Brodhi's absence, Karadath had grown in power and Brodhi scented it. He *tasted* it, as a beast might. Within himself he fought to maintain the pride and arrogance that shaped him, as it shaped all primaries and *dioscuri*s. Before his sire, whom he had not seen in four human years, it was difficult to do so. He felt himself a flicker of flame before a roaring conflagration.

Rhuan, not privy to those thoughts, laughed and shook back unbraided hair. "Is it truly my doing? Did I *force* you to enter Alisanos?"

But Brodhi ignored Rhuan now. He stared at his sire, realizing just how small, how young, he himself was. That he would one day kill Karadath to assume his place seemed impossible, a figment of undisciplined dreams.

He wrenched his thoughts away from that. "Rhuan's sire is plotting against you."

Karadath's expression didn't change. "Alario is consistent, if nothing else."

"That is why I came," Brodhi continued. "To warn you. Not to end my journey precipitously." He cast a venomous glance at Rhuan, who sat down casually upon the floor and rested his back against a wall with bound hands balanced atop updrawn knees. Ends of loose hair touched the floor. It crossed Brodhi's mind to wonder how that hair had come to be unbraided, but his attention returned to Karadath. "Punish me as you will . . . I have broken my vow not to return before time. But there is reason for it. Valid reason: to warn you of Alario's plans."

Karadath said, "What leads you to believe I am in need of such a warning? Alario and I have battled since we were younglings in the creche."

It was meant to shake Brodhi. He refused to allow it. He was Karadath's son, Karadath's *dioscuri*. He had his own measure of certainty, of entitlement, and employed both to shade his tone. "That may be," he allowed, "but there is more." Hands bound, he gestured instead with a jerk of his head, indicating Rhuan. "This weak one poisons us all. Even Alario realizes it. He has decided to take another human woman, to make a *dioscuri* who is strong, who honors his heritage." The startled look on Rhuan's face pleased Brodhi. "Yes, Rhuan, he intends to replace you. That leaves you with a choice: kill the child or challenge the sire." He bared his teeth briefly in something that was not quite a grin. "But we know you are capable of neither."

"And you?" It was Ylarra, Karadath's current mate, stepping through the doorway. Braid ornaments glinted in candlelight. "Of what are you capable, Brodhi?"

"Anything," he answered promptly, conviction paramount. "Anything at all."

"Even if it means you return to the human world for another five of their years?" She glanced at Karadath. "It's the only way, of course. He can't remain here or his journey will truly end. That is a result neither of us desires."

Brodhi was stunned. "You can't do that. Send me back to the humans? For another five years? I refuse!"

"You," Karadath said, "have no say in the matter." He met Ylarra's eyes; something passed between them. Complicity and agreement. "It is a solution."

"It keeps him intact. It buys him time. And us."

Karadath's abrupt grin was unnerving in someone who rarely showed emotion. "So it does."

Brodhi felt his flesh warm as the membrane dropped over his eyes. Pure, unreasoning instinct took hold of his body. The impulse to challenge was so strong he bit deeply into his bottom lip to dampen the response that fought for release.

Not yet. Not yet.

He looked away from his sire, stared hard at the floor, fixed his gaze upon a pattern in the rug and followed it from one end to the other, fighting for self-control.

Karadath's tone was amused. "You may challenge, if you wish. We can settle your future here and now."

Rhuan laughed. "I would enjoy watching that."

Brodhi, lowering his head, forced the words past clamped teeth. "I make no challenge."

His sire stepped very close to him. They were nearly of a height, but Karadath was a mature male in his prime, and his body reflected that. He exuded strength, power, and a terrible grace. "Look at me."

Brodhi did not.

"*See* me."

Brodhi steadfastly stared at the ground, face averted.

Karadath moved again, pressing closer yet. "Challenge me, *dioscuri.*"

Brodhi's breath ran ragged. "I make no challenge."

Karadath closed a hand over Brodhi's jaw and forced his head up. "*See me.*"

Brodhi closed his eyes.

Rhuan laughed. "Oh, do try, Brodhi! Then Karadath will kill you, and he, too, must look to sire another *dioscuri.*"

Brodhi held his tongue and did not meet his sire's eyes. After a moment Karadath released his jaw and turned away.

"Get up, Rhuan," Ylarra said. "Get up from there. You have disgraced yourself quite enough."

Brodhi held his silence as Rhuan contemplated refusing. He saw it in the eyes so like his own. But Rhuan rose in silence, and Brodhi realized his own moment of rebellion was ended. His skin cooled, the membrane withdrew. He could meet Karadath's eyes now, though he did so only briefly.

Ylarra drew her knife and sliced Rhuan's hands free. "It was given to Karadath and me to determine the punishment. It is decided. Resume your journey, both of you. Five additional human years, living among the humans." She cut the thong at Brodhi's wrists. "You are not ready," she told him quietly, "as you have seen. He would kill you in an instant. But when the journey is completed—" a smile flickered briefly "—perhaps you will be strong enough to bring down your sire and ascend to his place." Now she looked at Karadath. "Perhaps."

Brodhi heard in her tone a delicate disbelief. Ylarra favored him, he knew; Ferize had told him so. But in the meantime Ylarra bedded Karadath; could he trust her in anything? Was her suggestion that he return to the human world truly intended to keep him intact? Or was she playing a game with both sire and son?

For a moment, a moment only, he allowed himself the vision: Karadath defeated, himself ascending.

It was sweet, that vision. But also fleeting, banished by the truth. Were he to challenge his sire before his journey was ended, Karadath would indeed kill him in an instant.

Not yet. Not yet. I am not ready.

One day, he would be. And challenge would be made.

RHUAN, HAIR LOOSE, wrists tied, had walked with as much pride and dignity as he could dredge up, climbing the shallow steps out of the round, high-sided Kiba pit, prisoner among his own kind. Karadath, who followed him, forbore to touch him now, having tied Rhuan's wrists before him; the kin-in-kind who humans would name "uncle" wanted no physical contact, as if he believed he might be contaminated.

A corner of Rhuan's mouth jerked briefly; well, if he were to be sentenced to castration and to become a neuter, Karadath *would* be contaminated by his nephew's touch.

The human woman, Audrun, had protested such rude removal before all the primaries, shouting that Rhuan had more honor in him than any primary. She had courage of the kind most primaries had never seen in humans. But then most humans, in Alisanos, were rendered mindless by the physical alterations beginning in their bodies, by the challenges of remaining alive in a world both alien and dangerous; even, Rhuan believed, by the shock of meeting a primary, if they survived long enough to do so. Audrun was fearful, he knew; but that was yet another element that made her so different. She was afraid, but she confronted the nine hundred and ninety-nine gods who gathered in the Kiba, seated upon carved stone blocks. She confronted, challenged, and demanded of them things they would not do, knowing they would not do them.

Return her children, she asked. Five of them, missing, scattered throughout the deepwood. One taken by demon.

Walking steadily, aware of Karadath close behind upon the stone-paved pathway, Rhuan broke into a smile. It stretched into a grin. The primaries had refused Audrun her demand. But Brodhi—*Brodhi*—had brought four of the missing children to the Kiba and to their mother.

Karadath's son. Karadath's last *dioscuri*. Equally guilty of reentering Alisanos well before time.

Rhuan laughed aloud.

Oh, it was rich, that knowledge. He knew full well that he himself was considered weak by most of the primaries, if not by all. Alario had made no secret of his disappointment in his last *dioscuri*. It was ironic, Rhuan felt, that in the human world he had an undeserved and inaccurate reputation for killing and yet, among the primaries, Rhuan was believed to be too human to challenge Alario's other *dioscuri*. In fact, he had killed none of them; they had managed, instead, to kill themselves. None remained but himself.

Karadath, on the other hand, was arrogant with the awareness that Brodhi was markedly promising. Brodhi had, before setting out on his journey, killed two of his *dioscuri* brothers. Brodhi would one day challenge his sire; and if he defeated Karadath, he would ascend to his father's place. It was *expected* that one day Brodhi would do so.

But Brodhi, like Rhuan, had come home too soon. And he, like Rhuan, would be punished for it.

THE ANGER THAT had bolstered Audrun's courage and provided the words with which to challenge the primaries in their own Kiba, drained from her body as she climbed the steps. Now there was joy; joy and intense relief and other emotions too tangled upon themselves to name. The Shoia courier had brought her children to her.

All save one. The baby stolen by a demon.

That child, for now, was mourned more quietly than otherwise, because the children she knew best, the children she had raised, were alive, and present.

The courier had been sent away before she could thank him, even as she took Megritte from him into her arms. Darmuth, one of the karavan guides—but seemingly at home in the deepwood, which made her suspicious—also departed after murmuring something about the children being damaged but "safe for the time being." Megritte in her arms, Audrun told the other children—Gillan, Ellica, and Torvic—to stay close as they all followed a man whose features, height, and coloring marked him kin to the primaries. The difference was a certain softness to his face, as if his skin didn't fit as tightly as it should. He was braidless, this man, his dark coppery hair cut short at the nape of his neck. It was without the ornamentation that wove through the multiple braids worn by the courier, by all of the folk called primaries, and by Rhuan. No—that *had* been worn by Rhuan, before she undid them and married herself to him. Without speaking, this braidless man led them away from the Kiba along a paved footpath to a huge, spreading tree beside the towering cliffs. A massive stone bench had been placed under the leafy canopy; Audrun had already marked that everything in this place was of a larger scale than in her own world. But then, she had discovered in the Kiba that the primaries themselves were of a larger scale.

Gillan, she had already noted, limped badly. Ellica clutched against her breasts a small sapling wrapped in homespun skirts. Audrun wanted badly to know what had happened to them while they were lost in the deepwood, but there would be time to ask them later. For now, the only thing that mattered was that all of them were safe.

And Davyn, her husband, was not in Alisanos! "Thank the Mother," she murmured; yet there was a selfish portion of her that wished he were.

The braidless man left them. He said nothing, merely made a gesture she recognized as a request—or a command—that they remain here.

Meggie, no longer infant or toddler, was heavy, and Audrun too weary and worn to continue carrying her no matter how much she wished to. She leaned down and settled Megritte on the stone bench then turned and put out her arms to the others. As one, they engulfed her, Torvic in tears, Gillan laughing brokenly in relief and release, and Ellica, still clutching her sapling as if it were an infant, rested her head against Audrun's shoulder. There wasn't room enough in her arms to hug everyone at once, but she did her best. All of them were in tears, even herself, but no shame, no shame in it. She brushed hair out of their faces, briefly cradled their cheeks. They were filthy, thin, faces gaunt beneath the grime, clothing torn and stained. But they were whole. Whole and alive, and no longer missing, no longer lost in the deepwood.

"Thank the Mother," she repeated fervently.

Tears rose, stung, spilled. Cradling the heads of her children one by one, Audrun kissed each on cheeks and brows, then turned back to Megritte. She sank down upon the bench, gathered Meggie close, and began the efforts needed to bring order to tangled blond hair. Her own needed care as well, but she would rather tend her child.

Torvic found room on the other side of the bench next to her, so that she was between her two youngest, while Gillan hobbled to a wide shelf of stone and collapsed upon it, hissing in pain. Ellica sat down upon the earth, taking care to cradle the sapling and its rootball in her lap. Her manner was, Audrun realized, akin to her own when she tended an infant. To see it in her daughter, who had no child, struck her as odd; odder still to see that her charge was a tree. Ellica's tears had dried, and now she wore an expression of serenity, as if she drew strength from the sapling.

Audrun caught movement from the corner of her eye and looked up from Meggie's head. She registered braids and ornamentation as well as clean, sharp features, a severe expression, and a form incontestably female. Rhuan had called her Ylarra.

Ylarra halted before them. She looked at each of the children individually, as if evaluating them. Then she looked at Audrun. "The challenge has been accepted. We shall make you this road through Alisanos. Until there is a place for you upon it, you shall remain here."

Audrun could not curtail the bitterness in her tone. "As prisoners."

"We do not keep prisoners," Ylarra replied. "Those who are our enemies, we kill. But you have taken yourself a *dioscuri* as husband, and there are obligations in such things. Thus you and your young will remain as guests until there is a place for you on the road."

Audrun had denied that Rhuan was her husband several times within the confines of the Kiba, before the assembled primaries. She denied it again, now, but this time with neither anger nor rancor. This time she maintained self-control and spoke calmly. "You heard me before, in the Kiba. Let me say this again, since it appears you have not yet grasped the meat of the matter: I did not marry Rhuan. I unbraided his hair to cleanse his wounds. I have a husband, a human husband, in the human world."

Ylarra's smile was thin. She was a tall, elegant, powerful woman, larger than many men in the human world but no less feminine for it. A light kindled in brown eyes. Amusement, Audrun believed, and an arrogance so plain as to overwhelm a human. But Audrun refused to be overwhelmed. *She is not a god; a demon, perhaps.*

But no, not demon. Were she to attach that label to Ylarra, it would attach also to Rhuan. And that Audrun refused to do.

"Believe as you will," Ylarra said. "But here you are subject to our customs."

Audrun realized that she should be afraid. She was meant to be afraid. It was true she was apprehensive, but that emotion was as nothing compared to the others that motivated her. She was wife and mother, and such responsibilities superseded fear. "And if I refuse to abide by your customs?"

"It would be best," the primary said, "that you do not. We have no obligations to a human who is not—by our customs—married to a *dioscuri*. And we do not guest humans here, in the heart of our people."

No threat colored Ylarra's tone, no promise of punishment. A handful of words spoken quietly, evenly, with no trace of emotion. But Audrun felt it, and she understood: So long as she was believed to be Rhuan's wife, sealed by Alisani customs, she and her children would be safe.

"You will be looked after," Ylarra continued. "A neuter will be assigned and a private chamber with certain amenities."

Rhuan had said time ran differently in Alisanos. "For how long must we remain?"

"As I have said: until there is a place for you upon the road." Dismissal was implicit as Ylarra began to turn away.

"Wait!" Audrun wanted to jump up from the bench, but she could not bear to let go of Torvic and Megritte. "Wait," she repeated, and was gratified when Ylarra turned back. "You say until the road is built. But how long will that take?"

"Always time, with you. How long this? How long that?" Scorn underlay her tone, a gesture waved the question of time away. "And the answer is what, in Alisanos, the answer always is: That which is made here is completed when it is completed."

Yet again Audrun forestalled her departure. "Are we . . . will we be safe from the poison while we're here?"

Ylarra's brows rose. "The 'poison'?"

"The wild magic," Audrun answered. "Rhuan called it a poison."

"There is no poison here." The primary smiled. "Only power."

"Rhuan said it would change us. That we could never go home because of what it would do to us." She steadied her voice. "If you can make this road, surely you can see us safely home. We are as yet unchanged. Wouldn't you prefer to have us gone, we humans? Then your home would be uncorrupted."

"Home?" Ylarra echoed. "Go home to the human world?" Braid ornamentation glinted in the light of double suns suspended above the tree, above the cliffs. "They would shun you, your folk. Is that what you want?"

Abruptly, Audrun recalled the old man, the ragged stranger in the tent settlement, who had come up to the wagon. She recalled his clawed, scaled hands. He had begged for her aid, had begged to return to Alisanos, because he was no longer welcome in the human world.

But Audrun was adamant. *"Before* the change begins." She stretched out a hand and displayed it, wishing she could still the minute trembling. "See? Nothing. I am human. My children are human. There is no poison in us. Show us the way . . . take us to the border between your world and mine, and we will go."

Ylarra said, "Ask your eldest."

As the primary intended, Audrun instantly wanted to look at Gillan. But she would not allow herself. Not before Ylarra.

Ylarra smiled and departed. Audrun waited tensely until she was gone then looked at Gillan, asking without words.

All of the color leeched out of his face. Wordlessly, he peeled back his homespun pant-leg, stripped away the bindings, and showed her the discolored flesh, the terrible patchwork of demon-scaled skin.

Already, it began.

Too late, too late, too late. Chilled flesh rose on her bones. Grief engulfed her, yet she shed no tears. Not before the children. She was all they had, until their father came.

But inside, Audrun wept: for what they might have become, for what they once had been.

RHUAN'S HEART LEAPED as Ylarra entered the chamber he shared with Brodhi and pronounced sentence. It was so like the primaries to assume that denying him their presence was a punishment, when in fact, it was what he would have requested, given leave to do so. Darmuth, the demon who traveled with Rhuan, reporting his journey's progress to the primaries, had evidently told them nothing of Rhuan's heart; the half-human heart that longed to live among his mother's people for the balance of his life. Darmuth's discretion was unexpected. Darmuth owed loyalty to the primaries; his task was to stay with his charge and monitor his doings in the human world, then divulge those doings to the primaries.

Like all *dioscuri,* Rhuan was expected, at the completion of his journey—providing the primaries found him worthy—to challenge his sire so that he might ascend to Alario's place, were Alario defeated. He fully expected to be found unworthy to challenge his sire, but he was still *dioscuri*, and a successful completion of the journey would buy him a boon nonetheless and well before any challenge might be mounted. It was that boon he strived for, not the chance to challenge his sire, but the opportunity to inform the primaries, without reprisal, that he was departing Alisanos forever.

He might have lost the opportunity altogether, had the primaries decided his premature return to Alisanos was worthy of castration. He had come close, Rhuan knew. Closer than was comfortable.

It was a gift, this sentence. Five additional human years in which to inhabit the human world. A new journey begun among humans he knew, humans he valued, humans he counted as friends.

With Ilona, who was more.

And it was time that she knew it. Time she knew *him*.

ALARIO KNELT BY the shaded streamlet, leaning down to scoop water with one broad hand into his mouth. But drinking, rinsing his mouth, was not enough to wash away the bitter taste of annoyance—not regret; regret suggested weakness—and the acknowledgment that he had acted hastily, far too hastily; that he had, in a brief but overwhelming moment of fury, undone all his plans.

The edges of the streamlet were choked by ground cover aprickle with hair-thin, hollow thorns, pale-to-invisible barbs that insinuated themselves through one's clothing into flesh. Disturbed, the thorn-guarded heart of the plant fed poison into the barbs, injecting the flesh of anyone—demon, beast, or wayward human—with killing venom.

But Alario was a primary and more powerful than most. Where he knelt, ground cover bent itself away, withdrawing from him in something akin to obeisance.

Quite against expectations, his mind fed him a vision of the woman. The human woman, called hand-reader.

Infuriated, as angry as Alario had ever been in all of his many years, he had hurled her against the steep wooden steps of her wagon. In the instant her body struck, the moment the bones of her fragile human neck snapped, he regretted his actions, regretted his anger.

No. No, not *regret*; primaries had no regrets.

He merely wished it undone.

Alario, kneeling, nodded. Wished it undone. That was acceptable.

Self-control, even in the midst of unalloyed instinct, was paramount among the primaries. But he had allowed the woman to rouse his anger and the unreasoning instinct to destroy. Wished it undone, indeed; she offered everything he needed to defeat Karadath, to destroy Brodhi, his brother's get. And to replace the weakness that was Rhuan.

His first human *diascara*, Rhuan's mother, had never angered him. She was compliant and subservient in the months leading to the birth.

Perhaps *that* was why Rhuan was a failure. The dam had been too meek. Temperament mattered.

He had taken that particular human woman because her scent was correct. Her pheromones appealed. She would give him, he was certain, a sound *dioscuri*.

Rhuan, he knew, could do no such thing, could not choose based on scent. Worse, Rhuan had no *desire* to do such a thing.

Temperament was all.

The woman called hand-reader by superstitous humans, was neither compliant nor subservient. That was why he had, in fury, flung her against her wagon. And thus ruined his plans for a new *dioscuri* worthy of the title.

The war within was ancient, formed of blood, bone, instinct; of the *drive* to sire get who were stronger than oneself. And yet everything in the primary cried out to survive, to destroy every threat. And yet also to sire that which could kill its progenitor or be relegated to the position of neuter, his manhood cut away.

Alario smiled. And then as the demon leaped from the shadows, he effortlessly caught the scaled neck in one broad hand. He closed on the throat. Squeezed. In a frenzy, the demon attempted to twist free, to double up hind legs and rake through clothing at flesh, but Alario swatted away those legs and claws with his free hand. He felt the sudden cessation of movement as the demon's body went lax, and he threw it aside easily. He rose, smiling again. Such a small, inconsequential demon, foolish enough to believe it might attack a primary with impunity. Now the dead demon made but a small pile of meat in the shadows beneath the trees, mostly hidden by spike-leafed brush. Others would come to feast upon its remains, of course. Nothing would be left but a scattering of bones, unless they, too, were consumed.

Alario stood quite still, *very* still, listening to his body, giving understanding over to his senses. The body always knew, when the mind did not. Instinct guided every primary.

That woman, the hand-reader, had appealed far more than Rhuan's mother. He wished it undone, her death.

He *wished it undone*.

Was he not a primary, to wish a thing and thus gain it?

Fierce joy rose up in his body. Alario smiled, baring white teeth in the coppery tint of his face, his indisputably beautiful predator's face.

Chapter 1

*B*ETHID AWOKE JUST before sunrise, clear-headed and alert and instantly aware of a lurking sense of unease. Something, somewhere, was wrong. She heard the snores of fellow couriers Timmon and Alorn; the two had patched storm-torn oilcloth the day before and raised the common tent all couriers shared while at the settlement. It required additional attention, but she was grateful for any cover at all in the aftermath of the terrible storm.

She sat up, assuming a cross-legged posture. With neither full sunlight outside nor lantern light inside, the interior of the tent was markedly dim. She was aware of a sick feeling in her belly, the kind she felt when something had gone wrong or she had to do something she dreaded—and then memory abruptly spilled through her; memory and grief.

The hand-reader.

Oh Mother, the hand-reader was dead.

And another memory: Rhuan, surviving Alisanos only to discover that Ilona was dead. Such grief and shock in a man's eyes Bethid had never witnessed. She had left the wagon then, departed to give him the opportunity to master himself, to provide Ilona's body company through the night.

Morning rites. *Mourning* rites.

Bethid closed her eyes and planted elbows on her thighs, leaning

down into the heels of her hands to rest her brow, to apply pressure
to her eyelids as if to banish the recollection. She wanted nothing
more than to blot out this moment, the day before, and the vision of
the karavan-master, sitting on wagon steps, cradling Ilona in his
arms.

She scratched her scalp with rigid, short-nailed fingers, understanding the poignancy. Rhuan of the many women now wanted
only one.

The night before, with Naiya, a Sister of the Road, Bethid had
dressed Ilona in a burial shift, combed and braided her hair, settled
her atop her narrow cot beneath a multi-hued coverlet. Now it was
time to wrap the body and bring it out for the rites and the burial.
Ilona had crossed the river; it was time to say goodbye.

Her mouth twisted briefly. Conducting rites was the responsibility
of diviners and priests. But neither had survived the terrible storm
engendered by Alisanos, and Ilona, too, was dead. Now the duty fell
to Jorda, the karavan-master, who had known Ilona best.

Bethid glanced at the two forms hidden beneath bedclothes. "Up,"
she said, then cleared her throat and tried again. "Timmon. Alorn. We
have rites this morning, remember?" All would attend, tent-folk and
karavaners alike.

Snoring eventually broke off. She saw Alorn's brown curls appear
at the edge of a blanket as he pulled it down. Timmon, a long lump
beneath bedding, mumbled something with typical morning incoher-
ency.

"Up," she repeated, flipping back bedding to reach boots at the
end of her pallet. She had slept in her clothes, too tired, too depressed,
to change into her sleeping shift upon her return the night before.
"Gather up the folk," she said, tugging on her boots. "I'll go to Ilona's
wagon. . . . Mikal and Jorda are meeting me there." The bottoms of
her trews she tucked into boot-tops, then cross-gartered leather riding
gaiters around her calves and tied off the leather thongs.

Both men were awake, she saw, truly awake now, and were not
inclined to joke as they usually did, or to complain about too little
sleep. They said nothing as she untied and slipped out the door flap.

The sun was a lurid glow along the horizon. With its slow climb came first birdsong from the groves. Most of the trees in the younger grove had been uprooted in the storm, thrown down against the earth with rootballs bared to the day, limbs and branches stripped, offering no shelter to wildlife. But the larger, old-growth grove had mostly been spared. It was there Jorda had brought his karavaners to camp temporarily, until it was sorted out what they would do and what Jorda advised. All had been bound elsewhere, attempting to put distance between themselves and the brutal Hecari warriors who had overrun and conquered Sancorra province. But Alisanos had gone active, destroying everyone's plans, reducing fears of the Hecari to, for the moment, mere inconvenience, despite the fact the warriors were dangerous. The Hecari were *men*. Alisanos was far worse. Alisanos swallowed people whole; those it gave back, if rarely, were no longer human.

And, she remembered uneasily, Alisanos now nearly surrounded them.

The haphazard appearance of tents pitched willy-nilly without regard for order no longer shaped the settlement. In the handful of days since Alisanos had gone active, tent-folk and karavaners alike had heeded the advice of Jorda the karavan-master, and Mikal, the ale-keep who ran the largest and busiest tent. It had fallen to these two men, natural leaders both, to make recommendations for the safety of the survivors. The tent-folk had repaired what they could with belongings rescued from the storm and with aid and contributions from the karavaners. Tents had been raised once more, but this time they stood in ranks of circles around a massive stone-ringed bonfire. Instead of a tangle of footpaths, a clear grid of trails had been laid down.

And so it took less time for Bethid to reach the grove and Ilona's wagon than it might have otherwise. She saw ahead of her two large men walking more slowly than was their wont. Jorda and Mikal were in no more of a hurry than she to converge upon the wagon.

"Wait," she called, breaking into a jog. "Jorda . . . Mikal . . ."

At the edge of the grove, both men paused and turned back. They were of like height and similar width, though swarthy, one-eyed Mikal carried more bulk in his belly. Ruddy-haired Jorda kept fit by the duties of his position as karavan-master. As she came up, Jorda opened a mouth mostly hidden by bushy beard, then closed it as an expression of realization crossed his features.

Bethid answered the unspoken question. "Yes, Rhuan sat vigil. I wanted to give him privacy . . . I went back to the couriers' tent."

Gray strands threaded the fading russet of the karavan-master's hair, bound back in a single plait. Most of his face was hidden by the flamboyance of his beard, but in the flesh between beard and lower eyelids, Bethid saw weariness etched, and sorrow. She had been thinking only of Rhuan. But Jorda had known Ilona longer. Friendship, she knew, was as powerful in its own way as love.

Mikal cleared his throat. "We've made preparations. We'll see her buried with as much honor as possible."

He, too, had known Ilona better than she. Her path and the hand-reader's had not crossed often, save occasionally in Mikal's ale-tent. She had been attracted to Ilona but knew the hand-reader was a woman for men; Bethid simply had never cultivated a friendship. "I'm sorry," she blurted. "I wish I'd taken the time to know her better."

"She was worthy," Jorda declared. "Worthier than most. She'll cross the river easily enough and be at rest in the afterlife."

Bethid cleared her throat. "Timmon and Alorn are rousing folk to attend the rites."

"Mother of Moons," Jorda murmured raggedly. "I'm not prepared for this. I'm *never* prepared for this. There were always priests and diviners . . ." He dashed sudden tears from his cheeks. "I'm not worthy of this."

Mikal briefly placed a hand on the karavan-master's shoulder. "You better than any." Pressure urged Jorda into motion.

As they reached the hand-reader's wagon, Bethid felt an abrupt tightening in her belly. She realized how very much she dreaded seeing the door open, seeing Rhuan's expression. It was a private thing, such grief, and yet custom now required that Ilona's body be taken from him.

The grove was lightening from shadow into daylight. As karavaners awoke within their wagons, one or two dogs barked. A nearby horse, picketed by the Sisters' wagon, snorted heavily. Elsewhere, a baby cried.

Bethid and Mikal stopped simultaneously near the wagon steps. Jorda took one more step, placed a booted foot on the bottom step, wiped a hand across his bearded face. Then he made a fist of that hand and knocked quietly upon the closed door.

"Rhuan?" Jorda's voice cracked. Bethid wished she could offer some kind of relief, but it was Jorda who knew Ilona and Rhuan best. She did not wish to intrude upon that, and Mikal's expression confirmed his deference to the karavan-master. "Rhuan. It's time."

For a long moment there was no response. Then the wagon creaked as someone inside moved. The latch rattled. The door was pushed open.

Sunlight fell fully on Rhuan's face, limning his features, the scratches on his face, and the brightness of his eyes. Bethid had forgotten that his hair was unbraided. As he broke into a grin, deep dimples appeared.

It was wholly incongruous, Bethid thought, shocked that he should look so *happy*.

Until he moved aside, and Ilona took his place.

 DARMUTH STOPPED SHORT in the doorway of the stone chamber. "You as well?"

Ferize, in human form but with the scale pattern upon her, briefly bared her teeth in a response more animal than human. The pupils of pale blue eyes were slitted. He felt his body respond, the faint itching of his skin that accompanied the emergence of his own scale pattern. In the human world their transformation was under their control; here in Alisanos, their original forms exerted far more influence. Wild magic ran in their bones, was carried with them into the human world, wielded as they wished. But here the magic was far more potent. It wished to wield them.

She wore human clothing, a gown of dark, rich indigo, with

chains of braided gold wrapped around her waist. Black hair was loose and long. Her skin was pale, shining with the pearlescent hue of the scale pattern, delicate, almost fragile. The gown was cut low, so that as she breathed he saw the glistening of scale edges rising and falling from breasts to throat.

Darmuth crossed his bare arms, planted a shoulder against the doorjamb, and leaned, affecting a nonchalance he didn't truly feel. The itching of his skin subsided; he was fully human again, exerting more self-control than Ferize. "You're afraid, aren't you?"

Something flashed briefly in her pale blue eyes. He supposed humans would find her beautiful in her human guise; to him, it was alien. He preferred her demon form.

"So should you be," Ferize declared.

"Primaries will do what primaries will do," he said lightly. "What profits us to worry?"

"And if *we* are blamed?"

Darmuth lifted his left shoulder in a half shrug. "The risk is no greater now than it was before."

Her slight human body was stiff, tense. "You don't know that, Darmuth—"

But Ferize broke off, looking past him. Darmuth felt the familiar presence, the pressure of a primary in full command of the magic. He straightened and moved away from the door, taking his place at Ferize's side as he turned to look at the doorway.

Ylarra stepped lightly into the chamber. Her smile was cold. "Perhaps you should be blamed," she said. "Now, tell me why."

Ferize's voice was low. "Brodhi returned before time."

"And could you not prevent that?"

"I could not."

Darmuth felt his breath catch briefly as Ylarra looked at him. "And you?"

"Alisanos took Rhuan," he answered. "Would you have had me defy the deepwood?" He grinned briefly. "I was but a victim, Ylarra. As much as Rhuan was. It was Brodhi who willingly returned to Alisanos."

As he expected, Ferize erupted. "And so you shift the blame? Attempt to distract? Brodhi had his sire's welfare at heart! The welfare of a primary." She looked again at Ylarra. "That is why he came. To warn Karadath of Alario's intentions."

"To get a child, another *dioscuri* on the human woman; yes, we know." Ylarra's slight gesture was dismissive. "It was not necessary for Brodhi to come here; Karadath is prepared for any action Alario may undertake, any threat he intends. They have been battling for two hundred human years. But we have taken into account that Brodhi did indeed act in his sire's best interests, not through any desire of his own to give up his journey. And Rhuan indeed had no control over Alisanos; that, too, we have taken into account."

"What punishment for them?" Darmuth asked. "And what for us?"

The primary smiled. "For them, and for you, in equal measure. It begins again, their journey. Thus, so does yours."

Darmuth exchanged a quick glance with Ferize; she seemed no more the wiser than he. "And?"

"And," Ylarra echoed. Amusement laced her tone. "Five additional human years in the human world. You may take that as punishment deferred or punishment levied. That is your choice. You are once again to attend your *dioscuri*, to monitor his behavior, his thinking processes, to hear him as necessary, and to report to us. In the meantime, you escape the unmaking. But if either Brodhi or Rhuan again returns too soon to Alisanos—by any means, and for any reason—punishment indeed shall be levied. They will be neutered, and you both shall be unmade. So, it is in *your* best interests to see that neither returns before time." Her eyes were cold. "I suggest you hasten. Brodhi and Rhuan are back among the humans."

Eyes fixed on the floor, Darmuth waited until Ylarra departed. Then he looked at Ferize. Her scale pattern faded before his eyes even as his own came up to the surface of his flesh. "Did you hear what Rhuan's farm wife suggested in the Kiba?"

"Who? Oh." Ferize scowled at him. "I was not there."

"She suggested that they may not be gods."

Ferize's eyes hazed briefly yellow. "They wield the wild magic. If not gods, what are they?"

"*We* wield the wild magic."

Her scale pattern bloomed. "Not as they do!"

"Perhaps not, but what if she is right? What if the wild magic has poisoned them?"

"Does it matter?" Ferize walked by him, heading toward the door. There, she turned. "Darmuth, they can *unmake* us. If that does not define a being who is a god, I don't know what might."

Smiling, he let her go without further questions or comments. Ferize had always been more excitable than he, and occasionally, it was enjoyable to provoke her.

Then his smile faded. It was true that only the primaries could unmake those like him, like Ferize. Being killed was one thing, but being *unmade*—? A shudder coursed through his body. He wasted no more time on suppositions but departed the chamber. Time he returned to Rhuan, and to the human world.

Five more years, as the humans gauged time. While it no doubt displeased Brodhi, and thus Ferize, it was not anything Rhuan would consider a punishment, but in fact a reprieve.

Chapter 2

*I*LONA. *ALIVE.*

Jorda literally fell back a stride from the steps. Bethid felt her own mouth drop open inelegantly, and a shiver ran down her spine. She heard Mikal murmuring a fervent prayer to the Mother of Moons, fingering the string of charms at his throat.

Ilona still wore the plain linen burial shift Bethid and Naiya had put on her the night before. Her dark hair was loose of the single braid, reverting to the exuberant array of long ringlets usually tamed by being wound against the back of the hand-reader's skull and anchored with ornamented hair sticks. Her olive complexion was smooth and clear, hazel eyes warm and bright and most definitely alive, but encircling her throat was the unmistakable print of a large man's hand.

She had been dead. She *had* been dead.

"I wasn't dead," Ilona said. "Or . . ." An odd expression passed over her features. "Or I *was* dead, but I'm not now. It's—" She broke off, making a gesture of helplessness. "I'm sorry . . ." She turned her head. "Rhuan—? Can you explain? I'm not sure I understand everything yet!"

Jorda's voice sounded strangled. "Ilona."

"Yes, it's me. Rhuan? Please, before they all drop dead of shock!" Then Ilona gestured apology, making a face. "Poor choice of words, wasn't it? Well . . ." Barefoot, she descended the steps and stood on the ground, making room for Rhuan to exit the wagon. Her eyes were worried, Bethid saw; tension crept into Ilona's expression and posture.

Bethid's words came out completely different from what she had intended. "This isn't possible. *You were dead.*"

"Ilona," Jorda repeated. "By the Mother, girl, your neck was broken! D'ye think I don't know death when I see it? When it's in my arms?" He looked at Rhuan. "I would never tell you she was dead if she were not. Do you think I would? Do you think I could?"

Rhuan descended and sat down upon the middle step, resting elbows on thighs. Hands dangled loosely. "No," he said. "No, Jorda, you would not. You told me the truth last night." His eyes swept them all. "She was truly dead when I came here last night . . . as Shoia are before they—before *we*—resurrect."

"Shoia!" Mikal blurted.

Bethid began blankly, "But Ilona's not Sh—" She paused. "Is she?" She looked at the hand-reader. "Are you?"

Rhuan smiled wryly. "Have you another explanation?"

"I didn't know," Ilona said, drifting close to Rhuan. "What do any of us know about the Shoia?"

"Rhuan might know something," Jorda said mildly, "being as how he is, after all, Shoia himself."

Rhuan and Ilona exchanged a brief, sidelong glance that was quickly banished. Bethid abruptly had a very clear memory of Ilona telling her that Brodhi wasn't Shoia at all, but Alisanos-born; it was a short step from that to the realization that Rhuan was as well. And yet obviously, here and now, he supported the fiction that he was Shoia. But—Ilona? *She* was Shoia?

The hand-reader shrugged. "Then Rhuan must be correct. He would know, of course, as you say." She met Jorda's gaze. "I remember nothing. Not after Alario threw me down. That moment, yes, I recall it clearly; and then I awoke in my cot with Rhuan muttering at me." Her smile was faint and fleeting. Then delicate color suffused her face, and then Bethid knew precisely how Rhuan and Ilona had affirmed her resurrection.

Mikal frowned. "Who is Alario?"

"Oh, Mother," Ilona groaned, pressing hands against her head. "There is *so* much to explain . . ."

Jorda stared at Rhuan. "How did you make it out of Alisanos?" He paused. "You were there, were you not? I was given to understand the storm took you." Ruddy eyebrows shot up. "Or were you off elsewhere shirking your duty, as is occasionally your habit?"

Rhuan sighed. He glanced sidelong at Ilona. "There is indeed so much to explain."

Ilona looked at each of them; lastly at Jorda, where her gaze dwelled in a silent but poignant appeal. "It would be somewhat encouraging were you *pleased* that I'm not dead."

Jorda stared back in shock, then blinked. He took a step, then another, and pulled her into a bearish embrace. "Oh girl, I *am* pleased! Indescribably pleased! But you *were* dead!"

When he eventually released her, Ilona remarked, "You've seen Rhuan resurrect before."

"I knew he was Shoia! But even then, the first time came as a shock. As this does." Laughter rumbled. "Shoia or no Shoia, it's the Mother's doing." He tipped his head back and stared up at the sky. "Sweet Mother, I thank you!"

Bethid reached out and poked Mikal. "We should go. We need to tell everyone, to cancel the rites." Instinct told her it was time to let Ilona, Rhuan, and their employer discuss matters best left to them. Her own curiosity could be satisfied later. "Let's go, Mikal."

The ale-keep started. "Yes. Of course. We can—"

But a high, shrill scream cut through the grove, cut off Mikal's words. Another followed, and another.

Each of them, as one, stilled abruptly, then turned and ran toward the sound.

 DAVYN AWOKE WITH a start. He lay wrapped in blankets atop a thin mattress spread over wooden floorboards, shielded from the elements by the wagon and canopy. With the broken axle replaced and the backup oilcloth stretched over the roof ribs, it was home again to him, albeit a temporary one. But it lacked others. It lacked his children and his wife.

Trapped in Alisanos, all of them. All save himself.

Once again he was swamped by fear, anxiety, and guilt: he was not with his family. Better that they be together, even in Alisanos, than separated. But the Mother had inexplicably kept him free of the deepwood, while Audrun and the children were swallowed.

The hand-reader had seen it clearly: his youngest, Torvic and Megritte, together with the courier, Brodhi. She had seen nothing of Audrun or their two eldest, Gillan and Ellica, but she had told him that the child was born. Before time, well before time, victim of the power of Alisanos. So, in truth, *five* children were lost in the deepwood.

His body ached. Over the past several days too much had occurred, too much had affected his life, his plans; plans he and Audrun had made.

Huddled in blankets, he heard a rooster crowing in the day, then scattered barking. Nearby, a baby wailed with hunger, or the need for a fresh clout. The morning was perfectly normal in all ways, except that he was alone. Brodhi, the courier who had gone into the deepwood, was to bring him word. Brodhi was to restore at least the two youngest to their father, according to what the hand-reader saw.

A call rang through the grove, summoning everyone to dawn rites. And then he remembered. The hand-reader was dead.

Davyn groaned aloud. His right hand found the string of charms around his neck. Clenching them within a fist, he pictured the hand-reader in his mind, recalled her care and compassion. It was her vision of the courier, Brodhi, with two of the children, that convinced Davyn his only course was to ask Brodhi to go into Alisanos after his family. The courier had rebuffed him with distinct rudeness, but he had, in the end, entered the deepwood.

"Let them be found," Davyn murmured fervently. "Mother, let

them be found, all of them, and let them be kept safe and unharmed. Bring them back to me."

Again he felt a twinge of guilt as he made the petition. The karavan guide had made it clear how much danger they courted if they took the shortcut so close to Alisanos. But fifteen—*fifteen!*—diviners made the decision for him. It was the only way to reach Atalanda in time for the baby's birth.

His fault, then. Wasn't it? That Audrun and the children were taken by the deepwood?

His chest ached with grief, his throat felt tight. Tears stung his eyes. Still he clutched the charms, concentrating on what he begged, not on what he had done. "Mother of Moons, let them be found. Let them come back to me."

A dull headache nagged as Davyn threw back tangled covers from his pallet. Tension returned to his neck and shoulders, knotting muscles. He felt used up, emptied. Depression was palpable. What in the Mother's name was he to do now? Atalanda province no longer beckoned, the need to reach it lost with the loss of his family. He might as well remain in Sancorra, remain here in the settlement even if it was nearly surrounded by Alisanos. Worth the risk, for his family. And if the deepwood move again and take him, perhaps he could find his family there.

Or perhaps one day, one year, his wife and children would find a way out of the deepwood. He dared not depart in case they should do so. And there was work for him here, he realized, tasks to be done. The boundaries between safety and Alisanos were to be mapped and marked, crops planted, livestock raised, river fished, people fed. The wagon carried the makings for a new life. It would not be impossible to begin again; that was precisely what he and Audrun intended when they elected to move to Atalanda.

Not impossible but difficult, oh yes, and exceedingly painful, because he would be alone.

Davyn climbed down from the wagon. Throughout the grove other folk were stirring. He heard again the echoing call for rites for the hand-reader and reflected that tea could wait. Afterwards, he would approach the ale-keep and the karavan-master to offer aid.

Then he heard the shouting, the screaming, and broke into a run, heading for the bonfire.

ALARIO STOOD IN the borderlands in the verge between the human world and Alisanos. Here, the shadows were pale, the trees less shielding. Much had happened since last he visited. The woman he killed, then resurrected, had entwined her heart with his worthless get, a *dioscuri* not worth the name. His get took great joy in the world among the humans, turning his back on his heritage, even on his blood. Alario could not fathom how *his* get could so easily reject the traditions of Alisanos. He found it both infuriating and perplexing.

There was no sound, but he knew Ylarra's scent, her step. He did not bother to turn. "And now you must wait five more years," she said in her husky voice.

Alario spun around. "What?"

"Five more years," Ylarra answered, allowing a delicate disbelief to color her tone. "Ah, but I was forgetting. You were not present when we discussed what to do with Brodhi and Rhuan." Her smile was faint, but he saw the amusement in her eyes, heard it in her voice. "For differing reasons, they broke their vows and came back into Alisanos," she said. "But circumstances were judged to matter, so it was decided that they should begin again. Five more years before they may return to the Kiba."

Alario let the red scrim in his eyes drop down. His flesh warmed on his bones; he knew very well that his skin had darkened. "I should kill him now. *Now.*"

"And break with ritual? You?" She raised her brows. "That would cost you your place among us. Is that what you wish?"

"He is unworthy."

"Of course he is. And you will have the opportunity to kill him for it . . . in five years." She was nearly as tall as he, and equally able to intimidate when she wished. "A weak seed, Alario. You selected the wrong woman. You would do better to select one of us."

He smiled thinly. "You?"

Her shrug was casual, insousciant. "Karadath would not take kindly to that."

"And yet you give him no child, no *dioscuri* of your own making."

"The human woman will. We know she is fecund."

It startled him, though out of long habit he showed nothing. "Has Karadath found another woman? A human woman?"

"He has. Alisanos swallowed her then spat her out. Rhuan— himself swallowed and spat out—brought her to the Kiba. We saw her mettle. She dared to suggest we aren't gods at all."

"And that is a recommendation for breeding?"

"Of course it is, Alario. And you know it."

"It was a human woman who gave me a worthless *dioscuri*. If Karadath takes this other woman, how certain is he that the same won't happen to him?

Ylarra laughed. "It wasn't Karadath whose seed was weak. He sired Brodhi on a human woman, and no one may argue that Brodhi is worthless. That title falls only to Rhuan."

She judged him, he knew. As did all of them. Brodhi had killed all of his siblings to claim the favored place, the honor of challenge when the time came; Rhuan killed no one. There was no denying it: Alario's get disdained the ritual, repudiated their customs. "When we engage, he and I," Alario said, "there will be an end to it. I'll kill him immediately."

"I would assume so," Ylarra agreed. "No one will take that wager. But you have no other *dioscuri*." Her mouth quirked. "Is it better to raise up a weak one? Or to begin again?"

Karadath had Brodhi. Brodhi was all any of them were, and strongly favored. But as Ylarra suggested, it was a wise plan for Karadath to sire another *dioscuri*, in case Brodhi should fall. A wise plan indeed.

And nothing to persuade Alario from doing the same himself.

RHUAN WAS FIRST out of the grove, running to the screams. He, Ilona, and the others spilled out of thick-bolled, storm-wracked trees into the cleared central area that surrounded the hub of the new bonfire ring. Folk had been on their way to morning rites for Ilona. All had been arrested in motion, originally heading toward the swell of hill between the damaged grove and the old-growth trees, exiting tents and wagons, crossing new footpaths and the circumference of the bonfire ring. But now all were frozen in place. Rhuan thought initially a Hecari culling party had arrived, but then he realized that everyone was staring into the sky, many of them pointing overhead. Something black flew out of the rising sun.

The shadow was huge. Despite thin morning sunlight, it flowed across the ground. The wingspread was enormous.

Rhuan knew. Instantly.

"Down!" he shouted, hands cupped around his mouth. "Everyone down! Lie still! Don't move!" He spun in place, gesturing sharply to Bethid, Mikal, and Jorda as they came up behind Ilona. "Down—down!" He closed urgent hands on Ilona's arms and pushed her to the ground. " 'Lona—down. Make no movement, no sound." Once again he raised his voice. "*Everyone down!* Mothers, keep your children still!"

He did not himself flatten, but dropped to one knee. Movement here and there caught his eye as some folk followed orders while others gathered up children and ran for the grove, for the tents, for the wagons. For any shelter they might find in the new-laid settlement.

Too much movement— "Be still!" he roared. "No one is to move!" He saw one woman, frozen in place by panic, standing in the open like a single stalk of corn in a flattened field. Cursing, he plunged to his feet and ran to her, still shouting. "Lie flat! Everyone!"

Ironic, he thought, when he himself was doing precisely what he told the folk not to. But there was no choice.

Rhuan caught the woman, shoved her down without warning or apology. She landed hard, one arm trapped beneath her, and he went down beside her. He understood the impulse that cried out for motion, for flight, but movement was too dangerous.

From the corner of his eye he saw a young boy darting near the bonfire ring and a woman racing after him from the shelter of the tents. The shadow against the ground loomed close, loomed large. The wingspread swallowed woman and boy. In the light of the new sun, scales gleamed russett and ruddy and gold.

The beast came down. Rhuan smelled the odor of it, the musky scent of Alisanos. Talons closed in flesh. Whirlwinds of dust eddied in the air as massive wings beat toward the heavens. Horrified men and women screamed in disbelieving terror. The woman next to him ceased her noise only when he clamped a hand across her mouth. "Be still! Be still!"

But panic infected the folk. Some followed orders and lay flat, shielding their heads with hands and arms, but others, in the open and unable to stand it, scrambled to their feet and ran.

"No!" Rhuan cried. "Don't move!"

But they moved. They ran this way and that, filling footpaths, darting across the central area surrounding the fire ring.

Already he grew hoarse, his throat burning. "Be still!"

But they were not still. They tempted, tantilized, though unintentionally. The bodies of the woman and child were dropped from overhead and thumped into the earth, dead limbs asprawl as people screamed. The beast canted right, scooped. This time a man was yanked up into the air.

Chaos. Any chance Rhuan had of controlling the people vanished. He knew the beast, knew its instincts. In Alisanos, Audrun had listened to him. Audrun had done as told. These folk were frightened out of their wits and running for their lives.

A quick glance showed him that Ilona, as instructed, lay perfectly still, face-down against the ground. She made no sound. Nearby, Bethid followed suit. Mikal and Jorda were slower, heavier, and flung themselves down at the fringe of the grove several paces away. Too many fled this way and that. From the air, all that frenzied movement would further incite what was already a deadly prey drive.

Now the man's lax body was dropped. The beast altered direction.

Sprawled humans wailed, shrieked, sobbed, prayed. Cursing, Rhuan saw the massive body lower, clutch, then rise. This time, a girl. Her thin, piercing scream cut off sharply. The beast's pungent odor lingered in Rhuan's nostrils, bathed the back of this throat.

Four were beyond help. Three of them lay broken against the ground, and the last, limp, was clasped in talons. But now, finally, movement ceased. Humans were sheltered by tents, by wagons, or lay very still. At last, they listened.

Too late for four.

Expansive wings stretched, flapped, lifting the sinuous, coppery mass into the air. The girl's body remained clutched in talons.

Somewhere a woman wailed in tones of desperate grief.

ILONA LAY FLAT, face down, one cheek pressed into earth as both arms cradled her head. As she breathed, she felt puffs of floury dust rising against her mouth. She tasted grit, salt, astringency. A stone cut into her cheek. Every instinct in her body screamed at her to get up from the ground, to run, *run*, run to shelter. But Rhuan had told them all to go down, get down, to remain still. As exposed as she felt, she trusted him. So she lay pressed into the dirt, every measure of unshielded body aprickle with dread, with the stark awareness that death hovered just overhead.

Mother, Mother, Mother. She was afraid to speak it aloud, to make any noise at all.

The beast's scent was strong, and yet she did not find it unpleasant. It was a melange of odors that struck her as toweringly male. She felt pressure in the air, saw from the corner of her eye that shadows moved. And then the pressure lessened, the shadows withdrew, and the scent of the beast faded. She felt a hand in her hair, briefly cupping her skull, and knew it was Rhuan's.

"All right," he rasped in a voice roughened by shouting. "It's gone." Then he raised his voice once again, pitching it to carry. "It's all right! It's gone! We're safe!"

Ilona pushed herself to her knees, shaking back her array of tangled ringlets. She brushed dirt and debris from her face, spat out grit, wiped it from her lips with the back of one hand. Rhuan was standing next to her. For a moment, as had the beast, he blocked the sun. Then he leaned down, reached out a hand, and she let him pull her to her feet.

Others came out of tents, climbed from under wagons, picked themselves up from the earth. Children wailed. Women keened. Voices were raised in frantic questions.

The sun now showed its entire face above the horizon, warming the day. Beneath it, three bodies lay sprawled near the fire ring, fragile, broken, flesh torn by talons.

Bethid came up beside Ilona, backhanding grit from her bottom lip. "Mother of Moons," she murmured blankly, staring at the bodies. Then she turned to Rhuan, asking exactly what Ilona meant to ask, "What *was* that?"

"A draka," he said.

Bethid's eyes were intent. "From Alisanos."

Rhuan's tone was purposefully light, but Ilona saw a brief flicker in his eyes. "Where else?"

Bethid looked shaken. "Will it come back?"

Mikal and Jorda joined them. Anticipating the questions, Rhuan said, "A draka. Deadly, as you saw. And no, I can't tell you with certainty whether it will return, though it's possible, but I *can* say that we have a reprieve. For a while."

"How do you know that?" Bethid asked. "How can you be so certain?"

Rhuan's expression was grim. "First, it will feed."

The flesh tightened on Ilona's bones. "Oh Mother . . ." She knew. She knew, and it sickened her. It sickened all of them, who had seen a child's body carried into the air.

"You must understand," Rhuan told them, habitual humor absent. "Learn this lesson now and remember it: *anything is possible.*"

"But—" Mikal began.

"Anything," Rhuan repeated, cutting him off decisively. "The world you knew is altered. When Alisanos moves, it swallows some and disgorges others. For days, months, years, it remains unstable."

Jorda's eyes were full of horror. "Might there be others? Of, of—" he flapped an arm toward the sky, "—*that?*"

Alarmed, Bethid fixed on something else. "Are you saying Alisanos might move again?"

Rhuan's expression was grim. "Anything is possible."

Mikal gestured. "Then we should pack up the settlement and move!"

Rhuan nodded. "That is certainly understandable. But I would strongly recommend that you let Brodhi and me sort out where the boundaries are first. It serves nothing to pack up and move until we *know where safety lies.*"

Ilona was aware of others straggling up, tent-folk and karavaners alike. She understood why: Mikal and Jorda had established themselves as leaders, and Rhuan had been the one to issue orders when the draka attacked, clearly familiar with its habits. Dusty faces were stunned, tense, and frightened. Everyone spoke at once, asking questions, demanding answers in tones of desperate insistence.

A glance at Rhuan proved he was as aware of it as she. "I promise," he said to the folk, "I do promise to answer your questions as best I may. But for now—" He broke off, brows arching sharply, attention once again drawn away. Ilona turned and followed his line of sight.

Brodhi. Out of Alisanos.

He paused, saw the gathering of folk, the bodies, Rhuan in the center, and swiftly altered course.

He *walked away.*

Ilona couldn't believe it, even of Brodhi.

Rhuan's mouth stretched into a taut line, but he continued smoothly with what he had started to say, ignoring Brodhi. Ilona understood why Rhuan did so: expressing any curiosity about Brodhi's appearance might lead folk to question where he had been. And just now there were too many other questions to be answered. Addressing the fact that Brodhi had been in Alisanos searching for Audrun and her children would undermine any calm Rhuan might achieve. "But for now," he said, "we'd best look to rites for the dead."

Ilona felt a chill. Rites that had been originally intended for her.

And it was nearly tangible, the weight of questions in everyone's eyes. How could she be standing among them, clearly alive?

Chapter 3

*I*LONA BLURTED THE first thing that came into her mind. "I wasn't dead. I *appeared* to be dead, certainly, but I was only unconscious." She realized that laid blame for the mistake at Jorda's door, and hastened to absolve him. She was a diviner; there were many things about divining and its different sects that folk did not know. "I was dream-walking." She infused her tone with confident matter-of-factness. "Lerin taught me how, before she died in the storm. I struck my head." Ilona touched her temple briefly. "I wasn't dead after all . . ." *Oh Mother, help me find a way through this tangle!* And then she found it, altering the topic. "—but Rhuan is correct. We do need to hold rites. For the others."

Bethid raised her voice. "She's a diviner. She can officiate. We're lucky she isn't dead. Now we have a link to the Mother, even if not all of us are accustomed to relying on a hand-reader."

Ilona smiled inwardly with relief. Nicely done. She owed the courier her thanks, when the opportunity presented itself.

"I'm going to Brodhi," Bethid told Ilona, touching her elbow briefly. Then she circled around the crowd to take the shortest route.

"Dawn rites," Jorda announced, promptly assuming Bethid's lead. "Tomorrow."

It would allow time for the bodies to be cleansed and made ready, two more graves dug, and vigils held. It also bought Ilona time to sort out a more detailed explanation for her resurrection. She couldn't contradict her story and tell them she *wasn't* Shoia; and people would certainly ask when they came requesting she read their hands in the wake of the draka attack. It bought, as well, a day for Rhuan to prepare answers that would calm them. To nearly all tent-folk, he was mostly a stranger, but he had warned the settlement of the deepwood's imminent shift, saving lives. The karavaners knew to trust him and would say so. Rhuan was believed to be Shoia, as was Brodhi; like diviners, they were *expected* to know things others might not.

Ilona reflected that she could not look less like a hand-reader had she tried, clad in a wrinkled, dusty burial shift with grit on her face, and hair a tangled mess. But she summoned a professional demeanor despite her disarray. "We will see to it that the dead are given proper rites as they cross the river. At this time tomorrow, we'll meet at the burying place."

Where she herself, this morning, would have been interred.

"Wait!" called a voice. "Brodhi—wait! Did you find them? Did you find my family in Alisanos?"

The farmsteader, Davyn. Of course. With exquisite timing, hastening toward Brodhi as he exited the grove. "Sweet Mother," Ilona murmured as a stirring ran through the crowd. Shock was palpable.

A man blurted what all of them were thinking. "He was in the deepwood?"

And another. "He was in Alisanos? *Came out* of Alisanos?"

BETHID CAUGHT UP to Brodhi not far from the couriers' common tent. She could tell from his posture, an indication she knew well, that he had no intention of explaining anything, but she had to ask. "Ilona told me you'd gone into Alisanos. Are you all right?"

When he continued his determined striding, Bethid jogged after him and caught at an arm. "Brodhi—I know. I know you're not Shoia. Ilona told me."

He did not tear his arm out of her grasp, as she expected, but he nonetheless impressed upon her, with his expression, the rigidity of his jaw as he halted and turned to face her, that her inquiries were not welcome. She let go of his arm instantly. "The hand-reader knows nothing. She is a charlatan."

Bethid shook her head. "No. She's not." She drew in a breath and ventured, "You risked Alisanos . . . I simply want to know if you are all right."

Before he could answer—provided he intended to answer, and that was not a certainty—the farmsteader arrived. "Did you *find* them? Are they all right? Did you bring them out?" Restrained desperation was evident in his tone, his face. His clothing was soiled and wrinkled, and his hair lay damply against his head. "Where are they?"

Bethid saw something briefly flicker crimson in Brodhi's eyes. The faintest trace of ruddy color suffused his skin. It was the closest he had ever come, in front of her, to overt anger. He could be a cold man; she had seen that. But this? This heat was not Brodhi.

But Brodhi, she remembered as her belly spasmed with the thought, was unlike anyone she knew. Not Shoia, Ilona had said, but from Alisanos. *Of* Alisanos. Rhuan also.

Were they even human?

Brodhi's words were clipped. "I did not go into Alisanos to find your family."

"I know that, but *did* you find them? Unintentionally?" The farmsteader put out a hand, as if he intended to touch Brodhi. But the expression on Brodhi's face repudiated the impulse. Davyn's hand fell slack at his side. He repeated, "*Did* you find them?"

In the face of Davyn's desperation and Brodhi's indifference, Bethid blurted, "For the Mother's sake, Brodhi, *tell* him if you know something!"

The faint ruddiness disappeared from Brodhi's skin. His eyes, once again, were brown, and implacable. "Your wife and your children are together."

"Alive?" The farmsteader was hoarse-voiced, close to tears of frustration.

Brodhi said, "Perhaps not, anymore, as you would describe living." He shot a glance at Bethid, challenging her to speak again. "They are now of Alisanos."

A harsh, inarticulate cry broke from the farmsteader's mouth. He wavered on his feet a moment, turned unsteadily as if he meant to walk away but abruptly swung back. "*You* came back! *You* came out!"

"So did Rhuan!" Bethid, shaken, stared at Brodhi in disbelief. "How can you say such a thing? Obviously there is a means to leave Alisanos. It's been done!"

"Rhuan . . ." the farmsteader said in a flat, stunned voice. "He was with—he was with my family when Alisanos moved." His eyes on Bethid were abruptly alive with hope. "Rhuan has returned also?"

Calmly, Brodhi said, "Perhaps you should discuss this with him."

Bethid opened her mouth to speak again, but shut it as Brodhi turned and began walking once again toward the common tent. A painful ache centered itself in her chest, right behind her breastbone. She liked Brodhi. In spite of his moods, his self-imposed isolation, she *liked* Brodhi. He had done her a great favor in seeing to it she could enter the courier trials. But this. . . . In the midst of so much grief and panic, how could he be so indifferent?

"Do you know where he is?" The farmsteader looked beyond her, toward the fire circle. "Rhuan?"

Bethid glanced back. "He was right there—" But he wasn't anymore. Neither Rhuan nor Jorda nor Mikal nor Ilona. "The ale-tent," she said abruptly. "I would look there."

But she did not. She went after Brodhi.

ONCE BEFORE, JORDA and Mikal had found select men among the tent-folk and karavaners. All were older, all unlikely to panic, and all had wits enough to grasp salient points without making judgments or assumptions. Those men, summoned out of the tide of folk who still clustered near the fire ring, now gathered in Mikal's tent. Seats were found on stools, chairs, and benches. Hastily erected after the storm, the tent showed signs of battering with torn cloth and cracked timbers hastily wrapped with ropes to keep them whole. But then, so did the men show signs of battering; mental if not physical. Mikal found tankards and cups enough to serve them and charged nothing for the ale and spirits.

The plank across the tops of two heavy wooden barrels was thick enough to support a man. Rhuan boosted himself atop it, legs dangling, boot toes touching the earthen floor. He drank his own share of ale, then set the tankard aside. Quietly he told them what a draka was, described the habits of the beasts, and did not downplay the outcome when a person was taken. "If you see a winged shadow, lie down. Immediately. Wherever you may be. Don't move, don't even twitch, until you are absolutely certain the draka is gone. Movement attracts them. *Prey* attracts them, and that means infants, children, adults, as well as livestock. Crying, shouting, and screaming merely provokes them further."

And eventually, as expected, one man asked what all of them were thinking. His hair was a mix of brown and gray. Smile lines webbed the flesh near his blue eyes, though at present no humor touched his face. Rhuan recognized him as a karavaner. Sandic, he recalled. "How do you know so much about Alisanos?"

As a Shoia, as they knew him, Rhuan replied with casual ease, "Draka are legend among my people. It isn't Alisanos we know, but the beasts." Twenty pairs of eyes stared back at him. "There are tales of a time when Alisanos moved, and two draka were disgorged. Many of my people were killed."

"And resurrected?" Sandic asked. "It would seem your people have a greater advantage than we do. Those who fell from *our* sky will never live again, nor the child who was taken."

It prompted murmuring among the others. Rhuan nodded. "That is true. But a truth is also that when killed repeatedly, even Shoia die."

That, too, roused murmuring. Concerned glances were exchanged.

It was Jorda who asked the obvious question before anyone else could. "What happened to those draka? Did you find a way to kill them?"

The lie came easily because it had crossed his mind the moment he saw the draka. "We fed cattle on thornapple," Rhuan said. "They went mad from the poison. The draka then ate the cattle—" But he broke off. His vision grayed out and all the hairs stood up on his body. Swearing, he swung himself off the wooden plank. His suggestion to the men was succinct. "Out. *Now.*"

The earth rippled beneath his boot soles. A shiver shook the ale-tent. A strong shudder followed it, pewter tankards clanking as they tipped over, were knocked one against the other. Others fell and rolled off the tables, spilling ale. Canvas trembled. The earth beneath groaned. The rope holding one of the poles together came unwrapped, and the tautness caused it to whip through the air. One man, struck, cried out.

Poles cracked. The tent leaned to one side. Shallow guy-line anchor irons were pulled from the ground. Outside, Rhuan caught at poles and billowing canvas, attempting to hold open an escape route. Mikal, as expected, was the last to leave, fighting his way through falling canvas. Throughout the grove so close to Mikal's tent, amidst the ranks of tents surrounding the fire pit, Rhuan heard screaming. In a matter of moments all of the assembled men had dispersed, running for tents and wagons, seeking families. Dogs barked frenziedly. A horse, broken rope hanging from its halter, careened through the center of the settlement.

The ale-tent collapsed. Then the undulations of the earth died away. All was still again, save for the sound of weeping and a woman's raised voice, demanding explanation of a husband who knew no more than she.

"Sweet Mother," Mikal said hoarsely, staring at the mass of canvas and broken poles, "how much more can we endure? How long before this stops?"

Falsehood served nothing. Rhuan gave him the truth. "Weeks. Months. Possibly even years."

"*Years!*"

Rhuan hung onto his patience with effort; he wanted badly just to *tell* Mikal how he knew the answers. But not yet, if ever. "There is no predicting it, Mikal. Alisanos does as it will do."

"Then we should leave," Mikal said sharply. "We should pack up and go as far from here as possible."

Rhuan shook his head. "As I told Jorda, until we know the precise boundaries of Alisanos, it's too dangerous to test its borders."

"But Brodhi made his way here," Mikal protested. "There must be a safe way in. *And* out. He can show us."

Rhuan clamped his teeth closed on a sharp retort. Patiently he said, "There is danger here from Alisanos, of course, and we should leave when we know more. Remember when Brodhi arrived accompanied by Hecari from Cardatha? Would you have us risk culling parties? That's precisely what will happen if we leave."

"And in the meantime we risk Alisanos?" Mikal shook his head. "At least the warriors gave us clean deaths."

"Clean?" Rhuan asked. "You saw what they did, Mikal. Is it truly a clean death for a child to have his brains dashed out by a warclub?"

Beneath a coating of dust, Mikal's face was anguished. "Then what can we do?"

"We wait," Rhuan said, "until we know a safe route out of here. Then we can leave. But for now—" Rhuan squatted down and took into his hand a cracked pole. "—we'll raise this tent again."

DAVYN FELL TO hands and knees as the earth shuddered beneath him. He was aware of movement, of people once again running who had run from the flying beast. Cries and screams filled the air, as did shrill protests from horses and the barking of dogs. Tents began leaning. He saw the ale-tent shaking, heard the cracking of poles, saw canvas begin to billow into collapse even as men ran from the tent.

And then he saw Rhuan. Sweet Mother, he would get answers from the guide. Even now.

Davyn thrust himself to his feet, staggering as the earth shifted beneath his boots. Then it steadied, and he ran.

"Rhuan!" he cried. "Wait—"

The karavan guide turned toward him, holding a broken tent pole. Breathless, Davyn slowed to an ungainly stop beside Mikal. "Wait," he repeated, showing the flat of his hand in a gesture of delay. "He said you were in Alisanos, too. The other Shoia." For a moment color suffused Rhuan's face, then faded. "And *she* said so. The woman courier." Davyn tried to regain self-control, but all he wanted to do was shout at the man, to demand an answer. "The courier said they were there, all of them. My family. Did *you* see them?"

The guide's face bore an expression of compassion. It struck Davyn that he knew very well what he said offered no hope. "I did."

"And they were alive?"

Rhuan nodded. "They are in a safe place."

Davyn expelled a rush of breath and words upon it and closed one hand around his string of charms. "Oh, thank the Mother! Oh Mother, bless you!" He reached toward Rhuan, then recalled how Brodhi had reacted. He let his hand fall back to his side. "Please," he said. "Are they all right? Are they—whole?"

"They are safe. When last I saw them, they were safe."

Davyn's belly felt tied in knots. "But—you couldn't bring them out? "

"I could not."

He attempted to keep his tone casual, not accusatory, but failed. "*You* came out. You and the courier both. If you could do so, why not my family?"

Mikal frowned, looking at Rhuan. "What's he talking about? Where were you? Where *are* his folk?"

"In Alisanos," Davyn declared.

"But—" Mikal's frown remained, "You and Brodhi came out. You told us that."

Something flickered briefly in Rhuan's eyes. His face was still, composed of angles and hollows. "Alisanos occasionally gives up what it has swallowed."

"And they're no longer human!" Davyn cried.

The ale-keep scrutinized Rhuan. "But you're not human anyway. Is that why you escaped?"

Before Rhuan could answer, a wave of fear and desperation rose in Davyn's breast. "Why didn't you bring them out with you?" He drew in a tight breath and tried to reknit the fraying shreds of his dignity. "Put yourself in my place. If you saw them, if they are well—" He broke off and lifted his arms then let them fall slack. He felt very much like crying. "Put yourself in my place."

Compassion softened the guide's expression and tone. "I'm sorry. It was not possible to bring them out."

"I don't understand." Davyn's mouth felt numb. "How could you leave them there?"

Rhuan glanced briefly at Mikal, then nodded as if to himself. To Davyn he said, "Is your wagon whole?"

"Yes, but—"

"Then let us go there." Rhuan handed the tent pole to the ale-keep. "There is much to tell you, to explain. Let us do it in private."

Davyn thrust out an arm in the direction of the old grove. "There."

Chapter 4

STRIATED, RUDDY CLIFFS rose up from the earth, loomed as concave palisades over the Kiba. Audrun shaded her eyes against the double suns and squinted upward through the spreading limbs of a wide-canopied tree where she and her children had been summarily escorted.

The massive cliff face was infiltrated by a seemingly haphazard assembly of natural caves as well as hollows chiseled by hand into clean, precise lines and angles. Dwellings were stacked side by side and one atop another, interconnected by a skein of staircases running up, down, and sideways, and wide, arched openings that formed passageways leading more deeply into the cliffs. She could not tell how deeply the caves reached into the cliffs, but all of them were fronted by walls formed of chunks of stacked flat red stone mortared together, mudbrick facades, and beamwork. Colored cloth fluttered in many of the square windows, while tall doorways were warded by shimmery scaled hide or loomed hangings.

Audrun could not begin to count how many dwellings the cliffs hosted. The network of caves, dwellings, staircases, and passageways was vaster than anything she had seen, including the tent settlement where she and her family had joined Jorda's karavan. Awed, she could not imagine how long it had taken to build the cliff dwellings, to refine the extant caves and make homes of them. Many years. Many hands. Many tools.

"Mam." It was Torvic's voice, and plaintive. "Are we just supposed to stay here?"

Here was the stone bench beneath the tree; the sloping rock table immediately opposite the bench; a pathway of russet paving stone and red-tinged dirt. *Here* were her children, trapped as she was, amid beings she had never imagined even in her dreams. Primaries. Firsts. Gods, they called themselves.

Audrun called them captors.

My poor children . . . Yet looking at them one by one, making note of tattered and soiled clothing, fair hair tangled, and a gaunt tautness in their faces, she knew they mirrored her own appearance, her own unspoken desperation. She was exhausted, hungry, thirsty, and had given accelerated birth not long before. Her overused body was beset by trembling. Everything ached. Her skin, hosting uncounted scrapes and scratches, burned. She wanted to collapse into a bed and sleep for weeks. It was what her body needed, but her mind, she knew, would be too busy.

Audrun's mouth twisted as she recalled how she had stood before the primaries assembled in the Kiba and challenged them to act, to find her demon-abducted baby. They clearly held humans in disdain, and she had presented a most unprepossessing figure. But she would do it all again, in the name of the Mother; would do it daily, if necessary. And she would declare to them, repeatedly, that they were not gods at all.

Rhuan's people. The resemblence of one to another was striking, with identical dark-copper hair, clear brown eyes, the faintest ruddy sheen in skin. She wished he were present to guide her, to offer advice on how the primaries thought, on what mistakes she should not make. It was her task, she knew, to change their minds about humans. If she and her children were to be prisoners here—and she believed wholeheartedly that it *was* captivity, regardless of Ylarra's claim—she would make certain the primaries came to understand how humans thought. To understand that difference need not be weakness.

But Rhuan was gone.

Desolation and despair. She thought she might choke on both as they swept into her chest, rose to fill her throat. *Here* was her childrens' future, and her own.

Audrun closed her eyes as tears threatened. She would not allow the children to see their mother weep. Regardless of how frightened she might be, how overwhelmed she felt, she dared not let the children see it, feel it, sense it.

And then memory rose to banish those emotions. Her eyes snapped open. While lost in despair, overwhelmed by their circumstances, she had lost track of a most vital and valuable piece of information. It unfolded before her, and in that memory was strength.

A *road* would be built. A road leading safely through Alisanos from the settlement to . . . elsewhere. Atalanda? She had seen Davyn's crude map showing the shortcut edging around the borders of Alisanos. Atalanda province, on that map, lay due west, on the far side of the deepwood. If the road ran from the tent settlement in Sancorra to safety in Atalanda, it offered freedom to those in Sancorra province fleeing the depredations of the Hecari warlord and his people, just as her family had.

A safe way through Alisanos. That, Rhuan had gained for them; because of her, because of her children, because of the husband who, undoubtedly, was now frantic with the need to find them.

There was purpose in Rhuan's challenge to the primaries, and she had not seen it. Purpose and solution.

Acknowledgment replaced despair. Tension began to subside, replaced by fragile hope. A road meant she and her children could leave the deepwood, could find Davyn and put this nightmare to rest. . . . Rhuan had said he would bring Davyn to her, once the road was built

And if there were a road through Alisanos, they could travel upon it to safety. Away from Alisanos, away from the Hecari. To security, to a new life. Perhaps once on the road any change begun by the deepwood would dissipate.

Except . . . except there was the infant. She must be found. Before anything else.

As she thought of the child, her breasts ached. A glance down showed damp patches where the milk-soaked breast bindings had failed. Her children had seen it before; it meant nothing to them. But Audrun was embarrassed to think of the primaries seeing milk stains. Heat rose in her face. She had defied them in soiled clothing and tangled hair. That, she could do again. But that the obvious signs of lactation were perhaps amusing to the primaries irritated her.

Then again, it reinforced her demand that they find the child. It was difficult to put a missing baby out of one's mind when so obvious a reminder was before them.

"New bindings," Audrun muttered. Tighter bindings. For comfort if nothing else.

Movement caught her eye. Gillan, perched on the table-like formation of stone directly across the path, tugged his homespun trouser leg back down to his ankle, hiding the the ruin of his leg, the area in the flesh of his calf that resembled an imperfectly stitched patchwork of bruising that was, in fact, scales.

Scales. Human flesh made into—what?

Audrun recoiled from that picture in her mind. Instead she answered Torvic. "No, we will not stay right here. We are to be given accomodations." She rose, pulling Megritte up into her arms. The girl was heavy, but at that moment Audrun did not care. "Let us go find whomever is responsible for giving us these accommodations."

Torvic asked, "Are we ever going home?"

She did not know if he meant the cabin where he had been born, burned by Hecari, or the wagon that had become their home on the way to Atalanda. And she dared not ask him. There was no purpose in frightening a boy.

"Not yet." Audrun retained a casual tone as she hitched Megritte into a better position on one hip. "But we will. I promise it. The Mother of Moons will see us home."

And Gillan, shocking her with the raw anger in his tone, said, "This is Alisanos. How do we know the Mother is even here? How do we know any moon is here? Mam—*this is Alisanos.*"

Audrun held Megritte more firmly even as she met her oldest

son's blue eyes, his bitter and wet blue eyes. Because of those tears, she modified her own tone from the snap of authority and impatience to a gentler assurance. "We are to have a road, Gillan. Safe passage. When it is built, when enough of it is built, we will walk out of here to your father." She nodded firmly, settling the topic. "Now, everyone up. Ellica, come along. Without the sapling, please."

Ellica, still seated, glanced up, startled. Pale hair was a rats' nest, with snarled braids and loosened locks in tangled communion. "But—my tree. I can't leave it. It's too young."

"Sweet Mother . . . it's a *tree*, Ellica, not a child!"

Tears filled Ellica's eyes. "I have to tend it."

Audrun gritted her teeth. Now she had two children in tears—and the two eldest at that, who should offer strength of will, not doubts, for the sakes of the youngest. It was up to her, then, how everyone fared. "Then bring the tree with you. We'll plant it wherever the primaries see fit to house us."

AS HE PASSED by the battered old grove on his left, Brodhi sensed a presence behind him and stopped short. Bethid nearly ran into him as he swung around. "What now?" he asked and felt a brief spark of surprise that he was actually annoyed. *Annoyed.*

She re-established balance by taking a step backward. Her delicate features, so incongruous in view of her wiry strength and physically demanding employment, were sharp beneath tanned skin. In her eyes he saw an expression that surprised him: contempt. Anger, he had seen in her; frustration more often, when he behaved in ways she felt were rude. But contempt? Never.

Contempt . . . from a human. For *him*.

The realization delayed his answer until he could summon a tone of nonchalance. "I repeat: What now?"

"That farmsteader has lost everything," Bethid answered in a clipped voice. "How dare you? How *dare* you? Have you no compassion whatsoever?"

"Compassion," Brodhi said, his tone bland, "is a useless emotion. I avoid it." As he avoided all others. Except for that flash of annoyance. He would have to consider that. He would have to consider why Bethid's contempt meant anything to him.

And it had.

"Yes," she said. "Yes, I can see that. However—and I may only be able to count the occurrences on the fingers of one hand—you have proved *helpful* now and again. Why not help a man desperate to locate his family?"

"I told him the truth," Brodhi answered. "Is that not helpful? I understand humans esteem truth."

"But there are *ways* of telling—"

He overrode her. "Yes, Bethid; yes, I am all too aware that humans also esteem emotions, having a raft of them to use as needed. His family *is* in Alisanos, Bethid. I merely told him so."

"Brutally."

He ignored that. "Now he knows. He will come to terms with it."

"But why did you have to be so cruel? Why say what you said the *way* you said it?"

A brief flicker of amusement at her convoluted question died out. "What did I say?"

She gestured frustration by lifting upturned arms away from her body, then let them slap down against her thighs. "I can't quote you . . . but it was something to the effect that they were no longer living the way *he* would recognize living. Mother of Moons, that's harsh, Brodhi. Is he supposed to accept that with no questions? With no pain?"

"He wanted to know. He knows." Brodhi lifted his hand in a sharp motion to cut her off as she opened her mouth. "I have learned, among humans, that false hopes can be every bit as painful as hard truths. The truth requires less time and less effort." He raised his eyebrows. "Would you rather be struck to death by a Hecari warclub all at once, or have your flesh flayed bit by bit over a handful of your days?"

Bethid scowled at him, offering no answer.

"What would you do," he began, "if this family were to come out of Alisanos?

"Rejoice," Bethid snapped. "What would you expect me to do? I'd welcome them. Of course!"

"You would mourn them," Brodhi told her, "once you were over your shock and disgust. No doubt you would send up prayers to your Mother of Moons. Alive the family may be but no longer human. Not anymore."

"Of course they are still—"

"*No*, Bethid. Here is the truth of it: Alisanos transforms humans. The wild magic seeps into flesh, into bones, into blood. I have seen what humans do when one of their own returns. There is no 'compassion,' Bethid. There is no kindness. There is no welcome. I have seen humans vomit, so upset by the horror of what their kin have become. I have seen rocks thrown. I have seen backs turned. I have seen a woman screaming at what once was her husband, telling him to go away and never come back. Would you have this Davyn do the same to his wife? To his children?" He shook his head. "My compassion is truer. It saves him from the grief, his family from excoriation and abandonment."

Her prickly frustration faded into shock. "*How* transformed?"

"How is it done? Or what is done?"

"Sweet Mother, Brodhi—*How will they be changed?*"

"The mechanism is the will of Alisanos. As for the change itself?" He shrugged. "It depends on how long a human is in Alisanos and where. The wild magic is inconsistent."

" 'Inconsistent,' " she echoed with explicit clarity, glaring at him. "How *in*convenient."

"What would you have me say? Should I lie to him? Mislead him? Is that not cruel?" He saw color rise in her face. It was the edge of anger, born of a depth of empathy that he could not comprehend. "Bethid, you know nothing about Alisanos. I do."

"Because you're from there."

It was statement, not inquiry. Ah, yes. She knew he wasn't Shoia. The hand-reader had told her so; the hand-reader who had, unaccountably, drawn the attention of Alario, his sire's brother. Possibly the hand-reader knew more than any human alive about Alisanos.

But not enough.

Bedthid's hands went to her hips. "Alisanos is a place, not a *being*. How can it have a will?"

He stared into her eyes and saw an implacability equal to his own. It was far more than curiosity—this was a demand. And yet he could not explain Alisanos to her, because he lacked the human words. Alisanos, to those born of it, simply *was*. Every child of his people was taught from the creche that Alisanos was omniscient and sentient, and terrible in both. Alisanos was greater than even the highest of the primaries.

Who was, at this particular time, Karadath, his sire.

Five years. Five human years. Until that time was up, he could not challenge his sire. He could not prove himself. He could not ascend. He could do nothing, now, save repeat his journey to complete his journey.

"I'm not in the habit of betraying confidences," Bethid said, "as you well know. And I can't see that my knowing additional details would harm this settlement more than it already has been harmed." She made an expansive gesture with her right arm, as if presenting the entire settlement to his attention. "See what Alisanos has already done? Tell me why, Brodhi. And if it's a *who*, not a *what*, tell me that, too. I deserve it, don't you think?" She tapped her chest. "I am here at the edge of the deepwood, within striking range. If I am to be taken by Alisanos, to be transformed by it, I want to know why and how." And then the demand dropped away from her voice and posture. Bethid looked tired as she raised a hand, palm out. "But—not now . . . later. I suspect it will take all of my attention, and I haven't it to spare just now." She *was* tired; it was most unlike Bethid to let go of either argument or passionate discussion before its natural conclusion. She looked past him and sighed. "I see our tent is down again . . . Timmon and Alorn are mired in canvas." Her gaze returned to his. "Repairs are more easily made by four in place of two." She slapped him on the arm with the back of her hand. "Now, Brodhi. *Before* the sun sets."

He turned to watch her as she moved past him, striding toward the collapsed tent. She was a small person, small even for a human woman, and yet her personality and determination were greater than any human he knew. Brodhi considered for a moment, eyebrows arched, then hitched a shoulder in a brief shrug and followed her. It served him as well to put up a tent he intended to sleep in come nighttime.

And at least Bethid's attention had been appropriated.

Chapter 5

*T*HERE HAD BEEN no time, no time at all, nor room in Ilona's mind to truly comprehend what had happened to her. First, death. Then, life and a night in Rhuan's arms; and then harried, blundering explanations to friends and strangers about her resurrection. Now she stood alone in a soiled burial shift, hair a mass of tangled ringlets, feet bare and dirty, with nothing *but* time to sort out the turmoil in her mind.

They had left her, all of them, their minds on other things: Rhuan departing with the farmsteader whose family was lost to Alisanos, Mikal and Jorda marshaling men to again raise the ale-tent, Bethid following Brodhi, and the tent-folk and karavaners once again turning their attention to their damaged belongings.

She was alone, yet surrounded.

Ilona put out her hands. They trembled, even as a shiver ran through her body. Now, now there was time, and her body knew it. It overtook her, shook her, weakened her knees. She was altogether, and suddenly, hungry. Thirsty. Utterly exhausted.

Nausea rose. Ilona pressed both trembling hands against her mouth. *No, no—please, no.*

She ran. Shaking, shivering, hungry and not, in need of privacy. In need of a bath. In need of . . . *something*. Something as yet unrecognizable.

She had been dead. She had been murdered. Yet lived.

Shoia, Rhuan said. That was the glib explanation; and the only one, he said, that others would understand. He was not Shoia, nor the courier, but she apparently was.

Shoia.

She had no idea what it actually meant, to be Shoia. Or if, beyond offering a person seven lives, it meant anything at all.

As Ilona reached her wagon parked beneath one of the old-growth giants, she stopped at the bottom of the steps. Nausea subsided. Now she had time to send an appeal skyward, something unconnected to her mundane belly but wholly connected to emotions, particularly self-doubt: *Oh Mother, help me. Guide me in this.*

She climbed the steps into a wagon, no longer tidy in the wake of the earth's violent upheaval. For a moment she stood just inside the door, noting with empty interest the tumbled array of belongings and supplies spilled across the floorboards, across the blankets she and Rhuan had shared. But her chaotic surroundings were of no moment. Other concerns filled her mind.

Slowly, she folded her shaking body and sat down on the blankets. She pulled the coverlet from the floorboards, from under those things fallen. She wrapped it around her, clutched it close, but could not still her trembling.

She had Rhuan . . . was that not enough, to have the man she desired?

No. It was not.

Too much, too much in her mind. Time, now, to parse the thoughts and realizations gathering behind her eyes.

She hugged the coverlet, hugged the body beneath it, and felt tears rising.

Ilona let them fall.

 THE FARMSTEADER MENTIONED the need to relieve himself, so Rhuan was alone as he climbed the steps into the family's wagon. He paused just inside the door, noting that the contents of the tall, huge-wheeled conveyance were no longer set perfectly into their places, as was required to host two adults and five children. And the rib-supported canopy listed to one side, as if the earth's shaking had pushed everything out of true.

At the front of the wagon, wood planking formed a large, elevated platform. Atop it lay thin, straw-stuffed mattresses, muslin sheets, and a tangle of coverlets. Room for four children, Rhuan realized, but the boards had shifted and were no longer evenly aligned. Trunks filled the area beneath the platform. A child's cloth doll lay face down in the center aisle.

The wagon shifted as the farmsteader climbed up, ducking his head to avoid the ribs overhead. He paused, then gestured Rhuan to take a seat upon the bedding platform. He himself sat down upon the floor crosslegged. As Davyn picked up the doll, Rhuan saw that his hands shook. A quick glance at his face betrayed tears in the man's eyes.

A wholly human compassion rose in Rhuan. He shoved the platform boards back into order, then sat down. "It is the truth, what I've told you. They are safe."

But that was not enough. Not for husband and father. He saw it in Davyn's eyes as tears dried.

Rhuan moistened his lips, drew in a breath that fully expanded his lungs, and continued. "It is true that Alisanos occasionally gives up what it has taken almost immediately, but we simply cannot assume that will happen in this case. Hope, yes; of course we will hope, but we must not be frantic with it."

" 'We,' " Davyn echoed. Something glinted in his eyes, something akin to a potent anger suppressed, and Rhuan realized he had erred in words meant to reassure. " '*We*' assume nothing," the farmsteader declared flatly, with a sting in every word, "and I will indeed hope, and pray, in any display of emotion I wish. Frantic? Oh yes, I may be frantic. I may be desolate. I may be naked in my despair. But you have no wife, no children. How in the Mother's name can you even begin to comprehend what I think and feel?"

It was a natural reaction. Rhuan opened his mouth to say that according to the customs of his people, he actually was married to the farmsteader's wife. Then he closed it, abruptly aware that such a statement would not, in the least, bring ease.

Davyn continued to stare at him fixedly. Rhuan saw the tautness of his face, the pallor of his flesh, the anger in his eyes. "Did you send us the wrong way?" Davyn asked in a raw tone. "In the storm. Intentionally. Did you send my family the wrong way? Those I've asked have said you would never do such a thing . . . but I know nothing about you. What if you had a reason for giving them up to the storm? And is it just bad fortune that I was left behind to ask such questions?"

It had not crossed Rhuan's mind that he might be blamed for the loss of the farmsteader's family. For several moments he could not think of a proper answer, until at last he said, "No. No. And I will swear that to your Mother, if you wish."

Davyn flared, "You are not worthy of the Mother."

Oh, indeed: anger and hostility. Rhuan owed nothing to this Mother of Moons; she was no deity of his, but he offered because he believed it might mean something to the farmsteader. Clearly, it did not. And, strangely, it hurt to have it stated so definitively. Unworthy. He, the son of a primary. *Unworthy* of the Mother.

And perhaps he was. "I attempted to send them to safety. They were my responsibility. I am a karavan guide. I *do* care. I do. I sent them to what I believed was safety. And you as well." He shook his head and was reminded that as yet his hair remained unbraided. There had been no time to instruct Ilona in the intricacies. "Alisanos does what it will do, goes where it will go. I could only do what I believed was safest."

Davyn leaned forward as he shut a fist around the cloth doll. He raised it, displayed it. Shook it at Rhuan. "My *entire family* is lost."

Rhuan teetered on the brink of explanation. He liked, admired, and respected Audrun; her loss was indeed devastating to the man who loved her. Because he knew Audrun, he understood how much this loss hurt; understood better than Davyn believed he did. He owed the man, he felt, for Audrun's sake, for the sake of the children lost to Alisanos; owed the absolute truth and clear, unequivocal answers to all of the farmsteader's questions. This man was a caring, responsible father who dearly loved his wife. He was indeed devastated. Anyone possessed of compassion would wish to help this man.

Compassionless Brodhi could withhold all information, Rhuan reflected, as the rules of the journey required, but now, here, he himself could not. Not when he looked into Davyn's eyes and saw the naked pain, the agony of not knowing. And that pain kindled a share of its own in him. Empathy, he recognized; a purely human emotion.

What would I do, had I lost so much? Had I lost what I most loved?

And he realized that he could be empathic because he *had* lost what he most loved. When he saw Ilona, dead.

It was time to offer whatever words, whatever explanation he could to assuage a fraction of the man's pain. He would no longer keep secrets from him even if it was forbidden to tell him of Rhuan's heritage, the dictates of the journey. After all, Darmuth wasn't present to hear him. *Too much divulged*, Darmuth would say; and the demon would then be required to tell the primaries what Alario's get had done.

Could he lie to Darmuth? Could he lie during a Hearing? To do so abbrogated everything about the journey. And it put Darmuth in danger.

Rhuan looked at the doll with its stitched-on face, button eyes, hair of yellow yarn, then met the farmsteader's gaze. There was no question in his heart but that he had to ease this man's pain. Despite the risk to himself, he was wholly comfortable with his decision. "They were together when I left them. Where they are, no harm will come to them."

Davyn's face was taut. Jaws flexed as he gritted his teeth. "Tell me why you left them there. How you could come out, but they could not. Are you immune to this wild magic?"

"No," Rhuan answered. "No such escape exists. In Alisanos, I can die."

"Then how is it you're untouched by this transformation?"

And now the crux. "My mother," Rhuan said in a carefully calibrated tone, "was human."

Davyn blinked, momentarily diverted by an apparent non sequitur. "Your mother?"

"My sire—my father—was not. *Is* not. It is the absolute truth that I was taken by Alisanos even as Audrun was; I can avoid its caprice no more than anyone. But because of my father's blood, I have more resources."

"Sweet Mother, you're talking in riddles! What do you mean, 'resources'? Why does your father's blood mean anything? And if he's not human, what *is* he?"

"A god," Rhuan said dryly.

"A *what*?"

Rhuan drew in a deep breath, then blew it out in a noisy gust. "What I am about to tell you will sound fantastical—well, I suppose it *is* fantastical. But it is not fantasy. There is a difference."

Davyn scowled. "Speak directly; I have neither time nor patience for dramatic elaboration."

Rhuan continued at his own pace, in his own way. "Of course it is all *so* fantastical that not a soul would believe you—and if anyone asked, I would say you were lying. But no one would believe you anyway. So—"

"*Rhuan!*"

"—so why bother to tell them?" He let his skin color deepen faintly, his eyes glint red; summoned a subtle trace of the *presence* all primaries commanded. "Why bother to tell them?"

Davyn understood. He eyes flickered and he pressed his lips together, then said clearly, "Nor have I time to tell fantastical tales."

And so Rhuan explained. He told Davyn what he could of—everything. More than he had told to any human, save Ilona. It required a good while, even abbreviated to the mere facts, facts without personal observations, without nuances in his tone.

When he finished, his voice roughened from so many words, Davyn sat there with his mouth partly open and the thoughts behind his eyes working frantically. Rhuan suspected the farmsteader had so

many questions that he could settle on none of them. Some, anticipated, had been answered, but in turn led to other questions, other
explanations.

"She is a strong, confident, self-sufficient woman," Rhuan said,
"as well as an exemplary mother. Alisanos may not distinguish among
those it has taken and those who were born there, but I do. And,
regardless of what they say, the primaries do as well. She is someone
to contend with, Davyn. Neither weak nor lacking in courage. She
will withstand them all."

Davyn dropped the doll to his lap. He bent forward, dug elbows
into his knees, covered his eyes. Rigid fingers encroached into his
hairline. The fair hair he had bequeathed to all his children was stiffened from dried perspiration and pressed back against his head.

Regret was an unexpected knife in Rhuan's abdomen. He realized
that no matter how well meant, regardless of how carefully he framed
them, his words hurt Davyn to his very soul. It was true that Rhuan
himself had no wife, no children; but he was human enough—yes,
human enough—to take into his heart the farmsteader's grief and to
know that empathy was also a gift he might offer.

What would I do in this man's place? But he knew no answer. He
could not anticipate how he would react, what he would feel. To the
primaries, he was as yet a child, an adolescent. Perhaps they were
correct. A child could not completely understand as an adult might.

Or perhaps only a *dioscuri* who took upon himself the expectations of his people, who celebrated all of the arrogant assumptions of
his race, could understand the world as an adult. Perhaps that was
the explanation for Brodhi's attitude, his unspoken certainty of su-
premacy, of ascension. Brodhi simply *knew* one day he would kill his
sire. His confidence was unwavering. Rhuan knew he himself wanted
no part of the ritual—and that certainty had nothing to do with fear
Alario would kill him. Nothing existed in him to kindle potent instinct into pure challenge, into the overwhelming need to kill his sire.
No part of him felt the slightest urge to ascend.

He wondered if, in human terms, that made him a coward.

Davyn straightened, hastily wiping tears from his eyes with the back of a hand. His voice was raw. "She is everything you described. So strong. But she will be transformed regardless, yes?"

Rhuan banished personal musings and returned to the only topic that mattered to the farmsteader. "She less than others. Of that I advise you to be certain." He recalled Audrun's exhaustion, and the mental strength required to continue on and withstand the primaries, even as her body, all human, began to flag. The woman had experienced accelerated labor, had given birth prematurely, yet still faced down the primaries.

Davyn's voice lost its edge. "She was fifteen when we married. But she has always been strong, and confident, and self-sufficient." He met Rhuan's eyes. "The children . . . you say they are more vulnerable to the wild magic."

It was not a question, and in any case, Rhuan had already answered it. But he recognized the ongoing process of Davyn's mind. It would require time to truly grasp the magnitude of what he had been told. "They are more vulnerable. Anyone new to life is so."

"Then the newborn is lost . . . Sarith. She's lost."

Rhuan refused to lie for the sake of calming fears. Davyn deserved the truth. "She may be."

"And yet—a road?"

"A road that will, upon completion, take you to your family and on to Atalanda. Your family may not come to you—and I have told you why—but you may go to them."

"And will I, too, be changed?"

Rhuan shook his head. "Not upon the road."

NOW AND AGAIN, a stream ran before the tiny dwelling. Now and again, a river. Occasionally no water ran at all, merely a webwork of trees all woven together, canopy to canopy, branches so tightly tangled there was no parting tree from tree. Roots broke free of the soil and encroached upon one another, braiding themselves together into a massive woody lattice against the ground.

Blackened lichen furred boughs and rocks. Fern, bracken, grass, and fallen broken leaves layered footing beneath the trees. But footing was not necessary when one had wings.

It was little more than a hut, knit together from layers of cut sod, crooked courses of wracked branches, and upright, twisted timbers; from streambank mud, sinews from beasts, succulent vines wrapped around all and dried into snug ropes. Grass and bracken grew from the outer skin of the hut until it was clothed in vegetation, indistinguishable from the forest. Behind it, forming the back wall, was a massive outcropping of stone, black and gray and roan, veined with glinting chunks of brittle, cloudy crystal. It loomed over the roof of the low hut. Here all was damp beneath the trees, dryness denied because the double suns of Alisanos were made nearly invisible by the thickness of the canopy overhead. This dampness had never troubled the demon, whose wings lifted it above the trees into the brilliant warmth of the suns.

But now it had a child.

Now it had a daughter.

This day, a stream ran before the hut. Sweet water was plentiful. The demon landed gently on the ground, folded its wings, cradled the infant against its chest. It cast a glance at the tight-woven canopy overhead, air-scented briefly, then ducked beneath the low lintel and entered the hut.

The interior appeared larger than the exterior. Coals glowed in the fireplace against the rock wall across the back, where hearth and chimney had been built of stone ruddy and gray, piled one atop another and mortared into place. Holding the child one-armed, the demon bent and tossed tinder into coals, letting a foreshortened sweep of barely spread wings serve as bellows to raise flame. Twigs, sticks, limbs, all added as the fire grew. The demon would make the hut warm for the child.

Fragile human child.

Wings again were folded away. The black, open hide jacket hung askew, so the child, wrapped in dirty cloth torn from a woman's skirt, was pressed against demon flesh. Cold demon flesh, white as ice, except for a bloom of darkness rising from beneath hide waistband to breastbone, shining scales the color of bruised human flesh.

Now, the child began to fuss. Swaddled in cloth, it squirmed restlessly as if it would escape. The head was bared. Pale, white-blond hair, mere fuzz against the skull. Rosy silken skin, until the child began to cry, and then the face reddened. Cries rent the air.

Hungry, it thought. The child was hungry.

The demon cast a wild glance around the hut. There was no food. It hunted when hungry. But the child, so young, could not do so. It was the demon's task to feed the infant.

It sat down upon hard-packed earth, close to the fire. It bent its head down over the child, and long black hair, shining in the firelight, fell down upon the infant, who startled from the touch. Crying now was fear, not mere hunger.

"Tha tha," the demon said. A clawed hand moved the sheet of hair aside, closed gently over the fuzzy skull. "Tha tha."

No. Not *tha.*

"There," the demon said. "There, there."

Poor hungry child. Poor hungry human.

The demon closed its pale, slit-pupiled eyes. For long moments it sat there cradling the child, legs folded crosswise, fire warming the hut, wings folded against black hide. And then as the child continued to cry, the demon pressed a single claw against its own chest just below the black nipple, and drew a line.

Blood welled. Spilled.

"No." That much, it remembered. Milk, not blood. "No."

The demon tipped back its head. Its mouth fell open. A single convulsion passed through its body.

Beneath the blood, a breast began to grow. The infant knew. The infant nuzzled until the nipple was found. White milk flowed.

And as the child suckled, the demon remembered when it had been human.

When it had been a woman.

Before Alisanos.

"There, there," it said.

Chapter 6

*I*T WAS, AUDRUN decided, beautiful in a way she'd never encountered. Beneath the towering, hollowed cliffs grew trees both sparse and spindly, robust and elegant, forming close-grown stands and copses and the occasional solitary spears. Significant time had been lavished on the grounds of the Kiba. Pebbles, rocks, and soil were mostly russett-colored. Carefully hewn sections of stone paved looping pathways, mortared together into patterns with an equally ruddy substance. Everywhere she looked, she was surrounded by the color, as if the Mother's palette had been limited. And yet the trees and shrubbery were rich green jewels against a backdrop, while flowering plants cascaded from raised gardens. All of the bare ground she could see had been raked, creating thin, shallow striations; and the rocks pulled out by the raking had been arranged alongside the paved pathways as intricate mosaic borders. The *tidiness* of the Kiba was amazing. Even the shrubbery and trees were neatened by careful pruning.

It was bright. Too bright. Here the double suns were not blocked by thick, massive forest canopy. She and her children, following a pathway beneath the looming cliffs and dwellings, were fully exposed. Squinting, Audrun felt the heat beating on her scalp and knew if something were not done to curb the sunlight, her fair-skinned, pale-haired children would soon burn badly. Having experienced that herself, Audrun wished to spare them the pain and the peeling.

"Here." She stepped off the paved pathway near a clump of bushes and a singleton tree. Depending from the tree's drooping branches were wide, pleated fronds. She recognized the tree and its fronds as one she had seen frequently while following Rhuan through the thicker forest. "Take Meggie, Gillan." She set her youngest daughter down, relieved to be free of the weight. Then she stripped frond after frond from the tree and handed them out. "Use these to block the sun. *Suns.*" The plural was difficult to remember. "We'll have to take time later to make ourselves hats. For now, these will work." She handed Gillan a second frond. "Will you see to Meggie? She's so young; her skin is more vulnerable." She fixed Torvic with a minatory eye. "You as well, young sir."

Ellica stood clasping her small sapling in one arm while the frond dangled loosely from her right hand. The expression on her face was of startled grief. "How could you hurt it so?"

Audrun, assisting Torvic to adjust his frond, glanced at her. "Hurt what?"

"The tree!"

"The *tree*?" In disbelief, Audrun looked at the tree from which she had liberated six fronds. Then she turned back to her eldest daughter even as she plopped a frond across her own head. "Ellica, don't be ridiculous—"

"I am ridiculous because I know that it hurt the tree? Imagine having your fingers torn off one by one!"

"Sweet Mother, Ellica—"

"It *hurt* the tree, Mam!"

Audrun could think of nothing to say. Words were lacking because the entire experience was wholly beyond comprehension at this particular moment. Her mind was blank. All she knew was her tall daughter clutched a cloth-wrapped rootball against her chest as if it were a child, part of Gillan's leg was now scaled, Megritte hadn't said a single word since arriving at the Kiba, and Torvic—well, Torvic seemed wholly Torvic. Ellica, obviously, was not quite Ellica.

But Audrun instantly rejected her own judgment. Of course Ellica was herself.

It was hot on the paved pathway, even utilizing tree fronds as haphazard sunshades. "Come," Audrun said crisply. "We can learn nothing of these folk if we stand here arguing over whether a tree was injured by my actions. I need information. Leaving the deepwood as soon as possible is the first order of business, but apparently this is impossible until a road is built. And *that* will take time." She waved an arm at them in a gathering gesture. "I want to find someone in control, someone other than that arrogant female. Gillan, Torvic, go. Take Meggie. Ellica, now, if you please. And cover your head!"

Tears ran down Ellica's dusty cheeks, but she raised the frond over her head and followed the others. Audrun, aware of the odd picture she and her chicks presented to the world as they paraded down the pathway with tree fronds held over their heads, realized that with Davyn not present, all such parental decisions and issues now fell to her. Each and every one of them.

Audrun sighed as she brought up the rear, rubbing absently at her chin with the back her left hand. *Blessed Mother, aid me in this. Or I'll surely die of frustration before a week is through!*

And then their straggling parade came to an abrupt halt. Audrun, bringing up the rear and lost in thoughts of the Mother, nearly collided with Ellica. Instead of arranged neatly in single file, her children gathered in a clump, clogging the pathway. Mute Megritte, once again, was in Gillan's arms. Audrun opened her mouth to ask in aggravation what had caused the sudden halt but closed it instead. Some several feet away, centered precisely in the walkway as if he fully intended to block it, stood one of the primaries. Arms were crossed, legs were spread. He stared at them all out of predatory eyes, as if considering that they might make a good meal. His expression was austere, but also intrusively calculating.

Audrun registered that he was nearly a mirror image of the primaries she had seen in the pit. Clothing made of gleaming, scaled hides, skin touched with copper, and hair—all those beads and braids!—the same. The angles of his face, the shape of his body, even the tilt of his head . . . such a strong resemblance to each other was not even present in her children, who were very alike. And then she realized that she recognized him despite the likeness to all the other primaries. Something set him apart. Something very powerful.

"Ah," she said. "You were the one who wished *not* to help us. You are Karadath, Rhuan's uncle, I believe. Or whatever you choose to call it." She remembered Rhuan's reference. " 'Kin-in-kind,' isn't it?"

He looked at her children one by one, studying each closely, then raised his eyes to hers. The timbre of his voice was beautiful; she had forgotten that. "You are a very stubborn little human."

Audrun did not permit herself to flinch from either tone or observation. "So I have been told. Well, not that I am a stubborn *human*, nor particularly little—to us, that is—but yes. Stubborn. Particularly in defense of my children."

"Are all of them yours?"

Feeling somewhat at a disadvantage because of her generally unkempt appearance, damp bodice, and the incongruity of a tree frond balanced on her head, she attempted to summon dignity and stood up straighter. "Of course they are."

"By different sires."

Audrun was shocked. "*No*, not different si—fathers! One. Only one. My husband."

"If they are of the same litter, why such disparity in their sizes?"

A gust of incredulous laughter escaped her. "Humans don't have litters! We have . . ." she paused, rethinking, "but no, that's not entirely true. There are such things as twins, and I've even heard of a triplet birth many years ago, though none lived, nor did the mother. But we don't refer to them as 'litters.' They are children. *Child* is singular; *children* means more than one." And then she wondered what in the Mother's name she was doing parsing words with him. "So long as you are here, imitating a wall, would you be so good as to explain what is expected of us? Where we may stay?" She gestured. "My children are exhausted, as you can see, and I gave birth some while back. It takes its toll, such things, especially here. We would like—"

He cut her off. "You are fecund."

"I . . . well, yes. Five children does suggest fertility."

"We do not have litters. We have singleton births. And only one for each dam."

Audrun's eyebrows rose. As the mother of multiples, she asked, "Why only one for each mother?"

"They die."

His matter-of-factness shocked Audrun. "The mothers die? Each time?"

"But you are fecund. You haven't died yet. I think we should make a *dioscuri*, you and I."

THE TEARS WERE gone, the wagon neat, tea was ready for drinking as the sun went down. Ilona knelt beside the modest fire and took up the kettle with a rag wrapped around the handle, then filled a wooden mug playing proxy to pewter. She dropped two precious mint leaves into it—as drawers slid out in the quaking, much of her hoard of herbs and spices had spilled and were now mixed with dust—then retired to a fat cushion placed up against the massive wagon wheel, where a second cushion warded her spine against the hub. She sat down with a sigh, thumped her head lightly against the yellow-painted wheel spokes, and reflected that she needed nothing so much as a bath in the river, where she could cleanse her body as well as wash tangled, grit-encrusted ringlets. But she was too weary. Changing out of the burial shift into clothing of the living, for all it was a simple thing, stripped her of her last remaining reserves of strength, physical and emotional. More discouraging, tears always gave her a headache that lingered, sometimes beyond a night's sleep.

It was just after sunset. Nightsingers one by one joined in a ratchety, ringing chorus. She heard the flutter of birds looking for purchase in the old grove, the flap of wing against leaf. Dogs throughout the grove barked, answering dogs in the tents, and Ilona heard the squealing comment of a horse at Janqeril's picket lines. Across the grove cookfires sprang up, and soon a veil of smoke drifted through, followed closely after by the odor of meat, wild onions, and spices. The shouts of children playing echoed amidst the great old trees, as did the voices of mothers as they called respective children in to dinner. Her belly, too, was empty, but she was disinclined to eat. She sat upon her cushion, leaned against another, and sipped tea as twilight fell and the moon and her acolytes rose.

A twig snapped. Without even thinking, Ilona scrambled to her feet, and as the mug tumbled down it emptied the remains of warm tea all over her skirt. In the deepening dimness of twilight, she saw Alario and yanked the knife from her waistband, holding it low and underhanded, as she had been taught. She had killed no man, ever, but had meted out a slice here and there for those who grew too insistent.

And then she realized that the intricate braids were missing, as was prime maturity. "Blessed Mother, it's you!"

Rhuan, who had stopped moving altogether upon sight of the knife, observed, "You cut the drawstring of your skirt."

She felt the heat of a blush. Indeed she was standing ready to stab, cut, or slice with the big knife, completely committed to action, but she thought the fierce tableau was much undermined by the pile of fabric puddled around her ankles. Still gripping the knife, she peered down. "So I did."

"Might I recommend a scabbard if you mean to keep such a vast knife on your person?"

"Perhaps a scabbard would be best." And as she met his eyes, laughter bubbled up. She was so tired she surrendered wholeheartedly to laughter, and after a moment he grinned and stepped close. She felt him take the knife from her loosened hand, heard the clunk after he tossed the weapon aside, and then the warmth of his arms encircled her. But she protested. "I need a bath. I badly need a bath."

"Well, I daresay I do, as well. Everyone is eating, including the livestock, and not likely to stir any time soon. We could retreat to the river unburdened by watching eyes."

His last sentence sent a wholly unexpected chill streaking down her back. She felt the prickle of it in her flesh. "Not at night!"

It startled him into arched brows and questioning eyes." Why not at night? No one will be there."

She bent, grabbed the fallen skirt, pulled it up where it belonged. Indeed, the drawstring was cut. Ilona hung onto the waistband to preserve a little modesty. She was a diviner; tentfolk and karavaners might very well be planning to visit her, even those who did not follow her faith. "Not now. Please. I'd rather wait until daylight."

Another man might have questioned her further. Another man might have mocked. But after a moment Rhuan bent, retrieved the dropped mug, scraped the interior with his fingers, and knelt beside the fire to refill it.

Then, he paused. Ilona saw the motions of his hands change. He knelt beside the fire, mug clasped, and murmured words she did not know. When at last he looked up at her, she saw the laggard return of his senses, of his awareness of surroundings.

She ventured a question, if very quietly. "What is it?"

When he looked up at last, she saw a quick flash of red in his eyes. "I thanked it. I apologized."

She was not certain she had heard him correctly. "You—thanked it? And apologized?" She paused. "A *mug*?"

"That once was a tree."

"A . . . tree. Well, yes. Many things are made of trees, including this wagon."

"It lived once. Blood ran in its veins, just as it runs in ours. Humans tend not to think of that."

She wondered if the observation included her among those who did not think. But a mug? A simple wooden mug?

He refreshed the tea, then rose and offered the simple wooden mug.

Ilona took it but did not immediately drink. She studied the mug, noting scrapes and gouges. With gentle fingers, she explored the exterior as she had never done before. Fingers found smoothness. Fingers found divots. Found ill usage, compared to what it had been before axes, sledges, and saws took it down.

When the warmth was back in her hands, the familiar aroma rising, she felt tension slowly relinquish her neck and shoulders. "Then we'll wait," he said, referring to the bath she had forgotten about.

Ilona blew out a long breath. "I'm sorry. I thought you were—him."

"My sire?"

She nodded. "I forgot your braids were undone."

"Well, I believe we can remedy that." Firelight gleamed on the smooth flesh of his face. "How nimble are your fingers?"

"My fingers?"

"Devoid of knife, that is." He lifted one of her hands and guided it to his head, where sheets of hair hung almost to his waist. "I asked you last night if you would braid my hair."

"There is a lot of it," Ilona observed. "It would take half the night, at least."

He grinned, and dimples appeared. "I suspect we can find something else to do with the other half." Then the dimples faded, as did the laughter in his eyes. "I started to explain this last night but got sidetracked."

Ilona smiled widely. "So we both did."

"But if you do braid it, you must know about the repercussions."

She tried to school her tone out of skepticism into mere curiosity but failed. "There are repercussions for braiding hair?"

"Among my people, yes." His expression, she noted, was a carefully constructed mask, but the brown eyes, reflecting flame, burned. "It's a ritual undertaken to seal a man to a woman, a woman to a man."

She put her free hand to the disarray of her own hair. "Then I would braid mine?"

"There are different braiding patterns for a woman. I would braid yours."

Now she touched his hair, letting it slide through her fingers. It needed washing, as hers did, but despite the ripples left by braids it hung nearly straight. "How did yours come to be unbraided?"

Night encroached, but she could see fleeting expressions in the glow of the campfire. Something very akin to guilt. "It was not to be done, but was."

Obscurity had always been a part of him, but this night, after all that had happened, she had no patience for it. "What in the Mother's name does that mean?"

He touched his scalp, pushing fingers through his hair. "I was injured. Furrows, here, from a demon's claws. They're gone now, but she wanted to clean the blood away. I was unconscious, or I would have stopped her."

"Why does it matter that she unbraided your hair? Oh. I see. That's part of the ritual, too. "

"Among the primaries, if a woman wishes to marry a man, she unbraids her hair. If he accepts her suit, she then unbraids his."

"And then you braid it back again?"

"Yes."

"So whoever unbraided your hair was asking you to marry her?"

"I was unconscious."

That sounded suspiciously like an excuse. "So you have said."

"She didn't know what it meant."

"Sweet Mother, Rhuan, just say it, would you?"

"Audrun."

"*Audrun?*" She stared at him. "The farmsteader's wife?"

"The storm took us together. I led her to safety. Well, eventually— first I had to wrestle with a demon who wanted the infant."

"What infant? What demon? Rhuan—"

He placed two fingers against her lips. "If we are to have this conversation, may we have it in your wagon? For privacy's sake?"

She removed his fingers from her mouth. "Yes, we shall, but first one thing."

"Augh, Ilona, not another *thing*—"

He was so anxious, so worried, that Ilona had to stifle laughter. "If I have it right, then according to your people, you're married, aren't you? You and Audrun?"

Hastily he said, "It doesn't *mean* anything. Not here. It's not a human ritual. It's what the primaries do, but it means nothing here. Nothing at all."

She raised her brows and spoke with an overly dramatic tone. "But you've asked me to braid your hair. Here. So obviously there *is* some significance to the ritual, even by human terms. Yes?"

The conflict in his face was clear. "But we're not married. Not here. Audrun's already married, here. So I am free, here."

"Here, here, and here. But the primaries think otherwise."

"I'm not there, Ilona. I'm here." He stretched out his arms. *"Here."*

She laughed, tugged gently on the lock of his hair still grasped in her hand, then tugged harder. He followed the pressure on his scalp until their faces were level. She rested her forehead against his. "Yes, you are. Here." She pointed to the wagon. "But let's go *there.*"

Chapter 7

*B*ETHID WAS SOUND asleep until the earth shuddered and the tent fell down. It startled her so much that she sat up, thrashing, and got herself entangled in billows of heavy canvas. What she uttered was in no way polite. And then, "Sweet Mother, the lantern!" Timmon and Alorn were absent, staying late at Mikel's ale-tent, and it was routine to leave a lantern burning until all couriers returned to the tent. She smelled oil and smoke. "Where—?" It was difficult to make her way through the yardage of canvas. "Oh Mother . . . Brodhi? Are you here?" She had glimpsed him as she'd rolled up in her bedding. "The lantern's fallen. Brodhi?"

From somewhere came his voice, clear and concise, unmuffled by fallen tent. "I have it."

Relief. Now she could afford to be frustrated instead of worried. On hands and knees she made her way through folds and billows until at last she reached an edge of fabric and stuck her head out, yanking canvas aside. The settlement animals, yet again, were in an uproar. Across the grove, throughout the ranks of tents, she saw banked fires glowing. Above, the moon shed enough luminance to see shadowy bulks of nearby tents. She wondered if any others had fallen or just the one she slept in.

The earth stilled. Bethid crawled out from under the edge of fallen canvas and rose. Not far from her stood Brodhi, who had already made his escape. The extinguished lantern hung from his hand. She tried to restrain her tone, but failed. "How many more times is this going to happen?"

"Alisanos does as it does. It will take time for the land to ease."

"No, I don't mean that. I mean: how many more times is the tent going to collapse? Someone did a piss-poor job of pitching it. *Re*-pitching it, that is. What does it take to keep it upright if only for one night? That's all I ask." She raised a pointing finger in the air to emphasize the number. "One night. One undisturbed night. If Alisanos wants to shake the world again, why doesn't it do so in the daylight?" Aggrieved, she shoved fingers through her short-cropped hair, scrubbing violently, and glared at Brodhi. "Do something."

"*Do* something? I?"

"Yes. You. You're from there. Do something."

For a moment he ignored her, inspecting the lantern's oil reservoir. Then he bent, took something from the ground, tossed it at her. Bethid caught it, saw it was a slim stick. "*You* do something," he told her. "Flint and steel are buried beneath the tent. Go lift a light from another fire."

Bethid scowled at him. "My boots are in the tent. *Under* the tent."

"You have feet."

"Sweet Mother, Brodhi—you can't expect me to go traipsing barefoot through the dark!" She peered at his own feet. "You have boots on!"

"Yes," he agreed. "I have land-sense. I knew it was coming, this shrugging of its shoulders. And your first thought, as well, should have been to pull your boots on."

"If you knew this was coming, why didn't you tell me? A warning would have been good. I'd have appreciated a 'Bethid get up and put your boots on before the tent falls down on your head,' *before* it fell on my head."

"By then I was out of the tent. With my boots on."

"Don't sound so smug." She inspected the stick again, then tilted back her head to look up at the moon. Some light, but not enough. Barefoot, she went off to find the closest fire, swearing each and every time her feet struck rocks.

JUST BEFORE DAWN, the rain began. Davyn was wrapped in blankets on the floor of the wagon beneath a canopy given him by a karavaner with one to spare. He was perfectly dry, except for his tears. He had repeatedly dreamed of Audrun and the children throughout the night, getting little true rest. The karavan guide's words about a road, and safety when one was upon it even in the depths of Alisanos, left Davyn with a mix of relief and worry. *When* would the road be done? *When* might he take it into the deepwood and find his family? *When* could he once again hold Audrun in his arms, embrace his children? *When* might he meet the smallest one, the infant named Sarith?

Unanswerable questions, he knew. Rhuan could not predict when the road would be completed. The only action Davyn himself might take was *in*action, as he waited. And waited.

He rolled over onto his back, peering up at the oiled canvas of the wagon canopy. Outside the dawn grew stronger. He could see rain striking the canvas, as well as hear it, see the fragile light of a new day. Another day without his family.

Davyn pressed his hands over his face and rubbed. He had not shaved in three days, and his jaw itched. Fingertips found stubble and scratched.

The rain was, as far as Davyn could tell from inside the wagon, perfectly ordinary rain. Not the searing, steaming rain that had, in that unnatural storm birthed by Alisanos, struck the ground like spears and left divots of earth overturned. And it was not, as yet, a drenching rain.

It had been the promise of heavy storms that had set all folk in the karavan to better speed in order to reach their destinations before the rainy season, the monsoon, set in. When his family joined the karavan, Jorda the karavan-master had been plain with regard to their oxen, known to move more slowly and ponderously than horses or mules. He'd explained that, in another year, all the karavans would have already gone, but Jorda's was late, as was one other, which meant that he and Audrun and the children found a place. Jorda put them at the very end, where oxen would not slow the others; where he and his own ate dust.

But now it was rain, welcome for its cooling properties, the abatement of dust, the filling of barrels put out for such purpose; but it would be unwelcome after a handful of days and the roads transformed to mire, a sucking mud that could trap heavy wagons. Even if his family were here, they could go nowhere now. Best to stay with others beset by the same delay than set out alone. He and Gillan together still would not have been strong enough on their own to lever a wagon mired down, even with the oxen pulling. Better to stay here, he knew—as much to wait for the road through Alisanos to be completed as to sit out the monsoon.

Outside, rain fell harder, faster. No one would be going anywhere. It was time to break out the weather clothing, the trousers and shirt made of oiled canvas, though of a lighter hand than wagon canopies, and a rope-belted, hooded coat against the worst of the rain. Months, it would be. Months in one place. But for Davyn, alone, good weather would do nothing to urge him on his way. The child was born. Reaching Atalanda now lacked the relentless drive to get his family to safety, as the diviners had all urged before the baby was born.

The baby *was* born.

Blessed Mother, his children, his Audrun, all of whom were his life. Precisely the kind of life he had wanted and had, before now, beneath the Mother's weeping skies.

AUDRUN STARED AT the primary, stunned beyond words. He wanted *her*? To make another *dioscuri*? To make a child who would, at its birth, cause her death?

But she found her tongue as well as renewed strength, and schooled her tone into matter-of-factness, refusing to allow the primary to provoke her before her children. She sensed the shock of her eldest, Gillan and Ellica, who knew how children came into the world; Torvic and Megritte, as yet too young, knew nothing of such things in humans, only in livestock.

"I didn't realize you were insane. My sympathies for your condition."

She saw a brief flicker of surprise in his brown eyes, the faintest spark of red, though nothing showed in his face. "Untrue," the primary said.

In the same matter-of-fact tone, she said, "Oh, I think you are. Without question." Then she realized that possibly the same could be said of her, standing with a tree frond balanced on her head. She lowered it to her side. The double suns were blinding. Hats. They needed hats. "You stand here before me—before my children, no less—and declare we'll make a baby, you and I." She stared into his eyes, putting as much conviction into her own as was possible. No wavering. No flicker of concern or fear. Primaries exuded physical and mental strength, a nearly overwhelming power. But she refused to surrender to it. "You are impolite, to suggest such a thing. Before my children, if you please, you will mind your manners."

Ah. She saw it: she had provoked him.

"Human, do you know where you are?"

"Oh, yes. Rhuan explained about the Kiba."

"It is the heart of our people . . . do you mock that? Do you mock me?"

She drew in a careful breath, trying not to let it shake, and released it as carefully. "I never mock children. It serves no purpose."

He was, abruptly, *there*, standing in front of her, nearly touching her. The children, now, were behind him; a glimpse showed eyes gone huge and mouths open. She felt his power, recognized that she could not truly withstand it. It took great effort to hold her ground. His height, his bearing, his eyes, the sheer power of his presence nearly beat her down. Her legs were weak, trembling. She did not know for how long she might remain standing. She dug the fingers of her right hand into the frond at her side, realizing as she did so, completely inconsequentially, that two fingernails were broken.

The back of her neck prickled, but she did not give ground. He wanted her for breeding; he would not kill her when a child of his would do it for him.

The timbre of his voice tightened. "Would you, human woman, mock a *god*?"

He would not kill her. That gave her strength. "Probably not. I was taught good manners."

"Yet you mock me."

"Well, yes. You are deserving of it. How dare you come to me, a guest of the Kiba, and say such things? That is most rude. I was led to believe better of you, but apparently Rhuan was wrong."

"Rhuan—? Rhuan is a child. He speaks as a child."

"In my world, I rather think he's an adult." She wished badly she could see more of her children behind him, but by standing so close, he blocked her. She had to tip her head back to look into his face. She did so, meeting his eyes. "And why, when you already have a *dioscuri*, do you want to get another? Isn't Brodhi enough?"

He smiled. "Alario means to do it."

It took her aback. "And does that mean you must?" She shook her head. "Is everything here a competition?"

"Of course."

"And what will you do with two *dioscuri*?"

"What we have always done. We let them fight."

"You would risk Brodhi?"

"No risk," Karadath answered. "If Brodhi should fail, it would be because the other was more fit. And if *that* one dies, then Brodhi's worth is assured."

Audrun did not understand. She couldn't. But because Alario meant to sire a new *dioscuri* to replace Rhuan, now *she* was made part of the plan. Karadath, too, would make a new *dioscuri*, and would get it upon her.

"Human women can be difficult, overly emotional," he said, "and so we have learned to teach them much of us before we lie with them. You won't be harmed. Physically you must be well, as the pregnancy lasts twice nine."

She added it up instantly. "Eighteen months!"

"Twice nine. Eighteen months." He shrugged. "The words mean the same."

"*Eighteen months.*"

"Yes."

His words threatened her fragile courage, but she took shelter in disbelief. "No wonder they die in childbirth! I cannot even imagine how a woman could carry a child that long. Nine months—nine *human* months—is difficult enough." Audrun shook her head. "Short of forcing me, there is no way I would agree to such a thing."

Again, the primary shrugged. "Your agreement is not necessary. Just your womb."

Chapter 8

*R*HUAN AWOKE WITH the dawn, always. But this time his thoughts were not for his task as karavan guide nor for the responsibilities of the settlement, which had never, really, been his. Of a sudden, as he opened his eyes to the day, his mind ran backward. Memory rose up within him, memory of Brodhi, of Karadath. Ylarra. All of them in the chamber, as Karadath and Ylarra told him and Brodhi what their punishment was to be for returning to Alisanos much too early.

Brodhi's voice, telling him. Telling him with pleasure in it, in the customary mocking tone.

With eyes unfocused by thought and memory, Rhuan stared at the mother rib of Ilona's wagon, absently noting the string of charms and beads, the fetish animals.

His sire intended to make another *dioscuri*.

And Brodhi's words: *"That leaves you with a choice: to kill the child, or to challenge the sire."*

Ilona shifted, drawing his mind away from Brodhi, away from anything else but her. Joy superseded unsettling memory.

Despite the closeness of the wagon—he was accustomed to sleeping under the stars—Rhuan was supremely comfortable upon the floorboards with Ilona in his arms. A doubled mattress lay beneath them, and a tangle of bedding provided some padding against unforgiving wood. They had neither of them shed all of their clothing, but it had not been required. They made shift as they could in haste and would again, he knew.

Ilona lay on her side even as he did, body snugged against his. She rested her head on his bent arm.

Ilona's tone was delicately wry. "We should have done this sooner."

He smiled. "Much sooner." They had in fact wasted years apart, albeit in friendship; other years stretched ahead. For now they could take joy, take comfort, find the truths of bodies and souls. "You know why we didn't," he said. "I was afraid of you."

She lifted her head. "Afraid! Of me?"

"Of course. You're a hand-reader. A true hand-reader. From what I know, all diviners can sense things in a person even if they don't go through the ritual, and some more than others."

Ilona's tone was thoughtful as she lowered her head once more. "True."

"Though things are much clearer in a ritual, of course," he continued. "The Mother knows, my own people are bound up in hundreds of rituals."

Ilona rolled her head on his arm so that she looked upward to the canopy. " 'The Mother'? Have you become a convert?"

"Well, I believe the humans' Mother of Moons to be kinder than the primaries. But no, I'm not a convert. It's impossible for us to convert."

"Who is 'we'?"

"Primaries. *Dioscuri.*"

"Why?"

"Because we are gods." He paused. "Well, I'm not a god yet. Only one in training. Nonetheless, it wouldn't do to worship a human god when we have our own. Such as my sire."

"Your sire is hardly my idea of a god!"

"Primaries are unkind, as I've said. But that truth does not strip them of godhood."

"But what do they *do*, as gods?"

Rhuan reflected that the conversation was moving toward the line of inquiry Audrun had raised. In fact, he could see Ilona also facing down the primaries in the Kiba. The image made his grin renew itself. "It's complicated. But—"

"Rhuan!" Someone banged loudly on the wagon's latched door. "Rhuan, Jorda wants you. Now."

Ilona said a word most impolite.

The banging went on. "Rhuan!"

He released an aggravated but quiet growl, tempted to strongly suggest that whoever it was should go away. But then realization arrived. He freed his arm from Ilona's head and pushed himself upright into a seated position. "Darmuth? You're back!"

"A meeting has been called. Jorda wants us at Mikal's tent." Darmuth's voice paused, then continued with an underlying note of dry amusement in his tone. "I see you and Ilona have at long last allowed baser instincts to overcome your ridiculous reluctance to copulate."

"Baser instincts!" Ilona divested herself of bedding, then yanked a blanket around naked legs and hips. Before Rhuan could do it, she made her ungainly way to the door and unlatched it. One shove threw it swinging open on its hinges; it thudded against wood smartly, then swung back. Ilona stopped it with a hand and hung onto the latch. "Since you apparently believe we waited much too long to begin with, may I suggest you go away so we may make up for lost time?" She paused, then continued in a surprised voice. "It's raining!"

Rhuan looked past her and saw that it was, as yet, a thin rain, and the tree canopy offered decent shelter. Nonetheless, Darmuth's tunic was slowly darkening across the shoulders as droplets ran down his shaven skull.

"Rain is one of the subjects Jorda would like to discuss." Darmuth's pale, icy eyes reflected amusement. "Perhaps you should attend as well, hand-reader. You do hold a position of some importance in this motley assemblage."

"So I do, and so I shall." Whereupon Ilona yanked the door closed. The latch clicked into place. "I think first I will put on some clothes."

Rhuan grinned. Still abed, he shinnied back into hide leggings, knotting them low on hips even as he considered suggesting she do no such thing. Then his amusement faded. "I suspect I know what this meeting is about."

"The rain."

"The rain."

And in unison, "Monsoon."

Ilona found fresh smallclothes and a clean, if somewhat wrinkled, skirt. Everything in her wagon was askew; she would, Rhuan realized, have to spend a goodly amount of time reassembling it. There were advantages to sleeping in a blanket or two upon the ground. Nothing needed sorting or rescue.

"I suspect we're all staying put for awhile. No one is going anywhere," Ilona said, fiddling with a drawstring, "if that was in anyone's mind." Drawstring tied, she found a length of ocher-and-amber woven fabric and wrapped it around her shoulders over a beltless, wrinkled tunic.

Rhuan found a length of twine and tied his hair back. Regardless of such meanings as an intent to marry and its associated, intricate rituals, he wanted it braided and out of his way, but this would do in the meantime.

Ilona, muttering, started searching through bedding. "There must be a hair rod somewhere in this mess."

"Let it be as it is."

"My hair? Blessed Mother, no! It always wants taming. I think— ah! Here." Swiftly she twisted riotous ringlets into a thick rope of hair, coiled it deftly against her head, anchored it with an intricately carved rod. Then she studied him. "Perhaps your suggestion—offer? invitation?—of braiding it is a good idea." She checked for loose strands, found none. "Or I could cut it off. I've considered that before."

"You will do no such desecration!" Rhuan found his belt under a blanket as Ilona laughed, slung leather around his tunic, shoved the curved length of horn through a loop of sinew and snugged it into place. Boots, no hindrance to love-making, remained on his feet.

Ilona, however, had at some point tugged hers off and now sought them. Rhuan rose onto his knees, pulled one boot from beneath his insulted buttocks, offered it gravely. Ilona worked her right foot into it, tugged it into place, and finally unearthed its mate.

Rhuan unlatched and pushed the door open. Ducking his head against a canopy rib and canvas, he descended the wooden steps. The morning was young, rain-grayed, cool. He smelled dampness and woodsmoke, the subtle tang of wet stone and crushed grasses, the familiar breakfast aromas of oatmeal, sausage, eggs, fresh bread, frying bacon, and other equally savory foods. It made him hungry.

Darmuth was gone. Rhuan turned back, offered a hand to Ilona as she climbed down, gave in to sudden impulse, and leaned to kiss her. "Later," he promised against her mouth. "Darmuth is right; we've wasted too much time."

"Yes, I think so." Ilona pulled the wrap up over her hair and swung the long ends around her torso. "We shall have to make up for all that lost time."

And it was perfectly natural, supremely comfortable, as they fell in beside one another, hands interlocked, and made their way out of the sheltering grove and into the steady rain.

AS THE OCCLUDED sun broke the horizon behind a thick scrim of darkening clouds—rain was imminent—Brodhi surveyed the collapsed courier tent: billows and folds of canvas intermixed with poles, rope guy-lines, and personal belongings. He shared Bethid's opinion, her earthy complaint that a "piss-poor" job had been done raising the tent following the killing storm. Of course, it had been done without his supervision. His mind ticked over requirements for recovery: more rope for additional guy-lines, poles needed buttrussing, anchor irons should be pounded more deeply into the ground. Or, he knew, all of this would have to be done over again. Alisanos wasn't finished with them.

Bethid was picking through the collapsed canvas, attempting to find whatever she could of personal belongings and various para-phernalia vital to a temporary tent home. She peeled back what she could of heavy canvas, attempted to roll it aside. But for all her wiry strength, the weight and mass of the downed tent defeated her. She had, however, freed a loose pair of trews—which she tugged on over her sleeping tunic—two of the iron hooks that ordinarily hung from the central roof rib, and a boot. One boot.

"Mine," she muttered, and set it aside with the hooks. "Now, where's the other one . . . ?"

Brodhi was moved to comment. "This would be better done with more hands. More strength."

"*Male* strength?" she asked acerbically.

"Of course."

"Of course," she echoed, mimicking his tone. "But the only male in sight is doing nothing more than criticizing." She glowered at the downed tent. "It needs Timmon and Alorn, too."

"Of course," he repeated. "More hands. More strength."

Dark clouds gave birth. Bethid swore, tipping her head back to look up into the sky. "Augh, here comes the rain." She wiped moisture from her brow. "Well, it's the season for it . . . but, sweet Mother, enough is enough." The thin fabric of her night tunic, freckled by droplets, began to wilt and adhere to her skin. She rose, brass ear-hoops swinging, but dulled by the gray of the day. "We've got to get this tent erected *before* it becomes a downpour."

She stood before him, small, slim, wiry, exceedingly competent. And underestimated by those who did not know her. He clearly re-called speaking on her behalf before the Guildmaster, convincing the man to allow Bethid to participate in the demanding trials that di-vided the wishful thinkers from promising candidates. Then, Brodhi had done it because it amused him to challenge the Guildmaster and the precepts of the courier guild. It mattered less than nothing to him that the girl might truly be good enough.

Horses don't care if the rider is man, or woman, Brodhi had said. *If anything, a lighter person in the saddle is less wearing, allowing the horse greater efficiency. She can go farther in a day than the heavier men.*

And she had been good enough, and now stood before him because of it. No more a wishful thinker, no longer merely a candidate,
but a courier worthy of the Guild. And while there were more men
than less who still felt a woman should not be allowed, no one could
charge that she was incapable. She won her place fairly.

And the horses she rode *did* go farther in a day.

Her attention was drawn to an approaching man. "Timmon!
About time you came back. As you see, we need you. *And* Alorn. Has
he drunk himself senseless?"

The courier shook his head. "We're wanted. Mikal and the
karavan-master have called a meeting."

"Why should we be wanted?" Brodhi asked, annoyed. "Whatever
it is Jorda wishes to do makes no difference to us, as couriers. It isn't
necessary to go."

Timmon shrugged. "I'm only telling you what was said. You can
argue it with both of them, for all I care. But I was asked to fetch
you."

Bethid bent to canvas again. "I have to find my other boot—ah!
Here it is. And weather garb, if this is the beginning of monsoon."

Brodhi watched her balance neatly in place as she tugged on one
boot, then the other, stamping to settle the fit. "Did they say what
this meeting is about?"

"Plans," Timmon replied. "The immediate future. Safety. There is
much to discuss."

"Not for us," Brodhi declared. He wanted no part of human plans.

"Us, yes," Bethid said succinctly. "We are a part of this settlement
when we stop here. We eat their food, drink their ale, share their
company, do we not?" Her gaze on him was level, unwavering. "Do
we not?"

"And we *pay* for eating their food, for drinking their ale. It isn't
done in friendship."

Bethid glared. "Mikal is as much a friend to all of us as can be
expected of any man. We share his company far more than anyone
else's."

"Because he happens to run the ale-tent." It was an inane argument, not worthy of his time. Bethid had, once again, lured him into a somewhat testy discussion about humans. He wondered if she had set herself that task, to make him see in some way that humans were in truth worthy of his company, worthy of his care. "Were he merely a farmsteader, we likely wouldn't even know his name."

"Oh, stop." Timmon, disgusted, placed hands on hips. "Come on, Beth. Leave him here to deal with the downed tent. He wouldn't appreciate our help anyway."

Bethid hitched a shoulder in a brief shrug and turned away to accompany Timmon. Brodhi stood there a long moment, debating, then swore inwardly and set off after them. His longer strides brought him even with Bethid easily.

"Ah," she noted. "Curiosity has gotten the better of you."

"Nothing," Brodhi declared, "as you so inelegantly put it, gets the better of me."

"Except for Alisanos."

Well. That was true. But he had not expected such insight from Bethid, or that she would speak of it in front of Timmon. He cast her a frowning glance, but said nothing. Later, he would.

Bethid, however, snickered, and gave him a sunny smile.

 YOUR AGREEMENT IS not necessary, Karadath had said, *just your womb.*

Audrun felt the rush of ice through her body. Her mouth dried. She stared back at him with trembling limbs and a myriad of thoughts and fears so drowning her mind that speech was impossible. Indeed, he would not kill what he required to bear his child, but that did not mean he would treat her kindly.

Yet she dared not show him her fear, or he would play on it. *Blessed Mother, lend me the strength.* "Then may I ask what you intend to do with me before I am expected to conceive? Since now you 'prepare' human women?"

"We will provide for you and your get."

"Do you expect that to alter my opinion of you?"

The primary's brows arched up. She had seen that expression on Brodhi's face: a palpable arrogance coupled with a delicate but disturbing disbelief. "Your opinion of me is of no import. It has nothing whatsoever to do with whether you can conceive."

Audrun gritted her teeth. She was resolved not to give him any ground. "In my world—the human world—a woman lies with a man for three reasons. First, they are wed and love each other. Second, a woman accepts payment for it. The third, we call rape." Then she reflected that she had left out a fourth reason: bedding without marriage. Not every woman took coin for it. But she wasn't about to mention that to Karadath.

His eyes read her. She saw it, saw what he registered. She was sweaty, grimy, battered, exhausted, sunburned, and, compared to him, most insignificant in the world. Tears prickled, but did not fall. Insignificant? Yes. But she was also, in this world, the only predictable certainty her children knew. That gave her the strength of will to withstand anything he said, anything he promised.

She raised her chin and met his eyes. "Please move aside," she said briskly. "I would like to see my children. I would like for them to see *me*. You are impeding that."

With no visible warning, Karadath caught and cradled both sides of her head in big hands. The startling pressure was enormous. Audrun feared he might well crush her skull.

"No—" But that blurted word was all she could manage. She clung to his wrists, tugging at them, but her attempts to remove his hands were wholly unsuccessful. He was simply too big, too strong.

He pulled her up onto her tiptoes. Most of her weight now depended from her head. She felt her neck stretch, heard and felt the cracking of her spine that would ordinarily bring relief were she not practically hanging from the primary's hands. Yet another lift and her toes left the ground. *Mother of Moons, help me.* She pointed her toes, stretched them downward in an effort to gain even a toenail's worth of purchase. Other than the occasional weak scrape against the paving stones, she could do nothing. She gulped painfully. She believed any moment her head might, like a melon, burst through its skin. *Blessed Mother* . . .

"It need not be rape," he said, "when it's a question of whom and what you will eventually become. Do you care to see?"

The heels of his hands, set just below her mouth, dug into the hollows beneath her cheekbones, pressed painfully against her jaw. She could barely open her mouth. The protest she longed to make was merely a twisted blurt of sound that did not pass her lips. She yanked at his wrists, clawed at them, using what fingernails remained to her. The primary merely shook her.

"Yes," he said, "I think you should see it." He lowered his head, pressed his brow against hers, and a world she didn't know opened before her. "Look well," he said, still squeezing her skull, "that is indeed you. That is what you will become."

She saw scales instead of flesh, claws instead of nails, fangs instead of teeth. The pupils of her eyes were slitted, not round. Most of her hair was missing; what remained were thin, tangled strands. Her nose had altered, forming serpent-like slit nostrils. From her mouth ran saliva but also blood.

"Ah," Karadath said, his breath brushing her mouth, "I see you have fed."

She tried to cry out, but could not. She could not open her mouth widely enough to do so. She could only emit a sound that was a strangled, terrified, inward wail.

"Shall we see your prey? Yes, I think we shall."

The vision was of Meggie.

Half-eaten Meggie.

The primary released her. Audrun fell and fell hard. But it didn't matter. Nothing mattered but the vision in her mind.

She scrabbled against the paving stones on hands and knees, tangled within the vision, trapped in her own mind. But at last she sat upright. She clapped hands over her eyes. The cry came as much from her soul as from her mouth. *MotherMotherMother*— She bit into a wrist to keep herself from screaming. The vision, the knowledge, filled her mind, threatened to extinguish her soul. She could not check her tears, could not stop the keening that escaped her mouth. Whatever courage she had once relied upon, the determination to withstand anything he said, was banished. She could not escape the horrific vision of her bloodied mouth, of the fangs, of her jaws un-hinging, so she might take in more of her daughter.

Karadath loomed over her. He reached down, caught a wrist, and turned the joint so that she saw her palm. "You had best keep watch on your skin. Once the scales break through, it won't be long before the hunger rises."

A thin, terrified screaming began. She knew it wasn't her. And then, with a mother's ear, she realized exactly who it was.

"Meggie—oh Mother, *Meggie*—"

The screaming continued. "There," the primary said in mock kindness. "The little one saw the vision, too."

Ah, not Meggie.

Meggie, half eaten.

Audrun bent over the walkway and vomited.

Chapter 9

*M*IKAL'S TENT HAD been propped up hastily to provide shelter against the rain. It was a haphazard job and Ilona knew they would have to erect it all over again if it were to remain upright. For the moment, it stood. For the moment, people—all of whom she knew—ducked into it, all with damp hair and clothing. She herself slipped in before Rhuan, pushing clammy woven fabric from her hair. The rain had worsened during the short walk from wagon to tent. To offset the gray of the day, Mikal had set out lighted, drooping candles in cups on the tables along with battered plates of bread and cheese for all. The interior was hazy with muted glow; fragile wisps of smoke twined upward.

Mikal stood in his customary place behind the plank bar, propping himself on thick arms planted against wood. To his left, at the end of the plank, Jorda was setting down two lengths of iron bars. The longer was hollow, the shorter solid. After years on the road with Jorda, she knew the sound of the Summoner's chimes very well. When he rang the Summoner, everyone responded.

Darmuth was already there, appropriating a table for himself with arms propped up and chin resting in his hands. His shaven skull gleamed with rain. Alorn, one of the couriers, was seated at a table. She knew none of the couriers well, only by name. Then Brodhi came in, and Bethid, rubbing short wet hair into its usual spiked, untidy cap, took a seat at the table inhabited by Alorn; Timmon did the same. Brodhi did not join them, but gravitated to a corner of the tent where he stood with arms crossed against his chest, looking for all the world like a man irritated by something he wished not to do, yet did nonetheless.

Rhuan sat next to Ilona. As he sliced and then handed her bread and cheese, she smiled crookedly. They were so different, Brodhi and Rhuan, despite shared blood, despite similarly shaped faces, identical height and weight. She glanced sidelong at Rhuan and a wide, private smile blossomed. No, regardless of what Darmuth said, they had not wasted time in a friendship that was precursor to intimacy. If anything, it strengthened their intimacy.

Jorda, one hip set against the end of the bar and a full tankard close by, sounded almost matter-of-fact. "We have Brodhi's map through the passageway. We can escape being trapped here."

Brodhi's expression was ironic. "Can you?"

Jorda's tone changed to concern. "Can't we?"

"Should you?"

"We can't stay here!" Mikal declared.

"The warlord will send more Hecari when the four warriors don't return," Brodhi said. "You had no choice but to kill them, because they would have carried word immediately. For a little while, you won't be in danger. But in time they will come. Many will come."

"Then you can lead us through," Jorda stated. "We'll go back to the grasslands now and avoid the Hecari."

"That is a great risk, Jorda." Rhuan's voice was quiet. "We will be in the border. So many wagons, most of them large and thus closer to the trees. Possibly scraping the trees. A child steps off the path. The mother follows, or the father. All are taken by Alisanos. Others panic, and more are lost. Animals wander and are chased. Another lost." He paused. "And there is more reason to stay here the season. Monsoon. We left the settlement late, and then Alisanos delayed us even more. Even if we survived the passageway and the Hecari, it's too difficult, now, for horses and mules to pull the wagons in such mud, and levering bogged wagons out of it requires too many men and too much time."

Jorda stared hard at his guide for a long moment. Then he rubbed a wide hand across the top of his head. His tone was weary. "Alisanos. Hecari. Monsoon."

Rhuan nodded. "Three dangers. There really is no choice."

Jorda opened his mouth to speak but broke off as another man entered the tent—the farmsteader, Davyn. A moment later a woman Ilona recognized: Naiya, a Sister of the Road. Silence fell. The farmsteader found a stool at a table, but the woman remained standing near the untied door flaps, a length of rich green fabric wrapping her torso over russet tunic and skirts. Honey-colored hair was damp, curling, tied back from her face. She wiped rain from her brow and cheeks.

Jorda went on. "Nearly all of the younger trees in the smaller grove were uprooted and torn. That saves us the effort of cutting several trees down, and provides firewood enough to last us a very long time. Also, planks may be cut out, shaped, planed. We will build a rough boardwalk in the open spaces where there is no shelter, leading to both the grove and throughout the tents. New poles must be cut and trimmed for the tents, stronger rope is needed, and the irons will be pounded more deeply. Weather garb must be made for those who have none. We'll need barrels set throughout the tents and old grove to catch the rain so no one needs to walk all the way to the river and back when the storms are bad. We can't plant in monsoon, so those who are skilled at making and setting snares will be called upon to do so; others will hunt; some will fish."

The Sister made a sound of disbelief. "We're *staying?*"

"We have no choice," Jorda answered. "Monsoon is upon us. When the season is over, we'll depart. But for now, best to stay put."

The woman shook her head. "We're surrounded by Alisanos!"

"Nearly," Jorda corrected. "Not entirely."

The farmsteader, in the midst of cutting slices of cheese and bread, asked the question in nearly everyone's mind: "How dare we hunt when we don't know where it's safe to go, what to avoid?"

Jorda looked at Rhuan, who nodded. "That is my task," Rhuan said. "I have land-sense, as I have said, and can tell when I am close to the border between safety and Alisanos. We will raise cairn markers to warn you away from danger with significant space between the deepwood and the cairns. And we will map it as well." He indicated Brodhi with a tilt of his head. "Brodhi has already created a rough map of the way leading here. We can build upon that and map the perimeters. It's vital that we set to work, which is why I will begin sorting out the border from the actual deepwood as soon as may be. Rain or no."

"While it rains?" the Sister asked.

Rhuan shrugged. "We can't afford to wait out the rain each day."

Naiya registered disbelief. "You're saying it will rain every day?"

"Monsoon," Mikal said matter-of-factly.

Rhuan nodded ruefully. "Let us say the cessation of rain would be more worrisome." He smiled. "I take it you're not from this area."

"No. From the west." She raised her chin. "Yes, we may lie with men for coin rings—none of us has a home or family—but should we remain here so the Hecari can *take* what they want of us? Perhaps even kill us?" She shook her head. "It's not just families who wish to go to safe environs."

Rhuan smiled wryly. "No, I can see—"

"But what if Alisanos moves again?" Davyn asked, interrupting. "Then neither map *nor* cairn will apply."

Naiya shook her head. "It's too dangerous to stay here. We should leave and find another place."

"Would you have your wagons bog so deeply they can't be moved until the monsoon is over? That is weeks from now. And would you live there, mired in the open where Hecari may find you?" Rhuan shook his head. "Safer to remain here. We'll map the border, as I said, and raise cairns." He indicated the karavan-master. "And we can warn people with Jorda's Summoner."

To demonstrate, Jorda rose, picked up the bars and lightly tapped the longer one. It raised a deep, rich, chime, familiar to karavaners, until Jorda silenced it with a hand. "Different rhythms for different threats," Rhuan went on. "For draka, for other beasts loosed by Alisanos, if I sense that the deepwood is close to moving. . . . Everyone will have to learn what the different rhythms mean. If it's draka, you don't want anyone running for shelter. If the land is shaking, we must avoid being trapped in an earthfall. All must know the differences."

Jorda set the Summoner down atop the bar planks. "It's true that we will need supplies if we are to remain here. Much has been shared out, as the Mother requires us to do in times of trouble, but there is not enough to see us through the monsoon and, if necessary, beyond." He looked at Brodhi. "Could a few get through the passageway, if we are careful and follow your lead?"

"A few," Brodhi answered. "Possibly. But danger still exists."

Jorda nodded. "Then I propose that some of us travel to Cardatha immediately, before all the earth is mud. We will buy what we can of foodstuffs, new canvas, rope, awls, and other needful things. We will take two wagons and two teams of horses for each. And yes, we may bog down; this is why I'm taking extra horses. For any reason other than replenishing crucial supplies, I would not go. But I must, if we are to survive. If we leave very soon we'll escape the worst of the rain and mud. When the monsoon ends and the land dries, I will reorganize the karavan and lead folk to safety, if Alisanos and the Hecari allow it."

"We'll go with you," Bethid said, and everyone turned to look at her. "Timmon, Alorn, Brodhi, and me. It's time we returned to the Guildhall anyway. We can help with the wagons on the way there."

Ilona saw a flash of irritation in Brodhi's face before implacability returned. It made her grin at the tabletop.

Jorda nodded his thanks then gestured to Mikal. The one-eyed man took up the discussion. "This tent will now serve as more than a place for ale, spirits, tale-telling, and rumor-mongering, though of course all of those activities will continue." He smiled faintly. "News will come through me, and when a summons is rung, select men of the folk will assemble here. It's not efficient to call everyone out and too slow with only one or two men carrying news to the others. Then we can spread the news throughout the grove and the tents in a way phrased not to panic folk. Panic may be the most dangerous thing of all, living so close to Alisanos."

Davyn raised his voice. "What about the road? The road through Alisanos."

Rhuan snapped his head around to stare at the farmsteader, who belatedly recalled he was not to speak of such things to the others, yet, as it could well lead to questions Rhuan didn't wish asked.

"What road?" Bethid asked, even as Ilona put her own unspoken question into her eyes as she turned toward Rhuan.

He merely shrugged. "I think he meant *a* road, not *the* road. And I agree that it would be most helpful were there a safe road through Alisanos," he cast a hard glance the farmsteader's way, "but there isn't one. Much too dangerous to risk ourselves forcing a way through the deepwood."

Ilona caught a subtle undertone to Rhuan's statement. She was about to lean sideways and ask him a quiet question, but his glance at her told her no.

Jorda said, "We know that Alisanos surrounds us except for one opening, relatively narrow, like the neck of a bottle. It forces a large party to ride strung out, not bunched. And that gives us an advantage where the Hecari are concerned." He looked to Brodhi. "How long is the opening? How long would the warriors—or anyone, actually—remain hemmed in?"

Brodhi shook his head. "Who can say? It depends on how quickly the mount, or the person's feet, is able to move."

"One hundred paces?" Jorda asked, annoyed. "Two hundred? More? Surely you can estimate."

Brodhi did not speak at once but lifted one shoulder in a half-shrug. "Until it's walked, we can't know, only guess. Perhaps the responsibility of counting should be Rhuan's task in addition to setting out markers."

"Unwise," Rhuan countered at once. "Cairn markers throughout the neck of a bottle would identify what's safe, and what's not. We should not give the Hecari any information, visible or otherwise, that divulges such things."

"Then how do *we* get through?" Naiya asked.

It was Bethid who answered. Ilona reflected that a courier should have sound knowledge of such things. "There is no recognizable track yet, but I should think staying in the middle—keeping the deep-wood's edges equidistant from one another—would serve. Brodhi and those warriors came through without harm."

A flicker of lightning and resultant thunder momentarily stopped the discussion until Davyn raised his voice over pouring rain. "It's all well and good to discuss the merits of bottling up the Hecari," Davyn interjected, "but I suspect you have forgotten the reverse of that; a narrow pathway such as you describe could just as well keep us *in*."

Jorda smoothed his beard. "A road through Alisanos from here would be most helpful; unfortunately, it's also impossible. Who could survive to build it in Alisanos? But as before, we will post watchers, with runners bringing warning if Hecari approach." He paused, nodding at the Sister. "I understand your fear. It's not misplaced. It will take time to sort out what must be done and when. We know the Hecari *will* come. We merely have no knowledge of when."

"Brodhi might be able to find out," Rhuan suggested. "He reports directly to the warlord, rather than the Guildhall, because he of all the couriers is not Sancorran. The only knowledge the Hecari have of this particular settlement is what Brodhi tells the warlord."

Naiya's challenge was delicate, with careful inflection. "They found us before."

Rhuan leaned forward against the table, resting forearms upon the surface. "But Alisanos has moved. The terrain in this area is now completely different. It's true a culling party might find their way here, but they've never grappled with Alisanos." He glanced at Brodhi. "You can shape the truth with falsehood."

Brodhi was most annoyed, Ilona saw. He wore his habitual mask, but his eyes gave him away. Such enmity, she reflected, between close kin. They were alone in the world save for one another, Rhuan and Brodhi, but their hearts were completely different. When she had briefly read Rhuan's palm on the night they met, she had seen *maelstrom*. She wondered what Brodhi's hand would tell her and knew she would never see it.

"*I* would tell lies to the warlord," Bethid said pointedly, and then added in dramatic tones, "but a woman would never be admitted to his presence."

Ilona smiled to herself. Clever Bethid. And it was wholly effective in prompting Brodhi's response.

The courier shrugged. "Yes, he will listen to me. I told him about Alisanos. He sent four warriors to be certain what I said was true. I will now have to explain that the deepwood took them, not a mismatched assemblage of karavaners and tent-folk."

"*Organized* assemblage," Bethid countered.

The idea, the knowledge, the vision unfolded in Ilona's mind so clearly, so abruptly, at first all she could do was blink as her lips parted. Then a twinge of understanding, of anticipation, sent a faint shiver through her body. "Could we use Alisanos," she began, "to rid us of Hecari?" She glanced at the faces turned her way. "Could they be led to the deepwood and enter it on their own?"

Davyn straightened sharply on his stool and set the tankard down with a thunk. He said, with a note of discovery, "If so, we might stay in Sancorra. Return to our homes, if any remain." His blue eyes shone and color seeped into his face, easing tension and weariness. "We could all go home. Or build new homes, with no fear of Hecari." He looked at Rhuan. "What if *we* built a road? A false road that would draw the attention of the Hecari. They could follow it, thinking folk are hiding, only to be swallowed by Alisanos."

"And who could build it?" Brodhi asked in an acerbic tone. "Who risks being taken by Alisanos while in the midst of building a road, even if it's false? There is no safe way through Alisanos; it's a waste of time to even discuss it. Besides, the Hecari are too many." He shot a glance at Rhuan. "How do you think they were able to take three provinces so swiftly, so completely? They sweep the plains like an ocean. Many of us drown."

Ilona arched her brows in surprise. Brodhi had said *us*. She looked at Rhuan, who had caught the word as well. He smiled crookedly and leaned close to whisper, "There may be hope for him yet."

Ilona whispered back, "Do you truly believe that?"

"Well," he said, "no. But it's still an improvement."

Davyn's voice was confident, now that hope had been retrieved. "But we could be rid of *some* of the Hecari. Is it not worthwhile to let Alisanos kill them, no matter the number? One less, two less, twenty less . . . well worth it, I say."

Brodhi shook his head. "You are a fool. What do you think will happen when warriors begin to regularly disappear? I am to report to the warlord—"

Abruptly the candlelight was dwarfed by a sustained series of blinding flashes outside the tent, followed by an enormous crack of thunder. Everyone in the ale-tent jumped. Ilona slapped a hand over her heart. "Sweet Mother . . . !"

The two bars of Jorda's Summoner rolled together, producing a chime muted by wood planks. Mikal glanced upward, assessing the central tent pole with one squinted eye. Canvas trembled beneath the onslaught of rain. Naiya, closest to the door flaps, moved forward hastily to avoid rain spray that made its way through the gaps. Ilona noticed that the first tendrils of water crept their way inside beneath the hem of the door flaps.

As the thunder died out, Bethid resumed. "As we've already said, Brodhi will report to the warlord and tell him whatever serves us best."

Had Ilona not been looking directly at Brodhi, she would have missed the faint flicker of red in his eyes. He was most displeased with Bethid. But before he could respond, Darmuth spoke up.

"It's worth doing," he said lightly. "After all, you're *Shoia*, Brodhi. You can afford to lose a few lives."

Ilona nearly laughed at the cheerfully sly expression on Darmuth's face. Baiting Brodhi, she discovered, had its own measure of amusement.

"Could you do that?" Naiya asked of Brodhi. "Could you control the warlord's actions by giving him lies?"

"No. He's not a fool. He is clever, arrogant, ruthless, and he knows how to manipulate men."

"Sounds rather like you," Rhuan observed dryly. He grinned as Brodhi shot him a dark glance. "Aren't you cleverer than he? He's human, after all; surely you—a *Shoia*—could manipulate him."

Always the emphasis on Shoia, Ilona noted, as if it had become a private jest among those who knew of the pretense. Which struck her as odd, because apparently *she* was Shoia. And realization reasserted itself: *Blessed Mother, I have seven lives!* No. Six. Rhuan's father, Alario, had already stolen one.

Ilona forcibly pulled her attention back to the matters at hand, which happened to be talking Brodhi into feeding lies to the warlord. She nodded, affecting innocence, "Of course you are cleverer than he, Brodhi. I'm sure of it. And not necessarily because you're Shoia . . ." She let it trail off suggestively. "but because you're, well . . . *you.*"

Brodhi knew very well what she meant. The alteration of a single word: Shoia, in front of the others, in place of *dioscuri.* She saw it in his eyes, in the tensing of his face. "None of you has met the warlord," he said sharply. "You have no idea of what he is capable."

"Oh, I think we do." Davyn threw crumbled bread back onto the platter for emphasis. "He is capable of destroying a province. Three provinces. Many of us decided to leave, to run away, in effect—and I include myself among them—rather than face his warriors. But now he squats in Cardatha. He can't, by himself, keep track of one province, let alone three. He depends and acts on information brought to him by his warriors and, apparently, by Brodhi. *Purposeful* false information might give us an advantage, give us time to prepare."

"That's exactly what I have proposed," Bethid said, slicing more cheese. "Couriers come and go freely; we might as well be invisible, because we are *expected* to come and go. Couriers worth our trust, committed men, can also carry word of the warlord's plans so people may be prepared. Information is vital; there would be no Guild without it." She gestured toward Timmon and Alorn at the same table. Just as she began to place the cheese into her mouth, she said, "We've already discussed it, in fact, the four of us here."

Lightning again flashed outside the tent, followed almost immediately by thunder that obliterated speech. Ilona winced. Until the thunder faded, no one spoke; then Brodhi said frigidly, "I am not privy to the warlord's plans. Nor are any of you."

"There are ways to make ourselves so," Rhuan said lightly, and as Brodhi glared at him, Darmuth's grin stretched wide, displaying the gemstone drilled into one of his teeth.

Ilona was as mystified as anyone else, save for Rhuan, Brodhi, and Darmuth himself, all of whom appeared to be talking of something specific. She opened her mouth to ask *why* Darmuth could do what others could not, but a pointed glance from Rhuan and a slight shake of his head suggested she keep silent. And so she did but resolved that Rhuan had better provide details when they were away from others.

"Can it be done?" Bethid had to raise her voice over the noise of heavy rain. "Whatever it is that you're talking about, I'm assuming it concerns a means of learning the warlord's plans."

Darmuth's grin renewed itself. "Oh, it can be done."

"How?" Jorda asked sharply. "And, if so, why has it not been done before?"

"Because no one thought of it before," Rhuan said wryly, then sobered. "And that I will lay at the foot of fear, because the Hecari have trained us to fear. But circumstances have changed now because of Alisanos; this is no longer the transient, temporary settlement that drew the culling party. And there is change, too, because of the four warriors Brodhi brought here. The warlord knows that Alisanos exists." He looked steadily at Brodhi, shredding bread. "There was no choice, of course; you had to tell him. But now that he *does* know, we are likely in more danger than before. I think it wouldn't be just a decimation, next time the Hecari come, but a massacre."

Ilona did not need to read hands to sense the tension between Rhuan and his cousin. Their gazes were locked, precursor to what, she could not know, but she *did* know neither would give ground.

Unless she made them.

She raised her voice over the pounding of rain on sagging canvas overhead. "We all of us know how dangerous is Alisanos. But the warlord doesn't. He sent only four warriors." She caught Brodhi's eye, breaking the unspoken challenge between him and Rhuan. "If he truly believed what you told him of the deepwood, would he not have sent more?"

"Four Hecari warriors is not a token number," Brodhi answered. "Four Hecari can account for far more than four of us."

"But they didn't," Ilona said. "We killed them when they came. *We* killed them."

The Sister, Naiya, resettled her wrap. "If we are not to travel because of the monsoon, what about the Hecari? Will they all stay in Cardatha like good little chicks seeking shelter beneath the hen?"

Rhuan smiled. "And that brings us back to the beginning. We need to know the warlord's mind. That can be aided by Darmuth."

Darmuth shrugged. "First we will have to prepare. And it would perhaps be best if none of you know anything about how we will do it, should Hecari come here and ask. Though their habit is to kill, rather than to ask."

It did not satisfy Jorda, Ilona knew, looking at his stern, bearded face. Mikal, too, was troubled. Jorda might ask no more questions in front of others, but elsewhere, oh yes. And Rhuan would be his target.

"Well," Naiya said quietly, "I can offer aid . . . my two Sisters and I are skilled at needlework. If you bring back clothing-weight canvas as well as what else you need, we can fashion weather garb."

Without glancing at faces, Ilona knew exactly what the men were thinking. She wanted to say something, to remind them of manners, but the Sister did it for her.

Naiya's mouth twisted briefly in acknowledgment. "Well. We must fill the time not spent in bed with *some*thing, mustn't we?"

The farmsteader had the grace to looked ashamed, staring at the tabletop rather than at Naiya, and Ilona wondered what image his mind had painted as the Sister spoke.

Chapter 10

*E*VEN TO HERSELF, her voice sounded strange. "Gillan . . . Gillan, see to Meggie."

Oh, Mother. *Meggie.*

Audrun wiped the back of her hand against her mouth, spat out the residual taste of vomit, and from her sprawled position upon the paving stones, from behind a lock of tangled, crusty hair, she looked up into the face of the primary. And it was enough, more than enough, to goad her into motion.

She gathered herself, gathered her aching, battered body, and thrust herself to her feet. She braced them apart so she would not fall. With a great effort she stilled her trembling and stared up into his face, meeting arrogance with a powerful pride. She knew very well what she risked; she also knew she had to do it. For the sake of her children. For Meggie.

Though several sentences filled her mouth, she spoke none of them. Not in anger, nor in fear. She bit them back, swallowed them down, and straightened the body that wished to hunch in pain. She was no primary, with power at her beckoning. She was merely a woman, a human woman, a mother. And in this moment, such was enough, entirely enough.

Beneath the double suns Audrun faced Karadath. She put everything she wished to say into her eyes. She gave him defiance. She confronted. She made him truly *see* her, to know that she was strong enough, no matter the condition of her body, to take any assault, by word or by violence, any assault at all, that he wished to bestow upon her.

The words in her mind said most clearly: *I defy you. I deny you.* And he heard them perfectly well, despite the fact she did not speak them.

Karadath smiled. He turned and reached out swiftly, so swiftly, to grab a fistful of Ellica's tangled hair. By it, he yanked her close. She cried out in shock and fear, clutching the sapling even as her head was forcibly tilted. Tears ran down her sun-flushed face.

"This one is of an age," he said, "to be bred."

Audrun knew she dared not hesitate lest she give him a victory, or show him weakness. "Which is the better wager," she asked evenly, "to provide a child? A woman who's carried five to term and beyond, or a girl whose courses have not yet begun?" Startlement passed through Ellica's eyes, but she faced her mother, not Karadath, and he didn't see it. "So, it comes to me," Audrun said, "after all."

BECAUSE OF THE storm, almost no one wished to depart Mikal's tent. Brodhi left, not unexpectedly, and the Sister, pulling her wrap up onto her head before ducking out the door flap. But everyone else stayed put. Mikal served more ale, waving away payment. Rhuan rose, tankard in hand, and strolled idly over to Darmuth's table. He bent down just beside Darmuth's shoulder, taking care to keep his voice low. "I assume Ferize will accompany you?"

Darmuth smiled. "She will enjoy the challenge."

"Then you can do this? And survive to talk about it?"

Darmuth shrugged. "Too many variables to predict. Emulation will be effective for a short time, but we can't truly *be* Hecari, so we dare not stay long. Remember, Ferize and I, unlike you, can be killed in this world. Permanently."

Rhuan hooked a stool over with his foot and sat down facing

Darmuth. "We need information. We need knowledge of the war-lord's plans."

"Are you trying to talk me into it, or yourself?"

Rhuan planted an elbow on the table and scratched at his hair-line. "It was easy to say when in the midst of the discussion. Perhaps it isn't such a good idea after all."

"Of course it's not a good idea. But it's the only one we have, is it not?" Darmuth ran the palm of his hand over his shaven skull, rid-ding it of the last sheen of moisture. "It's worth trying. If it fails, we haven't lost anything . . . and be quite certain Ferize and I will con-trive whatever it takes to remain alive."

Rhuan considered that, rubbing his bottom lip in bemusement. "The head of the serpent."

"Cut it off?" Darmuth threw back a gulp of ale, brushed foam from his lip. "It's a thought . . . if one were to ask Brodhi how the serpent likes to sleep. That is, if he knows. But neither Ferize nor I can kill him. We can't hold the false form *and* kill a man. Our power is limited here in the human world, it can't be doled out to different tasks. And if we let go the illusion, we very likely would be killed immediately. They are fearsome warriors, our Hecari, and I don't doubt that the warlord has men aplenty whose sole task is to guard his body."

Nodding thoughtfully, Rhuan glanced around. He saw the farm-steader, Davyn, deep in thought, wrinkles across his brow, drawing circles in spilled ale. He blamed himself for saying anything about the road through Alisanos if he were so poor at keeping secrets. But the man had needed *some*thing.

That gave him an idea, and he rose with a brief grasp of Dar-muth's shoulder, then took himself and his tankard to the bar where Jorda spoke quietly with Mikal. "Have him go." Rhuan tilted his head in the farmsteader's direction. "Take him with you to Cardatha."

Jorda straightened. "Why?"

Rhuan very much desired to say he wanted Davyn out of the way before he let slip anything else. In the meantime, seeming idleness would do better than insistence. "It will fill his time. Distract him.

Here, all he can think about is his family. Take him with you, and he can help if the wagons bog down, help gather supplies in Cardatha. We're losing all the couriers to the Guildhall—the trip back will need another pair of hands."

Jorda frowned. "I thought Darmuth would accompany me."

Rhuan kept an eye on the farmsteader, answering Jorda absently. "Then have a *third* pair of hands to assist on the way back."

The karavan-master stared hard into Rhuan's face. Rhuan knew very well when he was being weighed, when someone attempted to sort out what was in his mind. He also knew that at some point he was going to have to be painstakingly honest with Jorda. When he and Darmuth had been no more than hired guides for the karavans, there was no need for Jorda to ask more of them, to know their origins beyond a cursory explanation. But now, with the world upended and Alisanos on the doorstep, Jorda would not let anything slide by.

Rhuan forestalled the emergent question by lifting a staying hand. "I know. And I will discuss this. But first—take the farmsteader with you. I'll tell him you've asked for his help."

"Then wouldn't it be best if *I* ask for his help?"

"He might say no if you do it."

Jorda frowned. "*No* to me, but *yes* to you?"

Rhuan smiled crookedly. "Yes."

Jorda raised his tankard and took down the last swallow. When he thumped it on the bartop again he fixed Rhuan with a steady gaze. "My wagon," he said. "Soon. A matter of moments. You and no one else. Not even Darmuth."

That surprised Rhuan. "Not even Darmuth?"

"Does he need to know your secrets, too?"

"Darmuth knows most of them. But we can discuss that, too, at your wagon."

"Soon," Jorda repeated, as much a command as a suggestion.

Rhuan nodded. "I'll speak to the farmsteader and come over immediately after."

"No lies," Jorda declared. "No more disguising things with dimples, a shrug, a lazy observation."

Jorda knew him better than Rhuan had believed. "You'll have the truth of me."

Jorda stared hard at him for a long moment, then turned to Mikal. "I'll leave the Summoner here . . . once the rain has died, you may as well ring it out by the bonfire. That will bring everyone out, and we can begin gathering volunteers for the tasks."

Rhuan glanced back at the farmsteader as Jorda walked by on his way out of the tent. Davyn had pushed his stool away from the table, midway to rising. Rhuan said sharply, "Wait," and after two long strides sat down across from him. He knew very well that the motion coupled with the word would be effective.

And indeed, Davyn sat back down after a moment, blushing red in embarrassment. "I know. I—know," he said. "I shouldn't have said anything about the road. I'll govern my tongue more closely after this."

Rhuan fixed Davyn with a stare as hard as Jorda's. "Yes, I think you'd better. Fortunately the idea is so preposterous that no one will think about what you said, this time. Next time, they might." He pulled his meat knife and speared a chunk of cheese. In front of Davyn's face, he waved the knife and cheese. "Unwise," he said. "Most unwise." Before tucking the cheese into his mouth, he said, "Why not go with Jorda? He could use your hands and strong back on the return journey. The couriers will remain in Cardatha, so he will be short of help."

"No." Davyn shook his head. "I won't go so far from the deepwood. Who's to know that my family won't somehow find their way back? I need to be here, in case that should happen."

Inwardly Rhuan sighed, but he kept his tone casual even as he meticulously enunciated. "As I have said, until the road is built—and it will be built—they can't come to you. Nor can you go to them." He sliced off another hunk of cheese, chewed neatly, and swallowed. He washed all down with a measure of ale, then said with great clarity, albeit couched in offhandedness, "Jorda could use you in my place. I have to stay and begin mapping the border."

"Then I'll stay here and help you with that."

Rhuan shook his head. "I'll risk no human to the deepwood's whimsy. You don't have land-sense; Alisanos might merely shiver, yet take you into it. And no, you wouldn't find your family that way. It's most likely you'd simply be eaten."

"*Eate*n?"

"Very likely." Rhuan tore a hunk of bread off the loaf. "Alisanos teems with devils and demons, all kinds of beasts, even humans who have been perverted by the wild magic. No one there will guard your life." As he had guarded Audrun's. Once done with bread and cheese, Rhuan slid his knife back into its scabbard. "In Cardatha, you won't be eaten."

Davyn scowled. "You're trying to get rid of me."

That truth Rhuan felt safe in telling. "Yes. I am."

Lightning shot across the heavens. On its heels came a massive explosion of thunder. Davyn winced and covered his ears. When he uncovered them, he asked, "Does it rain like this in Cardatha?"

"No. Cardatha's rain is gentle." Rhuan grinned. "No monsoon where you lived before?"

"Not like this." When lightning crackled so closely outside the tent that its odor could be smelled, Davyn once again covered his ears. Sure enough, thunder rumbled behind the flash. "All right. All right." He pushed away from the table. "I'll go with the karavan-master."

"Jorda will see to it you'll have meals and coin rings for your trouble."

Davyn nodded, but his mind was clearly on something else. Rhuan waited until the farmsteader exited the tent, then returned to his own table and slid onto his seat beside Ilona.

She studied his face. "You have the look of a man pleased by his actions."

"I am."

"What *were* they, exactly, these actions?"

Over the rim of his lifted tankard, Rhuan said, "I told the farmsteader he should accompany Jorda, and that the rains are gentler in Cardatha."

"You didn't!"

"I did."

"He'll know you for a liar when he gets there."

Rhuan smiled at her. "But in the meantime he won't be *here*."

"And that matters?"

"It will fill his mind with something other than worry about his family."

"For a while, perhaps, but—"

"*But*, it's enough. For now. And Jorda could truly use his help. Darmuth has a task in Cardatha emminently more important than buying supplies and loading a wagon."

"Doing whatever it is neither of you would discuss in front of everyone?"

"Doing exactly that." Rhuan leaned close for a quick kiss, then scooted back his stool as he rose. "I'm wanted at Jorda's wagon. I'll come to you after."

Ilona propped her chin against the heel of her hand and smiled lazily. "Do."

BETHID SAT WITH Timmon and Alorn as they finished their ale and chewed at her bottom lip as she thought. She looked first at Timmon, then Alorn, with great intensity. "We have to do this."

"Do what?" Timmon inquired.

"What we said we'd do. We're going back to the Guildhall. We must discover how many of us are trustworthy . . . and who might betray us." She played a quiet tattoo against the tabletop with her fingertips. "So long as the Guildmaster doesn't immediately send us back out, we could sort out those in the Guildhall who would support us." She frowned thoughtfully. "But I guess even if we are sent back out, we could test those couriers we meet on the road or at settlements. It's vital, I think, to let the people know there is a safe place available."

"Against Hecari?" Alorn asked. "What safe place?"

"Here."

Timmon's brows shot up. "Here?"

"You heard the discussion. The terrain now favors us. We could either provide directions for folk to come here, or lead them here ourselves."

"*You* heard the discussion, Beth." Alorn shook his head. "It would invite a culling party."

"This is still a much safer place than out on the plains, wouldn't you say?"

Alorn's mouth twisted. "I suppose."

"And the Mother knows there is plenty of room for more folk."

"For now," Timmon agreed. "But at some point there will be too many for this settlement to sustain. How do you propose to choose who comes here and who doesn't?"

"Hmmm," Bethid murmured. "That does bear some thought."

Alorn said, with a mix of fond amusement and exasperation, "That is your abiding fault, Beth."

It startled her. "What abiding fault?"

"You throw yourself wholeheartedly into one project or another, committing yourself—and, in this case, us—before you've thought your way through."

"But we *talked* about this! You agreed we should do whatever we can to keep people from harm, to lay down the first planks of rebellion."

"Yes," Timmon said. "But that was before you said anything about bringing people here."

"They'll come anyway, some of them. Everyone wants to leave Sancorra because of the Hecari."

"You know," Alorn said thoughtfully, "there may be another way. If we are very selective and only send men here who would be in deadly earnest about undertaking this rebellion, it could work."

Bethid frowned. "You mean build our own army?"

"In a way," Alorn replied. "Certainly we overcame the four warriors Brodhi brought back with him; and yes, I understand that four hardly constitutes a major victory, but the point is that we all of us were organized. That's critical. If we can build on that, smaller numbers may prove more effective than one might think."

Timmon looked doubtful. "Even against the Hecari?"

Bethid understood Alorn's intent and pounced upon it. "We train as many Sancorrans as we can, then send them back out to find others willing to fight. And then—" she sat up straight upon her stool. "And then we can begin killing Hecari patrols. Possibly even culling parties. We could meet the Hecari on their own ground." She waved Timmon into silence as he opened his mouth to speak. "Yes, we would have to be certain of our numbers in those circumstances. We must be judicious about this." She chewed briefly at a hangnail. "Brodhi could keep Hecari numbers down, perhaps. At first."

"Exactly: but only at first," Timmon said. "And if the warlord sends a thousand warriors? What then?"

"Brodhi said the passageway is narrow, like the neck of a bottle," Bethid replied. "That means a thousand warriors couldn't all squeeze through at the same time. It gives us an advantage. And if they try to push through, all of them, well . . ." She grinned. "A fair number would likely run smack into Alisanos. To them, it would be a forest. Nothing more, until it was too late."

Alorn shook his head. "I agree some would be lost as you describe, and that others might be killed by us, but we couldn't account for the deaths of a thousand warriors. We may have men, but we can't truly assemble an army. Not to withstand the numbers the warlord will throw against us. Can we kill a few? Kill a culling party? Probably, once we've trained a fair number of men. But we'll never have enough to defeat the warlord's armies."

Bethid considered for a moment, then looked at both men. "If Hecari keep disappearing here, specifically *here*, I'd think the warlord himself might decide to take a personal interest."

"Sweet Mother, Beth, you're out of your mind!" Timmon shook his head vigorously. "If he comes here, we might as well kill ourselves rather than die beneath the warclubs!"

"Maybe," Bethid agreed, "and maybe not." She gave herself the luxury of a big, back-cracking stretch, thrusting both arms in the air. "In the meantime, I think we'd better go raise our tent."

"In the rain," Alorn said gloomily.

Bethid rose. "When I left it, everything we had in the tent was covered by the canvas when it fell down. I suspect it won't be as wet as you might be inclined to think. We may very well sleep dry tonight. And besides—we're going to Cardatha. They have *buildings* there."

THE CHILD CRIED in a thin, wailing voice. Demon cradled her in its—no, in *her*—arms, wishing peace to the infant. She had fed, and fed well. Still, she cried.

Demon had made a small nest of tattered blankets. The baby had slept there for some time but awoke with a demanding cry. Demon at first felt completely helpless, but she took the child up into her arms, head resting in the crook of her left elbow, and began to rock the infant in small arcs. It came easily, the action. It *fit*. Empty arms were empty no longer.

Woman. Woman. She had been.

Was.

As yet it was alien to Demon. The child's cries did not quicken her breasts. She had borne no baby and her body knew it. But she had called milk from her breasts nonetheless. Thin, watery milk. There was something of a woman left in her, deep inside. That woman longed for the baby, longed to hold and comfort, to ease her own heart that had been stone for so long. Longer than she could count.

"Tha tha," she said, then corrected herself once again. "There, there."

The alteration from human into demon had been lengthy and painful. At first she understood what she had been and what had happened to her, trapped in Alisanos. But in time memory died. Even as scales formed from breastbone to genitals, as the nubs erupted from bone through flesh on either side of her spine. The pain of it had nearly driven her mad. She had no knowledge of what was happening to her, of what she was becoming. She knew pain, and nothing more. And when she had tried to rub her back against a tree, searching for relief, the pain of that had dwarfed all other discomfort. She had not tried again, but bore it. Bore it.

Eventually she had twisted her arms behind her back to just barely reach to her spine, and found more than nubs. There was thick *skin*, and none of it her own. She felt where layer upon layer of muscle had spread, knitting itself from her body into what was growing upon her. The substance was leathery. But she could reach so little of it, even twisting her arms behind her back; she knew only that she was changing. She was not the woman she had been the day Alisanos took her.

Claws, black and curved. Eyes that fed her richer colors, brighter sunlight. Too bright, as it could be in a world with double suns, and she felt something in her eyes, a brief stab of . . . *otherness*.

Still the infant cried, and it came to Demon that babies required more than food. She set the child down into the nest of tattered blankets and undid the clout. Very wet. The odor was astringent. At first all she could do was crouch down over the newborn, wishing her to be well. She was puzzled. Her mind felt empty of what she should do. And then something inside her, something buried human years before, guided her.

The child was wet and should be dry.

Demon smiled broadly. She *knew* what to do. And as her mouth opened, as her mouth stretched, fangs appeared.

Yes. She knew what to do.

Chapter 11

RHUAN DUCKED OUT of the ale-tent into rain. The day remained gray and depressing. Puddles had begun to fill in the low spots where no grass grew, where livestock and humans had pressed the grass and weeds out of life into packed dirt. For now, wet ground was an inconvenience but within a matter of days the surface would soak up so much water that no more could be assimilated, and the top layer would become slop running with rain. The only choice was to build a boardwalk, as Jorda suggested, unless people wished to fight the bog-like mud every time they attempted to go anywhere.

With the young grove destroyed, the grandfather grove now offered the only exterior shelter for the karavaners against the rain. Tent-folk were already under cover, save for those few whose tents had fallen during the latest incursion of Alisanos's birth pangs; all worked in haste to get in and escape the rain. Wagons were scattered throughout the grove, parked under thick-bolled, wide-canopied trees. The karavaners had begun to set up awnings from the sides of their wagons, tying the oiled canvas to wagon ribbing, then stretching it out to full length. Staves were driven into the ground, and the loose ends of the awning were roped into place and knotted, providing rough but effective cover so long as someone kept an eye on the awning and tipped off the water before the canvas grew too heavy. In addition to general shelter, awnings provided a place where cook fires could be built and survive the rain, where families could eat a meal together.

As Rhuan headed into the grove, here and there he saw some folk donning weather garb, oiled clothing-weight canvas, seams sealed with wax. Rough trousers were cuffed at the hems with drawstrings to keep the mud out, and the upper body was clothed in coat-shaped, belted garments with hoods, and sleeve cuffs also pulled tight with drawstrings. While the weather gear rendered the rain less of a bother, it also rendered the karavaners into identical human shapes with no distinguishing characteristics. Children were obvious because of their size, but a tall woman could easily be mistaken for a man. Some womenfolk, however, had nothing but knitted shawls; the karavaners had not expected to be at the settlement during monsoon and hadn't prepared for it. The majority of people Rhuan saw had nothing to ward their bodies against the rain. He reflected that the Sister of the Road had a sound idea in mind when she offered her hands and those of her fellow Sisters to make up weather garb.

Striding through on his way to Jorda's wagon, he was recognized. Some karavaners raised their hands in greeting, and a few asked him to blossoming fires for food and drink. It was nearing midday now and flatbread would be baked in treasured iron skillets, tea set to heat on the stone fire rings, and sweet beans flavored with molasses would go into pots that also sat on the stones. Each wagon carried in its gear a clay pot into which folk put coals and small dried twigs, kindling for when they stopped upon the road. Usually a child was designated to keep the coals alive by carefully adding twigs during the journey. Flint and steel might start a fire without need of the coal pot, but in the wet, no. The flat stones ringing cookfires, as had the coals, traveled with each wagon. One could never be certain of suitable rocks out on the plains, and yet setting a fire without them could be dangerous. So each time the ring was built, the fire-blackened stones were fitted together like masonry, lacking only mortar.

Rhuan saw that children had already been sent out to gather up wood and bring it back beneath awnings to dry. While some complained, others foraged bravely without comment. Rhuan could clearly see the image of Ilona marching through rain, sleet, or snow to gather wood. When the rain stopped later in the day, the men would set up chopping blocks near the wagons and cut dying limbs into managable pieces. Wood was one thing they did not need to ration with the young grove down, but it was vital to dry the limbs.

A pack of dogs ran through very close to him, yipping, barking, growling, and leaping joyously at one another in vociferous play-fighting. The smaller dogs hung off the ruffs or even the lip flews of larger dogs. In a matter of minutes they had taken their play-fight right into Rhuan, who stood still as the dogs leaped upon one another or rolled on the wet ground. His knees were slightly bent and legs were spread to hold his balance, which he very nearly lost when one of the larger dogs ducked between them.

Rhuan swore, flailing to recover balance and decorum. Leather leggings were smeared with mud and whipping saliva. "All right," he said. Then, raising his voice over the growling and barking, "All *right*, I said . . . I am not one of of your brethren! Can't a man walk where he wishes without being inundated by canines?" He waded through the dogs, pushing some aside with his legs and hands as he sought footing. In a matter of moments the pack was off again, tearing madly through the grove. In its wake was raised a child's high voice trying to call back one of the dogs. Rhuan grinned wryly; it would be hours before the dogs returned to their respective wagons, worn out but hungry.

By the time he arrived at Jorda's wagon, his boots were caked with mud, and he was wet from head to toe. The door stood open above the rough wooden steps that, as did Ilona's, folded away when it was time to move on. The wagon sat on big axles and high wheels, and was large enough to house a family such as Audrun's.

The exterior of Jorda's wagon was much plainer than Ilona's with its yellow-painted wheels and the canopy bearing diviner runes. Jorda's was as efficient, plain, and practical as its owner.

Rhuan could hear the karavan-master moving around inside. The wagon creaked. He drew in a deep breath, held it a moment, then blew it out into the drizzling rain. It was time for truths and frankness, an explanation that would illuminate, not frighten. But Ilona had taken the truth quite well; perhaps Jorda would do the same.

Like so many others, Jorda had put up an awning off the side of his big wagon. Though the rain fell steadily, the thick canopies of the elder grove offered a measure of shelter, keeping the worst of the rain off the awning. Jorda stood slightly bent in the doorway in stocking feet, gripping either side to avoid knocking his head against the roof-ribs. "Boots off."

Rhuan nodded. Removing footwear was usual during monsoon. He worked off his boots, set them side by side on the bottom step, next to Jorda's. The karavan-master frowned. "Perhaps I should ask you to strip down—all of you is muddy."

"Yes, a pack of dogs decided to include me in their play, which was not my intent." He slipped the curved horn fastener from a loop in his belt. "I'll strip down, of course, if that's what you want." And he meant it. Nudity, public or otherwise, did not bother him. But he knew Jorda was different.

And indeed, disgruntled, he waved the offer away. "Come in, then—but sit on the floor."

As Jorda moved back, Rhuan ducked down to avoid the canopy rib, brushing his head against a string of dangling charms. Another thong of charms depended from the Mother Rib. A third was strung around Jorda's thick neck. The bedding arrangements were different than those in Davyn and Audrun's wagon. Several planks ran the length of the wagon, covered by blankets, to form a man-sized bed. It was a very spare wagon with few possessions, as unlike Ilona's as could be.

The interior of the wagon, because of the rain, offered poor light that leeched through oiled canvas. A lantern hung from the front end of the wagon, but was as yet unlighted. Jorda resumed his seat on his bed; next to him lay the square plank he used as backing for number-ing and supply lists. Rhuan could see marks on the rough paper pinned to the board, but not well enough to read them. He folded his legs and sat down in the aisle, atop a thin woven rug.

Even seated, Jorda was a big man. His tunic sleeves were rolled back to display thick, red-fuzzed arms. Hands and forearms were scarred from the hardships of the road. His entire face Rhuan had never seen; Jorda wore a heavy, wiry beard that reached high on his cheekbones and inches below his chin. Russet hair streaked with silver was drawn back into a thick, doubled-over braid. Green eyes were fixed upon Rhuan. No patience lived in them, only a command for the truth. Now.

To stall the inevitible Rhuan pulled the binding thong out of his hair and let the curtain of it fall in front of both shoulders, hanging to his waist. He raked fingers through it, splitting sections, so it would begin to dry. Perhaps that night he and Ilona might see to the braid-ing. Well, unless other tasks made it impossible. Or Jorda did.

"Start at the beginning," Jorda said, so calmly that it moved Rhuan to try for levity.

"I don't think we have the time to explain all of it before dinner."

"Then we'll have none." Jorda's eyes were steady; no levity, there. "The beginning, if you please. Or even if you don't please."

The beginning. The night he had died, only to awaken with a slim young woman bending over him in an alley behind Mikal's tent. It was Ilona who had taken him to Jorda, saying the stranger who named himself Shoia was fit to take on a guide's job, to replace a guide killed by Hecari. A man who had been Ilona's lover.

But that beginning was not what Jorda desired.

"Well," Rhuan said, diving into the conversational whitewater, "what would you say if I told you I wasn't Shoia?"

Jorda considered him darkly, brows lowered, and did not respond to the bait.

Rhuan smiled crookedly. "I'm not Shoia."

After another long moment of contemplation, Jorda shrugged. "I'd never seen a Shoia before you and that courier came here. I be-lieved you when you explained your race and multiple lives. Why should I assume you were telling a falsehood? Ilona brought you to me—"

Rhuan broke in hastily before Jorda might jump to the wrong conclusion. "She didn't know, then, what I am. She made assumptions also. That was what I wished from you both. Assumptions. No questions asked, that way."

Jorda studied him again. Rhuan knew very well what kind of picture he presented: very human*like,* but when one looked hard, somehow a little . . . *other.*

Jorda looked hard. Rhuan saw the faint shift in the eyes, the almost infinitessimal flicker of eyelids. Jorda looked. Jorda saw. He just didn't know what to name it.

Rhuan was careful to control the reddish scrim that, when dropped, sheltered his eyes against the ravages of the deepwood's double suns. It also appeared when he was angry. But a stinging in his flesh was not so well controlled, and the faint warm flush intensified the hue of his skin. With effort, he maintained and displayed a wide and cheerful smile and put into it a certain amount of charm. His nature tended that way anyhow, but he also relied on the smile to draw attention away from that which was not like them. That which was not human.

Rhuan could see the tension tightening the skin around the karavan-master's eyes. "Very well. You're not Shoia." Jorda smoothed his mustache. "Then if you're not Shoia, what in the Mother's world are you? Some other legendary tribe no one knows much about?"

And now it arrived, the time to confess all. To alter forever Jorda's opinion of his guide.

"Well, yes—as a matter of fact." Rhuan drew in a deep breath and blew it out slowly. In a steady voice that did not give away how much Jorda's opinion mattered, he said with great clarity, "And what if I told you I'm not fully human?"

Chapter 12

*K*ARADATH WAS HIS name, Audrun recalled. Brother to the man who was Rhuan's father; *sire*, he would call him. They were all of a piece, the primaries. So very similar in appearance. One could not tell that either Rhuan or his cousin, Brodhi, were half human. It was as if the primaries' blood was prepotent. It simply overwhelmed any other influence.

Karadath stood before her, blocking her children from view, save for Ellica. He had a fistful of her hair in his left hand, and Ellica pulled very close against his body. Audrun could not help but notice that his posture was one of ownership, of total domination.

But now, abruptly, he released Ellica's hair and with a hand across her back shoved her forward, toward her mother. Audrun half caught Ellica, feeling the infant tree between them. "You'll be all right," Audrun murmured, steadying her daughter with hands on her shoulders. "You will, Ellica. You're strong." Then she once again met Karadath's eyes. It was easier, she thought, to withstand a man with impunity when what he wanted required her to live. She used that knowledge to her advantage, did not even now, after the horrific image he had put in her head, shy away from him or show submission.

"If you want me," she said, "you will see to it my children are not harmed. Not in any way, by you or your brethren."

He smiled. "Is that your price?"

"We humans don't assign prices to people. We are all worth the same."

"*She's* not." Karadath's gaze settled on Ellica, who stood next to her mother. "She's isn't worth anything until she can bear a child."

It nearly took her breath, such a threat to her daughter. "If you want me," Audrun repeated, squeezing the words through a constricted throat, "you will do nothing to harm my children. Do you understand? *Inviolate*."

Karadath inclined his head in agreement, though his tone was ironic. "For now."

"*And*," she said firmly, "you will find my baby."

His brows rose. "Will I?"

"If you want me, yes."

Karadath smiled. "Anything else?"

Audrun drew in a careful breath. Saying what she intended might prove terrifying to the youngest children, but it was required. "You will see to it that we are not changed. That we remain human."

His expression froze. She didn't know whether to feel triumphant that she had learned primaries had limitations, or more frightened than ever of the deepwood's power and what might happen to them all.

"You claim to be gods," she said. "Gods can do anything."

Karadath stared at her. She saw the red in his eyes, saw the predator who lived behind the flesh.

"Can't they?" she asked.

He did not answer. He stepped aside so that she had a clear view of the remaining three children. Gillan, as she'd hoped, held Meggie in his arms; Torvic was standing very close to Gillan but trying to appear brave. She saw the awkward stiffness in his face that betokened great effort to hold back tears. She opened her arms and knelt on one knee, dismissing the presence of the primary. Torvic, tears now allowed and falling, went to her at once, folding himself into her arms. Gillan brought Meggie close, bending to set her down, but the girl turned her face into his shoulder, clutched at his arms, and shrieked piercingly.

It drove a stab of pain so deeply into Audrun's chest that she thought she might die of it. "Meggie . . . Meggie." She stood, keeping a hand as a cap on Torvic's head. The other she stretched out toward the youngest of her brood. "Meggie, let me hold you."

Meggie screamed.

Audrun's tears prickled and spilled. She knew. She understood. *Oh, Blessed Mother—she saw it, too, that vision.* "Meggie, Meggie, I swear, all will be well. It was a bad dream, nothing more." But she did not move to touch her daughter; to force the issue would upset Meggie even more. On the inside, Audrun felt like ice. Her thoughts were a litany of commingling hope and forced conviction. *She'll be fine, she'll be fine, give her time, it will take time; just let her be. She'll be fine.* And to Gillan, she gave her thanks. He nodded, shifting Meggie in his arms. His own face, beneath the grime, was taut with strain. *My poor children. Mother of Moons, keep them well. They need your strength. All of them do.*

"She's old for the creche," Karadath said of Megritte, somewhat distastefully, "but her behavior marks her younger than her age. She would do better there."

"No," Audrun said sharply. "She remains with me. We remain together."

He lifted one brow. "Another price?"

"There is no price! No price! It's been impressed upon me that we go nowhere until the road is built, but you do *not* have dominion over my family. Is that understood?" Karadath grinned. And she saw, with a twitch of shock, a shadow of Rhuan's dimples. "Is that understood?" she repeated with as much strength in her voice as she could wield. She was so tired, so very, very tired.

And the primary saw it. He smiled again. "This unworthy one will escort you to your quarters."

Unworthy one? What unworthy one? And then she looked past Karadath and saw a man very similar in height and coloring, but there was something . . . *faded* about him. His spirit did not burn so brightly as Karadath's.

Karadath turned on his heel and walked away, leaving Audrun

standing in the middle of the stone walkway, surrounded by her children, but no wiser about what might become of them all.

She looked at the other man, the faded man. His eyes were downcast; his posture one of submission, not independence. "Come," he said. His eyes briefly met Audrun's, then hid behind lowered lids once more. Karadath had called him unworthy. The one so designated appeared to believe it. "Come," he repeated. "It is a place where you can escape the suns."

And that more than anything prompted Audrun to move. The top of her head was burning. "We'll go," she said to her children. "But cover your heads in the meantime."

Tree fronds again were balanced atop skulls, hands holding them in place. Audrun followed the man, Torvic's hand clasped in her own. His nose was already quite red. *Hats. We must make hats.* Ellica was beside her, still hugging her tree. Gillan fell behind them, and she heard him speaking very softly to Megritte.

Tears prickled once again in Audrun's eyes. She blinked them away hastily, wanting her children to see none of them, to see no weakness. She was exhausted and close to collapsing, but refused to give in. Her children needed her. *Please, Mother, please . . . let Meggie be well.*

JORDA'S BROWS JUMPED, then knit tightly. His body stiffened. He studied Rhuan with honed concentration, weighing this confession against the other, the first. The one considerably less stunning than this.

As Rhuan waited for further reaction, he heard the rain bouncing off stretched canvas. His hearing, more acute than humans', told him the storm was letting up.

But not the burgeoning storm in Jorda's wagon.

"Not fully human," the karavan-master echoed.

"Half. My mother was human."

Jorda was incredulous. "Is this a jest? If so, it's ill-timed! Rhuan—?"

Rhuan shook his head decisively. "No portion of what I've just told you, and what I *will* tell you, is a jest." He glanced up at the string of charms hanging from the Mother Rib over his head, swaying slightly. "I'll swear it on whatever means the most to you."

The skin of Jorda's face tightened again at the corners of his eyes where crows-feet had taken dominion. As a redhead, he could not tan as other folk did, could not escape the sun's damage. It left him with a reddish tint to his face and forearms, and a seasoning of golden freckles. "Waste no more time in telling me all, then!"

Rhuan drew in a deep breath. "I was born in Alisanos to a human mother and a father who isn't."

Because of the beard, it was often difficult to see an expression on the karavan-master's face. One needed to learn to look into his eyes, to note the movement of his brows, his eyelids, to read what his body said. Just now, he was completely still. He had briefly gone into himself, Rhuan saw, as if sorting through the words, but that moment passed. Now Jorda's intense green eyes were fixed on his face. "And Brodhi?"

Rhuan nodded. "The same."

"The storm," Jorda said. "When you were missing." He said nothing more, but his eyes asked the question.

"Yes," Rhuan told him. "The storm took me. I'm not immune to Alisanos. My people come from there, but we're no more able to control the deepwood than you."

"But you came back out after the storm. And I don't see any change upon you." Jorda paused. "Yet."

"And you won't."

Jorda's frown was deeper than ever. "What *are* your people?"

"We're not demons, any of us. There *are* demons in Alisanos, but we are not counted among them."

Jorda was tense as he worked through the information. Finally he asked, "And Darmuth?"

"Ah." Rhuan said. "Well."

"Well?"

"Darmuth *is* a demon. I'm sorry—I didn't intend to mislead you."

"Blessed Mother of Moons." Jorda closed one big hand over the string of charms at his neck. I've been harboring a demon?" He was so angry now, Rhuan feared he might drop over dead. "I'm responsible for the lives of hundreds of people every season, and one of my guides is a *demon?*"

"He isn't here to harm humans," Rhuan told him hastily. "Darmuth isn't here for humans at all. He's here for me."

Jorda's color deepened. "What do you mean, he's here for you?"

So Rhuan told him about Darmuth, Ferize, and the journey, with as much brevity and clarity as possible.

Afterward, Jorda sat in silence, staring at him, marking everything about him that he had once believed was Shoia and now knew was not.

Jorda's eyes darkened. "Does Ilona know what you are?"

"Yes."

"And she just accepts it?"

"Yes. Which means, very likely, that you can accept it, too." Rhuan paused, seeing the disbelief in Jorda's eyes. "Some day."

Jorda's tone was deceptively light. "Ilona rose from the dead."

Rhuan knew what he was asking. "She is not one of my people. She is everything she has ever been."

"She rose from the dead."

Rhuan nodded. "I assume she must be Shoia. There truly is no way of knowing how many are left, Jorda. But we know they aren't myth. It's why Brodhi and I let everyone believe we are—were—Shoia, because we can't be killed in this world. It was easy to accept. People know about Shoia having multiple lives."

Jorda was silent for long moments. Then he lifted the plank next to him and placed it on his lap, finding his lead as well.

"Is it enough?" Rhuan asked. "Do you understand?"

"I'm not sure it will ever be enough." Jorda read over the marks on creased paper pinned to the plank. "I'm not sure I *care* to know more. Not at this moment, in any case. I may have additional questions for you later. For now, go and tend your duty."

Rhuan, knowing dismissal when he heard it, rose. He ducked his head to keep it from brushing rib and canvas. But one more thing must be said, to ease the mind of a man he respected very much. "Jorda, we're not here to harm anyone, Brodhi and I. Truly. Neither are Darmuth and Ferize."

"Rhuan, I have work to do preparing a list of supplies for the trip to Cardatha. I'd advise, *again*, that you take yourself off to wherever this border between the deepwood and this settlement is, and begin to build your marker cairns." Jorda glanced up. "Now."

Rhuan badly wanted to say more, to explain in more depth. To find something that restored the balance between them. But the finality in Jorda's voice welcomed no such explanation. Rhuan nodded, turned, and descended the steps. He donned muddy boots. Before he left, he cast a final glance back into the wagon.

Jorda wasn't writing. Jorda was clutching the charms around his neck, eyes closed, talking to the Mother.

Regret lodged itself in Rhuan. The comfortable relationship between guide and karavan-master was forever destroyed, he knew. As was everything in this world. It was part of his rite of passage as a *dioscuri*.

And when that passage was completed, and in Ilona's name, he would have to kill his sire.

Chapter 13

*A*S THE RAIN let up, Ilona dug out from storage a thick mat made of grasses, quilted between two pieces of heavy canvas, and spread it on the packed soil beneath the awning, beneath an elder tree. Then she retrieved cushions, a low table, rich cloths, candles, items that enhanced her position as diviner, and set all out beneath the awning. She placed at the two outside corners of the awning tall wrought-iron sherpherd's crooks, and hung lanterns. Tea kettle depended from a smaller hook over the fire, carefully laid beneath the awning so as not to be drowned in the daily rain. She stacked several small clay cups beside her table.

She had eaten her midday meal and knew various folk would come to her to have their hands read, especially under the circumstances. She sat down upon a cushion behind the low, laquered table, folded hands resting on the cloth-draped surface, legs crossed beneath a full skirt. Quietude was necessary. Going into herself was necessary. There had, of late, been too much turmoil, too many upended days. Such turmoil did not prevent her from reading hands, but it did interfere and often twisted the vision upon itself. She closed her eyes, slowed her breathing, and let the ordinary sounds of a grove, of folk within the grove, fill her mind.

A step intruded. Possibly a client. She opened one eye: Rhuan, ducking under the awning. Her other eye opened.

Smiling, he bent over the low table and kissed the top of her head, loose hair falling around his face like a curtain, then knelt on one knee and reached out to take a hand in his own. "I haven't the time to stay." He threaded his fingers through hers. "I'm to begin building cairns along the border between Alisanos and the settlement. But later, yes." Dimples appeared. "Oh yes."

The warmth of his hand brought recollection, and a stirring in her body. But there was no time, now, for either of them. Later, as Rhuan said. Oh yes. "Jorda's orders?"

Rhuan's expression was rueful. "He is most displeased with me."

A wave of love and longing rose up within her. But she knew very well that if she gave into it and kissed him the way she wished to, the cairns would be forgotten as would her intent to read hands. She distracted herself by asking a question. "Did you tell him the truth?"

"As much of it as I felt necessary, at that moment. All of the truth, no. As much as he could bear." He shrugged, intent upon her hand, gently massaging each of her fingers. "There was no sense in telling Jorda my sire is a god and that I'm halfway there myself."

Ilona laughed. "Well, no, I suppose not. I think you served him quite enough on his plate!"

"He knows now that Darmuth is a demon, and Ferize, though he's seen nothing of her. He knows about the journey, the rite of passage. I can't say he *disbelieves* any of what I told him . . . but he needs time to understand it."

She smiled at him. "Of course he needs time. Wouldn't you? Well, no, not you. But then you grew up with this knowledge."

He nodded absently. "Have you told anyone?"

"The courier, Bethid. Circumstances demanded it. But I'm sure she will be discreet. And you? Other than to Jorda, have you said anything?"

He released her hand and shook hair back behind his shoulders. "The farmsteader. Audrun's husband. The man was so lost, so desperate . . . I told him about the road so he might take some solace that he will see his family again, when the road is completed. I think it gave him some comfort. What I did not say is that his family may not truly *be* his family when they meet again, merely fading reminders of what they once were." Rhuan shook his head. "I wish I could give him peace about that, but I believe if I told him now *how* bad it might be, he couldn't bear it. Too much has happened in a very short span of time. And how should I know? Alisanos will do whatever it chooses to do. But so long as Audrun and her children remain at the Kiba, they will be safe." He paused. "They *should* be safe. Physically. Emotionally—I can't say." His eyes took on a distant look. "It isn't easy living among primaries."

"Even for you?"

"Particularly for me." He looked down, picking absently at a small rip in the canvas matting, and the unbraided hair slipped forward once more. "I cannot tell you how relieved I was when it came time for me to begin the journey among humans. It got me away."

"You couldn't have left before?"

"No." Rhuan shook his head. "*Dioscuri* are tied to Alisanos in some way before we begin the journey. It's like a dog on a leash. A very *long* leash but, nonetheless, a leash. We are unleashed in a ceremony and, as humans say, pushed out of the nest. We must fly or die." He paused. "You know what we face, if we fail."

Indeed she did. Brodhi had made it plain: castration. And abruptly impulse took her, sending a river, a spate, through her spirit. Words tumbled over themselves. "Rhuan, stay here! Don't return to your people. Half of you is human . . . you belong *here*! Repudiate the primaries. Repudiate this journey. Don't go back."

His face was tense. "I must."

"But why? Your father and uncle—and Brodhi as well!—have told you repeatedly you are inferior." And that might have been phrased more tactfully, but she went on in crisp determination. "Why should any of them care if you stay here?"

She saw color rise up in his flesh, a deeping of the pale copper she was accustomed to. For a moment the third eyelid dropped down over his eyes, red as blood. But the membranes lifted, disappeared.

The flush in his skin died away. "Ilona, you know primaries can come to this world. Alario did."

Indeed, she knew.

"All of them could come to this world if they wished . . . but they *don't* wish. Why should they? In Alisanos, they are gods. Here, no, though with certain physical advantages. No *dioscuri* wishes to remain in the human world once his journey is done."

"Except you."

"Except me. And I'm not even certain what might happen to a *dioscuri*-cum-primary who returned to this world intending to remain. That's something I will discover for myself. But if, in the meantime, I don't complete the journey, primaries will come to me here. Three of them. Probably my sire, Brodhi's, and Ylarra, a female. I am a child to them . . . they are full grown and would easily overpower me. They would devour my spirit. Unman me. Yes, they would leave me here, but *what* they leave would be nothing you know." He met her eyes, and she saw the acknowledgment in them, the undertone of bleakness. "I must return to Alisanos when my journey is completed and challenge my sire."

She drew in a slow breath, released it. She had never seen him so. Never heard him so. "But you *do* mean to come back here. You've said so."

"If I take the victory, I may do as I will. Then it's my choice. And that is indeed my goal—to return here. Because then I will be a primary, and no one can stop me." He shrugged. "But whether I *remain* a primary when I return to this world, I can't say. No one knows."

Fear edged in like a blade. She had met Alario. She knew how fragile was human life, compared to the primaries. But Rhuan? Yes, half of him was human, but the other half came of the same blood that resided in Alario and all of the primaries.

She did him the favor of not prevaricating, of not dismissing realities and difficult truths. "Can you defeat him?"

Rhuan's voice was stripped of emotion. He did not dissemble, merely stated facts. "I don't know."

CLOUDS TORE APART, leaving streaks of blue behind. The sun, unencumbered, turned a bright face to the earth. But everything was damp. Wisps of moisture steamed beneath the sun. The fallen grove imitated life, green leaves not yet dry and shriveled. The warmth of the day returned with the sun, but it was humid, cloying. Tent-folk would be rolling up canvas sides to let in the the air and karavaners the same with their wagon canopies. This was what all would face for weeks, until the monsoon withdrew. Everywhere was the scent of dampness, the odor of mud and wet and woodsmoke.

Despite his disinclination, Brodhi assisted with the re-pitching of the big common tent. He grudgingly decided that, much as he detested the argument, perhaps Bethid had a valid point when she said they ate food and drank ale in the settlement, and thus he owed it his participation in the current situation and long-term future. There were worse places to stay on the road. This settlement had always been one of the most habitable. And Mikal wasn't afraid of him or made ill-at-ease by his presence, the way some ale-keeps were in other places, tolerating him solely because he was a Guild courier.

Brodhi smiled with no little smugness. *Afraid of me as Shoia . . . what would they think if I told them the truth?*

He, Timmon, and Alorn, being male and therefore taller and stronger than Bethid—who was small even for most women—erected the poles and canvas, and drove iron anchors into the wet ground more deeply than ever before. They doubled up on rope guy-lines and knots and did their best to secure the tent. But all knew that if Alisanos struck again, the tent might collapse once more.

In the meantime, Bethid scrambled under the canvas as they raised it to gather up personal articles. These she deposited in a pile in front of the tent, on top of a sheet of oilcloth. As the men tied off the lines, she ducked back inside to hang hooks from the Mother Rib, to untangle the leather thong from wire. She spread bedding for all. Fortunately the boot-packed interior ground had not soaked up the water, as fallen canvas had protected the ground as well as most of their belongings.

When Bethid came back out of the tent, Brodhi saw her gaze shift to somewhere over his shoulder. "Ah. Hello, Rhuan," she said.

Brodhi swung around immediately, unable to control the whiplash reaction. Yes, there he was, his kin-in-kind, about three paces away. Rhuan had yet to braid his hair—or have it braided for him—so it hung loose on either side of his face and down his spine. He gave the newly-pitched tent a glance of assessment, then came to a halt not far from Brodhi. "Your map," he said. "If you've gotten a head start on marking where the border is, it would save me some time."

Brodhi felt the familiar antipathy kindle. At that moment he cared nothing about maps, markers, or the well-being of the settlement. His mind fixed on one thing. "You're a disgrace."

Rhuan blinked. "Why am I a disgrace this time?"

"You might as well cut off your hair like a neuter. You have no respect for our rituals."

Rhuan sighed. "You know very well how my hair came to be unbraided in the first place. My sending in the dreya ring, remember, when I was injured? Not that it convinced you to offer aid."

Brodhi ignored that topic altogether. "You could have had it rebraided at the Kiba."

"I could have, yes." Rhuan glanced briefly at the other couriers, who looked on with puzzled interest.

"You married that farmsteader woman," Brodhi said disdainfully, ignoring the others; they would believe this was a Shoia conflict.

Timmon expelled a blurt of surprise. Alorn caught Bethid's eye, pointed briefly at Rhuan, and mouthed a question: *He married the farmsteader's wife?*

Bethid shrugged and shook her head, indicating puzzlement akin to his own.

Brodhi continued. "With proper instruction, she could have braided it as it should be braided."

Rhuan, who was focused solely on Brodhi, stared at him in bafflement. "Why does it matter to you whether my hair is braided or loose? And no, I did not marry the farmsteader woman."

Brodhi spared a glance for Timmon, Alorn, and Bethid, now riveted by the exchange. Brodhi glared. Bethid, somewhat more intuitive than the two male couriers, abruptly waved a hand at them in a gesture that suggested they go into the tent so that the cousins—that human word—could speak privately. And they went, but she knew they would have many questions for her later.

Brodhi looked back at Rhuan, lowering his voice. "It matters," he said. "You dishonor us by being so lax."

"Who is 'us'? You?"

Brodhi scowled. "You know very well who I mean. Primaries and *dioscuri*. I don't know why you even bother to undertake the journey . . . you want no part of it. You want no part of us."

" 'Us' again. Still the primaries and the *dioscuri*?"

A slow pressure built up in Brodhi's chest. His skin warmed into what he knew was a faint coppery sheen. "You are a disgrace!"

A chill settled into Rhuan's eyes, dismissing the normal cheerfulness Brodhi also detested. "You said that once already. But as it matters so much to you, I have every intention of instructing Ilona how to braid my hair. As I will braid hers."

Brodhi wielded the verbal knife with a scornful laugh. "Can you even satisfy *one* woman? And now you'll have two?"

Heat and color rose in Rhuan's face and the red membrane flickered. Ah, that told much to Brodhi. "I didn't marry Audrun."

Brodhi's smile, shaped so carefully, he knew from experience, was infuriating. "But you did."

"I didn't *mean* to marry Audrun."

"But you did."

Rhuan said something that was, in human terms, entirely obscene.

Brodhi laughed, pleased. "You see? Disgraceful. Offensive. Weak. Entirely inappropriate for your rank. Perhaps I should do all of the primaries a good turn and end your worthless journey here and now."

And he had, at last, gotten under Rhuan's skin. His kin-in-kind glared at him. "This profits nothing," Rhuan said. "I came for the map."

"To save yourself some trouble?"

"Why repeat an action that doesn't require it?"

Brodhi shook his head. "You want to be oh-so-careful about protecting the lives of these fragile humans."

Rhuan's tone and expression were aggravated. "It's natural, Brodhi. I'd just as soon none of them die—or worse—by stepping into Alisanos by mistake. We have quite enough to deal with."

"Whereas I don't care."

"Whereas *you* are a disgrace," Rhuan declared, "*because* you don't care. A disgrace to me, to your dam. Oh, but let's use the human word for a human woman: your mother. Disgrace? Dishonor? Offensive? You describe yourself."

The tent doorflap was jerked aside. Bethid appeared in the opening. "Sweet Mother, will you stop? You sound like squabbling four-year-olds!" She glanced briefly over her shoulder into the dimness of the tent, then stepped out and let the flap fall. She lowered her voice. "Fortunately, I already know what you are. And I don't really *care* what you are, but—"

Brodhi cut her off. "This is a Shoia matter."

Bethid opened her mouth, then closed it. Finally she said, "Yes, I suppose that would be the assumption. But I just know we need to make shift to be as careful as possible, this close to the deepwood." He saw unflagging determination in her eyes. "Brodhi, just give him the map. It will help us all. We *humans* don't have this land-sense, remember? Rhuan's right about protecting what we can. You will ride out of here, bound for Cardatha, but what about everyone left behind? Do you truly *want* us all to end up swallowed by Alisanos?" She paused. "We humans, that is."

Brodhi shrugged. "It makes no difference to me."

"But it should," Bethid told him. "You live among humans. Shouldn't you attempt to get along with them?"

Brodhi said "No" at the exact moment Rhuan said "Yes."

Bethid glared at Brodhi. "Just give him the map. We're likely leaving in the morning anyway."

"I," Brodhi said with exquisite clarity, "don't have the map." That struck both Rhuan and Bethid into baffled silence. Brodhi smiled. "Mikal has it. Apparently he claims some gift for mapmaking . . . one gives him the rough sketch, and he makes it over into a true map. He would probably do well in the Mapmaker's Guild in Cardatha, rather than serving ale in this piss-poor gathering of unworthy souls."

"Fine," Rhuan said in a clipped tone. Then he turned on his heel and began striding back through a thin layer of wet earth toward Mikal's ale-tent.

Bethid watched him go, then shook her head at Brodhi. "A waste of time, that. You might have told him plainly without baiting him into an argument."

Brodhi examined Bethid a long moment. "You know what we are, you said."

"I do. Ilona told me."

Brodhi gritted his teeth. "Well, why don't we just ring Jorda's Summoner and make an announcement? You could explain how it is that Rhuan and I aren't Shoia—"

"—but demons from Alisanos. I know." Bethid nodded. "And if I did so, what do you suppose would come of you and Rhuan? I don't care how superior you might be, physically, but how do you think others would respond?" Her tone took on an edge. "How would you like it if the Guildmaster were told what you are?"

Brodhi scowled at her, truly annoyed. "How *much* do you know, to threaten me like this?"

"Compared to what there *is* to know? Oh Brodhi, I have no idea. But you are not Shoia. That, I do know. And I suppose it might make a difference if all the settlement folk were told what you are." Her pale brows rose. "Alisanos has changed everyone's lives. The Hecari culling party has changed everyone's lives. What do you suppose they might think—or even *do*—if they were told what you are?"

Anger ran high, crested. "You don't know everything!"

"I know just enough to plant the seeds of distrust in the folk."

Bethid smiled grimly. "Shall I do it, so that you understand the import of such actions?"

Brodhi had never struck a female, human or Alisani. At this particular moment, he wished to. But he was on his journey. Such actions would be reported by Ferize to the primaries. He believed that most primaries might well understand what drove him to violence against a human, but he *was* on his journey. It was expected he would be circumspect. It was part of the challenge.

Bethid stood her ground. He had seen her do that twice before, when it was the only defense against physical and mental incursions: when she faced down the Guildmaster at her examination, and when she had waited for four Hecari to charge her in the midst of the settlement.

Brodhi met her eyes and nodded slightly, acknowledging a game well played. "By now, Rhuan will have the map. It no longer involves us."

Bethid's body was still; her eyes were steady on his own. "It must be difficult for you, living among a race you find inferior."

He did not take it as a challenge, though he expected it might be. "Indeed. Very difficult."

After a moment Bethid shook her head, made a dismissive gesture, and ducked back inside the tent. Brodhi, deserted by her and by Rhuan, expected to feel amusement and a comforting superiority.

But he felt neither. It puzzled him a moment. He consulted the self-knowledge all *dioscuri* claimed, the inner confidence and power that so easily rendered humans to faded approximations.

And he realized, having consulted, that what he felt was *alone*.

Chapter 14

*D*EMON SAT BESIDE the creek that ran before the hut and combed through its wet hair with its—no, *her;* when would she restore to herself the proper gender?—*her* clawed fingers. Thick and black, *her* hair fell to mid-back. Daily, Demon washed her own hair with a soapy substance pressed from a root. It mattered to her that her hair be clean and glossy.

She was naked. The creek/stream/river—today it was a creek—provided water for regular bathing. Each morning she slipped from loose leather leggings and black hide jacket, anticipating the sensation of water running over her flesh—so sensuous, so blissful—cleaning impurities from her body. Now she sat upon the creek bank with wings spread, drying in the suns. She had placed the baby in the curl of a root atop the soil, well wrapped against chilling. She had been restless all night, the baby, assuaged by neither sustenance nor clean, dry clouts. By dawn, Demon realized what the matter was. A tooth had erupted from the baby's upper gum. Now the child slept, after an application of numbing herbs.

Vague memory told Demon it was too early for teeth.

She lay back upon the bank, flattening wings beneath her so as not to harm them, to avoid cramps or crimping. The wings were featherless, formed of a flexible leathery brown membrane stretched between black, shining vanes, vanes echoed in the claws of her hands, the claws of her feet. Gently Demon scratched the dark scales climbing from pubis to mid chest, where two human breasts used to be. Nipples were swollen, black and loose. Her body understood that an infant needed sustenance to live. From that first deep cut made by a claw, scaled breasts had grown. Strange, that she had not noticed when the first transformation took human breasts away. But, even scaled, these would do. They served the purpose.

It crossed her mind to wonder if, when the baby was weaned, she would lose the breasts again. Would become an *it* again.

But she could not dwell on that. She preferred to live in the moment. She stretched from fingertips to toes, loosening muscle fibers. Flight was her joy, but being clean nearly matched that elation.

Demon extended both hands up into the air, spreading long, narrow fingers to examine curving black claws thick as her little finger. Such long but strong fingers, with five joints apiece instead of the human three. Between thumb and fingers on both hands ran webbing of the same leathery membrane as her wings, but considerably thinner, letting a measure of dull light through. From her feet, as well, grew claws. She wore no shoes or boots because neither could tame the toe claws, nor the spurs growing out of both heels. In certain seasons she rubbed claws with river sand, shedding the old coating. It was painful, and the new layer of claw underneath was initially extremely tender, though a carapace-like top layer grew to protect them.

Demon sat up, studying her feet. It occurred to her that perhaps the baby, as it grew, might come to view her as something terrible. It was a human child, and Demon did not look as the baby did. Wings, scales, claws. Strong, pronounced jaws used to tear out throats, to shred and chew meat. Teeth were pointed where humans' were flat along the bottoms. Scales adorned flesh in several places. And her eyes. The creek, when still, had provided that truth: pale, pale eyes with vertical slits for pupils.

At first, transformation had horrified her. Terrified her. Human hands and feet shed nails. Human teeth fell out. Her eyes wept blood. And then the first nubs of wings erupted. Claws replaced nails. Fangs replaced teeth. Her eyes bled out their ordinary blue, losing all color, and the black roundness of pupils altered. Scales grew from her white, white flesh. Dark iridescent scales, most beautiful in the sun. Fear fled. Prayers died. She was what she was. What Alisanos decreed.

Demon, feeling liquid heat within her loins, tipped back her head, damp hair hanging between the roots of her wings, sliding down against the small of her back.

Oh, she was beautiful. And knew it. Surely the baby would see her beauty as well.

The call of her body was intense. She yearned for a male.

It had been so long, too long . . . so very long she could not recall what mating was about. Such things were—confusing. She knew something was wanted. Her body rang with it.

But she did not desire a human.

Once, Demon herself had been human. She remembered that now. But in Alisanos, humans died. Initially she had escaped death any number of times, keeping fragile flesh safe from beasts and demons. And then transformation began. No one, now, would call her human. And it was well; in Alisanos, humans died. Her new self was far better prepared to fight for her life. Her new self was easily able to kill.

But the child. The child. What would the child think? Would she cower from Demon in fear? Would she, when she could, run away?

Demon's eyes stung. Breath caught in her throat. Without rising she crawled to the infant, lifted the infant, cradled it in her arms. She sat cross-legged upon the earth, naked body drying, head bent over the child she pressed against her breast, urging the child to feed. Wings were brought forward, forming a tent-like construction around the infant. It was best, Demon knew, if the child was transformed also. Because then she would not be frightened of a winged creature, a creature with claws. She was Alisanos-born, this child; she might herself become anything. Was the tooth not early?

It would be well, Demon decided, if the infant grew to be like her benefactor, able to rise into the air above the treetops with strong wings spread, warmed by double suns.

"Feed," she said in her rusty voice, cradling the child more closely. "Feed on my substance. Then you will be strong and no one will hurt you."

Nor would any human want her, when they saw what she became.

Demon smiled. She began to sing. It was a private song, meant only for the infant.

And it was beautiful.

THE FADED MAN led Audrun and her children to the cliff dwellings, showing them up a twisting stone pathway against the cliff wall. Steps of stone climbed up to dwelling terraces. Stacked and mortared bricks formed chamber walls. Audrun was grateful that all had been built with the primaries in mind; the pathways and steps were wide for humans, allowing them some security as they climbed higher.

Up and up. Around and around. She learned to follow the faded man's habit of stepping aside when a primary wanted to pass, always to the outside of the pathway. She kept track of the four children, urging them out of the way when necessary but directing how to be most careful at the outer edge of the pathway. Her guide never looked up as primaries approached, never met their eyes. Head bowed, he halted and stood in a posture of submission, eyes fixed on the ground, hands folded over his abdomen. Audrun, however, made no such obeisance herself. Nor did her children; they merely stared. Stared hard at every primary.

And at last they were led to a doorway flanked by tall, narrow windows on either side of the hide-curtained opening. Again, all was on primary scale. The man slid the hide aside on its rod, then stepped back, inclined his head, and gestured Audrun to enter. She did so after gathering her children close. And very nearly gaped as she entered.

She came from the timber and sod of a farmstead, of chinking between logs, of wooden floor assembled with pegs to hold planks in place. She came *to* a house of stone, one large chamber, one small. Richly colored rugs covered every inch of stone floor. Carved wooden chairs with dark hide forming seats and backs were set against walls. A long table bore a hand-worked container, several cups. In the center of the large chamber was a fire ring built of dressed bricks mortared into place, and meticulous mosaics around the top edge. Intricate iron stands stood in each corner, supporting on their plates fat, carved candles. Light spilled in the doorway, in the windows, illuminating the main room. Three of the walls were constructed of stacked stone; the back wall was part of a cliff and bore carved reliefs, lines and angles intermarried with flowing curves and circles. Overhead, above the fire pit, light from two suns came down in a glowing column. She tipped her head back and stared up at the hole in the ceiling, seeing blue sky and sunlight beyond.

She could not help the most practical of questions. "What about when it rains?"

The man gestured. "The iron plate, do you see?"

She did. It was round, like the window in the ceiling, but set aside from the opening.

"It swings over the skylight. With this, see?" He took up a long iron pole, slotted it into the plate, swung it over the opening. "Like so."

"This is—beautiful." Audrun turned in place, taking in the rugs, the wall carving, the gleaming hide curtains hanging beside windows and door. And it was, though alien to her eyes.

"Through there is the sleeping chamber," he directed. "There are beds enough for you all. Water is there, on the table. I will bring you meals except for when you are summoned to attend a primary."

"Is that likely?"

The man met her eyes. "Oh, I would expect it."

For some reason, that made her nervous. She did not in the least feel submissive, but to sit down to dinner with one?

Ah, but she should not be intimidated. She had eaten with Rhuan. And that provoked another question. "Do you know Rhuan?"

"He is Alario's get."

"And Brodhi?"

"Karadath's."

She named the only other primary whose identity she knew. "And Ylarra?"

Color rose in his face. She saw the copper tinge of his flesh deepen. But no red flicker appeared in his eyes that she could see, because he stared hard at the ground. "Ylarra wielded the knife."

Audrun stared at him. Knife? What knife?

He seemed aware of her confusion. "I'm a failed *dioscuri*. In the ritual, it was done by Ylarra's hand."

Audrun shook her head. "I'm sorry, but I don't understand."

He touched his hair, cut short at the back of his neck. "This first. Then my manhood."

"*What?*" The shock of it doused her with a chill. "She . . . blessed Mother, *what* did she do?"

"Cut me," he replied. "Made me into a neuter. That's what all of us face who fail but survive."

IT WAS TRUE, Rhuan found, that Mikal had great skill at mapmaking. The ale-keep spread out what Brodhi had given him, a rough sketch, and set it next to his own work. The inking was superb. Rhuan, leaning across the table, lightly tapped Brodhi's ill-made map with a forefinger. "This mostly deals with the approach to the opening and the passage into the settlement. There's nothing here about the immediate surroundings, which is my job. . . . This isn't as helpful as I'd hoped." He straightened, meeting Mikal's eye. "Have you a backer board, tacks, and lead?"

Mikal's lips twisted briefly in a wry amusement Rhuan didn't understand. "Wait here."

Rhuan studied Brodhi's rough map again. The opening onto grasslands was indeed narrow, as was the twisting passageway leading to the settlement. He supposed one could ride three abreast, but that might put someone too close to Alisanos. Two abreast would be better. But he could definitely see the possibilities of an ambush. The abiding problem, however, was proximity to the deepwood. Where were men to hide without risking themselves? When Brodhi brought four Hecari, the settlement was warned by those who had stationed themselves in the middle of the passageway to avoid the deepwood on either side. It had proved successful because the Hecari expected nothing. Were they to repeat the actions, it could end in death, or disappearance, depending on the deepwood's whimsy.

Rhuan sighed, chewing the side of his mouth. He traced out areas on Brodhi's rough map. "Here," he muttered. "Boulders? No, too difficult. Trees. Trees set out to look like deadfall." And thus shields for those who would watch for Hecari, passing word along through whistles approximating bird calls, the cries of vermin, or even a runner, if necessary. Rhuan's mouth flattened with tension. It was critical that he get the cairns up as soon as possible. He foresaw a long night. Since his vision was better than that of humans, he could work longer.

Mikal appeared from the private portion of the big tent behind the bar, behind the barrels, hidden by canvas. He carried the backer board to the table, slid Brodhi's map onto it, then tacked it into place. He handed Rhuan a rough-cut length of lead. Rhuan, who had never paid attention before, noted the breadth of Mikal's palms, the thickness of his fingers. He also saw that Mikal's hands were exceptionally clean. No smudges marred the surface of the inked parchment. Brodhi's map was soiled, as might be expected for rough sketching on the road, in weather, but not Mikal's. It was pristine, despite threats from ale, spirits, cheese, smoke, oil, candle wax. In an ale-tent one would *expect* a map to be soiled. Mikal's wasn't.

Rhuan looked up and met the ale-keep's eye. He had never asked, because the ale-tent and its owner were familiar, comfortable, affable. Mikal kept to the habits expected of a man who ran an ale-tent. He served others, and was not served himself. He was remakable in no way, if memorable because of the eye-patch. A big, wide, dark-haired man, no longer young but neither old. His weathered face bore the shadow of a beard.

Curiosity overcame tact; though Mikal had in no way ever suggested tact was necessary. Rhuan simply asked. "What did you do before coming here?"

"Lived in Cardatha."

Rhuan indicated the map. "That is beautiful work."

"No," Mikal said, "that is competent work. Apprentice work." He smiled crookedly, looking down at the sheet of parchment.

The realization came swiftly. "You were in the Mapmakers Guild."

"I was."

Rhuan shook his head. "Why did you leave the Guild? Why did you leave Cardatha to come *here*, pouring ale and spirits for travelers?" He paused, realizing with a brief inward wince that in saying so, he insulted the work Mikal did now. "I mean, those accepted to guilds are known as gifted folk. As you are gifted." He indicated the inked map. "It's obvious."

"I lost an eye," Mikal said. "I was dismissed from the Guild. A one-eyed man lacks perspective in what he sees, in what he draws." His shrug was nearly imperceptible. "So I took up a new trade."

"And left behind an art." Rhuan shook his head; again, tact fell victim to disbelief. "They were fools."

"One might argue that," Mikal agreed, "but the Guild is most stringent. A permanent injury to eyes or fingers is cause for dismissal. All of us know that when we apply." He smoothed a finger across his eye-patch. "The irony of all ironies is that this injury was caused by an ink pen. It was a minor thing, an argument between two journeymen about something inconsequential. But it grew to something more physical. And this was the result." Again he shrugged. "An accident. Not intentional."

"But it ended the life you knew." No bitterness lived in Mikal's tone, merely honesty. "Yes."

"What became of the other journeyman?"

"He eventually advanced to master."

Rhuan was taken aback. "He wasn't dismissed? He blinded you in one eye, caused your dismissal, and was kept on?"

Mikal nodded. "But he had a true gift. An eye, you might say."

The tone was wry. "You don't dismiss a man who may one day rede-fine an art." He smiled, the remaining eye distant with memories. "I took a job in a tavern, there in Cardatha. I put aside coin-rings. And eventually I took to the road, looking for a good place to set up my own tent." A gesture indicated the surroundings. "And here I am."

Rhuan was intuitive enough to realize that if he said more about the loss, about the permanent alteration of Mikal's life from gifted mapmaker to ale-keep, he would diminish the man as he was now. And that, he could not countenance. "Then we will make good use of your gift, and thank you for it." He reached to pick up the board with Brodhi's rough map tacked to it. "As I set up cairns, I'll mark them on this. Each night I'll return it to you."

"Rhuan." Mikal's hand pressed the board down. "What did *you* do before coming here?"

His own words, asked in very much the same tone of casual cu-riosity. And yet he knew that was not its intent at all. Mikal suspected something. *I told Ilona. The farmsteader. And Jorda.* And Bethid knew because of Ilona. *At this rate, everyone in the settlement will know!*

Rhuan stared at Mikal, saying nothing; silence sometimes served better than replies. Prior to Alisanos going active, he had been thought a dangerous man. If necessary, he could call up a hint of that attitude to control the conversation. He could borrow something of his sire's arrogance. He had done it before.

But the ale-keep smiled. "What did you do before coming here?"

He could not reply, as Mikal, that he had lived in Cardatha. He shrugged off-handedly. "I've no place truly to call, or make, my own. The karavan is my home. The road."

The expression in Mikal's narrowed eye suggested he didn't be-lieve that. But the ale-keep let it go. He gave Rhuan the board. "The hands have not forgotten. I thought perhaps they had, when Brodhi gave me his map to copy. But no. Perhaps one never forgets what once meant the most." He reached for some fabric folded on the bar-top. "It's waxed," he said. "Keep it draped over the map when you're not working on it. We dare not let the rain ruin it."

Rhuan accepted the fabric. "That said, I think I'll go by Jorda's wagon to collect my rain gear. It might not rain again until tomorrow, but the beginning of monsoon is always unpredictable." He tucked the board beneath one arm and headed toward the door flap.

As he reached it, Mikal said, "It's wasn't a difficult question, Rhuan, what I asked."

Rhuan halted at the exit. All manner of explanations ran through his head as he stood there, deciding how to respond. He used none of them, however; resorted instead to truth. "No, it wasn't. But it's a difficult answer."

AS BETHID DUCKED back into the common tent, she saw precisely what she expected to see: Timmon and Alorn seated on bedding, staring expectantly at her. They had heard just enough of Rhuan's and Brodhi's heated discussion to incite intense curiosity. She sighed and knelt down on her own bedding, digging out the two heavy oiled canvas bags she used for her belongings on the road. It was a drawstring affair, leather thongs fed through stitched holes and tied off. An interior flap was tucked over the last item, and then each bag was snugged closed and attached to either side of the saddle.

"Well?" Alorn asked.

Bethid used the explanation that had satisfied her curiosity before she knew the truth. "It's a Shoia thing, I gather." She said it casually, hitching one shoulder up in a dismissive shrug. "Did I not know they were cousins, I'd say they were brothers, bickering so." She began to gather together clothing and other items, folding and rolling, then tucked them safely into the two drawstring bags. "All I can say is, they're very different from—" she caught herself before she said *humans*, "—the rest of us. But it's their business, regardless." She glanced at them both. "I suspect we'll be heading out tomorrow. Remember, Jorda said he wants to get to Cardatha as soon as possible, before the monsoon makes the roads completely impassable. You might want to start packing up. I'm taking everything . . . the Mother knows when we might come this way again."

For all she was speaking to turn their thoughts elsewhere, she also spoke the truth. It was up to the Guildmaster to give them new orders, handing them scroll cases containing fresh correspondence. Thanks to Alisanos, they had remained at the settlement much longer than was ordinarily the case. "He's a karavan-master; he'll want to leave at first light."

Timmon laughed briefly. "I'll be glad to see the inside of a brick-built tavern! The ale-tent here is better than nothing, but I do prefer the variety—"

"—of women," Bethid said wryly, finishing it for him.

"—of spirits," Timmon declared.

Bethid continued to pack. "That, too, I suppose."

Alorn snickered. "Preferably, both at the same time."

"Women and ale, women and spirits . . ." Timmon sighed blissfully. "An excellent pairing. After too long a time."

Bethid laughed briefly on a gust of breath. "For that, there are the Sisters. Right here in the settlement."

Timmon's eyes widened. "Sweet Mother, I forgot about the Sisters!" He shot Alorn a glance. "We do have tonight."

"First light means first light," Bethid reminded them. "Jorda is not about to forgive tardiness because you spent the night with a woman. He'll leave you behind."

Alorn scoffed. "It's not as if we couldn't find our own way to Cardatha."

"Maybe, once you made it beyond Alisanos. If you could," Bethid said. "But Brodhi will guide us through the passageway to the safety of the open plains. You'll forgo that if you depart later, on your own."

The mention of the deepwood silenced them. Both now wore glum faces.

Bethid shook her head, grinning crookedly. "There is plenty of time to visit the Sisters before we leave. Just be back before dawn."

A note of careful curiosity shaded Alorn's tone. "Bethid . . . what do *you* do?"

She glanced up, her mind on packing. "What do I *do*? What do you mean, what do I do?"

Color washed through Alorn's face. "For women."

She had never hidden her preferences from fellow couriers. But the question had never been asked so baldly. It surprised her.

"I mean . . ." Alorn's face was still red. "We can go to a tavern in Cardatha and find women. Or, as you said, to the Sisters of the Road. But what about you?"

Bethid smiled, savoring the moment. Both men were rapt, waiting for her answer. "I can go to a tavern in Cardatha and find women."

Timmon blinked. "But—"

She was matter-of-fact. "Women who spread their legs for men don't look for joy from it. Some of them—some, not all—look for that with another woman." A bubble of laughter rose in her chest. She struck a thoughtful pose. "Perhaps *I* should go to the Sisters tonight."

The observation had the effect she wanted. Timmon and Alorn recoiled in surprise, then glanced at one another. In accord they rose and went out the open door flap in some haste.

Bethid grinned, raising her voice. "Tell the ladies I might be by this evening!"

Chapter 15

*T*HE SINGLE SUN of the human world struck Alario as indicative of humans themselves. They did not live as brightly. Their spirits were dim. The same could be said of their sun. Singular. Tepid. Impotent. He did not have to drop the membrane over his eyes.

Alario stood in the shelter of tall poisonous shrubs, of twisted trees, thorny vines, sharp-edged ferns, as the weak human sun surrendered slowly to twilight. All primaries learned that stillness was often necessary in Alisanos, to hide oneself from threat. As now it was necessary, though for a markedly different reason.

He stood in silence on the verge of the deepwood, invisible to human eyes, if not those of other primaries, and watched his get mark out the borders.

Rhuan gathered no rocks just yet, but used limbs broken from trees as temporary markers. After testing where the border of Alisanos began and ended, he pressed the limbs down into the ground, leaving a vertical guide where cairns would be built. Once that was done, he marked each placement on the rough map, flipping fabric over the board when he wasn't drawing. It was a slow, meticulous process; clearly Rhuan wanted to be most careful in protecting humans from the depredations of Alisanos. Wasted time, Alario reflected. What did it matter that some humans were lost to the deepwood? They bred frequently enough that there were always replacements. He did not understand why they mourned. His people did not mourn a death. His people knew full well that any primary lost was not worth saving. He certainly felt nothing of what the humans called *grief* when the woman he impregnated died whelping the child whom he'd named Rhuan— back when Alario believed in the infant's future.

A muscle leaped in Alario's cheek. All but four get had died in the normal progression from adolescence into maturity. Two had managed to kill one another, while a third failed but survived, leaving Alario with no get at all save Rhuan. He could not accept that this might be *his* failure, this *dioscuri* who wanted nothing to do with the customs of the primaries, the advantages and power. Surely the human dam was responsible.

I should have exposed him at birth. Except that, at birth, no one could have predicted that the dam's blood would so heavily pollute the child. That only became known when Rhuan was old enough to challenge his brother-get and did not. When confronted by his sire, Rhuan said, quietly but firmly, that death was the central defining belief of his people and he wanted nothing to do with it. No challenges among siblings, and none intended for his sire, either.

Alario knew very well he would defeat his weak get in a challenge. With *dioscuri* who would not participate in the traditional challenges, it was less trouble, perhaps, to cull early. Adolescent get learned how to fight by fighting one another. It prepared them for the challenge of adulthood, when bodies and spirits were united in the insatiable drive to kill, to survive, to become a primary. To kill their sires. If they lost but survived the battles of get against get, then they were pronounced unworthy. And castrated, because they should not be allowed to breed. Gelded to remind them forever that from the highest of potentials, they had fallen to the lowest.

One of his get had been castrated.

But neuters were certainly useful. Alario admitted that. They planted and harvested, wove blankets and rugs, chiseled attractive shapes into rock walls, created the painstaking beauty of carefully assembled stone and pebbles into walkways. So many things, the neuters did. So that the primaries need not dirty their hands.

Amused, Alario glanced down at his upturned hand. No indeed, there had never been any doubt that he would triumph when he challenged *his* sire. At the age humans called fourteen, after he had challenged and defeated several brother-get and then his sire, he ascended; the youngest ever to become a primary in the history of his people. And he managed it *before* going on his journey in the human world.

One might assume a primary such as he would sire superior *dioscuri*. But his sole surviving get was utterly worthless, a stain upon Alario's reputation, his position among his people. "A weak seed," he knew, was the term among the other primaries. He could hear it in his head: *Alario's seed is weak. He gives us a neuter, and he gives us a dioscuri not worthy of the title.*

Alario respected tradition. It was what bound them all. He would thus not kill his worthless get before the time came for challenge. It was rather a delicious image, the failure of Rhuan. The death of Rhuan.

Whereas Brodhi, if he were successful in his challenge, ascended.

If Brodhi did so, it removed Karadath from the pantheon. That, Alario would relish; he and his brother-get had fought multiple times throughout the years, but despite injury, neither had been able to kill his kin-in-kind. Both were simply too strong. And now that Brodhi and Rhuan were on their journey, neither Karadath nor Alario could challenge one another.

Waiting those five human years was a challenge in and of itself.

Karadath had mated with a human dam, and got Brodhi. He, Alario, had mated with a human dam and got *Rhuan*.

But. But. Perhaps he could sire his own version of Brodhi on another human dam.

That is what brought him to the border between Alisanos and the human world.

Alario looked again at his get, efficiently marking the map. The sun now was nearly gone, dusk turning to dark. He raised hands to his head and began to undo the intricate braiding, stripping away beads and charms and golden rings.

AS THE SUN slid below the horizon, Davyn considered returning to his wagon. The rain had stopped, it was time for dinner, and he was hungry, but the idea of returning to a wagon empty of his wife, of his children, depressed him. He remained at the table in Mikal's ale-tent. With the arrival of evening, Mikal had put lighted candlecups on each table, sending drifts of smoke toward the Mother Rib of the big tent as well as casting a brassy, burnished glow. Men began to drift in, asking for ale.

Hunched at the table, Davyn leaned forward on his elbows and threaded fingers through his hair, cradling his forehead against the heels of his hands. His spirit wanted to cry out, to release the tension and grief. His eyes stung and throat tightened. But he withstood the urge to weep. He was a private man; there was no reason for him to display his emotions to others. Yet they hurt. They sat in his gut like burning coals, eating through tender viscera to muscle and flesh. The question he had purposely ignored rose to the surface, expressed itself against his wishes.

What will I do if I never see them again?

And worse, if what Rhuan said was true, *What will I do if they are no longer what they were?* No longer—human?

He flinched.

In his mind's eye he saw Audrun laughing, tawny hair loose around her shoulders. Gillan, eldest son, caught between childhood and adulthood. Ellica, lovely as her mother in her own way, though fairer of hair and complexion; that was his own contribution. All of the children were fairer than their mother. Torvic, missing two teeth in front and his shock of pale hair standing up from his skull, had a mischevous temperament that endeared him to everyone. And Megritte, his baby . . . just beginning to establish her personality as apart from her older siblings. Pretty Meggie with braids almost constantly half undone.

The guide had told him, *They will not be what they once were.* But Davyn could not imagine it, could not see either wife or children ever different from when he last saw them. It was impossible to believe a *place* could so completely alter humans

Oh, he had heard of Alisanos. But it had been a distant presence. His folk had always lived in the central portion of Sancorra province. And although he, like everyone else, had heard tales of the deep-wood's moving, no such thing had happened in his lifetime. Until now. Alisanos had never seemed real to him. *Naught but stories*, his father had once said dismissively, and he was not a man who countenanced daydreaming. As the only son, Davyn had grown up working long hours beside his father in the fields. His two sisters and mother harvested the garden, churned milk into butter, made everyone's clothing from fabric woven on his mother's loom; tended the goats, cattle, and chickens; and completed any number of other chores. It was hard work, but satisfying. Davyn was proud of what he had accomplished with his father, and when time came for him to marry, he was fully prepared to become master of his own house. And so he had with Audrun.

Audrun, who was lost.

He heard movement, the quiet thunk of a pewter cup set down on his table. He took his hands away from his face and looked up. Mikal slid the cup across to Davyn. "Stronger than ale," he said in his deep voice. "I think you're in need of it."

Davyn stared at the cup, then met Mikal's single eye. "Drinking spirits is not the answer."

"Now and again, it is."

Davyn watched the ale-keep move on to another table, asking what was wanted.

ALISANOS DESIRED HIM. With supreme subtlety, that yearning crept into his flesh, wreathed his bones, slid the membrane over his eyes. Sheer startlement opened him wide to the deepwood.

He was *of* Alisanos, Alisanos told him. Born there. Raised there. A shudder ran through Rhuan's body. His bones *twisted*.

Already bent to implant yet another stick where a cairn would be, it was a simple matter for him to collapse onto hands and knees. The earth was cool, still wet from the rain. Mud. Mud beneath his hands, sticking to his knees. The sun fell out of the sky.

He *belonged* to Alisanos.

Did he? Would he?

Rhuan inhaled sharply through locked teeth, breath hissing. Again, he shuddered. All the fine hairs on his arms and legs stood up beneath his clothing. Unbraided hair slipped down, dangled, dipped into mud.

Oh, but the deepwood wanted him. It beckoned. It begged. It seduced.

It put him in pain, with the promise of more to come. Rhuan reached into his soul, his sense of *self*, and found the strength to deny the deepwood. He could not say "no" aloud. He could not speak at all, aloud.

But inside his head he was not mute.

Rhuan released the drawn breath, hearing it hiss between his clamped teeth yet again. From his soul he told the deepwood: *You can't have me.*

Alisanos answered: *Yes I can.*

All the primaries and *dioscuri* had land-sense. It ran like a river in their veins. It provided them with the ability to know precisely where the border lay between Alisanos and the human world, where one step was the difference. But there was nothing precise about the border itself. It was fluid. Where in one place the borderline was narrow, in another it was wide. The lack of uniformity offered one of the deepwood's greatest threats. How was one to stay out of the border, away from Alisanos, if one knew not where to step? Here? There? Here again? One foot in the border, the other not? Infinitely dangerous to humans. But primaries and *dioscuri* knew exactly where the border lay, its breadth, its length, whether one foot might be in and the other out. Rhuan could easily have escaped as the great storm came down upon them, because he knew, he *felt* where the storm was going. Yet he did not escape.

Alisanos said, scathingly: *Because of a woman.*

Yes. Because of a woman. He could not leave Audrun, separated from husband and children, to be swept up in howling violence. And so he had done his best to save her, to bring her out of harm's way. But in doing so, blinded and deafened within the storm, he sent them both into danger. Both into Alisanos.

Come home, said Alisanos. *I miss you.*

The primaries had sent him back to the human world. Alisanos was disturbed by that. It *wanted* him.

Two steps. That was all. Two steps, and he would be home.

No. Not home.

Rhuan wrenched himself out of the mud, rising awkwardly. His bones buzzed with proximity to the deepwood. Flesh itched. Limbs twitched. Loose hair bore a burden of mud. He bent over, put his hands on his knees—

Something.

Something there.

Something that was not Alisanos, but *of* Alisanos.

Rhuan spun as he straightened. Slickness squelched beneath his feet. Wet, mud-weighted hair slapped against his spine.

His sire.

AS SHE EXPECTED, a great number of folk had come to Ilona for hand-reading. Most of them were adherents of different divinations, of different avenues to contact with the Mother, but Ilona knew the reckoning was that any diviner, in such extraordinary and threatening circumstances as these, would do.

Mostly men came. Nearly all of them had wives, children. Seated crosslegged on the other side of the lacquered table, hand outstretched, somewhat nervously looking at accoutrements unknown to them, they did what they could to downplay the need for Ilona's gift. It was their wives, they said, who sent them.

As always, Ilona hid any physical expression that her clients might find unsettling or insulting and accepted whatever justification they offered for the visit. In good times, times when life was predictable, it was the women who came, asking personal things, usually, such as whether an ill child would recover, whether a certain man was honest in his wooing, was she pregnant, would she *become* pregnant, would the child live. But these were bad times, and life was no longer in any wise predictable. Women's concerns were now set aside so the men could assume their duties as protectors. But not all the men were married, not all were in or seeking a relationship. Some had no one to ask for save themselves. And these were the ones Ilona found most honest in their needs. They had courage in themselves to visit a strange diviner, to trust that she could show them a way to the Mother; were not influenced by concerns about family. They had come to the settlement alone, meaning to depart Sancorra by horseback, wagon, or booted feet. Their road had been clear; their intent, to make a better future away from the Hecari. But now that road, that future, was deferred. It made men tentative or assertive, depending on whether they had anyone to be brave for.

Ilona found all manner of answers in their hands but also questions. She had long ago learned never to be too blunt when relating what she saw. She read true and told them the truth. Unlike charlatans who wielded falsehood like a scythe—to increase the number of their coin-rings, to make clients dependent—she did not believe aggression or exaggeration was the way to the Mother.

Maiden Moon found avenues through the tattered limbs of old growth trees, through broken branches, to elder roots loosened from the soil. Ilona stretched to unkink her spine, then rose. More tea, she thought. A soothing blend that would ease her but not cloud her mind. She believed no more men, no women, would come to her tonight. Darkness, in such circumstances as these, was best greeted by a retreat to wagons, to tents, to prayers and petitions from inside shelter.

Ilona, kneeling to fill her mug, smiled with a slow anticipation. Rhuan would come to her later, when he retired for the night from mapping the border between safety and the deepwood. Her smile widened, the knowing smile of a woman who knew herself desired. Desired by the man whom she herself desired.

The sounds of karavaners tending night chores eased her as much as the tea. The rustle of horses, mules, bedded down for the night with grain to supplement grass. The occasional bark of a dog. Children with high-pitched voices protesting the need for sleep. The faint creak of wagon stairs folded away for the night, denying easy entry to vermin. Somewhere, a woman sang to a child, lulling it to sleep.

Ilona's smile now was not one of sexual anticipation but of the comfort found in the familiar. These days, familiarity was something which all could seek, could cling to, trying to find a way to accept that their lives, for the rest of the rains, were tied to a place nearly surrounded by Alisanos.

No, no one else would come. Ilona began to collect and put away items used in her readings, folding away the table drape, blowing out lamplights depending from shepherd's crooks. One she left alight, to guide Rhuan, though she knew it was unnecessary. He saw better at night than humans, she knew, regardless of the Mother's light, or of a lantern or banked fire. He would come to her late.

And exhausted by her readings, she turned to mount the steps into her wagon. There she remade the pallet on the floor, folded blankets back, slipped out of her clothing. The thin chemise worn beneath tunic and skirts was enough, she knew, until Rhuan came and took it from her.

Tired. So many hands, so many visions. Tragedy and joy.

RHUAN STARED AT his sire, time suspended, time revoked. He was, in that moment of discovery and astonishment, rendered entirely mute.

Alario smiled. He took the two steps necessary to leave the deepwood. To enter the human world.

When he summoned the power of speech, shock stripped Rhuan's voice of its natural timbre, leaving rust in its place. "Why are you here?"

Alario shrugged. "You prefer the human world to the deepwood. Perhaps I feel the same."

Rhuan released a blurt of laughter and disbelief. "I don't think so."

"Perhaps not," Alario agreed.

Rhuan regained control over his voice. "What do you want with me? And why did you unbraid your hair?"

"Oh, I'm not here to see you. You're not worthy of my attention. You are—an insect." Alario waved his hand as if shooing away a troublesome fly. "No. I came for the woman."

He spoke so offhandedly that at first Rhuan just stared at his sire. Then a sharp stab of concern shot through him, coupled with wariness. "What woman?"

"The hand-reader."

Shock, and with it heat, sheathed Rhuan's flesh. The red membrane slid down over his eyes. Anger, not fear. A hard, unyielding, painful knot of desperate anger. "You are not—"

Alario's hand shot out and closed over Rhuan's throat, holding him in place even as his body jerked in response. "Not—what? Not to see her?" He smiled. "I think otherwise."

He had killed her once, had Alario. Was he returning to do so again?

With raw, unreasoning power, Rhuan jammed the heel of his hand up against the underside of his sire's chin, knocking Alario's head back. It caught him completely off guard. He staggered back two steps to regain his balance and lost his grip on Rhuan's throat. Rhuan promptly took himself several long paces away, putting more distance between them. His throat was on fire from the pressure of Alario's hand. He would be lucky to have any voice by morning.

Blood flowed from Alario's bottom lip. He blotted it on the back of his hand, stared at it a moment, then grinned at Rhuan with bloodied teeth.

And Rhuan knew, knew without question, what his sire planned. Not killing. Making. Remaking. And he understood. "She isn't Shoia at all, is she? *You* brought her back."

"I was angry when I killed her. Yes. I. Is that an admission of weakness to you?"

Rhuan could do nothing more but stare at his sire.

"Dead, she was of no worth. Of no use. But I *un*made what an earlier anger provoked." Alario's smile was mocking. "Shoia? No. There are no more Shoia in the world."

"Then—"

"Then she has no lives to spend. One death. One human death. That, only. I gifted her with a reprieve. But merely temporary . . . she'll die bearing me a *dioscuri*, of course. And so the reprieve is ended."

Rhuan's skin heated. *"No."*

Alario took two swift, long steps forward and smashed a fist across his son's face. *"Yes."*

He might be a *dioscuri*, but primaries were considerably stronger. Rhuan went down hard, limbs sprawled every which way. His head smacked the ground, a second insult to his skull. He felt blood run from his nose down along his cheek. Hearing seemed muffled.

Instinct told him to rise, that it was dangerous to remain in a posture of submission. He tried to hitch an elbow underneath to lever himself up. But now Alario stood over him. Still stunned, Rhuan was only vaguely aware of his sire's skin shifting to a warm glow, the third lid dropping. Alario was alight with power. He reached down, grabbed a fistful of loose hair, and jerked his get upright, much of Rhuan's weight hanging from his scalp.

Alario said, "You'll remember none of this."

Rhuan could no more avoid the second blow than he had the first. This time bones broke beneath Alario's hand.

Down. Down into the darkness.

Chapter 16

*A*UDRUN SAW HER children settled upon the cots, each sitting on the edge. On each, a packed straw pallet covered by bright bedding rested on tight-woven ropes, making the cots more bearable than a bed upon the floor. Gillan, tentatively stretching out on his back, was clearly exhausted and in some pain; Ellica, yet again, was distracted by her tree. Torvic and Meggie shared a cot for the moment, hunched against one another as their legs hooked over the edge.

Audrun, too, was exhausted. So much of her had been spent in accelerated childbirth, in confronting the primaries, in recovering her children. But it was not time to rest just yet, no matter how much she longed to. First, there was a task.

"Meggie," she said in a quiet voice tempered by a delicate patience. "Meggie, would you come over here? I would like to give you a hug."

Megritte sat stiffly upon the cot's edge, staring speechlessly at her mother. Her eyes seemed strangely fixed, lids stretched too wide. Audrun, who had briefly lived in the horrific vision conjured by the primary, Karadath, could well understand Megritte's consuming fear. Instinctively, she knew better than to force a close physical presence on her youngest daughter just yet. Maintaining control of her voice, carefully avoiding a command, she asked, "Meggie, could you come give me a hug? Could you come over here and climb into my lap?"

Torvic, seated so close to his younger sister, said, "She won't talk."

Audrun blinked as her brows rose. But Torvic had been with Meggie since the storm. He was the one to whom Audrun addressed her question. "Has she injured her throat?"

"No," he answered. "But she won't talk."

Audrun looked at Meggie. The child's face was gray, smears of dark circles below her eyes. Hair straggled from braids, her clothing was soiled and torn, the marks of trees and vines crisscrossed her lower legs, which, because her skirt was tattered, had not been shielded against the depredations of the deepwood.

Audrun kept her tone even, inflections carefully doled out. "Meggie . . . you don't need to talk just yet. Just come to me and let me wrap you up in my arms the way you've always liked."

"She won't," Torvic said.

Gillan, stretched out on a cot, sounded cross and impatient. "Let her be, for now," he said. "She needs a nap. When she wakes up, she'll be better."

Pain could do that, could bring about such a tone of voice Audrun knew, and his exposed leg showed scarring as well as scales with fiery margins.

With confidence and a trace of annoyance in his voice, Torvic said, "No. She won't."

Gillan shifted, resettling himself. Pain was reflected in his eyes, in the lines of his face. He seemed to have aged, Audrun saw, over a matter of days.

"You can't know what she will do or not do," she said to Torvic.

"She told me." Torvic looked away from Gillan to his mother. "Meggie told me." He touched his head. "In here."

"Don't be foolish," Ellica snapped, looking up from the infant tree in her lap. "This is not the time for one of your games."

"It's not a game." Torvic still stared at his mother. "It's not, mam. I can hear her in my head."

They were in *Alisanos*. She knew from Rhuan, from her own experiences, that anything was possible.

Audrun drew a quiet breath. "Can anyone else hear her?" She looked at Megritte. "May I hear you? Inside my head?"

"No," Torvic said. "No one but me."

THE SPIRITS WERE extremely powerful. Davyn discovered that very soon after the first few swallows on an empty belly. He increasingly felt oddly detached from his surroundings, wrapped in dullness, aware that his vision was affected. The ale-tent would not keep still. He widened his eyes to see if that would curtail the slow spinning, but no. So he narrowed his eyes. No. And yet he lifted the cup and drank again. At first, his belly had protested the burning, but no longer. He felt detached, distanced. But he did not stop drinking.

Others had come into Mikal's tent in search of ale and spirits. Tables filled. He saw two Sisters of the Road entering with two male couriers. Not Brodhi; the others. They had put off their blue cloaks, but both wore the silver brooch identifying them as couriers, as honest men who carried word to others. One of the women was Naiya, gold-streaked hair worn loose. Her eyes paused briefly as she saw him, but then her attention returned to the man who walked with her to a small table set in one of the tent's corners. Stools were found. They sat, the four of them, gazing at one another. Davyn saw a coyness in the women's eyes. He saw, too, the eagerness in the couriers' faces.

One of the men shifted on his stool so he could look at the bar. "Spirits," he called. "Four cups, if you please."

They drank for pleasure. Davyn thought he would never feel pleasure again.

But he might find relief, if not answers, in spirits.

He pushed his empty cup across the table, catching the ale-keep's single eye, and signalled for more.

Mikal delivered the spirits to the couriers' table, then eased himself onto a stool set across from Davyn. He put a tankard on the table; Davyn could smell the tang of spirits. "Feeling better?"

"I can't tell." Davyn leaned forward against the table and once again braced his head in one hand. "This is . . . strong. The spirits. But it doesn't make me forget."

"No," Mikal said. "Not you; I do see that. Nothing will ever allow you to forget." He paused a moment. "Your cup is empty. Have this tankard in its place."

"What are you here for?" Davyn asked, realizing his bluntness was rude, but it was the spirits talking. "What do you want that's worth a cup of spirits?"

"An opening," Mikal said. "Were I simply to sit down and start discussing your personal business, I would be taken as rude. Instead, I offer drinks. Courtesy has its rewards."

Davyn stared at him, trying to focus on the ale-keep's single eye. "Why in the Mother's world would you want to discuss my personal business?"

"You mentioned a road."

Heat climbed into Davyn's face. He picked up the tankard and drank, hoping it gave him time to rearrange his expression. The pungency of the spirits set his eyes to watering. He put the tankard down. "That was wishful thinking."

Mikal shook his head. "There's more to it than that."

Say nothing. Say nothing more of what the guide told you. Accordingly, Davyn shook his head. "No."

"Rhuan nearly broke his neck snapping his head around when you mentioned this road."

"And he explained that."

"That doesn't mean what he said was entirely the truth." Mikal shifted on his stool. "As was said, a road through Alisanos would offer safe passage to hundreds of those fleeing the Hecari."

"It would," Davyn said guardedly. "But of course it's impossible. Who would build it?" Which was a question he should have asked the guide. Well, later. Later he would ask.

"A road through the deepwood would offer safe passage for your family," Mikal said thoughtfully. "A way to Atalanda."

After pausing for another swallow of spirits, Davyn nodded. "Yes, if it could be done. But we all of us discussed that earlier. There is no way it could be done. Would *you* be willing to build it?"

The ale-keep smiled. "You're not particularly good at dissembling."

Davyn wasn't entirely certain if that were insult or compliment. "I'm not dissembling."

"You're an honest man, farmsteader. I doubt you have ever lied in your life."

"I'm not lying!"

"But you're hiding something."

Davyn glared at the man. "Why would I be hiding something? What is there to hide?"

"Knowledge. The kind of knowledge that would prompt you to say something about a road, when it would never occur to anyone else. And Rhuan was displeased."

More spirits slid down Davyn's throat as he swallowed. Ale he enjoyed now and then, but spirits, no. He had determined that years before, when three swallows had made him drunk. And sick the next morning

Davyn squinted into the tankard. *Am I drunk now?*

Possibly so. He didn't feel like himself. He found himself hoping that he would not be sick this time.

"Rhuan told you something, did he not? Something to do with building a road through Alisanos. Specifically."

Davyn surrendered pretense. "I will one day walk the road to my family. Or they will come to me."

Mikal grunted. Then, in seeming idleness, he observed, "Rhuan has never spoken much about himself. But I suspect he has said more of himself to you than to others."

Davyn shrugged. "Does it matter?"

"It matters if there is threat to the folk here."

Davyn stared at Mikal a long moment. "He wouldn't harm any-

one here. He's a guide . . . his sworn oath is to safeguard the karavan." And memory became vision: Rhuan facing down a Hecari party
at the karavan and killing each. "At which he is most efficient."

"He's efficient at most things," Mikal said in an agreeable tone.
"But he was in the deepwood and came out again. Looking precisely
the same as when he went in. Is there another man alive who can
say so?"

Davyn shrugged again, realizing that his words had turned slow.
Spirits, he knew. "The courier did the same. Brodhi."

"Yes," Mikal said quietly. "Two men went in, two men came out.
It's not often that anyone comes out of Alisanos, certainly no one
sane. Yet both Rhuan and Brodhi did. It may be no coincidence."

"Does it matter?" Davyn repeated, and drank down more spirits.

"I have never heard of Shoia going into Alisanos. Before Rhuan
and Brodhi arrived, I didn't know there were any Shoia left in the
world *to* go into Alisanos. Yet we took them at their word."

"Why wouldn't we?" Davyn asked. "You took me at my word
that I'm a farmsteader."

Mikal smiled. "That is very evident. But for those two?" He shook
his head. "The only thing evident about them is a very close resemblance—"

Davyn cut him off. "They're kin. Anyone who saw my children
would know they were related. Why would it not be the same for
Rhuan and the courier?"

"Perhaps it would be," Mikal agreed, "did I not smell something
of subterfuge."

The tent continued to revolve. Oh, he would be sick. To take his
mind off the urge to rid himself of spirits in a most uncomfortable
way, he turned to a question. "Why subterfuge?"

"You asked Brodhi to go into Alisanos and find your family."

"I did."

"What man would go into Alisanos for any reason?"

"I offered to pay him."

Mikal waved a big hand. "That's not significant. I doubt any man
would willingly go into Alisanos at any price."

"The hand-reader saw it. That he would go. And she reads true."

"Ilona is discreet," the ale-keep commented, "but she would never keep to herself a thing that might be linked to trouble."

"Exactly. She saw it in my hand."

"Did your hand also tell her Brodhi would come back out?"

"Considering I asked him to go into Alisanos looking for my family, and that the hand-reader saw him in the deepwood, I would assume so."

"But he came back without your family."

Grief rose. His voice was uneven. "Yes."

"Davyn—I don't mean to be cruel," Mikal said. "I'm sorry, but I need to know. I care for the people here."

Davyn took up the tankard and drank the last swallow. "Rhuan didn't go into the deepwood voluntarily. Alisanos took him. He was with my wife, trying to get her to safety."

Mikal shook his head. "Then why didn't he bring her out? *He* came out. Why did he leave her there?"

He thumped the tankard down sharply. "He said he had no choice. Why would he tell me this road could lead me to my family if it can't?"

"Perhaps a kindness, in his own way."

"*Kindness!*"

"To keep you in hope."

Davyn stared at him. Now he was blearily curious. "Then you think he lied."

"He may have," Mikal said judiciously.

It was not quite accusation. Davyn squinted at him, trying to still the tent from its slow revolutions. "I thought you were friends."

"Rhuan and I?" Mikal shook his head. "He comes here to drink. I am not friends with every man who does so."

"But you give credence to what he says. You did earlier today."

"Because I believe Rhuan is very experienced in many things. But that is part of the problem. He knows too much."

Davyn shook his head. "I believe he meant what he said."

"About the road?"

"About the road. About me safely meeting my family *on* that road."

"You are so certain."

"I have to be. For the sake of my family."

Mikal ran a thumb back and forth across his upper lip. "I don't like it. Why would Rhuan tell you about a road through Alisanos, but not any of us?"

Davyn rubbed one side of his face, elbow planted on the table. His skin felt tight. "I don't know. Ask him." Earlier he had let information about the road slip, despite promising he would keep it in confidence. Rhuan, now, was the only connection he had to his family. He could not betray him.

But disbelief tugged at him. *He said he is a god. A god*! Once again Davyn took up the tankard. This time he drained it. Oh, indeed, he was drunk. Was that why Mikal had given him spirits? To make him speak of things he shouldn't?

Davyn said with meticulous enunciation, "I have no reason to disbelieve Rhuan."

"Well. Perhaps not." Mikal leaned forward, lowering his voice. "You would do well to understand that, for all his affability, for all his charm, Rhuan is a dangerous man."

Memory found its way through the fog of strong spirits. The same vision in his head: Rhuan, killing Hecari with deadly accuracy; throwing long-bladed knives that cut into Hecari throats.

"To save us," he said as the tent continued to spin.

"Save you from what?"

"Hecari. You should have seen it. Him . . . matter of moments. And then all of them were dead." Oh, Sweet Mother. He was going to pass out. Or be sick. Perhaps even both. "—did this on purpose."

The one-eyed man smiled. "I did."

"You think I'll give up secrets."

"I do."

Davyn attempted to hang onto concentration. His eyes wished to close. "Why does it matter?"

Mikal smiled. "Rhuan exaggerates. He can tell a twisty tale when he chooses. But he was deadly serious when you spoke about the road."

"And I repeat: Ask *him*. Not me."

"I intend to. "

Davyn squinted. "Why ask me at all?"

"Because you are far more likely to tell me the truth."

He wanted nothing more than to go to sleep. But he was afraid he might be sick first. Well, better than being sick in bed.

His eyes wished to close again. "I told you. He said a road would be built. And I could go to my family."

"Did he say anything about why he came out of the deepwood with impunity?"

"He's a god."

Mikal froze, single eye widening. "A *what*?"

Davyn's eyes won the battle. Lids closed. "He said . . . he said he's a god." With great effort he managed to open his eyes, albeit the merest slit. "Half a god."

The ale-keep said nothing. He just stared from his single eye.

"Maybe he is," Davyn said thickly. A yawn overtook him. "Or not."

"Or not," Mikal echoed.

"I am quite drunk," Davyn said.

"Yes."

He pushed the tankard toward Mikal. "More."

"I think not."

Briefly it annoyed him, that the ale-keep would deny him. Was he not someone who sold spirits and ale to anyone who asked? But only one more question made it through the fog of spirits and profound sleepiness. "How will I get to my wagon?"

Mikal laughed softly. He rose, pushing the stool out of the way. "I'll take you there. It's a task I know very well. You are not the first to lose his wits to spirits."

Davyn sighed his relief. "Thank you."

"You're welcome." Mikal hoisted him up, steadied him.

"He *said* he was a god. Half."

"Well," Mikal said. "Either he's telling the truth, or it's one of his twisty tales." He set a shoulder under Davyn's, hooked a limp arm around his neck. "I'm not entirely sure which I'd prefer."

Davyn let the ale-keep take much of his weight. "I want him to be a god."

"Blessed Mother, why?"

"Because then I can go to my family. When the road is built."

Chapter 17

DESPITE HER INTENTION to go to the ale-tent, Bethid decided against it. She was tired in mind and body. It felt like she had been battered one way and another for days. She pulled off boots, stretched out on her pallet, dragged blankets over her body. Still clothed, she lay flat on her back, eyes fixed on the ridge pole, the Mother Rib, high overhead. And on the dangling string of charms that all couriers respected as a thing to ward them against dangers of the road.

She sighed heavily and draped an arm over her face, elbow jutting upward. Little by little she relaxed knotted muscles, one limb at a time. As always, it was her spine that took the brunt of stress; that and her neck. She felt dirty, gritty, itchy. A bath was called for, but she would not go to the river in the dark, even if she carried a lantern. She respected what Rhuan said about the dangers of the night, camping so close to Alisanos. So she would rise with the dawn, dunk herself in the river, put on clean clothes (though they would soon stick to her flesh) and join Jorda and the others heading for Cardatha.

Bethid badly wanted to sleep, but her mind would not permit it. And for the first time, she felt a faint flutter in her belly. What if she were wrong? What if none of the Cardatha Guild couriers wished to involve themselves in her plan? What if they declined to pass the word directing people to the settlement? She was, after all, inciting war.

Blessed Mother . . . am I wrong? Should I just let things go on as they have before?

Certainly that was the easiest course, but even as she asked herself that question, she felt again the surge of determination to strike a blow at the Hecari. She well understood the pervasive fear among Sancorrans trying merely to survive in a province now ruled by the Hecari. She herself had been frightened and still was. But now she had a task to do. Now she knew of a way to help her people.

If only she could convince other couriers about the need—well, no; they understood the need. And the danger. The Guild had a truce of sorts with the Hecari. If word of this were carried to the warlord, that truce would end, and the Guild would be destroyed.

Couriers would die.

Timmon and Alorn, her closest friends among the couriers: dead. Halleck and Gathlyn, both of whom she esteemed highly: dead. And even the youngest, the one whom she teased, Corrid: dead.

Bethid lifted her arm from her face and rubbed at eyes that felt hot and dry. *Blessed Mother, let me do this thing.* She pondered that a moment. *And let all of us survive it.*

EVENING SETTLED OVER the encampment like a shroud. Birds stilled, tucking heads under wings. Cook fires, banked for the night, glowed as if to light his way, but Darmuth did not need such aids. He walked as a man, as the man so many recognized when they saw him, not knowing what he was. Rhuan and Brodhi had established that they were Shoia; he was merely a man. He let no human know—or suspect—otherwise. And so he walked among the humans as if he were kin-in-kind. They saw what they saw, what they expected to see, marking him as eccentric, perhaps, with his taut-fitting, colorful clothing, winter-ice eyes, a green gemstone set in one front tooth; but one of them all the same and tasked with getting the karavan from the settlement to distant portions of Sancorra, where there might be fewer Hecari.

Walking as a man, he slipped through the elder grove, noting that lanterns glowing in the wagons' interiors were being snuffed out one by one. A dog barked; another answered, but the tone was not of alarm or aggression. Perhaps they, too, were saying goodnight.

Darmuth smiled crookedly. Maybe what he should do, at some point, was to take on the guise of a dog and learn what they knew of life, why they did what they did. There were no pets in Alisanos.

Except perhaps for the lesser demons. They might be viewed as pets by the primaries. In fact, they probably *were* viewed as pets by the primaries. Lesser demons, such as himself. Such as Ferize.

He did not wish to be a pet. He wished to be greater than he was. To gain respect. To ascend even as the *dioscuri* who killed their sires ascended, save that a demon had no hope of rising so high, or in the same manner. Demons were made. They were not born as infants, did not experience childhood, knew nothing of how a baby in the creche grew to young adulthood. They were *made* creatures, he and Ferize and hundreds of others.

Providing Rhuan and Brodhi were guided along their journeys in a way the primaries approved; providing they gained the insight and drive required to properly challenge their sires, neither he nor Ferize would be unmade.

Already, pathways were being formed in the elder grove. Grass was pressed to earth, showing where humans walked. Soon it would be torn, killed beneath boot soles, and the soil underneath the destruction would rise up through broken stems.

His own boots packed down the grass, tore it, killed it, as they pressed into soil. Odors permeated the grove. His sense of smell was far superior to that of humans. Odors of meat, bread, fire, smoke, spices, the barest trace of tea, warm horseflesh, herbs, grain, and grass, dampness, stone, earth, wounds in trees whose limbs were freshly broken; all, he smelled. And the scent of humans. To him, to a demon, lesser or no, the scent of living human flesh, human blood, was the most significant scent of all.

At night, he hunted. Rhuan periodically reminded him he should not take for a feeding the horses, mules, oxen, dogs, milk cows of the karavaners. And Darmuth was willing to leave them be, *if* he found other meat to eat, the meat of wild animals, of birds, of ground vermin, of snakes, of insects, and others. He was an omniverous demon; anything would do. But meat was what he craved. If a hunt brought little, he occasionally appropriated a chicken from karavanfolk, or a goat, taking care not to do so often. It did not please Rhuan when he did so, but the *dioscuri* did grudgingly understand that a demon, like any living creature, had to feed to survive.

Perhaps he and Ferize could dine on the two Hecari whose forms they took.

Trees grew sparse at the edge of the grove. Now he smelled the river.

And blood.

Rhuan's blood.

Darmuth broke into a run, following a scent that spoke of anger and injury, and of power.

Primary. Where none should be.

SHE CAME TO him on the cusp of night, that portion of time between dusk and dark. Brodhi waited for her at the edge of the elder grove in an area free of wagons. Maiden Moon illuminated that verge between grove and plains, and so it was easy to watch Ferize come down from the air, to see the blurry shift between demon form and human. This night she was red-haired, green-eyed, clad in a rich amber-dyed gown. A glint of gold flashed at her throat, where a pendant lay against pale skin.

She came up to him, smiling, and he took the initiative. He captured her arms, pressed them against her body, and caught her bottom lip in his teeth. Ferize laughed softly and then poured out of imprisonment into a woman who stood just in front of Brodhi. Before he could do anything more, she spread flattened hands against his chest and pushed.

An off-balance step collided with tree root. That step, accompanied by Ferize's push, set his spine against the wide trunk of an elder tree. And it hurt. Ferize, as all demons, was much stronger than he, even in human form. He opened his mouth to speak, but Ferize deftly undid his leggings and slipped a hand inside.

She gripped him. "Ah," she said. "I doubt you will last long tonight."

"I last as long as is needful," Brodhi retorted, stung.

Ferize laughed, locked arms behind the back of his neck, and pulled herself upward, against him, tucking legs around him. He embraced her as she rode his bared hips. "Now," she said.

He had brought a blanket for that very reason. He lay her down upon it, knelt, and covered her body with his own.

"Perhaps twice," she said against his mouth.

Brodhi grinned into darkness. "Oh, more. Certainly more. I'm a god, remember?"

Ferize laughed. "*Half* a god."

HEARING RETURNED BEFORE vision, and Audrun realized she had fallen asleep upon the cot. She remembered nothing of the movements necessary to lie down, only knew that obviously she had resorted to them at some point.

Eyes opened. She turned over onto her back, wincing from stiffness. It was dark in the chamber, no sunlight creeping between tapestry curtains covering the long, slotted window openings. Nighttime had fallen in Alisanos, as it did in her own world. But this nighttime, she did not doubt, was far more dangerous than the one she knew.

She could see little of the other chamber from her bed, save for a faint shaft of moonlight forming a delicate column from fire ring to skyhole. Reflecting her long practice with assessments and decisions made on a daily basis, Audrun realized that she and the older children would have to be vigilant about the hole in the chamber ceiling. First, there was the possibility of rain; secondly, light from two suns was dangerous, and the skyhole would concentrate it.

She felt groggy, still exhausted. Joints ached, limbs stung from cuts and slashes, and her abdomen was flaccid, sore.

She turned onto her side, looking for her children. Gillan was asleep flat on his back, injured leg baring scales, discoloration. Ellica slept with the infant tree, its rootball nestled against her side. Torvic and Megritte lay curled up on one cot, arms and legs intertwined. Audrun saw the bellies of both her youngest rising rhythmically as they breathed. They slept so deeply, blessed by innocence, as if Alisanos had never come upon them.

And then she realized that Torvic was not asleep at all. He lay in a tangle with Meggie, as she had noted, but his eyes were open and fixed upon her. And Audrun realized that while she had chosen Meggie to join her for a hug, she had not offered the same to her older children.

She sat up and swung her legs over the edge of the cot. She stretched out her hand to him.

Torvic came to it slowly, sliding carefully from under Meggie's arms and legs without disturbing her. First his hand slipped into his mother's. Then, as she guided him closer, all stiffness and reluctance bled away. He was her child again, her youngest son. And when he leaned into her, when he pressed himself against her and wrapped his arms as far around her as was possible, Audrun felt the upwelling of relief and a surge of love for him, as well as tears of gratitude that he was alive, and present, and unhurt.

She pulled him close. She pressed his head against her shoulder. She slipped one hand through his hair, pulling tangles back into something that resembled neatness. And then she hugged him. Hugged him hard. And felt the beat of his heart in time with her own.

"Mam?" Torvic asked, barely above a whisper.

"Yes?"

"When are we going to look for the baby?"

"I have asked that primary to find her for us."

"Will he?"

Audrun's mouth twisted. She wanted to say he would but how could she be certain? Well, if he wanted her to lie with him willingly . . .

She reached for the string of charms that lay against the hollow of her throat and found nothing. Nothing at all.

The thong was lost. She inhabited Alisanos without a physical connection to the Mother.

But before she could reflect on how disturbing and frightening a loss that was, Torvic pulled her attention back to himself.

"When is Da coming?" he asked. "He could help find the baby."

Audrun turned her head so he would not see her weep afresh. "I can't say, Torvic, but I know in my heart and soul that he's looking for all of us."

And what would he find when he reached them?

His children, Audrun told herself; his wife and his children.

ALARIO, IN DARKNESS, watched the hand-reader tend her belongings. What little remained of the tea still warmed at the fire, its kettle set on an almost level rock. But the hand-reader forgot it in the midst of putting away the accoutrements of her art. When all was done save for the forgotten kettle, the woman climbed up the steps into her high-wheeled wagon. He heard her moving inside, saw the freshly-lighted glow from the single lantern hanging from the door frame.

Smiling, he crossed to the wagon. It creaked as he mounted the steps. Alario blew out the lantern that depended from the wagon's door frame. The glow faded, no longer sparking off bits of metal. The spreading tree canopy blocked much of the moon. A human would say no one could see in the dark.

He was not human.

Alario adopted Rhuan's lighter voice. "I am late coming from the markers. Forgive me."

He needed no lantern to light the wagon's interior. He saw the hand-reader's smile, saw her pleasure in his company, saw the invitation in her eyes. She put out a hand. "Where are you? I can't see you."

"We need no light," he said. "Our bodies know one another."

Ilona laughed softly. "Not as well as might be expected. We spent too much time apart. Two nights is hardly enough time for either of us to learn the other's body."

Alario bared his teeth in a grin that would frighten her, could she see it. "Indeed," he said. "Two nights is much too soon to know anything of one another."

Her hand searched again. "Where are you?"

"Here." Alario caught her hand in his, pressed it against his breast. He knelt upon the pallet even as she did and cradled her head in his hands. "Here."

Chapter 18

*R*HUAN ROUSED TO wet grass, damp earth, and Maiden Moon glowing overhead, as if to judge him. That thought was not comforting; he was unsure if, in the human world, this Mother the people talked about endlessly was, in fact, a goddess or nothing more than a globe of light used to track the seasons. He squinted up at the moon/goddess, and then wished he hadn't. It hurt his face to squint.

Still muzzy, he took stock of his body. He lay sprawled upon his back, one knee bent upward, the other leg flat. Arms were splayed out. Parts of him ached, and parts of him seemed perfectly normal. The back of his head had apparently collided with something sharp. And his face hurt. He touched it gently, exploring tender areas.

"Ow," he muttered, having learned that complaint on his first day in the human world. "Ow ow ow."

"Oh, come up from there," Darmuth said, standing over him.

Before Rhuan could forbid him, Darmuth reached down, caught a wrist, and pulled him upright into a seated position.

"Ow! Darmuth—!" His complaint trailed off, muffled by the two hands he pressed over his aching face. "That hurts!"

"Of course it hurts. Your nose is broken."

"My *nose*?"

"And probably a cheekbone, maybe both. But all will heal." Darmuth paused. "And that missing tooth will grow back. You may not be as pretty as usual, but it's temporary."

Rhuan sought with his tongue, found the gap in the top teeth. He also found a swollen and split bottom lip. He pressed the back of his hand against it, and saw the smear of night-blackened blood when he took the hand away. "Did somebody kill me again?"

"You don't remember?"

Rhuan pondered that a moment. "No."

"Later," Darmuth said tersely. "Stay here. Your face will feel better if you remain seated."

"My face would feel better if you hadn't yanked me off the ground!"

"Stay here," Darmuth repeated, the first trace of urgency entering his tone, "and consign me to whatever punishment you feel is appropriate when I return."

"Darmuth—"

"Later. I'll explain when I return."

"But where are you—"

"*Later!*"

Rhuan stared after the demon until he could no longer see him. Then he eased himself back down upon the earth, spine against cold soil. "Ow." He counted up the injuries he knew about: face, nose, cheekbones, missing tooth, a split lip. And the back of his head. Possibly more damage existed, but he was in no mood to seek it out.

It was unlike Darmuth to sound so definitive. And yet Rhuan had to honor the request—no, the command—to stay where he was, because Darmuth only sounded like that on occasions of great consequence.

It hurt his head too much to sit up, and standing likely would be much worse. He would do as Darmuth commanded and stay right where he was, under the eye of Maiden Moon. He lay with boot soles planted and legs crooked up. Maiden Moon's observance of him did not falter. He realized it was his imagination suggesting that the moon was more than merely a thing in the sky at night. Nonetheless, he cupped one hand and set the edge against his brow, blocking the moon entirely.

"I don't understand," Rhuan muttered. "I don't understand. Why is it always *me* this happens to? It's just like people saying I kill people." Well, he had killed people. But only those whose death kept innocent people safe. He inspected the bridge of his nose with gentle fingertips, moving the cartilage back and forth with care. Another thought occured, hardened into certainty: "Bone hunters."

He was believed to be Shoia, and Shoia bones were worth much to practitioners who burned them to ash and grit and then read the resulting heaps. Opportunistic humans had learned that quickly.

Rhuan frowned, then wished he hadn't; it hurt. What would it take for a human, or two or three of them, to sneak up on him as he concentrated on his task of planting tree limbs to mark spots for cairns, or on marking the map pinned to Mikal's board? That they had proved unsuccessful might well be because of Darmuth's arrival. If so, the humans were probably dead. Darmuth, over the years in the human world, had actually killed more people than Rhuan.

"And they'll blame me for that, too." He wiped a trickle of blood away from his sore lip, tongued the gap between teeth. "There are others you might murder for *their* bones, not mine." And then he realized that such a thought was entirely inappropriate. He looked up at Maiden Moon once again, thinking aloud: "Well, best that no bones are taken from anyone. Of course. From anyone. But especially not from me." The idea of his being cut up for his bones and hauled off to the ant hills before he could resurrect from a temporary death was a horrible thought. "I would like my bones to stay right where they are, if you please, in the correct assemblage beneath my flesh . . . and *why* am I lying here talking to the moon?" He pressed fingertips against brow and massaged sore skin. "Of course it may be that I'm talking to myself and not to the moon at all, in whatever seasonal garb she—or he, for that matter—wears." Rhuan peered up at the moon again. "If you're truly up there in the heavens . . . or if *anything* is up there, actually—could you perhaps make this headache go away?"

DARMUTH FOLLOWED THE scent, the faint muskiness of a mature male primary preparing to breed. It was something no human would ever notice. Within moments he also knew where Alario was. Knew that the primary had bred a female. Knew that she was the hand-reader.

He paused beside the wide bole of an elder tree near Ilona's wagon and hid himself in darkness. Confrontation, oh yes, it would come. But Darmuth could perhaps make a larger impression if he had aid.

He quested for her, found her. With Brodhi, undoubtedly doing precisely what Alario did. *"Ferize. If you can, come."*

He felt the quickening of her interest—and her annoyance. *"Now? Why? Can it not wait until I have completely exhausted my* dioscuri?*"*

"Alario is here."

That prompted a flicker of curiosity. *"Why?"*

"To beget another dioscuri.*"*

Now she was clearly startled. *"Then he means to kill Rhuan before the challenge can ever go forth."*

"That is my thought. Ferize, can you come?"

"I'll come. Brodhi is half asleep anyway, poor boy."

Her presence in his mind faded. Darmuth set a shoulder against the striated tree trunk, crossed his arms, and kept an eye on the hand-reader's wagon. No illumination glowed from the interior, no silhouettes moved against pale canvas. All was dark, and all was still.

Alario had completed the act for which he had come. That much Darmuth could tell from the alteration of the primary's scent. He was a male satiated, replete. Ilona had been bred.

Whether she was fertilized, Darmuth couldn't know any more than primaries or *dioscuri*. She was human; knowledge would come later when her courses continued or stopped. That much he knew of human anatomy.

Alario could be nearly silent as he moved, and he was silent now. Darmuth saw the faint shifting of the wagon, the careful opening of the wagon door so it would not creak. The night was dark, but not black. Banked coals at each wagon lent pale illumination. But Darmuth's eyesight was superior to a human's, and he had no trouble recognizing Alario as he descended wagon steps.

"*Ferize?*"

He sensed her amusement. "*I'm here. I'm up a tree. I'll come down when it's needful.*"

"*And when might that be? When I am nearly unmade?*"

"*He won't unmake either of us, Darmuth. Not for this. Alario has always gone his own way, but in this the other primaries would not forgive him.*"

"*You mean if he unmade us beyond the borders of Alisanos.*"

"*Exactly. And since you and I are tied to our* dioscuri *while they walk among humans, he knows very well he can't unmake us here. It provides a measure of protection.*"

"*I do hope so.*" Darmuth stood up from the tree and intentionally stepped into Alario's way.

BETHID ROUSED. SHE knew Timmon and Alorn had returned earlier because she woke briefly as they came into the tent. But this was a single man whose entrance woke her, and she knew very well who it was.

"Don't forget to blow out the lamp," she said sleepily. "How were the women tonight?"

"I never forget to blow out the lamp, primarily because I am never the last one in."

Bethid snorted. "Tonight doesn't count?"

He ignored that. "As for the women you mention, I have no idea how or who they were. I wasn't with Timmon or Alorn."

Bethid grinned into the darkness. "Oh Brodhi, don't play the innocent with me. I daresay it's the woman I saw you with once before." A yawn captured her jaw. She waved a limp hand. "I don't care, Brodhi. I don't care if she's your mother. I am not one to judge." Nor was she, who preferred women to men in her bed.

Brodhi blew out the lantern and walked unerringly to his pallet. It always annoyed her that he saw so well in the dark, even when there were no lamps, even during Empty Sky when there was no moon at all. But it was Maiden Moon, and Bethid could see, albeit not necessarily clearly.

Bethid heard him slipping off his boots to set them neatly beside his pallet. Like her, he did not bother replacing day wear with night-time apparel. He lay down, turned onto his side, pulled blankets up to his ear.

Bethid's smile was both slow and anticipatory. "So. How was *she*, then? Singular. As you mentioned yourself, it is not like you to come in after Timmon or Alorn."

Brodhi held his silence. It was palpable that he had no intention of answering.

Bethid rested her chin on folded hands, elbows jutting from under the coverlet. "If she's not one of the Sisters, who is she? One of the karavaners? Tent folk? Those are the only two possibilities, after all."

"Bethid—"

"Oh, I forgot . . . you have alternatives. Is she from Alisanos?"

His tone was forbidding. "Shall you tell the entire encampment, then?"

That startled Bethid. She teased him, but hadn't truly considered that the woman *was* from the deepwood. But it made sense. Brodhi and Rhuan were here, and they were from Alisanos. So could the woman be. "I'm not talking that loudly. Besides, Timmon and Alorn passed out the moment they hit their pallets. I suspect it will be the midday meal tomorrow—or, rather, today—before either is fit to do anything more than scowl." She paused, then grinned. "Will you be in better humor, now that you've been with a woman?"

He said nothing.

"Sometimes that's all a man needs, you know. One night with a woman, and the entire world becomes presentable. Or so I've heard."

"Bethid—why are you baiting me?"

"Am I?"

"And don't be disingenuous."

She shrugged, though he couldn't see it. Well, maybe he could, come to that. "I guess I'm just looking for amusement."

"There is nothing amusing about me."

Bethid had to muffle laughter behind one hand. "Well. This is true. Usually."

"Do you wish me to *make* you go to sleep?"

That caught her off-guard. "You can do that?"

Brodhi said nothing.

"Can you do that?"

And then he swore. The language was none she knew, but the tone told her everything. He turned over onto his back; she knew because his voice was clearer. He said a few more words in his private language, but she recognized one of them. It was a name.

She levered herself up on one elbow, turning onto her hip. "What has Rhuan done now?"

Brodhi sounded very much as if he were gritting his teeth. "It's the Sending. Two Sendings, earlier. It's opened a link. Temporary but most uncomfortable while it lasts."

"What kind of link?"

"To him."

"Yes, I understood that. But what does it mean? You can read what's in his mind?"

"Bethid, you may know more about me than any other human—"

"No, Ilona knows more; she's sleeping with Rhuan, remember?"

"—but you don't know everything, and neither does Ilona."

"Do you think—" But Bethid cut off the balance of her question. Brodhi had gone very still; an almost preternatural stillness. She could sense it, feel it. Hair stirred on the back of her neck. "What is it?"

Silence.

"What did this link tell you? This Sending? Is Rhuan in trouble?"

Brodhi rose and bent to tug on his boots. "Usually the only time he ever Sends is when he's in trouble. But what I sense now . . .

there is more. Most decidedly more. It's someone who shouldn't be here."

It startled her. "Someone else?"

"Bethid, go to sleep."

"Do you want company?"

He made no answer. He passed by her pallet, deftly untied the door flap, and slipped out into the night.

Chapter 19

A SCREEN STOOD DIAGONALLY in a corner of the sleeping chamber; a wrought-iron framework filled with crisscrossed lengths of stripped tree branches woven together with copper wire to form a barrier. Audrun inspected the space behind the screen and found what she hoped for: a crock. It was formed of the same fired red clay and soil that permeated the Kiba. She put it to good use, and felt much relief.

Torvic slept again, this time in the cot that had become hers. Audrun resettled the woven coverlet over him. As was her habit, she mentally counted the children. And found that Ellica was missing.

For one fleeting moment, it raised no alarm; her children were sometimes up early and outside organizing chores or playing. And then recollection shot through her, turning body to ice and knotting up her stomach.

Audrun plunged into the larger chamber, telling herself Ellica was probably there. But no Ellica. She ripped aside the door curtain and stepped hastily out into the dawn light, beginning to tremble. She opened her mouth to shout for her daughter, and then saw Ellica sitting on a wooden bench beside the door.

"Oh, *thank the Mother* . . ." Relief was so overwhelming that she nearly dropped to her knees. She felt breathless. "Ellica, what are you doing?"

Her eldest daughter gazed up at her. "Eating."

And indeed, she was. A wide leaf set next to her on the bench contained some kind of puffy flatcake drizzled with honey, and a clay bottle was gripped in her left hand. "Where—" But Audrun broke it off. The sharpness of her initial fright, the dismissal of it in as powerful a relief, drained her of strength. Shakily, she took two steps and sat down on the bench next to her daughter, avoiding the leaf and cake at the last moment.

"He'll bring more," Ellica said.

Audrun blinked. "Who will bring more of what?"

"This," Ellica said through a sticky mouthful. "Omri."

Audrun leaned back against the brick-built front of the cave, settling her breathing. Two suns rose; though not yet hot, she felt the first warmth of the day more keenly than when she was in Sancorra. In the human world. She still trembled, she still felt weak. Her breasts ached, and her arms were empty of infant. But she was done with tears. She had children to care for.

"Where's your tree?" she asked. She had not seen Ellica without it since being reunited with her here in the Kiba.

"It's here." Ellica's gesture indicated the ground beside the bench, though Audrun couldn't see it. "Omri's bringing a pot."

It appeared her daughter had made a fruitful acquaintance with someone in a surpassingly short amount of time. "Omri who, and why is he bringing a pot?"

"Omri's been given to us," Ellica answered matter-of-factly. "And the pot is for my tree. For now. I'll have to plant it in the ground, of course, but not right away. Not—here."

"Given to us? Given? A man? Blessed Mother, Ellica, no one can give a person!"

Ellica shrugged. "That's what he said."

"Omri said?"

"That he'd been given to us."

Something to eat. And now a pot for a tree. "I'll talk to him," Audrun said on a sigh. And then she saw, climbing the pathway to them, the man with cropped hair who had escorted them to the dwelling. "That's Omri?"

Ellica nodded.

Indeed, he had a pot. When he reached them he carefully set the container down, then reached inside and removed a tray of leaf packets that smelled of cake and honey. And clay bottles like the one Ellica had. The bottles were capped by something; nothing had spilled.

Ellica rose, licking honey off fingers. "I'm going," she said. She lifted the sapling and very carefully placed the root ball inside the pot. "I have to find the ideal soil for it." Holding the pot against her chest, Ellica strode off.

Audrun stared after her a moment. Then she turned her attention to the man. "Omri," she began, "my daughter says you told her you've been *given* to us."

He nodded.

"We don't do that," she said. "We don't give people to other people."

"In the human world?" he asked.

"Yes, in the human world!"

Omri nodded understanding. "But we're not there. And everything . . . everything you know, have been taught to know, and have always known, does not exist here." He set on the bench beside her a stack of leaf-wrapped cakes, placed into her hands a bottle of liquid that smelled like berries, and squatted before her. "This is Alisanos."

"I know that!" she snapped. "So everyone keeps informing me. But it does not mean I and my children should simply dismiss everything we know from our world. We *are* human, Omri. We do have courtesies, and habits, and beliefs, and convictions. No matter where we are."

His expression was grave. "I do know that. I have been in your world."

That stopped her burst of anger and desperation. "You have?"

"I have. We take a journey when we are *dioscuri*—"

She waved a hand. "Yes, I know about that. Rhuan explained it. So you should very well know what our world is like, should you not, since you were there for five years?"

He nodded. "I do."

"Well then—"

But he cut her off. "It is less rigorous in your world, less danger-ous. Oh, you die from any number of causes, even killings by fellow humans. But here, it is different. Far more deadly. There, we resur-rect. Here, we do not."

Audrun studied the softened angles of his face, the faded look of his skin compared to Rhuan's. And he did not meet her eyes for long, but lowered his lids in what she could only describe as submission.

She gentled her tone. "You failed to kill your sire."

Omri nodded.

"And so . . ." There was no way she could describe the details. "And so you were—punished."

"Yes."

An idea occurred. Audrun stared at him for a long, still moment, saw color come into his face, and immediately looked away. She had been rude. But the idea . . . *the idea had occurred,* and it took prece-dence over everything. A cold prickle ran down her spine. If. *If.* Oh, very much an "if."

She drew in a very deep, very careful breath, held it a moment, then released it on a rush as she met his eyes again. "Why not return to our world?"

And the idea: *Take us with you.*

He met her eyes. "It's not possible."

The idea gripped her so tightly she thought he must surely read in her eyes what she truly wanted. "There, no one would know who you are, or were, or what you are—or what was done to you. You would be a man like any other."

And then what she could not speak, dared not, and her chest was so tight. *Please, say you'll go . . . say you'll take us with you.*

"I am not a male," Omri said. "I am a neuter. I am a failed *dioscuri.* I didn't die in challenge of my sire but neither did I kill him."

Once, she would have considered what she wanted entirely self-ish. But not now. Not in the deepwood.

She opened her mouth to attempt persuasion again, but he cut her off.

"Neuters *serve*. We weave, we plant crops and harvest them, we form and fire clay, we mortar small stones together, we carve designs in our walls, we raise children in the creche . . . We do everything here that is beautiful." He lifted his hand, indicating the cliffs, the dwellings, the entire Kiba. "Without us, there would be no beauty here."

"No one would know," Audrun repeated, wishing very hard not to let the desperation show. "No one."

He rose. Submission was no longer evident. "I give you back your words," he said. "We too have courtesies, and habits, and beliefs, and convictions. No matter where *we* are."

Oh, that struck home. Audrun said nothing, made no beginning of an answer, because she could not, and there was none.

Omri named himself a failed *dioscuri*. He served the primaries; he was not one of them. But for all his posture and lowered eyes spoke of submission, even though Karadath referred to him as worthless, Audrun saw in him the same innate sense of *self*. His was simply dimmer than Rhuan's, than Brodhi's. Dimmer than the primaries she had seen.

But dimmer was still a glowing coal.

After a moment, torn between despair that Omri could not help and resentment that he *would* not, Audrun gathered up the tray of leaf-wrapped cakes and carried them in to her children. To three of her children. The fourth was potting her tree. The fifth was— elsewhere.

Ah, but her breasts ached. As much, she thought, as her heart.

THE DEMON DELIBERATELY moved into his way, Alario knew, who stopped short to avoid a collision. For the first brief moment, he was speechless, and then annoyed that he was speechless. Especially in front of Darmuth. "Little demon," he said, "not the best course."

Beneath the moon, there was a hint of gleaming on Darmuth's skin; pale, pale glow outlining a scale pattern. And when he stretched his mouth in what was merely mimicry of a smile, elongated canines glinted white. The green gemstone glowed. "But the only course, I think," Darmuth said, "in view of what you've done. And yes, I know exactly what you've done."

This was sheer folly. "It's none of your concern, Darmuth."

The demon's brows rose. "Of course it's my concern. It may well affect my *dioscuri*, and I must protect him against incursions such as this. You are not to be here, Alario. You are not to interfere."

Alario smiled and made no answer other than the warming of his skin, the downward slide of ruddy membrane over his eyes. No words were needed.

But Darmuth did not hesitate, nor did he back down in submission. "You know this perfectly well, primary. It's been a rule since well before I was made. Possibly even before *you* were. You are not to interfere with a dioscuri's journey."

Alario took a step forward. His chest nearly touched Darmuth's. "In this world, I do whatever I wish."

"You're not supposed to *be* in this world!" Darmuth declared. "Not to confront me, not to harm Rhuan, and most especially not to impregnate a woman! I say again: You are not to interfere."

"My get makes it necessary to sire a *dioscuri* on a human woman."

"You have one of those, primary!"

"I want another. And I shall *make* another." Alario stepped closer yet to Darmuth. The faint flicker of Darmuth's scale pattern faded, overtaken by the powerful dominance of a primary's presence. "My current get is worthless, and you know it. His failure to exhibit the proper behaviors for a *dioscuri* make him weak—"

To Alario's astonishment, Darmuth cut him off. "—and that reflects on you, so you believe. I know that. What do you think a journey is for but to discover if a *dioscuri* is fit to become a primary? It isn't up to you to decide whether he is or not. It's up to him. It's up to the challenge. Up to *all* the primaries."

Anger rose and an inner annoyance that Darmuth could make him angry. "I may make whatever decision I wish, little demon. Such as deciding what is fit to be my get. Rhuan is not."

"He survived," Darmuth insisted coolly, not in the least submissive. "He is your only get left. That's all the customs ask, that a primary have *one dioscuri* to challenge him. And to take his place if the primary is killed."

"He survived because the remaining two killed one another. Rhuan did nothing save watch them die. And he could never defeat me. Never."

"It's doubtful," Darmuth agreed, "in which case you will defeat him, and all the questions of his fitness to ascend shall be answered. But you precipitate matters. Let it play out as it will. Anticipate Rhuan's death, yes, but don't effect it. It's not your place."

Additional heat spilled down through veins and flesh, limned even bone. "My place is as I make it!"

"In Alisanos, yes. Not here. You risk censure, if the others found out."

Alario leaned into Darmuth, chests pressing against one another. "And do you intend to carry word, little demon? You have leave to come and go so you may tell tales about how Rhuan fares on his journey." Alario smiled. "How would you do that thing, were I to unmake you?"

He saw the faintest flicker of startled withdrawal in the demon's eyes. Darmuth, speaking of Rhuan, was confident, protective. He could be nothing else. But now it was his own existence threatened.

"I should give you a taste," Alario murmured, and fixed upon Darmuth's eyes, his own in unwavering dominance. "Do you feel it?"

Darmuth's lips drew back as breath hissed between his teeth. His head tipped back, baring his throat; tendons stood out like rope. Slits appeared in the flesh of his face, but what he bled was not blood at all. It was light.

"I could flay you," Alario said carelessly, "and leave you alive to live without flesh. Would the humans accept you then? I quite doubt it."

Darmuth cried out. He flattened palms against his face, attempting to stop the flow of light. But then identical slits appeared in his hands, and light welled forth. Alario need only extinguish that light, let it bleed the body dry, so that the flesh fell off the demon, the viscera crumbled, and the bones were blown away as a fleeting shroud of dust.

"*Stop it!*"

That wasn't Darmuth. Alario looked up into the branches.

"And will you unmake me as well?" Ferize dropped out of the tree and landed lightly, abreast of Darmuth. The scale pattern was upon her, and her pupils were vertical slits. "Because unless you intend to unmake Darmuth *and* me, *and* to kill Rhuan, the primaries will at some point discover the truth. As Darmuth said, they will censure you." He saw her feral, malicious smile, elongated teeth glinting in the darkness. "Do you believe they would not? How many challenges do you think you could withstand before one of your opponents was the victor?"

And yet another new voice came out of the darkness. "If you like, I will send Ferize to the Kiba now. And then we shall know."

Alario was shocked as Brodhi stepped free of shadows, and then angry that the distraction of troublesome demons had kept him from sensing Karadath's get. He should have sensed Brodhi. That he had not would be remarked as a weakness in the Kiba. But, for now, he was *here*, and no one would know.

"She will carry word," Brodhi continued without inflection, "just as she is supposed to. And if you attempt to unmake Ferize and Darmuth, you will be challenged by Rhuan and I simultaneously. Can you defeat both of us acting in concert?"

Alario's third eyelid slid down, and a faint copper sheen rose up on his flesh again. Though this was not a formal challenge to the death, Brodhi *did* challenge him with provocative words and tone.

Alario laughed as Darmuth fell to his knees. Then he halted the bleeding light, closed and sealed the slits, and made him whole again. His amusement had palled, and now he addressed Brodhi.

"That is not how it should be. Not both of you. Single combat, by get and sire," he said.

"In the Kiba, yes. But we're not there. We're here. And if you intend to do as you please, regardless of the customs, then we shall as well."

He let contempt show. And certainty. "I would kill you both."

"Perhaps so." Brodhi paused, letting the moment build. "But then Karadath would challenge you in my name . . . would you survive that?"

Alario's flesh began to glow. "Karadath would do no such thing! In fact, Karadath has elected to make another *dioscuri*."

Brodhi could not hide his shock. The membrane dropped. His skin warmed, casting a faint ruddy sheen. His posture altered. He was so stiff now that Alario smiled. "Send Ferize. She will return with confirmation. Should it come to that, she may even return with Karadath himself."

Brodhi matched him stare for stare. And then Karadath's *dioscuri*, bitter, looked away.

"You see?" Alario said. "Do you see?"

Brodhi's tone thinned. "Ferize. If Alario kills Karadath's get, or even his own, you should immediately return to the Kiba to tell what has happened."

He looked again into Alario's eyes. This time, Brodhi did not lower his own.

Chapter 20

*B*RODHI KNEW IT was essential to stand his ground, to recover what he could of his pride; to banish also the shock of Alario's announcement and end his laughter. But now was not the time to consider whether the announcement was true; instead, he focused solely on the hand-reader, on what Alario intended for her. For Brodhi, play in the game had suddenly gone much deeper. He had to craft his words carefully, control his attitude, and shut down any avenue Alario might take—*would* take—to undercut him.

"She'll die," Brodhi said. "Your seed will kill her when labor is upon her."

Alario shrugged. "Does it matter? I want the child. Not her."

"The child is at risk as well. If the woman dies too early in labor—"

Alario detested Karadath's get almost as much as he hated Karadath. He let it show. "If she begins to die before the child is born, I will open her belly and take it."

"And if I summoned her here now, to hear this?" Brodhi gestured toward Ilona's wagon some distance away. "Human women have methods of ridding themselves of troublesome pregnancies. And she's a hand-reader . . . very likely she could see what was to come of her if one path is followed, or another."

"Then I will come again and again," Alario said, clearly amused.

"How many times could she rid herself of my seed before the very act of ridding cost her her life? Because it would. You know this."

Brodhi *did* know that. It was a choice between dying sooner, or dying later. But dying, certainly. And she would not resurrect.

He drew a breath. "If you took her to Alisanos now in order to remove her from the human world, it would be too perilous for her. She could well die before giving birth. Or the change might come upon her and render your seed entirely useless. Or twist it into something that could never be a *dioscuri*."

Alario scoffed. "My seed? Never."

"Then take her." Brodhi was delicately casual. "Take her to Alisanos and see what might happen. *My* human mother was taken to the Kiba. Oh, yes, she died—how could a human woman not die giving birth to a *dioscuri*? But that death came after I was born. If taken to Alisanos early, there is no certainty that the hand-reader wouldn't die before giving birth. Or before the child had the strength to survive."

Arms folded against his chest, Alario examined him. Brodhi saw it, knew it, hated it. While true that he could challenge Alario and be within his rights, those rights were his only after successful completion of the journey. If he and Rhuan should attack Alario in tandem, they might well defeat him. But that was not considered part of a successful journey. And Ferize and Darmuth were required to report the truth to the primaries. On pain of being unmade, they must be accurate and honest, detailed and precise.

"She may remain," Alario said abruptly. "Twice nine. But then I will come for her."

Brodhi had no stake in whether Ilona survived childbirth. Human females died often enough in labor, or after the child was born. In Alisanos, it was a certainty. In no way would it affect his life if Ilona were to die. But he had a stake in what might affect his sire, and therefore his own chances of ascending. If the hand-reader were taken to the Kiba, he could no longer watch the progress of her pregnancy. And it was vital that he should do so, so he would know when, and if, Alario's new *dioscuri* would one day be a threat to Karadath.

It was not impossible that here in the human world, in the characteristically violent birth of Alisani get, the halfling might die even as its mother did. But it was necessary that the child be *here*, where no one could save it.

"Eighteen months," Brodhi said, using the human counting method. "You've bred her; there is no more for you to do."

Alario smiled. It was a dangerous smile, and yet also one of agreement. One of certainty that, in due time, none of what was said here would matter. He took two paces away, then swung back. "You need not be concerned, Brodhi. It will be years before Karadath's new *dioscuri* is capable of challenging you."

It was meant to provoke him, to rob him of confidence. Brodhi ignored it. But he saw Alario look first at Darmuth, still kneeling, then at Ferize. Brodhi knew very well what such potent dominance would engender in them. They were but demons. By a primary's presence, they were diminished.

Darmuth struggled to his feet. Ferize set a steadying hand upon his elbow.

Alario bared his teeth in a feral smile. "Be quit of here."

Ferize and Darmuth shared a moment looking at one another, lean faces taut, eyes acknowledging they must do as a primary ordered. Ferize did not even so much as glance at Brodhi, and that concerned him.

Scale patterns bloomed, ran like water over every exposed portion of their bodies. Their faces, though shaped differently, took on eerie semblences of something other than human. Claws extruded from fingertips. The flesh of their backs flowed aside, granting room for wings.

And then they let darkness lift them from the earth. Let darkness take them.

As Brodhi stared after them, he heard Alario's quiet laughter. "One day," he said, "you will have the ordering of demons also. You will be able to make and unmake them. But for now, these two answer to me."

Brodhi watched as his kin-in-kind turned away from the light of the coals, turned away from the moon called Mother, and disappeared into darkness.

THROUGH DARKNESS AND moonlight, Darmuth went directly to Rhuan. As he landed, wings withdrew into his back. Scale pattern faded. Claws became fingernails. He felt the brief pain in his eyes that betokened a change of pupils from slitted to round. Inwardly, he was demon. Outwardly, human.

He caught his breath. Whole again, yes. But losing substance was infinitely weakening, infinitely dangerous. He needed meat. Tonight. Very badly. Very soon. *Now* was best, but "now" insisted he tend his *dioscuri*.

Rhuan, sitting up, appeared not to have noticed the method of his arrival. Bruises had begun to form on his face. Darmuth very nearly winced in sympathy. Rhuan would heal significantly sooner than a human, but in the meantime he would nonetheless be in pain. And others would see all the bruises and swelling and ask what had happened.

It mattered that none of them knew the truth. And mattered that Rhuan did not, also. He would challenge his sire. Well before time, he would challenge, and die in the doing of it. Darmuth dared not let that happen. He himself was too vulnerable.

"Hirelings," Darmuth said matter-of-factly as Rhuan raised his head, "or men who took it on themselves in hopes of finding a bone-dealer at some point. Everyone here still thinks you're Shoia; that remains a believable explanation for you."

Rhuan, muttering various vicious comments about hirelings, bone-dealers, and Kantic diviners, rose to his feet with great care. "That's what I thought." He paused. "Did you kill them?"

Darmuth wove the lie effortlessly. "I killed them and fed them to Alisanos. There are no bodies to be found." Which was perfectly true; there had been no bodies at all. "No questions will be asked."

Rhuan squinted at him, feeling a swollen cheekbone. "Oh, there might be questions. If they have families."

Darmuth shrugged. "No one has come looking for them. I think likely they were men traveling alone and believed they saw an opportunity. They all smelled of spirits; maybe they hatched the idea because of too much drink."

"How many?"

"Three." Darmuth bent, took the crude map and backing board from the ground, flipped oilcloth over it, and handed it to Rhuan.

"Three," Rhuan said in eloquent disgust. "Three humans against a *dioscuri,* and they won."

"But they're dead. For good." Darmuth put a hand on Rhuan's back and pushed. "Go to Ilona. Rest. Or don't rest . . . it matters little to me if you bed her twenty times a night."

Rhuan's response was a breathy blurt of sound as he tucked the map board under an arm. "Why not say thirty?"

"Because you're not a primary yet." Darmuth decided it was worth a tentative test. "Have you recovered any memory of what happened?"

"I don't even know *when* it happened. My brains are scrambled."

Clearly Alario had removed any memory of the meeting between himself and his *dioscuri.* Now came the most delicate falsehood of them all, and the most important. "You left Ilona because you had forgotten the map. The attack happened on your way back to collect it."

"Oh. Well, whatever you say. I don't remember any of it."

Darmuth nodded. "Try not to get yourself killed while I'm in Cardatha."

The canopy of the hand-reader's wagon glowed gently in the light of the Mother's moon. Darmuth slapped Rhuan on the shoulder and left him. But even as he faded away into the shadows of the grove, he felt a faint breath of cold air tickle the back of his neck.

Nine months. Nine months of life left to Ilona, if she were pregnant. And nine months left to—no. Not nine months left. Twice nine. He had been thinking in human terms. Twice nine bought Ilona and Rhuan more time. And more time before Alario came for Ilona.

Darmuth nodded to himself. More time to perhaps devise a plan for escaping Alario.

ILONA AWOKE AS the wagon creaked. Tangled in blankets upon the floor, she worked herself free, but did not rise. "Rhuan?"

"Yes."

A single word, and it kindled pleasure, joy, anticipation. Smiling, she lay back down on one side, planted an elbow, and propped her head up. Through a yawn, she asked, "Where did you go?"

He ducked in, bumped his head on the unlighted lantern, swore, pulled the door shut behind him, and promptly tripped over a fold of blanket. He caught himself even as Ilona lunged out of the way in case he fell. "I left the map out with my markers."

She heard him set the board and map out of the way and also heard a few well chosen words she hoped he would never speak in the presence of children. "Here Rhuan, light the lantern before you fall flat on your face. There is flint and steel, just by it, tucked in that leather pouch hanging from the doorjamb."

She felt the wagon rock gently as he moved, heard the rattle as he took the lantern down from its hook, heard also, and smelled, the scrape and spark of steel against flint, the astringency of the resulting bloom of flame, and then the wick was lighted. He cupped his hand around the vents for a moment, then lifted the lantern to hang it once again.

Ilona sat up abruptly. "Sweet Mother, Rhuan, what happened?" The lantern and its light were behind him, but all of the wagon interior was now illuminated to some extent, and she could see the blood and swollen flesh perfectly well. "You *did* fall flat on your face!"

"Not without help." He slowly lowered himself to his knees.

"You look terrible! What happened?" She moved closer and indicated he should sit down on the cot mattress and blanket-padded floorboards. He did so with teeth clenched, moving gingerly. When he at last was seated, leaning against a leather-wrapped trunk, she knelt before him, then gently cradled his jaw with both hands, searching his eyes. She saw pain there and a faint trace of shame. Even embarrassment. "Oh, your poor nose." She didn't dare touch it. "Is it broken?"

"Yes."

"You are going to be so bruised come morning!"

"Yes."

"Here . . . I'm going to wash your face. Your nose bled quite a bit, and I see you have a split lip as well." She took up the modest jug of water she kept beside her cot for middle of the night thirst, found a soft cloth, wetted it and turned back to Rhuan. She scrunched up her face in sympathy. "Let me do this . . . I'll be gentle."

He sucked in a sharp breath as she lightly pressed the wet cloth between nose and mouth. "You said you'd be gentle!"

"That *is* gentle. Hold still—Rhuan, let me do this. Stop pushing my hand away." And as he scowled, she added, "You're worse than a child." She was as gentle as she could be to remove blood that was nearly congealed. His nose was definitely swollen out of shape, as was one side of his face. No cause for a smile and dimples, but she did wonder briefly if the swelling would fill in the dimple. "The bruises are coming up already." She refolded the cloth for a fresh side and applied it once again to his face. "But if you don't tell me what happened, I may give you another one."

"Ow," he said. "Ilona—that *hurts*."

She eyed him critically. "Did you get into a fight at Mikal's?" If so, it might be difficult to find any measure of sympathy for him after all.

"No."

"You've done it before. I think I've lost count—or would have, had I been counting."

His tone was aggrieved. "But not this time! I wasn't even *at* Mikal's." He pushed away her hand. "Let it be, Ilona. The rest can wait until morning."

She shook her head. "You'll be worse in the morning, and this will hurt more. You can't go around with blood all over your face."

He smiled wryly then looked pained as he pressed fingers against his split lip. "I heal quickly. It's an advantage."

She stared at his mouth. "Are you missing a *tooth*?"

Now he looked guilty. "Yes."

"And will that heal by morning?"

Rhuan felt carefully at his nose. "Possibly not by morning. It may take a couple of days. But the worst of the bruising should be fading by dawn."

"Hmph," she said, considering him closely. "I don't smell any spirits on you."

"I said I was not at Mikal's. I wasn't at Jorda's supply wagon. I have been nowhere that I could drink spirits!" He paused. "Though possibly under these circumstances a mug would be medicinally helpful if applied to my insides."

Now she believed him. Rhuan teased, Rhuan exaggerated, Rhuan told tales as it suited him, but this time he was truthful. She heard it in his voice. "Then how in the world did this come to be?" She gestured. "All this damage?"

He adjusted his position against the trunk, then closed his eyes. Lantern light tinted his copper-hued flesh ochre. It set unbound hair aglow. "Darmuth says it was men after my bones."

That shocked her. "But there is no Kantic diviner here. I'm the only diviner, and bones are not my responsibility, thank the Mother. Why would anyone want your bones when they can't be sold or used?"

Rhuan was quiet a moment. "Bones are not perishable."

"Of course they're perishable. That's why the Kantic diviners want them. They break them up and burn them, don't they?"

"Bones are not perishable in the *usual* way," he emphasized. "They'd dump me on the anthills, and when all the flesh, organs, and tissue were eaten away, the bones would be perfectly clean. And easily packed up and carried away."

"Oh." He was so matter-of-fact about it. "But did they kill you? And how many deaths would this be?"

"No. At least, they never got the chance. Darmuth arrived."

Ilona sighed. "I suspect those men are now dead instead of you."

"Well—yes." He paused. "Wouldn't you prefer it that way?"

"I prefer it hadn't happened at all. But as it did . . . here—lie down. Just lie down. You may hurt too much to sleep, but at least you'll rest. Lie down, Rhuan."

Eventually, he eased himself down upon the bedding. "Ow."

"Here's a pillow for behind your head." She lifted his head even as he complained and settled it gently against the grass- and herb-stuffed pillow. "I'll brew willow bark tea in the morning."

He made an inarticulate sound of distaste. "Bitter."

"Bitter makes you better." She smiled as he looked at her, surprised. "It's what we tell the children when they have to drink it."

Rhuan grunted. She had the feeling he would not make a good patient. In fact, she had the feeling he would be a most difficult patient. It would be a very good thing indeed, if he healed quickly.

"If Darmuth stopped the attempt on you, then I assume he disposed of the bodies? Or are we to discover them tomorrow on a morning stroll?"

He gripped his brow with the palm of a hand. "He said he fed them to Alisanos."

A chill ran through her. "That's . . . Rhuan, that's horrible!"

"They were dead!"

"It's still horrible." Ilona put away the capped water jug and spread the damp, bloodied cloth out to dry atop the bed platform they were not using, its stuffed mattress and coverlets upon the floorboards. "Will they . . . ?" A perverse curiosity would not let the subject drop. "Won't they be—eaten?"

"You don't bury or burn anyone in Alisanos," Rhuan explained from behind his hand. "Demons crave meat. Of course they'll be eaten."

She stared at him, stricken. "*Human*—meat?

"Any kind of meat. Mine, for that matter. They are not discriminating. They just . . . feed."

Ilona lay down next to him, careful not to jab him or jar his head. "That's disgusting."

"Please, 'Lona, don't speak so loudly."

"I'm not speaking loudly . . ." But she lowered her voice anyway. "Couldn't Darmuth have just left them where they were?"

"So they'd be discovered on someone's morning stroll?"

Her mouth twitched in a tacit acknowledgment. "We could have given them rites and buried them decently. But to be *eaten* . . . It sat ill on her stomach. "What was Darmuth thinking?"

A breath of laughter escaped him, then he winced. Carefully. "Darmuth is a demon. What do you expect?"

Ilona sat upright abruptly, ignoring his blurt of pain. "You're not telling me Darmuth eats humans!"

"No, Ilona. Darmuth doesn't eat humans."

"Ever?"

"Ever."

She eyed him in suspicion, brows tightly furrowed. "How can you be certain? When he rides ahead to scout alone or hunt, how do you know he's not looking for human meat?"

"Because before he joined the karavan I made him promise he wouldn't eat any humans."

She was horrified. "Oh *Mother*, Rhuan . . . what if he ever breaks that promise?"

He lifted his arms and gently pressed the heels of both hands against his brow. "Can we talk about something else? Something that may not involve speaking?"

She was aggrieved. "What else can we talk about, in view of Darmuth promising not to eat any humans? Don't you believe it's a topic that might be of some concern to all the humans here in the settlement?"

"I think," Rhuan began, "that we might discuss collecting canvas and wooden buckets tomorrow, and asking people to fill them with stones suitably sized to erecting cairn markers." He lowered his hands. "Including you, if you would be so kind."

Ilona lay back down. "Of course. Children can help, too. It would be good for them. I think—" But she broke off abruptly as a shiver ran through the earth. Pots throughout the grove clanked against one another, dogs barked in alarm, voices rose in fright as people were awakened. Ilona grabbed a chest to steady herself as a long, rolling motion rode the tail of the first. At Janqeril's picket-line, horses screamed.

"That," Rhuan muttered from behind gritted teeth, "is of no help whatsoever in making my headache go away."

"Blessed Mother, Rhuan! There are matters of greater concern than your headache."

"Not to me." He reached out, caught one of her hands, threaded his fingers into hers. "It's gone now, 'Lona. The shaking. The rumbling. It won't repeat tonight. Possibly tomorrow, but not tonight."

"It *is* tomorrow, Rhuan."

He tugged. "Lie back down. No, closer. Let us both simply lie here quietly and await the dawn." He paused, yawning. "No matter how near it is."

Ilona lay down. Rhuan, clasping her hand with interlaced fingers, settled it against his chest. The quiet affection was pleasing. She warmed to it, moved closer yet. Felt the quiver deep inside. "Rhuan?"

"What?"

"Is your headache so bad that you would rather sleep?"

His voice sounded blurry. "What is the other option?"

"Something that has nothing to do with sleep." She freed her hand from his, slipped it between leggings and his belt buckle. "You just stay as you are. I will do the work." She smiled, feeling the upwelling of joy and wonder that this man was hers. *Oh, indeed, I'll do the work.*

"Ilona?"

She very nearly purred it. "Yes?"

"My head truly does ache."

"I would expect it to. But I'll make you forget about it."

He sounded unconvinced. "Can you be gentle? Very, very gentle?"

Her answer was to unbuckle his belt.

Gently.

Chapter 21

*A*UDRUN, LIKE HER children, sat crosswise on the cot so she could lean against the chamber wall. In silence, she watched her children eat honey-drenched cakes and drink juice. Megritte barely ate or drank anything at all, and when Audrun tried to encourage her, Meggie turned her head away as if putting up a wall between them. She refused to meet Audrun's eyes, refused to answer questions, refused to offer any indication that she would communicate. She was entirely passive, except when it came to Audrun's speaking to her.

Audrun was weak, exhausted, in pain; her breasts ached, and her daughter's actions drove her to tears. She did not sob, but silent tears broke over the lower rim of her eyes and ran down her face. Part of her wished badly to tuck Meggie into her arms, to reestablish the bond between mother and daughter, particularly so young a daughter. But Meggie had made it clear she wanted neither physical contact with her mother nor to meet her mother's eyes.

Time. It will take time. That's all. Just a little time. But what she told herself was not comforting. It was desperation.

Audrun wiped tears away, uncaring that she likely smeared grime all over her face. But the same was present on her children's faces. All of them were filthy, sunburned, scraped, scratched, and bruised. She would ask Omri where they might bathe. Gillan's beard was coming in, but in the golden stubble she saw black marks, a dispersed array of small black holes. After a moment she realized what they were: small, roundish burns. As if sparks had alighted on his jaw and burrowed into his skin.

As she looked at his face, thinned and taut with pain, she saw little resemblence to Davyn. Gillan's growth had come upon him of a sudden, and his body was making its own provisions for what it would be in adulthood. But his face was so stark, so rigid, that he looked like a stranger.

Audrun spoke quietly. "Perhaps Omri will bring us salve for your leg."

The desolation of Gillan's eyes met her own. "I want nothing from him. I want nothing from anyone here."

She saw, then, that he had laid aside his leaf-wrapped bread. "Gillan, you must eat. It will hinder the healing if you don't."

The sound that came from him rode a rush of breath, and in the undertone of his question she heard a trace of desperation. "Heal so that as time goes on my skin becomes hide?"

She had seen his bared leg, had seen the mottled, scaly island of hide as opposed to flesh, the reddened margins and rough edges. No one would mistake it for anything other than what it was: hide surrendered by a demon to provide a measure of wholeness to the leg. Audrun had once seen a man with terrible burns. Though he escaped the conflagration that had taken his home, he did not escape injury. The skin had dripped from his body as if peeled away, the muscles and veins burned to bone. He had not lived but a number of hours.

She could do nothing but assume that Gillan's leg had been burned as badly. It was lacking the firm curves of a muscled calf, appeared somewhat shrunken, as if much of the original leg was missing. The leg, she knew, would never be normal. But it was a leg he could walk on, and he would live to do so because of what Darmuth had done. What a demon had done in the belly of Alisanos.

Audrun said, "I need you, Gillan. We all of us must heal. We all must learn how to survive here until the road is built. If you starve yourself to death—"

Gillan interrupted in a choked but angry voice. "I didn't ask for this! I didn't ask him to do this to me! I had no choice, no say . . . and he has made me a monster." He bent, yanked a torn pant leg aside and bared his lower leg. "See that. See that! I'm not wholly human anymore, and he did it to me. On purpose!"

There was no way, now, to ask Darmuth his intent when he had bandaged Gillan's leg with some of his own flesh. Audrun believed it had been a choice between life or death, and Darmuth chose a course that would keep her eldest alive. That was a gift no one should look on with hatred.

But then, her flesh bore no resemblence to Gillan's leg. She could not truly put herself in his place. How would she feel if it were her leg patched together with the hide of a demon?

There was no answer for her. But what Audrun did acknowledge was her dedication to getting her children through the nightmare that was the deepwood and its denizens. She would do and say exactly what was needful, things she had said to them many times as she and Davyn raised them. Whatever it took for her to make them see the need for what she asked of them, she would do. The Mother had gifted them with life. It was up to them to honor her for it by living worthy, upright lives.

"Salve," Audrun repeated firmly. "And if you mean to die, you had best plan on a long battle. Because I simply will not allow it."

RHUAN AWOKE IN pieces. All of his parts appeared to be disparate. Pain here was worse than pain elsewhere—or rather, there than here. But by far what hurt the most was his nose and face. He explored each with care, pressing lightly in various places to see if the pain worsened. In all cases, yes. He had not believed a human, or even two, could bring him to such a precipice, but there was nothing for it other than to accept Darmuth's statement that three humans had defeated him.

Ilona was absent. And while she had been as gentle as was possible a number of hours before, lovemaking had nonetheless been painful. And he missed the deep kisses, denied because of the split lip and soreness in the socket where a tooth had formerly resided.

Dawn had come, had gone. Rhuan could tell by the amount of sunlight working its way through the canvas canopy. Nothing was hidden by day; he could see perfectly well. And hear also . . . Ilona, outside, very likely brewing tea, baking panbread in the skillet. He could smell both. And eggs.

Rhuan eased himself into a seated position. It hurt to do so, but he could not lie about in Ilona's wagon while others worked. He had tasks, and Jorda expected him to fulfill those tasks. Rhuan fully intended to continue marking the boundary between Alisanos and the human world. There were persons to gather, karavaners and tentfolk with canvas and wooden buckets meant now for carrying rocks. It was not only a prudent task, but something that should take their minds off the circumstances. Chores were understood. Chores were what everyone executed. The familar, he believed, would calm fears and erase a measure of worry.

He tongued the hole where his tooth had been. It was sore, as one might expect, but the more extravagant pain one would feel, were one human, was absent. His teeth had always grown back after someone separated root from gum.

He had been divested of clothing in the midst of night. Now he tugged on leggings and pulled them up over his hips. Thong drawstring was tied, his tunic pulled carefully over his head and pulled as carefully into place so he could avoid pain. Then the belt was buckled on, and with it his knife. The baldric of throwing knives. Now he gathered his boots, tugged one on and then the other, and essayed the difficult distance between a seated position and a body in the process of rising. The headache was much improved, but he was not free of it. He likely wouldn't be for a day or two.

Perhaps he could begin to build cairns very gently, clacking no rocks together. Perhaps he could inveigle the children into singing their songs, arguing their arguments, more quietly. But—not likely.

THERE WAS NEITHER wall nor fence, nor markers of any sort to tell her where safety left off and threat began. But Ellica, nonetheless, stayed reasonably close to the cliffs of the Kiba and did not go too far into the tangle of vegetation that was precursor to hostile forest. When she stopped, she was concealed from the Kiba and its people, left to tend her tree as she desired.

Carefully she set the pot down, then stood quietly and listened. No more than that. She heard a variety of noises, grunts, rattling, shrill cries, the swish of bodies through brush—so many she could not count. She recognized none, but was not led to believe that she or her tree was in imminent danger, be it from above or below.

Ellica lifted the sapling from the pot and put it gently aside, then began, on hands and knees, to scrape away leaf mold, creepers, any number of nameless plants until she reached actual soil. That, she began gathering up in both hands, along with scraps of aged leaves. Handful after handful she dropped into the pot and eventually felt it was ready for the sapling. Carefully she lifted it, keeping the rootball as whole as possible and, as carefully, set it into the hollow she had made in the pot's mounded dirt. She scooped earth around the rootball and pressed the soil around it. She began again to scrape up soil, and finished filling the pot.

Dirt was crusted beneath her fingernails. Thready lines and creases in her flesh were filled with soil. Her hands were cold from digging beneath the canopy of the close-grown trees. Skirt and tunic were snagged, laddered, torn, full of rents. She remembered watching her mother weaving the fabric, working the loom's treadle, passing the shuttle back and forth. Once, the cloth Audrun wove for this dress had been a pale, creamy yellow. But walking miles along a dusty road had imbued the fabric with a shroud of dirt, and kneeling on damp ground at streamlets to drink had formed two large stain blotches in the folds of the skirt. Snarls ruined the careful weave of her braids. Ellica knew she was filthy, but the acknowledgment did nothing to suggest she ask Omri where she might safely bathe. What mattered now was that the sapling came first. Before her, before her brothers and sister, before her mother. The tree took precedence.

Ellica closed a gentle hand around the central stem that would, when properly groomed and fed, form a trunk. She felt the life in it, the pulse of its blood. The tree contemplated whether to trust or not. Ellica cupped palms very carefully around each small leaf and kissed it.

"Be well," she told it. "Be well and grow strong."

The tree did not answer. Ellica rose, set the pot against one hip, and began the walk back to the Kiba. She would keep the tree beside her cot when she slept at night, and at the first light of dawn she would place it outside in the suns.

Ellica smiled. Watered, fed, groomed, the tree would thrive. And one day she would lift it from the pot, and she would set the roots deeply into soil, then cover and pat down the dirt. And then the sapling would grow up and up, would sprout its own canopy. But for now, it was an infant, requiring a mother's care.

Ellica began to sing a lullaby to the tree.

Chapter 22

DAVYN HAD SLEPT, but the rest he craved escaped him. Twice he had scrambled hastily out of the wagon in order to be very sick. After the two trips, he brought a bucket in with him.

He woke at dawn as always, turned over onto his back and stared up at the Mother Rib, at the charms dangling from it. Each morning he and Audrun, wakening on the floorboards, asked the Mother's blessing. He did so now, but was aware of a painful emptiness. He was a husband and father lacking wife and children, and each morning he rediscovered that truth, felt again the helplessness of being able to do nothing. The road, Rhuan said, would lead him to his family, but how long before the road existed? Months? Years?

With a growl of annoyance that he should once again give himself over to doubts, worries, and fears, Davyn sat up. He paused, afraid to move, as the canopy slowly revolved. But his belly settled itself this time, perhaps because nothing was left in it.

Moving more slowly now, Davyn took down fresh clothes where he had laid them out on one of the sleeping platforms and put them on. Before going to Mikal's tent to drink himself senseless, he had readied himself for the journey to Cardatha, packing a change of clothing, smallclothes, the comb and tin mirror he and Audrun shared, a straight razor, lump of tallow-colored soap, blankets for bedding. He had rolled all into lengths of oilcloth and tied the thongs.

Rain clothing was to hand as well as a packet of dried fruit, dried and salted meat, a chunk of hard cheese, panbread he'd cooked the evening before, and a small cloth bag of tea leaves. Lastly, he tucked inside one stocking the modest number of coin rings remaining to the family, saving two for a deep pocket in his tunic. Though Jorda said the supplies brought back would be shared out equally, Davyn thought it was possible he might find something more, something for Audrun. The coin rings had been intended to see them to Atalanda, but why should he save them now? Atalanda lay farther away than ever.

Davyn rose, slightly bent so as not to bump his head on the canopy ribs, pulled on his boots, gathered up his bedroll, packet, and rain clothes, and climbed out of the wagon into morning. Others, too, were awake. Wives prepared firstmeal; he could smell bacon and panbread, a hint of garlic and wild onions.

All smelled terrible to a man who had imbibed far too many servings of spirits the night before. All threatened the fragile stability of his belly.

Mother, what a fool he had been to drink so much! And powerful spirits at that; when he did drink, though rarely, he had been a man for ale. But it had been so easy to buy a little peace, find relief from the pain of emptiness. The spirits had numbed him.

He wished he was numb now but without a chancy belly, the weight of his aching head, the grittiness of his eyes. Oh, he longed for a mug of Audrun's willow bark tea, for all that it was bitter.

Davyn put up the steps with one agile foot, managing with the ease of long practice; he could not bear thinking about the consequences of bending over to fold them up by hand. Bundling everything under one arm, he squinted briefly across the grove, making note of where wagons were parked and children played. Then he walked a distance away and relieved himself. The pungent odor of spirits rising from urine nearly made him gag. But then his ears were assaulted by a reverberating clangor that rang throughout the grove.

Jorda's Summoner? It must be. What else could make such noise?

So, they were wanted. He knew it would be men who answered the call, those selected by Jorda and Mikal to carry messages to the rest, while women continued to work at the cookfires. Davyn tugged his clothing into something approaching presentability and began the journey out of the grove to Mikal's ale-tent. It took longer than expected, but he supposed that had something to do with the condition of his head and how it affected his balance. He was required to concentrate on where he stepped. Or even *that* he stepped, planting each boot with care. Thank the Mother, the Summoner finally stilled. It allowed him to think of something other than an aching head and delicate belly.

Cardatha-bound, he was. To a *city*. He had heard of but never seen a city. Had never seen stone dwellings. He knew wood planks, mud chinking mixed with grass and straw, split logs, and sod. He could not imagine how people lived within stone squares.

Caught up in his own thoughts, Davyn did not notice another man was approaching him. Nor did the other man notice Davyn. They very nearly ran into one another but stopped abruptly just short of collision. Each opened his mouth to excuse himself, and each lost track of that when he saw the other's face.

"What happened to you?" Davyn blurted.

Rhuan's brows rose. "What happened to *you*? Your eyes are all bloodshot—ah." He smiled lopsidedly, then winced and pressed a fingertip against his bottom lip. "You were in Mikal's tent long after I was. You carry the odor of spirits, my friend, and also . . ." Belatedly, he let the blunt observation die away. "Well. You probably know what else you smell of. That's often the result of too much drink."

Davyn made note of the blackened eyes, the swollen nose, the bruises all over Rhuan's face, a split and swollen lip. "And what is your excuse?"

Rhuan hitched one shoulder in a casual shrug. "Apparently three men decided they wanted my bones."

Davyn nearly recoiled in shock. "Why in the Mother's name would anyone want your *bones*?"

Rhuan's brows rose. "I take it a Kantic diviner was not among the fourteen you consulted before beginning this journey."

"It was not."

Rhuan's tone took on a note of instruction. "Well, they break up bones into chips, then burn them. Supposedly they can divine the future that way. And Shoia bones are much in demand because, I'm told, they provide clearer visions."

Davyn blinked. "But you're not Shoia."

"They don't know that. And best no one finds out, because who knows who might want other parts of my body besides bones."

It made no sense. "But you can't die."

Rhuan grimaced. "No, but that doesn't mean I'd like to die only to wake up chopped into bits."

"*Would* you wake up if you were chopped into bits?"

The karavan guide scowled. "I have no idea. It's never been attempted, and I'd just as soon leave it that way, thank you."

"Aren't you ever curious?" Davyn asked. "I mean, curious about how many ways of dying you could experience?"

"No, I'm not curious about how many ways I might die," Rhuan declared, affronted. "Would you be?"

"But I *would* die," Davyn pointed out. "The experiment would fail."

"I'd just as soon not experiment with my body," Rhuan said decisively, "because even if I do resurrect, it hurts to die."

Jorda's Summoner rang out again. Both men winced. "Go on," Rhuan said in a tight voice. "I am going elsewhere as fast as my poor head will allow me."

Gloomily, Davyn said, "And I have to go *to* it."

Rhuan clapped a hand to Davyn's shoulder. "Make the trip to Cardatha a safe one."

As the guide—no, the Alisani-born—strode away, Davyn turned to watch him go. Unbraided, all of the coppery hair hung down in a river to the small of Rhuan's back. Briefly, Davyn wondered why the hair was loose, but then went on toward the ale-tent, where he joined the crowd of men standing outside. Jorda stood before the door flap, as did Mikal.

"Today," Jorda began, green eyes and tone serious, "there are several tasks before us. With your willingness—and we truly have no other choice—some will cut planks from the downed trees and plane them for the boardwalk. Others can gather up any kind of bucket or pot available and begin collecting stones for Rhuan, who is marking the boundaries prior to building cairns. Older children are welcomed as well, providing they obey, and any women who care to join you. We badly need a boardwalk before the worst of the monsoon arrives, or we'll all be wading in muck. More importantly, because of the deepwood, we need to know where we are safe and where we are not. Do as Rhuan tells you."

"Why depend on him?" a voice asked. "He's a karavan guide, by the Mother . . . how do we trust him to know where this border is?"

Jorda did not look pleased to be interrupted. "Step out so I may see you." As a man stepped out from the knot of other men, making himself visible, Jorda continued, nodding. "Ah, you are tent-folk; you would not know, necessarily. Rhuan is one of my guides, yes. He has land-sense. He can sense where the edges of Alisanos are."

The man, frowning, asked, "How can he do that?"

Jorda paused a moment, then went on briskly. "He's Shoia. You've heard of Shoia, yes? Well, it allows him some abilities we don't have, such as land-sense." He caught Davyn's eye and continued, moving smoothly away from the subject. "Today some of us leave for Cardatha to buy supplies. We should be back in five days, unless the rains slow us. In the meantime, questions may be asked of Mikal regarding how to plan, for now, and if you hear the ringing of my Summoner as you did earlier, answer it. You will not hear it except when you are needed, or when you are at risk." Jorda lifted both bars and tapped them in a tattoo of deep, quiet chimes. "This sound is for flying beasts. That draka we saw. If this signal is heard, all who are outside should lie down at once. No talking, no shouting, no crying, but above all, *no movement*. Make this very clear to the children."

He looked over the gathered menfolk as if weighing each of them. "Understand me. There is no predicting if that beast will return, even Rhuan said so. But we must be prepared. And this—" Again he tapped a tattoo quietly, "—means find shelter. Tents, wagons, even beneath trees in the old grove. Anything that may be used as shelter. Make certain your women and children know this." He handed off the Summoner rods to Mikal. "We'll bring staples back from Cardatha. Meanwhile, have your women count up how much and what kind of food is left to us all. When I return, we will assemble all the food—yours, and what we buy—and store it here in Mikal's tent."

"Store it!" another man said in startled disbelief. "Why should we store it here? We have wagons and tents of our own."

This time, Mikal answered. "We must change many habits in order to survive here through the monsoon. We must be fair and equitable, until the season improves and we can plant crops. Meals will be cooked and served here, at my tent. This—" he raised the Summoner rods and tapped out a muted, brief rhythm, "—means meals are ready."

Davyn was unsurprised by the low-voiced grumbling and scowling among the men. He wasn't certain about this system himself.

Jorda raised his voice. "If you wish to leave, you may. We cannot keep you here. But for the sake of your welfare, I ask that you stay, at least through the monsoon. All of the land is altered because of Alisanos. All must be freshly mapped. I am a karavan-master, and *I* don't know what the terrain looks like or where the roads are now. Will you risk Alisanos as you navigate the passageway? Set off across lands you don't know? Face the rains alone? Risk being found by Hecari while alone in the grasslands?" Jorda nodded as no one answered. "As for the meal lines, it's the only way of insuring every person, be it a child, a woman, a man, has enough to eat. We can't afford to serve only ourselves, or only our own families, while others run out of food. Not now. Not with the Hecari on one side and Alisanos on the other."

Davyn nodded. That explanation settled his concerns. And from the expressions on the faces of the others, they understood as well.

Five days, Davyn reflected, thinking again about the journey to Cardatha. Five days when he would have no time to think only of his losses. Five days when he had a job to do, the means to aid tent-folk and karavaners alike. Rhuan had been correct to suggest he accompany Jorda. He saw that now. But oh, the condition of his head and belly would be made worse by today's journey.

"No more spirits," Davyn mumured to himself. "Ale, perhaps, and not often, only now and then—but no more spirits."

AUDRUN WAS AWARE of heat, of chills, of sweat, of a body ignoring anything she might wish it to do. It had come upon her of a sudden, a terrible fatigue that turned her bones to water. She remembered speaking to Gillan, remembered feeling weak, recalled seeking her cot. That she had reached it, she knew, because she lay in it now.

The bodice of her tunic was soaked with breast milk, but it was not enough to relieve her of the ache. She badly needed an infant to nurse from her. It would help, too, with the laxity of her womb. But there was no infant, no newborn who had issued from her body. Nothing to hold. Nothing to love. Nothing to begin life ignorant of Alisanos. The child had been born in Alisanos; Audrun vaguely remembed Rhuan saying that the baby was also *of* Alisanos. And she feared for her. For Sarith. The third daughter she and Davyn had made.

She lay upon her cot and shivered. Heat coursed throughout the interior of her body, but the exterior was cold. Her hands and feet were numb. Her mind, too, felt cold. She could not think clearly. None of her thoughts stayed put, neither new nor old. Everything drained out of her body, out of her head. She was stupid with exhaustion. There was nothing left of her save a shell of a body over which she had no control.

But she had four children to tend.

Four children who, she realized abruptly, were no longer present.

The other room—? Audrun, curled on her side against the chills, slowly worked herself upward onto a braced elbow and squinted into the common chamber. Even her eyes ached.

No Gillan, no Ellica. No Torvic or Megritte. No one at all.

She could not permit herself to stay in bed, no matter how ill she was, while her children were missing.

Mother, I beg you. Blessed Mother, care for my children. Let no harm come to them.

She did not ask for herself. Only for her children.

Tears came too easily.

Chapter 23

*B*ETHID COLLECTED HER mount, Churri, from the picket-line and made sure her bedroll and supply bags were snugged behind the cantle and tied on, along with her blue courier's cloak. She wore rain gear over her clothing, in anticipation of showers, and would don the cloak for added protection if necessary. Her silver courier's brooch, for the time being, was attached to the top of her weather clothing.

She, Timmon, and Alorn inspected tent pegs, sledging them yet again to drive them deeper. They checked the guy-lines for tension as well as fraying and tied the flaps closed. Storm-snapped poles had been replaced. The custom was to leave the common tent clean and ready for the next couriers to come through.

Bethid wasn't sure the tent would remain standing if the deep-wood displayed another temper tantrum. Against Alisanos, all they could do was their best.

She could not deny a fair amount of trepidation about the journey to Cardatha. Couriers knew the roads as well as karavan-masters and often better, as they took other roads in addition to the wagon routes. But this time they were riding without a road to follow and no knowledge of what might await them along the way. Brodhi had found the narrow passageway leading to the settlement on his way back from Cardatha, and she knew his memory was sound; it was one of the traits the Guild required of couriers. Once through, she would know the way as well, but for now they were wholly dependent on Brodhi.

Bethid counted off those who would be on the journey. Herself, Brodhi, Timmon, Alorn, Darmuth, Jorda, and the farmsteader. If the heavens opened and poured, there were enough people to break the wagons free of mud, but only on the journey out; Jorda would lose four of them once they reached Cardatha, leaving only Jorda, the farmsteader, and Darmuth. She did not expect them to linger in Cardatha; Jorda would want them back on the road as soon as possible to evade, if at all possible, bogging down. The rains had only begun yesterday, so perhaps there was, as yet, no danger of the heavy wagons getting stuck in the mud.

She cast a discerning eye at the sky to see if rain appeared imminent. It did not. But the sun had only just risen; plenty of time remained for clouds to build up. For now, all was dry save for a heavy film of dew.

Bethid put foot in stirrup and swung up onto Churri, settling easily into the saddle. The horse bobbed his head as she gathered reins, stamping with front hooves as he blew noisily through his nostrils. He had been picketed for several days, had survived a terrible storm, and was more than ready for a ride.

Bethid leaned forward in the saddle and smoothed a hand down his warm neck. "I know, sweet boy. We're going. I promise you a good ride to soothe the itch. But for now we go to where Jorda told us to meet. Then we'll head out."

She lifted reins and turned Churri in a tight half-circle, then rode him out of the grove. He had snatched at grass as she mounted and now had a large clump, roots still intact and clogged with wet soil, hanging off one side of his bit. Bethid shook her head. "Whatever dignity you may have had is now lost. You just look silly."

Churri was aware of the clump as well. He twisted his lips into a grasping sideways motion and yanked the grass out of his bit rings. A violent shake of the head rid the clump of mud, and then he ate it.

"Awww," Bethid drawled affectionately. "I thought you might

save that for a midday meal." She set him to a long-trot, transferring weight from the saddle through bent, flexing knees and muscled thighs, and cut across the center of the settlement between the bonfire circle and Mikal's tent, where men gathered. Jorda nodded at her as she rode by. She heard something about storing food at Mikal's but was out of range before she could hear any questions or Jorda's answers.

AWAY BY HIMSELF in the old but still surviving grove, Brodhi stopped. A look at his hands confirmed trembling. He felt ill, wishing to vomit. A chill coursed through his body. Finally, he allowed his legs to bend, to deposit him onto his knees. After a suspended moment, he settled back onto his heels.

Karadath intended to make another *dioscuri*? Karadath? Alario, yes, because Rhuan was not suitable. But he? He who had killed all other challengers for the favored position? He was more than suitable!

He heard the sound of leaves rustling overhead. Just as he glanced up, a Hecari warrior, painted and armed, came down through the branches. He landed in front of Brodhi, war club at the ready.

Brodhi sighed. "Ferize."

The warrior asked, in Ferize's light voice, "Will I pass?"

"Not to me."

"I know not to you." She scowled as the warrior guise simultaneously melted away and was replaced by a human form. Today her fine-loomed belted tunic and skirts were a deep purplish red, the color of mulberries. Hair was black, eyes as well. Brodhi had yet to see a guise that did not attract him. Or perhaps it was what lay beneath the clothing. Or maybe nothing more than the tease of sweet musk in her scent. "The question is, will I pass in the warlord's dwelling?" Then she waved the question away. She knelt facing him, knees to knees. She took his hands into hers. She was in human form, but in the back of her eyes he could see the demon, see the depths of a fierce, dangerous loyalty. See the ferocity usually kept restrained.

Ferize locked eyes with his. "You will kill him."

Brodhi shook his head slightly. "You know I can't. I'm not ready. I know it."

"Not your sire," she said with careful clarity. "The one who would supplant you. Kill him in the creche."

It painted a picture before his eyes. But he shook his head again. "He must be old enough for a true challenge. And for all that, he may be a she." Brodhi brightened as relief sparked in his belly. "A daughter. *Diascara* she might be, but she could not withstand me."

"Think," Ferize commanded. "Think, Brodhi. Only rarely does a female challenge a male. One another, yes . . . but almost never males. She would be no impediment to you. You will be back in Alisanos well before she is old enough to challenge anyone."

"But I would have to challenge Karadath."

"Of course! And if you win, the world is yours." Ferize shrugged. "If the offspring should be male and named Karadath's *dioscuri*, well, nothing changes. He would challenge you when he was old enough."

Brodhi's mouth hooked sideways. "And if he won?"

Ferize pronounced a vulgarity. Her hands pressed more tightly on his. "Impossible. It is, and would be. Impossible."

The concerns were serious, but he could not hide a smile. "You are dangerous in your dedication."

She squeezed his hands one last time, released them. "You are the best of all. I chose you."

That stopped the breath in his chest. "You . . . *chose*—?" It was unthinkable.

"Of course." She leaned forward and set a palm on either side of his face. Her eyes sparked. "Did you think we had no say in the matter?"

"Yes," he admitted flatly. "No say in the matter at all. I believed you were *assigned*."

"If I chose badly," she said, "and the primaries could not countenance it, then yes, I would be denied the *dioscuri* I preferred. But I chose well. And it was done." Her smile displayed fangs. "You allowed me to unbraid your hair and then to rebraid it. Even the primaries know when a bond should be left as it is."

Brodhi had never asked of Ferize how she had been made. One day, she just *was*. And she was beautiful in a way no human could understand. She wore the form at need, but never did he see a human in her place. Only a *seeming*. Behind the eyes, behind the smiles, behind the desire, much more lived in her. He had always simply accepted what she was. She was, in a way, a part of him.

"Now," she said, "Darmuth and I shall meet in Cardatha, and we will see what we will see of the Hecari, he and I." She leaned forward, planted a kiss on his brow. "Go to bed, Brodhi."

He smiled. "With you?"

"I think not. I think it best that you sleep with no one in your bed, even if that bed is under a tree." She smiled at him with a world in her eyes. "Good night, Brodhi."

"Ferize!"

But she was gone. He could not even sense her.

Karadath intended to sire another *dioscuri*. Tamped fury replaced desire for Ferize's company.

Male or female, he would kill it.

THE MEN AT Mikal's tent had dispersed, intent on relaying instructions to women and children regarding the Summoner tattoos, food disposition, and other things. Jorda and Davyn, too, were gone, joining those who would accompany them on the journey. It left Mikal alone in front of his tent with metal bars in his hands. He turned and ducked back in, put Jorda's Summoner in a convenient place, and strode to his bar. His morning tasks were always to wipe down the bar planks and the tables, check inventory— Jorda would return with sloshing kegs from Cardatha as well as supplies—wash cups and tankards, check the oil level and wicks in each candle cup or lantern, and make up new platters of bread and cheese.

He was working on the bar planks when a person entered the tent, and before he could say he was not yet serving, the woman walked quietly to him and paused on the other side of his bar. She met his eyes. There was no diffidence in her manner, no hesitation.

He knew her, if not by name. She was one of the Sisters, the one he had seen in his tent before. Tawny hair was drawn back, displaying the hollows and contours of a lovely face. She wore a dull green tunic and skirt he had seen before, and also the wide belt fastened by curved horn and loop. The length of fabric she wore as a shawl was a quiet amber, decorously shielding decolletage. There was nothing about her that bespoke her profession. And, equally, nothing about her that suggested she was a wife.

"I was not invited to your meeting," she said calmly, "undoubtedly because of who, and what, I am." She smiled faintly. "So be it, though you should realize that I can bring you additional custom. Men like to drink with a woman before sleeping with her."

The blunt speech, the dry tone, was not what he expected. Mikal, leaning against the bar on braced arms, drew in a deep breath to speak.

"But that's not why I'm here," she said before he could reply. "I did 'attend' your meeting, in a matter of speaking. I simply stayed behind a corner of the tent and listened. And now I have come to you with a proposition."

This time he spoke before she could continue. "I don't hire Sisters of the Road. You may conduct your business, of course, as you will—you have a wagon—but I won't hire you."

"I think perhaps you will," she demurred, "when you actually *listen* to my proposition instead of wondering what is under my wrap." Her smile took the sting away but left him with a burning face. "A food line has its place, and I think you explained it well enough, but there is something else you should consider. With all lined up here at the same time, three times a day, you will fall dreadfully behind in serving it. And also cooking and baking. Or do you intend to do it all? Yourself?" She pushed a stray tendril of hair out of her eyes. "We can bake, we can cook, we can serve, my Sisters and I. That is what I propose you pay us for."

He shrugged. "I could have tent and karavan women tend those duties."

"They have families and other responsibilities. As for us, we are three. One will bake, one will cook, one will serve."

He contemplated that, eyebrows knitted. "And you would not ply your trade?"

She laughed. "Oh, now and then, I suspect. At night, and in our own wagon. But know that while drunken men may sometimes forget themselves and become boors and beasts, a woman such as I, such as the three of us, would not. You catch more flies with honey." She shrugged. "Fewer men will come to us, you see. We are Sisters *of the Road*, not women who put down roots in the midst of a respectable settlement and set up business. But as cooks, bakers, and servers, I think we may be accepted for more than the obvious thing. The women, the wives, the mothers and sisters, will see us doing the baking, cooking, and serving, and they will perhaps come to realize that we are not after their men. It wouldn't matter what anyone thought if we could go on from here to find a new encampment. But we don't dare do so during monsoon. This would solve a problem for you, and for us."

Mikal considered. It was quite true that when he and Jorda discussed the need for a food line so that all were fed equally and adequately, they had not talked about who would take on all the tasks that Mikal himself did. He could not do those things by himself, with folk lined up and waiting outside his door flap.

"We will move on," she said gently, "when the rains are gone, and it's thought safe to go through that passageway. But while we are here, we could offer aid and lift from your shoulders the need to tend everyone at the same time."

He nodded. "Very well. A copper coin ring per month for the three of you."

"Per week, if it's copper." She paused. "Each. And don't tell me you can't afford it. You very well can. Since no one can leave until the rains are gone, you will have much more custom than usual. Those who might have paid you a ring for, say, two or three nights, are trapped here for weeks. Men will come here to forget the circumstances. They will do it in ale and spirits, and they will do it frequently."

Mikal knew when he was outflanked. "Very well. A copper each, per week."

"Thank you." The woman resettled her wrap around her shoulders, sparking warmth in his face yet again for wondering, just as she said he would. "We shall take inventory, I and my fellow Sisters. We need to know what is available now and what will be added to storage when the supply wagons return." She tilted her head in a brief goodbye, but turned back as she reached the door flap. "My name is Naiya."

Chapter 24

*I*LONA DRESSED, WASHED her face, tamed and coiled hair against her head, anchored it haphazardly with a rune stick, and opened the wagon door. She badly wanted an intimate visit with the river and a bar of soap. Mud-crusted boots yet stood on the second step from the top. She gathered them up, knocked heels against the steps to clear most of the mud, and bent to pull them on over stockings. She did not complete the motion. A woman stood not far from the steps, shawl wrapped so tightly around her torso it resembled swaddling clothes. Lank hair was brown, as were her deep-circled eyes.

Ilona knew exactly what she wanted and how soon she needed it. "Let me put on my boots," she said, "and spread a mat. Then we'll proceed."

The woman nodded. Her chin quivered. She bit her bottom lip so hard, pink blanched white.

Ilona yanked on her boots, climbed down the steps, took up the mat she had rolled and set away for the night, and with a practiced snap of both hands unrolled it. She spread it on the ground, wishing she'd had tea, but she dared not delay the woman longer. She was clearly desperate, clearly in need of immediate aid. Without it, she might well break.

"Now," Ilona said, gesturing, "we are protected against the dew. Please be seated."

The woman, now, was trembling. She made no move to follow Ilona's instruction.

It hurt even to look on her. Ilona took her by thin shoulders and guided her to the mat. "Be seated, please. Trust that I will guide you safely through the reading. What is your name?"

The woman sat down, shivers coursing her body. "Herta," she said shakily. "My name is Herta."

Ilona sat down arranging her skirts. It was a very spare setting, two women upon a grass mat; customarily she set out a table, cushions, runesticks, fetishes, dice, cards, and more to aid the ambiance. She had learned long ago that such things were expected and actually put visitors at ease. But there was no table between her and this woman, no tea offered, no gentle questions about such things as husbands, lovers, hoped-for husbands and lovers, or parents or children. Unlike charlatans—and there were many—she read true, even if the questions raised were much the same as asked of other diviners, the true and the false. This woman, Herta, had not come for tea, for cushions, or for any other accoutrements. They sat knees to knees in front of one another. Herta's hands tightly gripped one another within the folds of her skirt.

Ilona smiled. "May I?"

Herta nodded jerkily. Ilona reached for one of the woman's hands and gently turned it palm up. She saw calluses and a shallow scar running from the base of Herta's middle finger to the heel of her hand.

From long practice, Ilona kept her expression bland but friendly. "May I see your other hand?"

Herta stretched out a trembling left hand. "This one was burned many years ago, when I was a child."

The flesh bore the raised pucker of an old burn scar, filling her left palm. The fingers of that hand were permanently curved because of the tightness of the scarred flesh. It did not resemble a claw, but she lacked the flexibility of a normal hand.

—fire . . . screaming . . . heat . . . screaming . . . a child . . . a father's clothing on fire . . . screaming . . . mother's hair aflame—

It was enough to swallow Ilona. The memory was too strong, far too concentrated for a hand-reader. The woman recalled the experience every day because of the scarred hand. She could do nothing else. The fire had taken mother, father, brother, the cottage. In her memories, nothing was left of the fire *but* fire. She had never grown beyond the tragedy.

Perhaps because she couldn't.

With supreme mental effort, Ilona forced herself to thrust away the the vision of fire, of screaming, of human flesh burning. Her breathing ran hard. She broke her gaze from the burned palm.

"Is it all right?" Herta asked, voice fraying. "Can you read my hand?"

Ilona forced calm upon herself. "I can, yes," she told the woman. "The burned one, no, but the other, despite the scar, I can read. Wounds, even healed wounds, interfere to some degree—I read what made the scars, you see, whether I wish to or no. But the signs of hard work, such as calluses, do nothing but confirm that you have been most attentive to your tasks." Smiling, she released the burned hand without so much as glancing at it. Now she pondered the slice of scar cutting diagonally across Herta's right palm. She sensed the vague memory of an accident. She would have to go beyond that to more recent memories.

"What will you do?" Herta asked shakily.

Ilona met her eyes. "Have you never visited a hand-reader before?"

The woman shook her head. "Before my husband died, we were of the Kantica, though not devout. I did seek a Kantic diviner before we left on this journey—" But she broke off as tears brimmed over and began to run down her face. "My daughter was taken. That beast took her." Her voice was nearly choked into silence. "The flying beast," she said. "It took my child away."

Ilona remembered everything about the incident. The draka had taken a boy and a man but let them fall. It then had taken a young girl and flown away. The woman was heartbroken, as any mother would be. As any woman would be. And so close to complete collapse of mind and body.

"I have no words," Ilona said through a tight throat, meaning it. "I'm so very sorry."

Tears ran freely. "And my husband is dead, and I can have no more children. Not since Gaddi. I was hurt inside." Herta sucked air through her trembling mouth. "She was all I had. All, since my husband died. And now I am alone."

Blessed Mother, let me ease this woman's grief. Tears stung Ilona's eyes, but she blinked them away before they could fall. "Is there a certain thing you wish me to look for?"

Herta nodded. "I wish to know if Gaddi can be brought back. No, no, not alive—" What little was left of the color in her face now washed white. "I know the beast killed her. But her bones. Whatever may be left of her. So she may have proper rites before she crosses the river." Herta swallowed hard. "Can you find that in my hand?"

Again Ilona blinked tears away. "You must understand that my reading may not be clear to you. Some visions lack clarity, some require more time than others. But trust me to do my best. Trust my promise to you. I will find your daughter."

Herta nodded vigorously. She thrust her palm-up hand toward Ilona. "Please. For Gaddi."

MEN GATHERED, AS did a few women and children, where Rhuan stood beside one of the upstanding tree branches he had thrust into the ground. He watched as the group arranged itself according to their alliances: friend with friend, wives with husbands, fathers with children. But the anomaly was evident immediately. Three women stood in a clutch on one side of the men, while two others waited on the far side.

Rhuan's mouth twisted in irony. It didn't require a diviner to understand the marked separation. The larger clutch was of wives. The two others were Sisters.

He waited as all noticed his two black eyes, the swelling, the bruising. He had discovered in very short order that pushing limb after limb in the ground to mark where a cairn should go was painful. It meant he had to bend over, apply a little force, and doing so made his head pound. He knew that within a couple of days he would be healed, but in the meantime everything above his shoulders hurt. Still, the border must be marked clearly enough that a good amount of buffer zone divided safety from nightmare.

Rhuan grimaced. *Unless the deepwood moves again and undoes all our work.* But he had no sense of that, nothing that suggested movement was imminent. Alisanos might not move for another twenty-five years, and by then all would have escaped to Atalanda via the road.

A quick head count told him there were a dozen men, five women, six children. He had hoped for more, but a fair number of men were cutting and planing wooden planks for the boardwalk, while others set out with snares and fishing poles—though they would not go far. Not into the forest they knew as deepwood. They meant to go where Rhuan had told them safety lay. As for absent women, they were likely counting up stores in wagons and tents, as Jorda had suggested.

As asked, those who came had brought buckets both of wood and waxed canvas. All the adults looked curiously at the parade of sticks but said nothing. He had their complete attention, though he suspected it was more because of his injuries than of a wish to hear what he said.

He stood before them, arms folded across his chest. "Thank you," he said, "for coming. There is plenty for us to do, but we need not attempt to complete it all today. I doubt the rains will allow it anyway." He cast a glance at the sky. For now all was bright, but about the only thing anyone could predict in the rainy season was the rain itself. "Each stick marks where a cairn is to be built. Don't yet bother mudding the stones together, even with grass included, as the rain will simply wash it all away. Stack well, be certain the cairns are stable before moving on to the next. I suspect a regular chore will be rebuilding what has fallen, when necessary." He noted a couple of men nodding acknowledgment.

Now he looked to the children. Five boys, one girl, ranging in age, he guessed, from perhaps six to ten. The girl was a redhead; the boys were a mix of dark and fair. "As for you, I expect you to find the very best stones and carry them here. This large." He used cupped fingers to demonstrate the size he wished. "And flat is best. Bring me three to four stones each."

One of the men opened his mouth to say something, but Rhuan was certain he already knew what the man wished to say and overrode him with precision.

"Yes," he said, raising his voice, "it will take somewhat longer for the children, but what better way to become familiar with the terrain?" He looked hard at the man who had intended to speak. "They will know every inch of this ground."

The man, understanding, nodded abashedly. In addition to warnings heard from parents, these children would tell other children, and others, and soon every child in the settlement would know where safety lay, and where it did not.

Still addressing the children, Rhuan continued, "Take the buckets to each stick, each person. Pour out what rocks you have and go back for more. In fact—" he grinned "—we could make it a contest. Each day, whoever builds more cairns by mid-meal shall win a prize. But remember that the grownups can only build with what you bring. And—" he raised a hand to forestall questions from the children "—those who carry buckets will be part of the building team, and thus will share in the winnings."

Rhuan waited until the excited voices ran down into silence. He shed the friendly demeanor, briefly taking on a muted version of a primary's dominance. Even the adults responded, though he did not look at them. What he said to the children would remain in the adults' memories as well.

"Pay me mind," he said. "Oh, do pay me mind. Look there, and there. You see a forest, do you not?" Eyes flicked briefly to the forest but returned to his own almost immediately. The children nodded. "That," Rhuan said with careful clarity, "is Alisanos. We are marking a border between the deepwood and safety, do you see? But you must never, ever go past the cairns. Not when you bring the rocks, not when you dump out the buckets, not even if a grownup lets you place a rock. Do not go beyond the cairns. Ever." And then, as the dominance dissolved, he included what would undoubtly win their obedience: "Anyone who goes beyond the cairns forfeits his, or her, chance at the prize." He smiled into the six very attentive faces. "Promise me. Swear it. Make it a vow to the Mother of Moons."

The tallest boy spoke up. "When do we begin?"

"You have your buckets. Go."

And so they went, running off in six different directions on the hunt for rocks. Rhuan smiled and looked at the adults. Twelve men and three women gathered their buckets and joined the hunt for cairn stones.

Two women did not go. Two women stood waiting.

"Do you want my blessing?" he asked mildly. "I suspect you are able to carry stones, are you not? That is the only qualification I require."

One of the women, he did not know. She was dark-haired, dark-eyed, with a muted swarthiness to her complexion. The other he recognized as a woman who had come to Mikal's tent. A tall, tawny woman who named herself Naiya.

"This is nothing we did not expect," Naiya said. "In fact, it is quite commonplace. But they are not accustomed to being forced to consort with us." She made a belaying gesture. "Well, they won't *consort* with us, even under these circumstances. Not yet. But gathering rocks suitable for cairn markers makes us the same, I believe. Kitri and I will be as dirty-handed as they, with clothing every bit as muddy when we are done. No one will know wife from Sister."

The dark-haired woman, Kitri, drawled, "Except for the wives."

Rhuan grinned. "That is true. As far as I am concerned, you are most welcome."

Naiya touched the other Sister's elbow briefly. "Shall we begin? Rather than force anything, we will hunt rocks in a different direction."

Kitri displayed two buckets, handing one to Naiya.

On the brink of departing, Naiya looked Rhuan up and down appraisingly. "You're with the hand-reader."

He grinned. "I am."

She met his grin—and dimples—with a seductive smile. "Pity."

As they walked away, all Rhuan could do was laugh.

Chapter 25

*I*T WAS THE vision Karadath had given her. Scales instead of flesh, claws instead of nails, fangs instead of teeth. The pupils of her eyes were slitted, not round. Most of her hair was missing; what remained were thin, tangled strands, not enough to cover the gray-mottled skin over her skull. Even her nose had altered, forming serpent-like nostrils. From her mouth ran saliva but also blood.

She had eaten. She had eaten well.

Of Meggie.

Audrun opened her mouth to cry out but could not. The sickness was upon her again. This time hands helped her, hands grasped her shoulders and lifted her from the mattress, eased her onto her side, and held her head as she vomited into a bucket.

But nothing came up. She was empty.

Again she heaved, leaning over the side of the cot. Again, nothing. Her body simply didn't realize there was nothing left to be rid of.

She had eaten. Eaten well.

This time Audrun was not trapped in silence by Karadath. This time she was able to emit a strangled wail, but of no coherency; it was not communication in words, only of sound, of desperation. Eyes open or closed, she saw the vision Karadath had conjured.

A shudder ran through her body. *Mother, blessed Mother, make this vision stop.* She forced her mouth to form a word. "Meggie—"

"Safe. Safe. Whole. In your Mother's name, I swear it."

It was a voice she did not know. The hands, she did not know.

"Meggie—"

"Safe. I promise you. Whole."

It was difficult even to keep her eyes open, though it wasn't sleep she wished for. She had never felt so weak in her life. Her heart pounded so hard she thought it might burst.

"Here," he said. She heard the sound of a cloth being squeezed of water. Still bending over the edge, she allowed him to clean her mouth before aiding her back onto the cot.

"You have been ill for some days. But you will mend."

"Who—?" She peered up at him. But focusing hurt. "Oh. You." She closed her eyes. It was easier. "Where are my children?"

"Safe. Well. Unharmed."

"But *where*?" She enunciated as clearly as was possible, opening her eyes again.

Omri smiled. "Wait." He rose, left her.

Audrun tried to blink away grittiness. Her eyes ached from the pressure of vomiting. Abdominal muscles already sore from childbirth were even more painful now. Everything ached. Everything complained.

Another petition. *Blessed Mother*— But she got no farther. Omri was back. Meggie was in his arms. The others came in behind him.

"You see—" Omri began, but a piercing shriek cut him off.

Audrun's throat was so tight it hurt. "Meggie, *please*—"

Meggie screamed. Meggie tried in all ways to climb out of Omri's arms. When she could not do so, she turned her head away and pressed it into his shoulder, her mewling sounds muted. From beneath tattered tunic and skirt, urine ran down her legs.

Torvic shouted, "She wants you to stop! She wants away from here! She wants to be somewhere Mam isn't, because . . . because she knows Mam will eat her!"

"No," Audrun cried, horrified. She braced an elbow and levered herself up. "No, Meggie, I promise. I will not. I *promise* you. I will not!

Blessed Mother, child, I bore you in my own womb! I wouldn't harm
you—"

But Meggie screamed again. Again. Again. Omri, this time, set
her down. She ran stumbling from the chamber with Torvic behind
her, urgently calling her name.

Omri leaned over Audrun, resettled the coverlet. "I will care for
her. I will see her clean, calm. She will be unharmed."

Audrun had no strength to protest.

As he exited, she pressed hands across her mouth and cheeks so
Gillan and Ellica would not see how badly she wanted to cry out,
how her mouth opened to do so. Thoughts circled, chasing down
other thoughts. But of none could she make sense. It couldn't be. It
wasn't. She rejected it utterly. *Not real not real not real.* No, none of it
was real. Omri was not real. Karadath was not real. Alisanos was not
real.

But it was. All of it.

A wave of helplessness washed through her. *Oh Mother . . . oh,
Mother, please . . . make this no more than a bad dream.*

She wished it very strongly, did Audrun, yet knew no such dream
existed. It was real, all of it. Alisanos. Omri. Karadath.

The latter who, with a single conjured vision, had nearly destroyed her daughter. Meggie was so frightened of her mother, so
utterly terrified, that she could not hold her urine.

Audrun looked at her two remaining children, her eldest. Her
most sensible. Overwhelmed, she reached a hand out to Gillan and
Ellica. She needed to touch them, to feel their very human warmth,
the flesh and bone that she and Davyn had made.

Ellica said, "I must go to my tree."

"*Ellica*—" It was part astonishment, part command. All Audrun
could summon of strength, she put into that tone.

Ellica looked at her. "I have to."

"Ellica, please—"

But no. Ellica was gone. Now only Gillan was left.

He came forward and knelt close beside the cot. She saw the

worry, the weariness in his eyes. She reached out a trembling hand and touched his hair. Felt the texture, the tangles, the stiffness of dirt and sap.

She swallowed hard. "Don't leave me." *I can't do this—can't do this by myself.*

"No," Gillan said. "I won't."

That brought fresh tears from aching, stinging eyes. "It's just a vision," she said unevenly. "A *false* vision. Not the truth. Not real. I would never, *never*, harm Meggie—"

"Mam, I know. I know, Mam."

"Never, Gillan!"

"Mam, I know."

Everything within her cried out, "But *Meggie* doesn't know! She sees it, too! *And she believes it*!"

He nodded. "She will know. She will, Mam. I make that my task. Here, let me sit." Gillan turned and set his back against the cot, arranging his body carefully, as if he hurt. And she remembered that he did.

Fear. So much fear. By itself, the fear in her was overwhelming, but not for herself. For her children, yes.

So much wished of the Mother. Audrun, mute, again begged for aid. For peace.

But she didn't know if any such thing as peace existed in Alisanos. Nor whether the Mother of Moons existed in Alisanos, to hear her.

DAVYN SQUINTED AGAINST the sun as he walked. Too bright. Too bright for his head. He wanted to go somewhere and sit quietly in the shade, but instead he was walking across the settlement. Ahead he saw two outfitted supply wagons. Both four-horse teams were hitched and waiting in place, attached to the earth by no more than a rope and modest weight.

The woman courier was already there, bent low in her saddle to stretch out along the horse's neck as if in conversation. Even as Davyn headed for the wagons, two of her fellow couriers rode past him to join her. Neither man appeared to be feeling particularly good, or any better than Davyn, come to that. He had a hazy memory of the two men spending a great deal of time in Mikal's tent, drinking a great deal of spirits as they entertained two of the Sisters.

As the men reined in at the wagons, the woman's smile grew to a grin. She waggled a minatory forefinger at them, clicking her tongue as she did it. "You know better. You know you know better. You know you know better every time you do this."

One of the men squinted at her. "Bethid, don't expect me to parse that. Not this morning."

"Because you know it's true," the woman said smugly. She glanced at Davyn as if seeking agreement. But the smile died out of her eyes as she stared at him. "You, too? Did none of you remember last night that we're due to leave for Cardatha this morning?"

"I'm not sure," Davyn began, "exactly when I forgot."

Bethid shook her head. "You know Jorda will not coddle you." Looking at Davyn, she tilted her head in the direction of the two male couriers. "They at least know that. But you—"

Davyn raised his voice. "I won't shirk my responsibility."

"Hah," the woman said briefly, then looked beyond him. "Here's Darmuth. And Jorda." She glanced around. "Where's Brodhi?" Then she waved a hand as if to dismiss her question. "Never mind. He'll arrive when he feels like it." She smoothed a hand down the neck of her horse. "Of course he had a woman last night, so who knows when he might trouble himself to join us?"

The other couriers were astonished. "Brodhi—" one began.

"—has a woman?" the other finished, the final word sliding up his register.

Darmuth arrived on his horse. Davyn noted again the shaven skull, the length of silver braid doubled under into a club of hair and wrapped with crimson-dyed leather strapping. Davyn, who had seen him during the karavan's ill-fated departure, had forgotten the guide's eyes: pale as ice, with something lurking just behind the surface.

Demon. Davyn knew that now. He knew also that Darmuth was very much aware that he, Davyn, knew. The guide grinned, displaying perfectly normal human canines. The emerald set in one tooth glinted in the morning sun.

Jorda briefly assessed each individual. Then climbed up into the lead wagon, retrieved something, jumped down. He tossed the something to Bethid, who caught it. A leather-wrapped tin flask.

"Not me," she said. "My fellow couriers, yes—*and* the farmsteader. Alorn, catch." She tossed the flask a short distance to the courier.

Alorn uncorked the flask, drank, handed it to the other male courier. "Timmon?"

Timmon drank. Then he tossed the flask to Davyn, who caught it akwardly. "What is it?"

"A stirrup cup," Bethid answered. "Tradition."

"Tradition if you drink too much the night before," Jorda growled. "Drink it, farmsteader. They say it helps."

Davyn blinked, brows rising. "You don't know?"

The karavan-master unhooked the rope and weight from the front wheel-horse's bridle. "*I*," he said, winding the rope, "have never needed a stirrup cup."

That surprised Davyn. "You don't drink?"

"Oh, I drink." Jorda put the coiled rope and weight into the lead wagon. "But not to excess and certainly not the night before I'm to drive a wagon over terrain that has never, to my knowledge, seen a wagon wheel." He gestured. "I'm lead wagon. Drink your share, put away your weight, and climb aboard. We're wasting daylight."

Davyn observed the flask a moment. Spirits. After he'd sworn to himself he would not imbibe again. But a glance at Jorda showed him a man not much used to people delaying the execution of his orders. Davyn raised the flask to his mouth and tipped it, swallowing a goodly gulp.

Jorda grunted satisfaction and gestured for Davyn to toss him the stoppered flask. He climbed up onto the high bench seat, tucked the flask away, unwrapped the reins from their hook. Ruddy brows ran up. "Daylight?"

"Sorry," Davyn muttered. He gathered up rope and weight, put them away, then climbed aboard. "What about Brodhi?"

"He's there," Bethid said, gesturing with a thumb. "Waiting for us."

So he was. Out in front of the party at some distance.

"Oh," Davyn said. "I drank off the last of the spirits."

"Don't worry about him," Bethid drawled. "The last thing *he* needs is spirits."

Jorda set his team into motion with reins and voice. The lead wagon creaked as its wheels slowly began to revolve. Davyn hastily unwrapped his reins, sorted them out, and urged the team to fall in behind Jorda's wagon.

It was true. The stirrup cup had indeed settled his headache to some extent. He found it amazing.

His belly, however, was unimpressed.

Chapter 26

*I*LONA FELT SWEAT break out on her body as she found memory in a callused hand. The fabric beneath her arms was soaked. Droplets rolled down her temples, into her eyes. For a moment she was pulled toward the present, but a centering phrase sent her flying again, literally flying, as the draka lifted her in the girl's place and flew away from the sun.

Tight pressure against her body, enough to steal her breath; the clamp of claws around her torso, cutting flesh. Blood spilled, poured from body into sky. She opened her mouth but could not scream.

A low hill. A tumbled outcropping of stone piled one upon another. The draka flew closer, then backed air with huge wings shining red-gold in the sun. As it prepared to settle, Ilona knew she had no more time. She printed the outcropping in her mind, burned it there, and just as the claws around her torso began to loosen she reached for reality: her wagon with high, yellow wheels and new steps Rhuan had fashioned; the tea kettle sitting next to the fire ring; the elder grove, leafy canopies raised high against the sky. She wrenched herself out of the draka's claws and fell.

Ilona jerked her hands away, releasing Herta's. She trembled violently, wiping her palms against her skirt repeatedly, used a sleeve to blot her face. She heard her own breathing coming in gasps, in gulps.

Vision returned before hearing did. She saw the woman's pallor, the size of staring eyes, the mouth as it moved. Then hearing was regained, and she heard Herta asking again and again if she were all right.

No. She was not.

Ilona drew in a breath. "I have the place. I saw it." She pushed upward to her feet, stumbled three steps to wagon. She clung to one big wheel, clamping hands around the rim. "I'm sorry—you must go. I saw the place. Your daughter will be brought back for rites. But now . . . now you must go." Without the wheel as stability, Ilona knew she would collapse. "Please."

The woman rose, moved close. "Can I help you? Is there anything I might do?"

"I need . . . I need to be alone . . ." She knew it might sound rude even as she said it. But very few words were left in her mind. "I need to rest. Please, just go."

And so the woman did. Alone, Ilona hung onto the wheel and made herself move, hand over hand, step by step, to the back of the wagon. She nearly fell over the steps, but caught herself. Still trembling, she managed to turn, to sit, to plant feet and brace her legs, elbows on thighs. Ilona leaned forward and lifted her hands so she might rest her head in them. Her belly cramped. She gulped air then exhaled very hard through pursed lips. As saliva filled her mouth, she swallowed it back down.

I will not be sick . . . will not.

She pressed both hands against her mouth, sealing it. She could not stop herself from the slight rocking of her body. A childish thing, that. But she could not help it.

What she had seen . . . oh, what she had seen. A moment only, inside the draka's mind.

Maelstrom. Just as she had seen in Rhuan's hand, once. But worse. Far worse.

Nausea slowly receded without the results Ilona feared. Some small amount of strength seeped back into her body as she sat upon the wagon steps. She had best move now, she knew. She stood, turned, managed the last two steps into the wagon. Mattress and blankets remained on the floor, reminders of the intimacy she and Rhuan had shared. But this time she didn't smile in recollection. This time she knelt briefly, then followed the wishes of her body and rocked forward, letting outstretched arms take her weight. Then elbows. And finally she lay face down upon mattress and blankets, head turned so she might breathe.

Still, Ilona shivered. She wished herself warm but nothing came of it; that was not her gift. A searching hand found a loose blanket and pulled it over her body. She turned onto her side, drew bent legs close, tucked her jutting shoulder under the blanket. A hand pressed briefly against her brow found skin cold to the touch, abnormally cold. She dragged more blankets over herself and tucked her head down beneath a corner.

Memory swooped in, ignoring her mental effort to banish it. She lost herself again, saw the earth far beneath her feet, felt the bite of claws into flesh.

Maelstrom. Just as she had seen in Rhuan's hand, once. But worse. Far worse.

Then Ilona realized memory was repeating itself. Memories of flying, of draka. Of the outcropping upon a hill. Of a woman's hand, burned. And of the other hand, scored from finger to the heel. And of what she saw, so briefly, in Rhuan's hand, the night they met.

Of Herta. Of Herta's daughter, stolen by the draka.

For a suspended moment of time, Ilona had been that daughter.

"Stop," she whispered. "Mother, please."

The Mother did not please.

RHUAN PLANTED THE last branch marker for cairns and straightened, rolling tight shoulders, stretching his neck. He pressed thumbs into his spine, twisted his torso in two directions, all of which resulted in the desired and satisfying pops. He winced none-theless; sore spots left by the beating had stiffened. Possibly by to-night he might feel considerably better, but for the moment he ached the way any human would. And leaning over each time he planted a tree limb made his head feel heavy, about to burst. Which did his broken nose no good.

"Heal faster," he muttered. He looked down the long line of cairns and saw that his helpers had lost enthusiasm and speed. The smallest children now dragged their buckets, and the adults stacked stones more slowly than before. Rhuan could not blame any of them. It was not work anyone would seek out or find particular pride in. But there were plenty more cairns to build, and he would need all his helpers. And others, if they were willing to come.

The day turned gloomy. Clouds had come in from the east, smothering sunlight. Rhuan eyed them critically, then lifted both hands to his mouth to make a funnel. "Done for the day! Rain's com-ing!"

A familiar voice from behind sounded annoyed. "Trust me to ar-rive just as everyone else departs."

He turned, smiling. But the smile faded, replaced with alarm. "What's wrong? Are you ill? You look ill."

Ilona wore a deep indigo wrap pulled tightly around her torso, arms crossed and shoulders drawn up against cold. Her mouth sketched brief irony. "Such flattery. No, I'm not ill. I had a very dif-ficult reading earlier. And I'm cold." She shrugged. "A good night's sleep is all I need."

He frowned. The day was warm, not cold, not even cool. The steamy oppression of monsoon humidity was rising. The air was heavy with it. "Why are you cold?"

"I don't know. I just am." As had he, she studied the clouds. "Looks like the rain will last through dinner." She shivered. "Oh, I hate this time of the year. Everything is always so *muddy*. I'm tired of dragging my skirts through mud, tired of knocking it off my boots, tired of having boots sucked off my feet by mudholes. I'm tired of any number of other things."

It was not characteristic of Ilona to be querulous. Rhuan waggled his brows, hoping to replace her annoyance with laughter. "Tired of me?"

"Hah." She said it with muted irony that faded almost instantly. "There's something I must ask of you. But let's go to my wagon first. I've built a nice big fire beneath the awning. Tea will be quite hot when we return . . . perhaps it will thaw me out. I had considered a bath in the river, but not now. Maybe I should just stand outside and let the rain wash me clean." She tugged one of his sleeves. "Let's go, shall we?"

He wrapped an arm around her shoulders and turned her toward the grove. "There are means other than tea for thawing out."

"Of course there are, and I expect we'll get to that later this evening. Tea first, and there's also something we need to speak about."

"What is it?"

Ilona shivered. "There's too much to be said, to say it in the rain."

A large raindrop struck Rhuan's head. And another. He glanced up. "Well, we'd best hurry. Or you'll be colder yet." He slipped his arm from around her shoulder, took her left hand in his, and pulled her into a run toward the grove.

AUDRUN COULD NOT count the days. She lived in the haze of fever. She had a vague recollection of being lifted off the cot so bedding could be changed. She was given fresh nightclothes, and someone both fed her and bathed her forehead with a cool, wetted cloth. Her world had become limited to the sleeping chamber, shadowed by day, black by night. In the day, she heard voices. At night she dreamed.

She dreamed of Karadath's nightmare.

Of the infant taken from her.

ILONA FEARED SHE might fall down and be dragged through dampening grass. "Wait!" she cried, trying to keep up. "Rhuan, I can't run as fast as you . . . and besides, I'm wearing *skirts*!" Skirts that were weighted with moisture along the hems. Already the folds of fabric slapped through and around her legs. She tried to dig in her heels to halt them both, but her boot soles slid forward. She nearly sat down in wet grass and soil. "Rhuan—slow down!"

He slowed to a jog and, grinning, turned his head toward her. "It's raining."

"I know that. I suspect everyone in the near vicinity knows that. But it does me no good at all if I fall down, does it? I'll be wet one way or the other."

"Here." He stopped altogether, pulled her close, and flashed his dimples at her—something he used with devastating success. "This may help."

He leaned close to kiss her, but she placed the flat of her hand against his chest. "I'm wet, I'm cold, and I wish to have tea. I long for tea. If we stand out here in the rain I'll become even wetter and colder, and the tea will be delayed even longer."

"It was your idea to stop."

She brushed a raindrop from her cheek. "I didn't mean we should stop. I meant we should slow down. There is a marked difference between the two." The rain began to fall more heavily. She screwed up her face against it. "Let's go, then. It will be worse before it's better." Then she realized he was no longer looking at her. He was looking beyond her, beyond his row of stick markers. Toward the deepwood. She swung around to look as well. "What is it? I don't see anything." And she didn't, not out of the ordinary, just the crowded, towering line of the edge of Alisanos.

"Ilona, go." His tone was urgent, and his hands on her arms closed so tightly as to hurt. "Go to Mikal's. Tell him it's coming. I have to make sure the children who helped me are safely back with their parents."

"Tell him *what's* coming—?" Yet she broke it off. She knew quite well he was deadly serious. "Alisanos."

"Yes," he said tersely, releasing her arms. "A storm. We have little time for a warning. Go, Ilona."

Rhuan turned and ran from her.

Ilona, too, turned, and ran from him.

Chapter 27

*B*RODHI LED THE party out of the wide settlement clearing into a passageway that was very nearly a tunnel, so thick were the trees on either side.

While she felt it possible to ride two abreast, Bethid did not do so. Nor did Timmon and Alorn. Brodhi was followed by Alorn, then Timmon, then Jorda's wagon and, behind him, the farmsteader. Bethid brought up the rear.

The path was deeply shadowed. As she looked upward, her impression was of branches reaching toward one another across the passageway. It struck her that the trees leaned as if yearning to touch, to intertwine, to lock limbs; to wind leaves and roots together in what Bethid thought of as a discomfiting display of arboreal intercourse.

She shuddered, banishing the image. Not what she wanted to spend time envisioning.

Ahead lay sky and horizon. She could see the end of the passageway. It broadened into grasslands beneath bright sun. Already she felt better. Certainly safer.

Until she heard Brodi shouting. She saw him wheel his mount to face the short line of horses and wagons behind him.

"Go!" he cried. "Get out of here. As quickly as you can, get out of this. *Now.*"

Bethid saw Timmon and Alorn set their horses to a gallop, heading straight for the break at the end of the passageway. But Jorda and the farmsteader drove wagons with two teams hitched. It took time to hurry the horses.

She heard Jorda's raspy shout, the slap of reins brought down upon broad backs. The farmsteader was slower off the mark, but he, too, began shouting at the teams, wasting no time now. It did briefly cross her mind to ride on past the two wagons to reach safety more quickly, but she forebore. Not only was it selfish, but the teams needed nothing to distract their attention, and Churri going by at a gallop would do precisely that. So she hung back, fighting the urge, quietly telling Churri to mind his manners.

Churri did not. Churri, in fact, leaped straight up into the air, kicking powerfully behind. Bethid retained her seat and attempted to rein him in. Then she saw the cause of Churri's reaction.

After a frozen moment of shock, Bethid shouted, "Brodhi!" Surely he could do something. Shoia or Alisani, surely he could do *something*. He knew the deepwood. Ahead of her the break widened. She badly wanted to ride by, but it was particularly narrow here and the two wagons and teams were in her way. Churri stomped and kicked. "*Brodhi!*"

In front of her, roots snaked across the ground from trees on both sides. She saw the motion, saw how the roots quested after Churri's hooves. The wagons ahead now were free of the tree-hedged passage, but Churri refused to follow. He backed up in a humping motion, pushing more deeply into the shadows.

Bethid twisted in the saddle, briefly looking behind. Roots there as well. When she turned back, she found Brodhi close by. He leaped from the saddle, then knelt. A knife glinted in his hand.

Distracted by Churri's panicked behavior, Bethid caught only a glimpse of Brodhi's actions. The knife flashed again. Blood ran from his hand—she saw that. She saw, too, how he caught a writhing tree root and clamped his hand around it.

"Go, Bethid! Now!"

She gave Churri a taste of her heels. Even as she went by Brodhi, his horse broke away and went with her, running shoulder to shoulder with Churri.

It crossed her mind to turn back; Brodhi was now on foot. Being in the saddle provided some manner of temporary safety, but he was in contact with the ground, holding a root in the air as if it were a serpent to be strangled.

A horrifying shriek broke the air. Then another, and another. It was not in the least human.

Churri ran. And as he did, as he broke free of the shadowed passage into the bright grasslands, Brodhi's mount stayed close, as if finding comfort in Churri's proximity. Bethid stretched as far out of the saddle as she could without losing her balance. It took two tries, but she captured the reins of Brodhi's horse. She pulled up sharply, spun Churri away from the other horse, who followed along as Bethid now leaned away from him, most of her weight in the right stirrup. It was Brodhi she wanted to see. Brodhi she was worried about. That sound . . .

Then he walked out of the shadow into the light, sliding his knife back into its sheath. Bethid saw blood running from his hand. "Are you all right?"

Brodhi approached and took the reins from her hand.

"Brodhi—are you all right? What did you do?"

He held his bloodied palm up. Blood ran down it, down to the ground, and she saw the grass burn away into ash as droplets struck it. "That," he said.

The cut in his hand was deep. "You'll need that wrapped."

Brodhi shook his head. "It will take care of itself." He swung up into his saddle.

Bethid looked beyond him into the threshold of the narrow passageway. The shrieking had stopped. She felt her mouth drop open. "It was the *roots* making that noise!"

"When dying, things often do."

She turned back to him. "You burned them."

"Just two. One from each side." He gathered his reins. "Time we went on."

" 'One from each side,' " she echoed. "I don't understand."

"Poison from a snake bite can run all through the body," he said simply.

Bethid said it slowly, half in disbelief. "So you poisoned the roots."

Brodhi did not reply. He said something to Darmuth, who nodded after a moment and turned back the way they had come, returning to the passageway. It baffled her. She opened her mouth to ask another question, but Brodhi merely turned his horse and left her, rode past the two wagons, past Alorn and Timmon, to the head of the line once again.

Bethid scowled after him. She wanted badly to shout, but her fellow couriers had no idea what Brodhi was. Nor did Jorda and the farmsteader, as far as she knew. So instead of shouting she rode up to the head of the line and joined him there, speaking quietly, but in no wise less demanding. "If you can do that," she began, "why not do it to the rest of Alisanos?"

Brodhi was truly surprised. "I carry no more blood in my body than you do. So much drained would kill me long before there was any appreciable difference in the health of Alisanos."

She glanced briefly at Timmon and Alorn, out of earshot. She lowered her voice anyway. "But you wouldn't *stay* dead."

His expression was annoyed. "To burn enough to make a difference, I would have to be *in* Alisanos. There, even I can die. And no, we don't resurrect. Not in Alisanos."

After a moment, she said, "Oh." Then another question, one that set a chill in her belly: "Will we be able to get back to the settlement? Or will the passageway be closed off?"

"No, it won't be closed off; I sent Darmuth back to Rhuan. He can do the same."

"Darmuth can? Or Rhuan?" She paused. "Or both?"

"Rhuan. And don't ask me any more questions."

Bethid asked dryly, "Ever?"

Brodhi looked at her from under lowered brows, then turned and rode on.

Still grinning, Bethid fell in with Timmon and Alorn, contemplating what Brodhi had accomplished. Finally she said, "Huh," and let it go.

The skies were blue and sun streamed down. No hint of the deepwood remained, unless one turned to look back. Bethid did not.

GILLAN SAT ON the bench just outside the living chamber as Omri, inside, tended his mother. He was bent over, head down, injured leg bared to the morning sunlight. It still made him sick to look at the irregular patch of scaled skin grafted onto the flesh of his calf. And it itched. He could not keep his fingers from it. Already he had peeled back a tiny section of the edges just from scratching. A dribble of clear fluid crawled down his calf, freed by the violence of his scratching.

"Leave it be," Omri said.

Not having heard him approach, Gillan jerked upward in startlement, saw who it was, then reached down yet again to scratch.

"Leave it be," Omri repeated in a mild tone.

"And if I don't?" Gillan demanded. "If I keep scratching, can I rid myself of this?"

Omri squatted in the doorway, lifting his face to the double suns. "Are you sure you wish to do that?"

"Get rid of *demon* skin? Yes. I am quite sure!"

"And have no leg?"

"I can wrap it," Gillan answered sharply. "I can wrap it, splint it, use it, even if the muscle and flesh is burned away."

Omri's eyes remained closed. "What would you do then?"

It burst from Gillan's mouth, shaped by disbelief that such a question could be asked. "*Leave.*"

Omri nodded. "Of course. It was a foolish question, wasn't it?" His eyes opened, the same clear cider-brown as the karavan guide's. "Well, shall we say that you can leave? Yes, I think so, by the expression on your face. So. You will attempt to make your way through Alisanos to the human world."

"I think—"

But Omri overrode him. "One might wait," he said, "until the road is built."

Gillan was horrified. "I can't wait that long! The Mother only knows what will become of me if I wait." He shook his head. "No. I can't wait."

"You would risk your life, Gillan."

He had not expected Omri to know his name. After a moment, he said, "I will take that risk."

"And leave your kin behind?"

"No," Gillan declared, frowning. "No, that's not what I meant. All of them will come, of course. Everyone."

"Your mother is ill."

It seemed obvious to him. "When she is well."

"And if Ellica refuses?"

Gillan turned his head to look at the man squatting in the doorway. "Ellica wouldn't refuse. Why should she? Why should any of us refuse? Are you simple, not to understand that?"

"She has potted her tree."

All these questions annoyed Gillan. "She's been lugging that tree all over ever since she uprooted it. She can lug it out of Alisanos."

"Once she finds her ring, the tree will be planted permanently. Then she will go nowhere."

Gillan frowned. "What ring? She doesn't wear a ring."

Omri looked at him fixedly. It made Gillan highly self-conscious. He took his hand away from the scaled area once again. He tried to meet Omri's eyes with the same sharp focus, but failed.

Omri said, "The wild magic will alter all of you."

Gillan bent and pulled the torn fabric of his trousers over the patch of hide, hoping that doing so would halt the scratching. What he needed was wrapping. "That's what you say."

"I say the truth. She may well agree to go with you, but the tree takes precedence now."

Gillan hooted in amused disbelief. "My sister would never give up a chance to escape Alisanos because of a *tree*!"

Omri shrugged. "Ask her."

"And Torvic and Megritte will come, too, and Mam, when she's better." Gillan nodded. "All of us. All of us will leave."

Omri stood up so quickly it took Gillan aback. And then he felt the hand close around a wrist. Omri jerked him to his feet. Gillan nearly fell because the suddenness of motion put added stress on the weakened leg. He remained standing because Omri held him up until he regained his balance.

"It is possible," Omri said, "that you could blunder your way back to the borderlands. But not all of you—sisters, brother, mother—would live to do so. Is that risk worth taking? That Megritte or Torvic might be stolen by beasts and demons? That Ellica might find her ring and have to stay? That your mother would refuse to leave the infant?" Omri shook his head. "You are not the sire, Gillan. Making these decisions isn't for you to do."

Gillan hid desperation in anger. "Da isn't here. Mam is ill. I'm the oldest. I *have* to make these decisions!"

"It will not stop," Omri said.

"What won't stop?"

"Darmuth gave you substance of himself. Gave you living substance."

"I understand that, but—"

"You do not," Omri said. "You understand nothing. He gave you living substance, so you would not lose your leg."

"Yes, I know, but—"

"Your leg itches because that substance is knitting itself into your bone."

Gillan stared at him. "My bone?"

"The process has begun. You have wild magic in you, now. The substance Darmuth gave you will feed off that magic. It will grow, Gillan. *Grow*. It will overtake your human flesh."

He turned cold. So cold that he shivered with it. Sudden weakness took hold of his legs, tried to drop him to his knees. Gillan managed a single off-balance hop toward the bench, caught himself with braced arms before he could fall, and sat down hastily. He felt as if he could not breathe.

"You will remain yourself, Gillan," Omri said quietly. "You will not lose that which makes you human in your mind and self. You will be Gillan on the inside."

He stared down at his lower leg. Torn cloth had fallen aside, baring scales. "And on the outside—this?" He swallowed the painful tightness of his throat. "All over?"

As he looked up, Omri's eyes gave him his answer.

In panic, the words burst from him. "I don't want this! I don't want to be this! I want to be normal again. Even if it costs me my leg, I want to be normal again!"

"Do you think," Omri asked, "that I wished to be castrated?"

In shock, Gillan's mouth dropped open.

"Were you to go home, Gillan . . . were you to return to the human world wearing the skin of a demon, what would they do to you? The humans. Your people. What would they do to you?"

Gillan remembered the half-changed man, the man with scaled hands and claws, who had come to the settlement. His voice shook. "Hate me. Be afraid of me. Shun me."

"Or worse," Omri said. "They will neither understand, nor accept, that you are human inside the hide."

"Oh Mother. Oh Mother, Mother of Moons . . ." Tears started. He bent over, crossed arms hugging himself tightly. All of his bravado, his challenge to Omri's words, bled away. "I don't want to be that."

"Only on the outside."

Gillan dashed tears away and stared at Omri in a desperate appeal. "Is there nothing you can do? You say there's wild magic—can't you undo this?"

"Could I do that, I would have done it for myself two decades ago, when they cut me." His mouth was a flat, pale line.

Gillan drew a shaky breath. For the first time, he thought of Omri before himself. "Why? Why would anyone do such a terrible thing against your will?"

"Oh, it wasn't against my will. It was the price of failure. We are very well aware of that price."

Gillan could not grasp it. "You knew they would cut you?"

"If I failed, yes. And so I did. And therefore I was castrated."

"Oh Mother," Gillan murmured, appalled. "How can you live like that?"

Omri's mouth twisted a moment. "Living like this is part of the punishment for failure."

"But what did you fail?"

"To kill my sire."

Gillan stared at him. From the moil of thoughts, he said blankly, "You were to kill your father?"

"Yes."

"Why?"

"If we wish to ascend, we must." Omri put a hand up to forestall additional questions. "It is our way. Not the human way, I know well—I lived among you for five years—but *our* way. We are not like you." And then he repeated it. "We are not like you."

Gillan said the only thing he could think of. "Thank the Mother for that!"

Omri's tone was dry. "As well you might."

"Is that why you've been—given to us?"

"Of course. You could not be expected to remain here without me or someone like me."

"But, why?"

Omri sighed. "Language can be muddled. Let me say it this way, then. In your tongue, it's simple enough. We're slaves."

Gillan blinked. "What?"

"We're slaves. All of us who fail, but live. Neuters. Why, did you believe the primaries tend crops? Weave fabric? Build walkways, living chambers, make clothing? What, did you think the road would be built by magic?"

Gillan, quelled, murmured, "Yes."

"With our backs," Omri said. "With our hands."

Gillan stared at him, but no longer saw him. His vision was unfocused as he tried to stitch together everything, all the ideas, the visions, the questions, assumptions. And answers.

"This is one of the reasons why we challenge our sires," Omri told him. "Oh, there are other reasons as well, such as an unflagging physical drive, but don't you believe this is a powerful inducement? We challenge for our lives. For our manhood. For the right to breed. And for the get who are *dioscuri*, who will one day challenge *us*."

Gillan said, "Cruel. That's what it is. Horribly, terribly cruel."

Omri smiled sadly. "What else is there to be, when reared in Alisanos?"

Chapter 28

SHE STOOD JUST at the edge. Behind her lay the depths of Alisa-nos, before her a road. She judged it just wide enough for a wagon's passage. Tree canopies on either side overgrew the road so that a tunnel was formed. The brilliance of double suns were visible in patches, in narrow streaks stretching toward the ground, but the road remained deeply shadowed. It did not welcome her, but was none-theless a form of deliverance.

She heard axes. Heard the crack and scrape and whoosh of trees falling down, the massive thumps. She could not see the road being cleared; occasionally she heard the sound of beasts and outcries of men. In each instance, the noise of clearing stopped, then began again, when a man's cries died.

She lingered there on the verge, contemplating what might happen if she stepped out onto the road. Would she feel differently? Would it speak to her? Or would it be inert and empty, nothing more than a way through the deepwood?

And Davyn would come to her.

Someone said her name. And again. Once more, and she managed to open her eyes. They felt gritty and hot, as if scraped. Weariness yet plagued her, though she felt somewhat better.

Davyn would come to her, to their children, upon the road.

"Audrun, I have brought a cushion. Let us sit you up so you can lean against it. You have been flat too long."

It was the faded man. Omri. She saw kindness in his eyes. At no time since arrival at the Kiba had she seen any such emotion or appearance. For that kindness, she nodded and moved to sit up. She trembled, but his hands were on her, guiding her against the cushion. She managed to shift position enough to be more comfortable.

"Your fever is down," he told her. "You are recovering. I will bring a meat broth for you. But first, there is a service you might render me, if you will. . . . It won't require strength," he said hastily, as she opened her mouth to ask how in the world she could do anything for anyone at this particular time. He bent down beside the cot, lifted something, then peeled back wrappings so she might see.

A baby.

Oh Mother, a baby.

Audrun made a sound. It was not comprehensible, but Omri appeared to understand what she meant to say. Smiling, he offered the infant to her. "Will you care for this girl? Not for so very long. Only until she is a little stronger."

This time Audrun knitted actual words together. "Is she not being fed?"

"Her mother is dead. This one is a child of the creche, as we all are. But I think right now you are in need of a child more than the creche is."

She stared into his warm brown eyes. He was not, in this moment, deferential. Nor did he appear faded. There was compassion in his eyes, and hope.

A part of her wished to refuse. This was not her child. Her child was elsewhere. But her body in all matters cried out for the baby Omri offered.

Audrun nodded. Omri carefully placed the wrapped infant in her arms. She was, Audrun believed, only a matter of weeks in age. Red fuzz capped her head instead of the pale, pale blond of all her other children.

Her child, Sarith, was missing. This child was not. This child needed tending.

She is not mine. She is not mine.

Nor would she ever be. But until Sarith was found, Audrun would tend this child.

She reached up and tugged the neckline of her shift down. Omri murmured something and excused himself. She lifted the child to her breast. Tears formed and fell.

"I haven't forgotten," she murmured hoarsely. "Sarith, I haven't forgotten you. We will come for you. I promise it."

DEMON LIFTED THE naked child in the air and smiled, exposing fangs. It was pleasure she felt, not menace, not hostility. The child was no longer truly an infant, but still a baby, yes. She still needed care, she still needed guidance, and Demon would provide it.

The small cabin was built against a sheer cliff of stone amid a tumble of huge boulders. Outside, the river ran by. It had been a river for some time now. Demon didn't know the reason; she was not privy to the desires and decisions of Alisanos. Roaring river, flowing creek, barest trickle—it did not matter.

The baby was entirely the opposite of Demon. She had hair so pale as to be white, just a fuzz that stood up from cowlicks. Her eyes were a clear, wondrous blue. Nothing like Demon, who was all over a gray so dark as to be black, of black wings and black claws, of hair the same.

So carefully did Demon lift and hold the child. Always, most carefully. The child's flesh was fragile. Demon had scratched her once, all unintended, careless with claws. Now she took very good care, did Demon. She hoped the scratch across the child's collar bone would fade to insignificance. For the moment it was purple. Healing, but definitely purple. Easily visible.

Still smiling, Demon brought the child down from the air and held her close, tucking her into an arm, tucking her against the gray-black chest. Still, Demon had breasts. Still, she fed the baby. And remembered a time, now and then, when she had neither claws nor fangs, merely a woman's fair face, a woman's lissome form; remembered, too, that her hands and toes had borne thin, pink-and-pearl nails. They broke so easily, those nails. Not good for much of anything, Demon decided. But in those days, in the memory of human womanhood, all served. The body had served, then. It had been remade in the shadows of Alisanos, giving her that which a survivor of the deepwood required: the means to kill. Slashing claws, teeth that tore throats easily, wings that lifted her high into the air. She was a superior being now, so different from the days of weakness.

The child was human. All human. But one day, she, too, would be changed by Alisanos. She would become of Alisanos, just as Demon had.

"You will be strong," Demon told the child. "Most strong. And your body, your self, greater than any weak human body." Demon kissed the child's head. "Alisanos will be proud of you."

A WIND CAME up as Ilona grabbed handfuls of damp skirts and held folds of fabric out of the way. She heard it blow through the elder grove, from out of quietude and silence to a rushing, rising hiss. The heavens opened. By the time she reached Mikal's, mud and running water weighted her clothing.

She found him in front of his bar, leaning against it casually as he spoke with a handful of male customers. He looked up as she tore the door flap aside and stepped in.

One brow rose sharply; the other was contained by the leather thong holding his eye patch in place. "Blessed Mother, Ilona, you're soaked."

Out of breath, she nodded. "Yes. Wet. It's raining. Mikal, Rhuan says to sound the alarm. This storm isn't natural."

He shrugged. "It's just monsoon rain."

"The wind . . . can't you hear it?"

"Yes. But monsoon does bring wind with it, often enough."

It was most frustrating that he could not grasp the threat. She made her words more precise. "No, Mikal. A storm out of Alisanos."

His single eye narrowed. He rounded the bar, took from beneath it the two rods of Jorda's Summoner, then strode through the tent to the doorflap and stepped outside, banging the rods together. In the midst of pouring rain blown sideways, Mikal struck the rods again and again in a specific pattern of sound. The customers departed hastily, jogging off in several different directions.

Mikal stopped banging the rods as the lightning began. The Summoner's clangor was lost in the first crack of thunder. He ducked back through the door flap, wiping water from his face.

Ilona conjured the inflections of his own voice. "Blessed Mother, Mikal, you're soaked." But it was a poor joke, and his smile was merely a tightening of his lips.

The tent sidewalls flapped. Support poles creaked. Mikal set the Summoner atop the plank bar with a dull, metallic chime. "The wind is still rising." As Ilona nodded, he continued. "We need to cut more tent poles. Many. We'll have wood in plenty, with the grove down. But these tents can't stand up to repeated storms this powerful. We'll have to double or triple the poles, rig additional guy-lines. And we'll have to make sure everyone has canvas to lay down as flooring against the mud." He winced as another huge crack of thunder followed a slash of lightning. The air was acrid with it. "Did Rhuan predict how often we might expect storms out of the deepwood? The monsoon is bad enough. I assume these storms will be considerably worse."

Ilona shook her head. "He said nothing of it. I'll ask."

Mikal's own tent poles shuddered and creaked. Clearly concerned, he looked up at the underside of fabric stretched over a ridge pole.

Ilona picked wet strands of hair off her face. "I'm going back to my wagon."

He was surprised. "Now? Here, you're under cover." He cast another glance at the ridge pole as it shuddered beneath the storm's assault. "Well, temporarily. Mother, I hope this tent doesn't go down."

Ilona understood his consternation. The ale-tent was the largest in the settlement and had long been a place for meeting, not just drinking. "Do you have spare poles and rope?"

"A few poles, but not much rope. Rope is one of the supplies Jorda is bringing back." Wind blew the door flap open, making way for the hard, slanted rain to find entry. Mikal swore. "Are you certain you wish to go back to your wagon?"

She nodded. "I'll only worry about it if I stay here. Nothing there is tied down against the wind. And I can't get any wetter than I already am."

He nodded understanding. She shot him a quick smile of thanks, then ducked back out into the storm.

Immediately the wind yanked the wet wrap away from her, tumbling it across earth already running with water. Gone, too, was the lone rod she'd stuck through the thick coil of her hair. Freed ringlets weighted with rain straggled and slapped around her face and neck. With one hand she tried to hold skirts up, with the other she grabbed whipping hair so she could see.

Not far. The elder grove was not so far. Or her wagon in it.

The gloom of the storm was momentarily banished as the skies lighted up. Thunder assaulted her ears. "I hate it," she muttered, staggering against the strength of the wind. "I hate, hate, hate lightning!" She nearly tripped. "Especially when it comes down to earth instead of across the sky!"

She was nearly blind in such heavy rain and wind. Squinting while working hard to remain upright, she didn't see the broken plank flying through the air until the flat of it struck her head. The shock and force knocked her onto her back.

For a moment, disoriented, she lay sprawled as the rain beat into her. Then she pushed herself up into a sitting position, bracing herself on one arm while pressing a hand against her brow. Already the flesh rose against her palm, forming a large bump.

Sweet Mother, that hurts.

Now lightning chained itself across the sky. Thunder was ceaseless. Ilona rolled to her hands and knees, pushed herself to her feet, and shielded her eyes with one hand as the other again gathered up mud-weighted skirts. She could tend the knot on her forehead later.

There. Grove. Though limbs and branches whipped in the wind, though leaves were torn off and shredded, the grove nonetheless provided shelter. She made her way through other parked wagons, noting all were closed up tightly, and finally reached her own. The awning was gone and the grass mat with it. Ilona muttered an unkind word regarding the insolence of storms, especially when she discovered that the wind had also blown the wagon door open. She ran up the steps, ducked in, slammed the door closed and latched it. The rain, falling hard and fast, carried on the slashing wind, had wetted half of her floorboards as well as the mattress, blankets, and cushions she and Rhuan had placed upon the floor because her bed platform wasn't large enough for both of them.

Swearing yet again, Ilona dug into a trunk and pulled forth clothing, wrinkled from packing. She stripped down and dried off as best she could, wrung out her hair, pulled on dry clothing, grabbed up a long woolen wrap and wound it tightly around her chilled body. The wagon rocked and creaked, battered by wind and rain. Ilona climbed onto the bed platform, tucked up her legs, and prepared to wait out the storm.

"Come on, Rhuan," she murmured. There were questions to ask, and memories of a heartbroken mother who so desperately wanted her daughter's remains.

RHUAN MADE HASTE to find the wagons where the children belonged. Apparently all were where they should be. The wagons were buttoned down against the storm, and Rhuan was not about to go from one to the other in the midst of so much rain and wind. Now it was his turn to find shelter.

As he would with Ilona.

After a stop at Mikal's elicited the information that Ilona had returned to her wagon, Rhuan broke into a jog, rounding trees and shrubbery. Wet, unbraided hair slapped against his spine. Already torrents of water ran beneath his boots so that he splashed and slipped his way through the grove. Lightning was so near, thunder so loud, that he could not help wincing against both. And when he reached Ilona's tall, high-wheeled wagon, he noted at once that the awning was gone, torn from the canopy ribs. Something for him to repair once wind and rain subsided. For now, he just wanted to get in out of the rain and enfold Ilona in his arms.

Rhuan jumped up the steep steps and tried to open the door, but it was latched. So he banged on the door, shouting Ilona's name over the clamor of the storm. And at last the door was opened. She stood there all wrapped in a length of beautifully woven wool the color of a sunset. But the woman within the wrap had hair straggling down her shoulders and spine, and shivered.

She moved aside as he shut and latched the door behind him. "Here," he said, "let me warm you."

Ilona grimaced. "I'm not certain I *can* be warmed. This is the coldest I've been since joining Jorda's karavan." As if to balance the statement with something other than words, she shivered again and pulled the wrap tighter yet. She handed him a blanket. "Wrap up in that. Though you're not nearly as wet as I was. Did it soak through the leather?"

"No. One reason I wear it—though I do have weather clothing as well." He grinned. "If I strip out of these clothes to get dry, I suspect I would not don new ones any time soon. Besides, I have no clothing here. What I have is on its way to Cardatha with Jorda, as I neglected to retrieve my belongings from the supply wagon before it left." He shed the baldric of throwing knives, unbuckled his belt. Off came the boots; he set them neatly next to the door.

It had crossed his mind to take her down into the mattress and blankets with him, but he discovered all bedding was soaked. Instead, he guided her to the bed platform, climbed up and set his back against

the wooden partition, then pulled her down to sit in between outstretched legs, her spine against his chest. Despite dry clothing and
the woolen wrap, she was damp and icy cold. He shivered once himself from the initial contact, but set his arms around her, held her
closer and more tightly yet.

Summer was a time of high temperatures, humidity, and rains
that did nothing to cool the surroundings. "Alisanos has upset the
seasons."

"I know. You've said that before." Yet another shiver ran through
her body. "As you are a child of Alisanos, do you suppose you could
ask the deepwood to be less chilly?"

Rhuan grinned into the back of her head. "It doesn't listen to me.
I am a child to it. I don't count."

"Until you ascend to whatever position it is all the primaries appear to want?"

He rested his chin atop her skull. "Ascending is eminently better
than failing to do so. I would like to keep all my parts."

He felt her soft laughter against his chest. "Yes, I as well. I rather
admire your parts." But she pulled away and turned toward him before he could speak, tucking her legs under her. Even slightly damp,
chilled, wet hair in disarray, he found her beautiful. It was not a va-
pid, insipid beauty, but a strong, determined beauty. Weak men
would not see what she was, would not understand.

As he stripped out of his leather tunic, she set her hands against
his chest. "You're always so warm."

His flesh had jumped against the chill of her touch. "We all are,
we Alisani." He caught up his hair, pulled all of it forward over his
right shoulder and squeezed. "I asked you this once before. Now I ask
again. Will you braid my hair?"

"Sick of it loose, are you?" But her eyes did not speak of such
things as that. "You told me what it means."

"I did."

"Then—this is what you want?"

His smile was fleeting. "Well, perhaps not. Perhaps I only ask to
tease." But the smile returned, deepening dimples. From the belt he

had shed, he took a pouch. He loosened the drawstrings. "Put out your hands. Cup them."

Ilona did so, and he poured into them a stream of beads both metal and colored glass, coin rings, fetishes in silver and gold, drilled gemstones, metal clasps. In the light from the single lantern depending from the Mother Rib, glass glinted, gold glowed. She stared at the array, clearly stunned, then raised her head and met his eyes, keeping her tone light. "You have more fripperies than a woman."

Smiling, he separated a section of hair on either side of his face. "It will not be done all at once. But one begins with the sidelocks."

Chapter 29

RECENT RAIN HAD washed out hoofprints left by his return from Cardatha with the four Hecari warriors, but Brodhi's land-sense never led him wrong. It was a simple matter to ride across the plains with no thought to his route, trailed by two wagons and four riders. No one questioned his knowledge of such things; couriers always had a superior grasp of directions and routes, as did karavan guides. That land-sense had nothing to do with his role as courier, attributable instead to being a *dioscuri*, did not matter. It existed. He used it.

Here, trees were not so commonplace as in other areas of Sancorra. The grasslands spread before the small karavan beneath bright, broad skies. He heard the muted thunk of hooves against earth, the click of horseshoes striking stones, the metallic rattle of bit shanks when the horses shook heads to ward away insects.

"It's clouding up." Bethid, again falling in beside him. Her torso was twisted as she looked behind them. "That's downright ugly. They must be getting rain at the settlement." She turned back. "And I'll wager we'll probably get hit as well."

He did not need to look. He felt it in his bones. It wasn't the ache of age and injury, as with humans, but his increasing connection to the patterns of the human world, the workings of weather. He supposed he should tell Ferize. He supposed they should share a Hearing, so she might then report to the primaries that he was, at long last, allowing himself to begin to understand this world that wasn't his own, to understand humans. But he could not find it in himself to like them or admire them or view them as anything other than a weak, undisciplined folk. That was enough, surely. Wasn't it? The primaries would want no more than that. Would they?

Yet why the primaries insisted *dioscuri* spend time in the human world was completely beyond his ken. He had asked, as all young *dioscuri* did, but there had been no satisfying explanation, no details for him to grasp. Tradition. The journey was required because it always had been.

Tradition. Such weight in a word. It had the power to tame any *dioscuri*, any primary, who might otherwise choose a different path.

"Look," Bethid said. "Scavenger birds. Something's dead. And not far from here."

Brodhi looked. Ahead, the dark blot of birds circled repeatedly, then slowly began to descend. As they neared the earth, the flock broke apart. No more circling. No more waiting. They fell upon their prey. No one, now, could see them. Except for one still high in the air, still circling languidly with no apparent goal.

Brodhi sighed. *Ferize?*

Yes. Do you like me this way?

What are you doing up there?

He felt her distant amusement. *I'm not hungry.*

Why are you here?

You don't wish my company?

He glanced sidelong at Bethid, who was shielding her eyes against the sun with a raised hand. "What is that bird doing?" she asked. "Why not go down with the others?"

Brodhi said, "Perhaps it's not hungry."

Ferize laughed within the link.

Bethid frowned. "Scavenger birds are never *not* hungry. They're voracious."

Under the circumstances, it struck him as amusing. He smiled, still watching Ferize in bird form. "So they are."

The bird rode a swirl of breeze, flying higher and higher. Then it left its fellow scavengers on the ground and flew toward the small karavan. Its shadow flitted against the ground. All in the party looked up at it. Timmon made a warding-away hand gesture. This was not in the least normal behavior for a scavenger bird.

Ferize, you are confusing the humans.

Good. That is the intent.

Why?

Because otherwise I'm bored. Now she circled directly overhead. *I was not made to be patient.*

Brodhi smiled. *Well, no. So you weren't.*

He glanced at Bethid and saw what he expected to see: consternation. But he saw also a faint trace of fear, which surprised him. It wasn't like her. Wasn't like her at all.

"Bad luck," she murmured. "Oh Mother, don't let this unnatural bird be a harbinger."

"Harbinger of what?" Brodhi asked. "It's just a bird."

Bethid tipped her head back against her shoulders, staring upward. "It's wrong. It's wrong, Brodhi. It isn't 'just' anything."

"Superstitious nonsense." His mouth twisted. "I believed you were less likely to succumb to such, Bethid."

She completely ignored the disdainful edge in his tone. "I've never seen this before. This is unnatural." She turned her head to look directly at Brodhi. "I think one of us is to die."

He was incredulous. "Oh, Bethid, that's ridiculous. People don't die because a bird is circling overhead."

Bethid shook her head, still watching the bird as it dipped lower. "*Scavenger* bird, Brodhi. They eat dead things. There is no reason for this bird to be here, right here with us. Not like this. Not when dead meat is so near." She paused, then said, "Unless one of *us* is soon to be dead meat, too."

The shadow, wings outstretched, drifted over them again. Brodhi heard Timmon and Alorn speaking in hushed voices, but the tone of them contained a rising concern. He twisted in the saddle to look back at them.

"It's a bird," he said firmly. "And it's a foolish man—or woman—who imputes danger to such."

Their expressions suggested his mocking reassurance made no impact.

Brodhi sighed. *Ferize, stop playing with the humans.*

I find it amusing.

I don't. I have to ride with them.

Very well. I'll put their concerns to bed. But this really is ridiculous that they would believe a bird could bring bad luck.

Of course it is, he agreed. *But who can explain them? You can't. I certainly can't. They just are what they are.*

"Brodhi," Bethid said uneasily. "Where are you? You've gone away in your head."

Ferize, go.

She drifted in one more lazy circle, then flew swiftly back to the scavengers feasting on an indefinable carcass.

"You see?" Brodhi asked. "I told you. It's just a bird."

"I don't like it," she muttered. "It's a harbinger."

"It's no such thing, Beth—" But he broke it off. The stony expression on her face told him nothing he could say would make the slightest difference. Surprisingly, he found himself annoyed. But humans were a superstitious people. They worshipped the moon, visited any number of diviners, based much of their decision-making on nebulous predictions by charlatans. Brodhi shook his head.

"You think I'm a fool, don't you?" she asked.

He looked at Bethid. "Yes."

"But it's true," she insisted. "You saw how it came to us, how it circled over all of us. How it watched us. Someone's going to die."

He debated whether to tell her the truth. She knew what he was. His words might carry weight, might disabuse her of this notion.

"No," he said. "I don't think so."

They rode side by side again, horses matching pace. Brodhi felt the wind come up, felt the first contact with his clothed back. On the wind rode a scattering of raindrops. A glance back at the sky confirmed that the storm from the settlement was fast coming upon them. The day went gray, deep, ugly gray. Clouds boiled up, and the wind strengthened.

Brodhi frowned. There was something. . . .

And then out of the roiling mass of clouds came something else, something living. The wingspread was enormous. The clouds had blotted out the sun to a dim, insignificant smear so the flying thing cast no shadow. Everyone else looked ahead, curious, he believed, about the scavenger birds.

That was foolish superstition. This was real.

He wasted no time. "Bethid, get down. Get off your horse. Now." Brodhi wheeled his horse to face the others. "Draka! Get down!"

"Oh, sweet Mother," Bethid murmured.

He cast a sharp glance at her. "Get down, Beth . . ." But his attention shifted. "Halt those wagons. Stop moving. And keep your horses still!"

"You see?" Bethid asked. "It truly was a harbinger, that scavenger bird."

Brodhi had never seen such an expression on her face before. Her temperament was steady, her confidence sound. She dealt with challenges easily, almost dismissively. Perhaps it was because she had fought her way into the Guild. But now, as he looked at her, he saw fear. Abject fear.

And he did not like it.

"Get down," he told her sharply, then twisted again in the saddle to look at the others. Already Jorda's horses and the farmsteader's were restive, not wanting to halt. "Timmon! Alorn! Go to the teams! Now! We'll collect our horses later."

 DAVYN GAVE THE draka one glance. He needed no more. *Blessed Mother . . .*

He felt a cold shiver go down his spine as he heard Brodhi's orders. Stay still? How could they stay still? The beast was huge.

Clouds collided. A heavy, lashing gust of wind caught him across the back. The fine spray of raindrops quickened into a steady rain, then became a downpour.

Alorn was on foot now in front of Davyn's wagon, hands gripping the lead horse's bridle. What Alorn said in an effort to calm the horses, Davyn didn't know; nor did he have time to wonder about it. Part of him wished badly to leap off the wagon bench and flatten himself against the ground, which was quickly becoming mud. But Jorda, ahead, showed no signs of doing any such thing. Timmon was with the karavan-master's team, trying to calm them while Jorda worked with reins.

"Bethid! *Get down*!"

Davyn followed Brodhi's line of sight. The female courier was still in the saddle. The horse beneath her fought to be free, fought to run, but she would not allow it. "Churri! Settle! Easy!"

It wasn't a shadow. It wasn't a thing of the bright skies beneath a bright sun, but something dark. Something conjured of nightmares.

Busy controlling his team in concert with Alorn, what Davyn saw was fragmented, a series of images imprinted in his mind. Bethid, astride, her horse terrified; Brodhi, also astride, reining his horse close to hers. The courier leaned, clamped an arm around her torso, and yanked even as he urged his horse away from her own.

"Let him go!" Brodhi shouted. Too quickly for Davyn to see clearly, Brodhi slipped boots from his stirrups and half-slid, half-jumped down, taking Bethid with him. They landed in a tangle of limbs upon the ground even as all four courier horses fled.

"Mother damn you!" Bethid cried. Davyn could not make sense of the arms and legs heaped upon the ground. "Brodhi—let me go!"

He did not. And Davyn, open-mouthed, watched the draka, rather like the scavenger birds, fall upon its prey. It was a raptor's stoop, an abrupt, controlled downward rush. Not in the least slowed by the saddle, the draka sank claws through saddle leather and horse-flesh.

Bethid heaved her body out from under Brodhi, swearing at him in truly vile language. She was on her knees, then on her feet. She took two staggering steps against the wind. "*Churri*!"

But the draka beat skyward in the rain, horse clutched in massive talons.

The woman whirled to face Brodhi. Her face was pale and tight, cropped blond hair slicked against her skull. Wind battered her. "Damn you!" she cried. "Mother *damn* you for that!"

"Beth!" It was Alorn, shouting against the wind. "He saved your life!"

"He sacrificed Churri!"

"It's what any of us would have done," Timmon declared, shouting as well. "Mother of Moons, Beth—"

Her raised voice cut across his. "Leave it. Leave it be, Timmon."

Wind surged against them. The day had been clear; none of them had pulled up hoods from the necks of their rain gear. Rain streamed down faces, streamed down hair.

"It was a horse," Brodhi said, raising his voice over rain and wind. "A horse."

"Leave it, Brodhi—"

"Your life is worth more than that of a horse." His tone matched hers: icy and angry. "Would you rather I had let the draka take you both? Would you allow any of us to be taken by a draka if you could prevent it? *You* leave it."

She swung away, strode three long steps, stopped. Her back was to them, wet rain garb flattened against her in the gusting wind. She placed hands on hips and stood stiffly in the rain, looking at no one. Staring into the sky.

When at last she turned, her face was white to the lips. Perhaps she wept, but Davyn couldn't tell. Not in the rain.

Chapter 30

*I*LONA DUG UP the cracked hand mirror she used now and again. She raised it before his face. "Well?"

Rhuan very carefully considered his reflection. Again he wore temple braids, and again they were weighted with ornamentation. He turned his head from side to side, then nodded. "A beginning."

Ilona hid a grin. Vanity? She thought not. Tradition. Culture. It represented a part of his inner self. And maybe, maybe just a *little* vanity. "To do the rest will require days."

"It always does." Rhuan took the mirror from her hand and set it aside. "But we need not think about that just now. It's my turn to braid your hair." He smiled. "Just temple braids, like mine. A beginning, as I said." He rose, bent to keep his head from knocking against a canopy rib, and slid onto the bed platform. He physically turned her so that she faced him, brought her close. With care, he sectioned a thick, wiry lock from the rest of her hair.

"You look terribly serious," she observed.

He smiled back briefly, flashing dimples, but his eyes remained fixed on her hair. "It's a serious thing, isn't it? This announcement of our new relationship?"

"No one in the settlement will understand what it means. They aren't your people."

He stretched out the lock of hair, banishing the curl from it. Released, it sprang back into a ringlet. "This will be a task," he murmured. "And no, the others will not understand what this means, but we do." He stopped, looked into her eyes. "I've been selfish, haven't I? Would you wish a human rite, to say the same to your people?"

"Oh," she said thoughtfully. "I hadn't thought of that."

"Would you wish it?" He was even more serious now. "It would be fair, if you did. And I would do as you asked." He paused. "What do humans do?"

Ilona laughed. "Worried, are you?" She shook her head. "Not so much, Rhuan. We stand up before the people, invoke the Mother, exchange vows, and it's done."

He considered that. "Too easy."

"And then we walk away on our own, leaving all behind, and beneath the moon we cut one another's wrists and spill our blood onto the soil." He looked so startled that she laughed. "No, we do no such thing. That last bit, I mean. We do walk out under the light of the Mother after public vows, when darkness falls, and make private vows to one another."

He nodded. "But I would do the other, if you wished it. Except my blood would burn the grass."

"Somewhat destructive," she observed. "Not precisely what the Mother would expect."

"Well, no." His hands returned to braiding. "Probably not. Such a bond should be based on something growing, not dying."

She wanted to laugh at him. So very serious! But she muted her amusement as he once again concentrated on her hair, which was not terribly cooperative about being transformed from wild ringlets into an orderly braid.

And then she stopped smiling. She looked into his face. She again noted the clean lines and hollows of angled cheekbones, the fit of his nose, the shape of his mouth, the smooth warmth of his skin. He was beautiful. He had always been beautiful to her. But not as a woman was.

It was a straightforward question she asked, not a coy introduction to conversational foreplay. "Do you remember when we met?"

"Of course I do. I died."

A bubble of laughter rose in her throat. "Well, yes, so you did. But that isn't what I meant." Amusement faded. "I was mourning Tansit."

"And you found me quite rude and arrogant, but also charming."

"You *were* rude and arrogant. I did not find you charming. I found you insufferably proud of yourself—a man accustomed to women falling at his feet."

"No woman fell at my feet. Ever." He paused. "Well, except for that once. But she tripped."

"Looking at you, she tripped. Yes." But the irony faded. "You believed you could charm me into recommending you to Jorda, as he had lost one of his guides."

His eyes flicked to hers. "I was perhaps too forward in that. Then."

"Yes. Then."

Then: Tansit, Jorda's guide and her lover, had been dead for all of three days. Charm meant nothing when a woman grieved. She was in no way prepared for, nor desirous of, a man with Rhuan's undeniable appeal.

Neither was she prepared to see him rise from the dead.

"Don't stare," he said.

"I'm not staring."

"Yes, you are. It's very difficult to concentrate on your hair with you staring at me."

"I'm not staring. I'm looking. What else am I supposed to do with you right in front of me—roll my eyes back into my head?"

He winced. "Please don't."

"Then this." She closed her eyes.

"That will do."

And so it did; very much, it did. She had not expected it. But with her eyes closed she could give herself over to tactile sensation, a quiet exhilaration of the body. The touch of his hands upon her hair, separating narrow locks; the sliding of beads onto it; then the braiding of all, together. Already she could feel the weight of ornamentation, and she found it pleasing. More pleasing yet was the seduction of his fingers, the languid pressure against her scalp as he braided. For a moment she opened her eyes, wondering if he felt the same, but he was intent upon his handiwork. She closed her eyes again and gave herself over to memories.

AS THE TERRIBLE wind died, as the clouds broke apart, the sun resumed its strength. Bethid, bereft of speech, throat tight, rode next to the farmsteader on the wagon bench. Eyes stretched wide, she stared hard, almost fixated, at the rumps of the wagon team in front of her. By the sun, approximately three hours had passed since the draka's attack.

Three of the courier horses had been found, as expected, judged sound, and mounted by Timmon, Alorn, and Brodhi. Until she reached the Guildhall, she could only ride in a wagon.

Churri had not been hers. She had never owned him. All horses belonged to the Guild. In time couriers settled on one or two horses, and occasionally three, that they found pleasing. Although she had done so, the other mounts she rode had never pleased her as much as Churri. Since she had no intention of ever leaving the Guild, she understood that she would very likely outlast Churri's lifespan. Certainly she rode other horses—distances were too great for only one mount—but Churri was the one who held her heart.

It was strongly advised against, such bonds. Best, as a courier, to attach no importance to one horse over another. But she couldn't help it. The men, who seemed somewhat amused by her affection for Churri—one had even said it was expected of a woman—nonetheless stopped requisitioning him. Eventually, no one else used him. Only Bethid.

Only Bethid, who now was horseless altogether.

She rubbed at cropped hair, which had dried into spikes. Brass ear hoops swung against her neck. She wished, very strongly

wished, not to be sitting on a wagon seat. She should be free beneath the sun, riding horseback across miles of grasslands, along
wheel-cut roads. And that would come again, of course; she would
use one of the other horses on her journeys. But he wouldn't be
Churri.

"I'm sorry," the farmsteader said.

She stared straight ahead, preferring to neither answer nor em-
bark upon any kind of conversation about the loss of her horse. She
allowed purposeful rudeness to shape her tone into an aggressive
flatness that would cut off further comments. "Why should you be?"

He did not react to the rudeness. "Because it was a terrible thing,
what happened."

After a moment she swallowed back the tightness in her throat
and hitched one shoulder in a casual shrug. "You had nothing to do
with it. Why should you apologize?"

"Because one may feel badly for another. Because one may wish
to express regrets."

Again she altered the tone of her voice. Now she used Brodhi's
inflections. "He was just a horse. There are others at the Guildhall."

"I have four children," he said, "and not a one of them hasn't
cried over the death of something beloved. My youngest, only weeks
ago, cried over an old hen who crossed the river. One might say 'it
was only a chicken,' but that devalues what my daughter felt."

Bethid looked at him sidelong a moment, trying to read his face.
"You're suggesting I cry?"

"Oh, no, I would not make that suggestion. It isn't necessary. I
know you will cry, when you're ready. But for now you are a woman
among men, a woman who works only with men, and you would
want none of them to see you cry, lest they believe you weak. Lest
they use it against you in poor jokes."

Bethid heaved a sigh, surrendering her crumbling emotional wall
to actual conversation. "They will anyway. Some of them."

"Are they men you care for?"

She frowned. "No."

"Then does it matter what they think of you? What they joke about? Have you not proven your mettle to men you respect?"

She looked at him thoughtfully, chewing her bottom lip. They rode too near one another on the bench for face to face conversation to be comfortable, but she did now wish to see his expression. What she found was calmness, and compassion.

So his daughter had cried over an old, dead hen.

"What did you do?" she asked. "With the hen?"

He smiled briefly. "We held rites for it."

"And you believe I should do the same for my horse?"

He glanced at her. "You will do whatever it is you wish to do. Again, I make no suggestion."

"Then why are you telling me these things?"

"My wife cried when the cat died."

Frustration rose high and hard. "Why are you telling me these things? Are you saying only women cry because an animal has died?"

"When I was small," he continued, "a squirrel used to take acorns from my hand. Then one day our dog caught him. And I cried."

For the third time, now, in something akin to desperation, she asked, "Why are you telling me these things?"

"Grief," he said. "Happiness is from the Mother, and so is grief. There is room for it in the world." He worked the reins, made a clicking sound in his mouth to urge a bit more speed out of the team. "I have four children, as I said. They learned never to be ashamed of their grief."

"And you think I would be ashamed of *my* grief?"

He smiled slightly. "As I said, you are a woman among men, a woman who works only with men."

"I don't think any of them would cry over a squirrel."

He glanced at her briefly. "Or a hen?"

It nearly made her smile. "Well, no, probably not."

"But a horse, yes." He nodded. "Some would."

She shook her head. "How would you know? You're not a courier."

The farmsteader shrugged. "I'm a father."

Bethid stared at him for a long moment. She turned her face toward the muscled rumps of the wagon team. Eyes prickled.

She remained a courier. She would always be a courier. Nothing else in her life had she wanted, nor wanted now. The Guildhall was home.

With Churri, or without, the Guildhall was her home.

She allowed her eyes to fill. She allowed the tears to fall.

Chapter 31

*A*S RHUAN BRAIDED her hair, Ilona gave herself to memory.

She had seen, in her life, many deaths. It rode the hands of all humans, though few could read it, and fewer still could interpret the conflicting information. But this was Tansit's death. Never had she read the hand of someone she cared for as she had cared for him, only to see his death. Now she lived it.

Ilona had never *not* been able to see, to read, to interpret; when her family had come to comprehend that such a gift would rule her life and, thus, their own, they had turned her out. She had been all of twelve summers, shocked by their actions because she had not seen it in her own hand; had she read theirs, she might have understood earlier what lay in store. She was not, after all, their daughter. Not of the blood. They had taken her in. Now they turned her out.

In the fifteen years since they had done so, Ilona had learned to trust no one but herself, though she understood that some people, such as Jorda, were less likely to send a diviner on her way if she could serve their interests. All karavans required diviners if they were to be truly successful. Clients undertaking journeys went nowhere without consulting any number of diviners of all persuasions, and a karavan offering readings along the way, rather than depending on itinerant diviners drifting from settlement to settlement, stood to attract more custom. Jorda was no fool; he hired Branca and Melior, and in time he hired her.

That night, it had been cool. Ilona had tightened her shawl and ducked her head against the errant breeze teasing at her face. Mikal's ale-tent stood nearly in the center of the cluster of tents that spread like vermin across the plain near the river. A year before there had been half as many; next year, she did not doubt, the population would increase yet again. Sancorra province was in utter disarray, thanks to the depredations of the Hecari. Few would wish to stay who had the means to depart. The increased population would provide Jorda, as well as his hired diviners, with work. But she wished war were not the reason.

Mikal's ale-tent was one of many, but he had arrived early, when the settlement had first sprung up, a place near sweet water and good grazing and not far from the border of the neighboring province. It was a good place for karavans to halt overnight, and within weeks it had become more than merely that. Now merchants put up tents, set down roots, and served a populace that shifted shape nightly, trading familiar faces for those of strangers. Mikal's face was one of the most familiar, and his tent a welcome distraction from the duties of the road.

Ilona took the path she knew best through the winding skeins of tracks and paused only briefly in the spill of light from the tied-back doorflap of Mikal's tent. She smelled the familiar odors of ale and wine, the tang of urine from men who sought relief rather too close to the tent, the thick fug of male bodies far more interested in liquor than wash water. Only rarely did women frequent Mikal's: the female courier, who was toughened by experience on the province roads and thus able to deal with anything; the Sisters of the Road, taking coin for the bedding; and such women as herself—unavailable for hire, but seeking the solace of liquor-laced camaraderie. Ilona had learned early on to appreciate ale and wine, and the value of the company of others no more rooted than she was.

Tansit had always spent his coin at Mikal's. Tonight, she would spend hers in Tansit's name.

Ilona entered, pushing the shawl back from her head and shoulders. As always, conversation paused as her presence was noted, then Mikal called out a cheery welcome as did two or three others who knew her. It was enough to warn off any man who might wish to proposition her, establishing her right to remain unmolested. This night, she appreciated it more than usual.

She sought and found a small table near a back corner and sat, arranging skirts deftly as she settled upon a stool. Within a matter of moments Mikal arrived, bearing a guttering candle in a pierced-tin lantern. He set it down upon the table, then waited.

Ilona drew in a breath. "Ale," she said, relieved when her voice didn't waver. "Two tankards, if it please you. Your best."

"Tansit?" he asked in his deep, slow voice.

It was not a question regarding a man's death but his anticipated arrival. Ilona discovered she could not, as yet, speak of the former and thus relied upon the latter. She nodded confirmation, meeting his dark blue eye without hesitation. Mikal nodded also, then took his bulk away to tend the order.

She found herself plaiting the fringes of her shawl, over and over again. Irritated, she forcibly stopped herself. When Mikal brought the tankards and set them out, she lifted her own in both hands, downed several generous swallows, then carefully fingered away the foam left to linger upon her upper lip.

Two tankards upon the table. One: her own. The other was Tansit's. When done with her ale, she would leave coin enough for two tankards, but one would remain untouched. And then the truth would be known. The tale spread. But she would be required to say nothing, to no one.

Ah, but he had been a good man. She had not wished to wed him, though he had asked. She had not expected to bury him, either.

At dawn, she would attend the rites. Would speak of his life, and of his death.

Tansit had never been one known for his attention to time. But he was not a man given to passing up ale when it was waiting.

Ilona drank down her tankard slowly and deliberately, avoiding the glances, the stares, and knew well enough when whispers began of Tansit's tardiness in joining her.

There were two explanations: they had quarreled, or one of them was dead. But their quarrels never accompanied them into an ale-tent.

She drank her ale while Tansit's tankard remained untouched. Those who were not strangers understood. At other tables, in the sudden, sharp silence of comprehension, fresh tankards were ordered and were left untouched. Tribute to the man so many of them had known.

Tansit would have appreciated how many tankards were ordered, though he also would have claimed it a waste of good ale.

Ilona smiled, imagining his words. Seeing his expression.

She swallowed the last of her ale and rose, thinking ahead to the bed in her wagon. But then a body blocked her way, altering the fall of smoky light, and she looked into the face of a stranger.

In the ochre-tinged illumination of Mikal's lantern, his face was ruddy-gold. "I'm told the guide is dead."

A stranger indeed, to speak so plainly to the woman who had shared the dead man's bed.

He seemed to realize it. To regret it. A grimace briefly twisted his mouth. "Forgive me. But I am badly in need of work."

Ilona gathered the folds of her shawl even as she gathered patience. "The season is ended. And I am not the one to whom you should apply. Jorda is the karavan-master."

"I'm told he is the best."

"Jorda is—Jorda." She settled the shawl over the crown of her head, shrouding untamed ringlets. "Excuse me."

He turned only slightly, giving way. "Will you speak to him for me?"

Ilona paused then swung back. "Why? I know nothing of you."

His smile was charming, his gesture self-deprecating. "Of course. But I could acquaint you."

A foreigner, she saw. Not Sancorran, but neither was he Hecari. In candlelight his hair was a dark, oiled copper, bound back in a mul-tiplicity of braids. She saw the glint of beads in those braids, gold and

glass and silver, and heard the faint chime and clatter of ornamentation. He wore leather tunic and breeches, and from the outer seams
of sleeves and leggings dangled shell- and bead-weighted fringe. Indeed, a stranger, to wear what others, in time of war, might construe
as wealth.

"No need to waste your voice," she said, sitting again. "Let me see
your hand."

It startled him. Brows rose. "My hand?"

She matched his expression. "Did they not also tell you what I am?"

"The dead guide's woman."

The pain was abrupt and sharp, then faded as quickly as it had
come. *The dead guide's woman.* True, that. But much more. And it
might be enough to buy her release from a stranger. "Also diviner,"
she said. "There is no need to tell me anything of yourself, when I can
read it in your hand."

She sensed startlement and withdrawal despite that the stranger
remained before her, very still. His eyes were dark in the frenzied
play of guttering shadows. The hand she could see, loose at his side,
abruptly closed. Sealed itself against her. Refusal. Denial. Self-
preservation.

"It is a requirement," she told him, "of anyone who wishes to
hire on with Jorda."

His face tightened. Something flickered deep in his eyes. She almost thought she saw a hint of red.

"You'll understand," Ilona hid amusement behind a businesslike
tone, "that Jorda must be careful. He can't afford to hire just anyone.
His clients trust him to guard their safety. How is he to know what a
stranger intends?"

"Rhuan," he said abruptly.

She heard it otherwise: *Ruin.* "Oh?"

"A stranger who gives his name is no longer a stranger."

"A stranger who brings ruination is an enemy."

"Ah." His grin was swift. He repeated his name more slowly,
making clear what it was, and she heard the faint undertone of an
accent.

She echoed it. "Rhuan."

"I need the work."

Ilona eyed him. Tall, but not a giant. Much of his strength, she thought, resided beneath his clothing, coiled quietly away. Not old, not young, but somewhere in the middle, indistinguishable. Oddly alien in the light of a dozen lanterns, for all his smooth features were arranged in a manner women undoubtedly found pleasing. On another night, she might; but Tansit was newly dead, and this stranger, Rhuan, kept her from her wagon, where she might grieve in private.

"Have you guided before?"

"Not here. Elsewhere."

"It is a requirement than you know the land."

"I do know it."

"Here?"

"Sancorra. I know it." He lifted one shoulder in an eloquent shrug. "On a known road, guiding is less a requirement than protection. That, I can do very well."

Something about him suggested it was less a boast than the simple truth. "And does anyone know *you?*"

He turned slightly, glancing toward the plank set upon barrels where Mikal held sovereignty, and she saw Mikal watching them. She saw also the slight lifting of his big shoulders, a smoothing of his features into a noncommittal expression. Mikal told her silently that he knew nothing of this Rhuan that meant danger but nothing much else, either.

"The season is ended," Ilona repeated. "Speak to Jorda of the next one, if you wish, but there is no work for you now."

"In the midst of war," Rhuan said, "I believe there is. Others will wish to leave. Your master would do better to extend the season."

Jorda had considered it, she knew. Tansit had spoken of it. And if the master did extend the season, he would require a second guide. Less for guiding than for protection, with Hecari patrols harrying the roads.

Ilona glanced briefly at the full tankard. "Apply to Jorda," she said. "It's not for me to say." Something perverse within her flared into life, wanting to wound the man before her who was so vital and alive, when another was not. "But he *will* require you be read. It needn't be me."

His voice chilled. "Most diviners are charlatans."

Indeed, he was a stranger; no true-born Sancorran would speak so baldly. "Some," she agreed mildly. "There are always those who prey upon the weak of mind. But there are also those who practice an honest art."

"You?"

Ilona affected a shrug every bit as casual as his had been. "Allow me your hand, and then you'll know, won't you?"

Once again he clenched it. "No."

"Then you had best look elsewhere for employment." She had learned to use her body and used it now, sliding past him before he might block her way again. She sensed the stirring in his limbs, the desire to reach out to her, to stop her. She sensed also when he decided to let her go.

Chapter 32

RHUAN KNOTTED THE bottom of the temple braid into a silver clasp, then pressed it closed. Gently he let go of the braid, and it swung out of his hand to dangle before her ear. "Half done."

She didn't respond. Her eyes remained closed.

"Ilona? Where have you gone?"

She smiled faintly, eyes still closed. "Away."

"Away where?"

"Remembering."

"Remembering what?"

"When we met."

He grinned. "You've done that already. Remembering."

"It bears repetition." Her eyes opened. "May I see?"

He held up the cracked hand mirror. Ilona studied her reflection. "It's quite pretty." She turned her head to consider the beaded braid from a different angle. "I like it."

"Now the other." He set the mirror aside. "And remember not to stare."

Ilona laughed as she closed her eyes. "No staring."

After a moment he leaned forward, kissed her warmly, lingered on the lips. Against them, he murmured, "I couldn't help myself. You made me remember. I remember how you looked in the moonlight that night, when I resurrected. "

"Rather stunned, I imagine."

"But you cared. You were sorry I was dead. Well, when you thought I was dead."

"Of course I was sorry you were dead! Would you expect otherwise?"

"I was a stranger."

"That doesn't mean I wouldn't feel badly if you—if a stranger—died."

Wind roared, set the wagon to rocking. Wood creaked, canvas cracked. For a moment an explosion of lightning illuminated the interior of the wagon. Thunder came swiftly behind it. Rhuan waited it out, then said, "I had been an annoyance to you in Mikal's tent."

Ilona frowned. "Of course you had. You meant to be, and you were. But those are not reasons to wish a man dead." She opened her eyes. "Are you going to weave the other braid or not?"

He smiled, took up a wiry lock of hair, and slowly began to braid it, to weave into it glittering treasure.

IT BEGAN NOT far from Mikal's tent. Ilona had heard its like before and recognized at once what was happening. The grunt of a man taken unawares, the bitten-off inhalation, the repressed blurt of pain and shock, and then the hard, tense breathing of the assailants. Attacks were not unknown in settlements such as this, composed of strangers desperate to escape the depredations of the Hecari. Desperate enough, some of them, to don the brutality of the enemy and wield its weapon.

Ilona stepped more deeply into shadow. She was a woman, and alone. If she interfered, she invited retribution. Jorda had told her to ask for escort on the way to the wagons, but in her haste to escape the stranger in Mikal's tent, she had dismissed it from her mind.

Safety lay in secrecy. But Tansit was dead, and at dawn she would attend his rites and say the words. If she did nothing, would another woman grieve? Would another woman speak the words of the rite meant to carry the spirit to the afterlife?

Then she was running toward the noise. "Stop! *Stop!"*

Movement. Men. Bodies. Ilona saw shapes break apart; saw a body fall. Heard the curses meant for her. But she was there, telling them to stop and for a wonder they did.

And then she realized, as they disappeared into darkness, that she had thought too long and arrived too late. His wealth was untouched, the beading in the braids and fringe, but his life was taken. She saw the blood staining his throat, the knife standing up from his ribs. Garotte to make him helpless, knife to kill him.

He lay sprawled beneath the stars, limbs awry, eyes open and empty, the comely features slack.

She had seen death before. She recognized his.

Too late. Too late.

She should go fetch Mikal. There had been some talk of establishing a Watch, a group of men to walk the paths and keep what peace there was. Ilona didn't know if a Watch yet existed; but Mikal would come, would help her tend the dead.

A stranger in Sancorra. What rites were his?

Shaking, Ilona knelt. She did not go to fetch Mikal. Instead she sat beside a man whose name she barely knew, whose hand she hadn't read, and grieved for them both. For them all. For the men, young and old, dead in the war.

But there was yet a way to know what was required for his rites. She had the gift. Beside him, Ilona gathered up one slack hand. His future had ended, but there was yet a past. It faded already, she knew, as the warmth of the body cooled, but if she practiced the art before he was cold she would learn what she needed to know to give him the proper rites. She would make certain of it.

Indeed, the hand cooled. Before morning the fingers would stiffen, even as Tansit's had. The spirit, denied a living body, would attenuate, then fade.

There was little light, save for the muddy glow of lanterns within a hundred tents. Ilona would be able to see nothing of the flesh, but she had no need. Instead, she lay her fingers gently upon his palm and closed her eyes, tracing the pathways there, the lines of his life.

Maelstrom.

Gasping, Ilona fell back. His hand slid from hers. Beneath it, beneath the touch of his flesh, the fabric of her skirt took flame.

She beat it with her own hands, then clutched at and heaped powdery earth upon it. The flame quenched itself, the thread of smoke dissipated. But even as it did so, as she realized the fabric was whole, movement startled her.

The stranger's hand, the one she had begun to read, closed around the knife standing up from his ribs. She heard a sharply indrawn breath, and something like a curse, and the faint clatter and chime of the beads in his braids. He raised himself up on one elbow and stared at her.

This time, she heard the curse clearly. Recognized the grimace. Knew what he would say: *I wasn't truly dead.*

But he was. Had been.

He pulled the knife from his ribs, inspected the blade a moment, then tossed it aside with an expression of distaste. Ilona's hands, no longer occupied with putting out the flame that had come from his flesh, folded together against her skirts. She waited.

He saw her watching him. Assessed her expression. Tried the explanation she anticipated. "I wasn't—"

She cut him off. "You were."

He opened his mouth to try again. Thought better of it. Looked at her hands. "Are you hurt?" he asked.

"No. Are you?"

His smile was faint. "No."

She touched her own throat. "You're bleeding. Here."

He sat up. Ignored both the slice encircling his neck and the wound in his ribs. His eyes on her were calm, too calm. She saw an odd serenity there and rueful acceptance—perhaps that she had seen what he wished she hadn't.

"I'm Shoia," he said.

No more than that. No more was necessary.

"Those are stories," Ilona told him. "Legends."

He seemed as equally amused as he was resigned. "Rooted in truth."

She was highly skeptical, and she let it into her voice. "A living Shoia?"

"For now," he agreed, irony in his tone. "A moment ago, dead. But you know that."

"I touched your hand, and it took fire."

His face closed up. Sealed itself against her. His mouth was a grim, unrelenting line.

"I see." She paused. "You might come up with a more believable story. And is it a Shoia trait, then, to burn the flesh a diviner might otherwise read?"

The mouth parted. "It's not for you to do."

Ilona let her own measure of irony seep into her tone. "You are well warded, apparently."

"They wanted my bones," he said. "It's happened before."

She understood at once. "Practitioners of the Kantica." Who burned bones for the auguries found in ash and grit. Legend held Shoia bones told truer, clearer futures than anything else. But no practitioner she knew of used *actual* Shoia bones.

He knew what she was thinking. "There are a few of us left," he told her. "But we keep it to ourselves. We would prefer to keep our bones clothed in flesh."

She frowned. "But legend says no one murders a Shoia. That anyone foolish enough to do so inherits damnation."

"They murder us when they can. It's simply more difficult to do so."

Nor did it matter. Dead was dead, damnation or no. "These men intended to haul you out to the ant hills," Ilona said, and thought, *Where the flesh would be stripped away, and the bones collected to sell to Kantic diviners.* "They couldn't know you are Shoia, could they?"

He gathered braids fallen forward and swept them back. "I doubt it. But it doesn't matter. A charlatan would buy the bones and claim them Shoia, thus charging even more for the divinations. Clearer visions, you see."

She did see. There were indeed charlatans, false diviners who victimized the vulnerable and gullible. How better to attract trade than to boast of Shoia bones?

"Are you?" she asked. "Truly?"

Something flickered in his eyes. Flickered red. His voice hardened. "You looked into my hand."

And had seen nothing of his past or his future save *maelstrom*.

"Madness," she said, not knowing she spoke aloud.

His smile was bitter.

Ilona looked into his eyes as she had looked into his hand. "Are you truly a guide?"

The bitterness faded. "I can be many things. Guide is one of them."

It amused her to say, "Or dead man?"

He matched her irony. "That, too. But I would prefer not." He stood up then; somehow, he brought her up with him. She tensed, but he released her arm immediately. She faced him there in the shadows beneath the stars. "It isn't infinite, the resurrection."

"No?"

"Seven times," he said. "The seventh is the true death."

"And how many times was this?"

The stranger showed all his fine white teeth in a wide smile. "That, we never tell."

"Ah." She understood. "Mystery is your salvation."

"Well, yes. Until the seventh time. And then we are as dead as anyone else. Bury us, burn us . . ." He shrugged. "It doesn't matter. Dead is dead. It simply comes to us more slowly."

Ilona shook out her skirts, shedding dust. "I know what I saw when I looked into your hand. But that was a shield, was it not? A ward against me."

"Against a true diviner, yes."

It startled her; she was accustomed to others accepting her word. "You didn't believe me?"

He said merely, "Charlatans abound."

"But you are safe from charlatans."

He stood still in the darkness and let her arrive at the conclusion.

"But not from me," she said. "I read true, and that worries you."

"Shoia bones are worth coin to charlatans," he said. "A Kantic diviner could make his fortune by burning my bones. But a *true* Kantic diviner—"

"—could truly read your bones."

He smiled, wryly amused. "And therefore I am priceless."

Ilona considered it. "One would think you'd be more careful."

"I was distracted."

"By—?"

"You," he finished. "I came out to persuade you to take me to your master. To make the introduction."

"Ah, then *I* am to blame for your death."

He grinned. "For this one, yes."

"And I suppose the only reparation I may pay is to introduce you to Jorda."

The grin flashed again. Were it not for the slice upon his neck and the blood staining his leather tunic, no one would suspect this man had been dead only moments before.

Ilona sighed, recalling Tansit. And his absence. "I suppose Jorda might have some use for a guide who can survive death multiple times."

"At least until the seventh," he observed dryly. "But please don't tell him."

She considered that. Yes, it was information a man might not want passed among others. For now, it fascinated her.

"If I read your hand, would I know how many you have left?"

He abruptly thrust both hands behind his back, looking mutinous, reminding her for all the world of a child hiding booty. Ilona laughed.

But she *had* read his hand, if only briefly. And seen in it conflagration.

Rhuan, he had said.

Ruin, she had echoed.

Chapter 33

*A*UDRUN AWOKE SCREAMING. Screaming and screaming. Except she made no noise.

A tentative hand touched her shoulder, then closed and shook it. "Mam. Mam!"

Gillan.

"Mam!"

"Oh, Mother," she gasped. "Oh, blessed Mother . . ."

Morning. She lay limp, aching. Sweat pasted hair to her face. Gillian bent over her; Ellica and Torvic sat with Megritte on another cot. Meggie looked horrified—so badly horrified that she had soiled her shift with vomit.

She dreams what I dream. Audrun levered herself up on one elbow. She had pleaded with Meggie before, to no avail. Now she would not plead.

"It's not true," she told her youngest. "None of it is true, Meggie. I would not eat you. I *will not* eat you. I promise it with all my heart and soul. I vow it in the name of the Mother. Never, never, never, Meggie. These are dreams. Terrible dreams; I see them, too. I know. Believe me, Meggie. I tell you the truth. These dreams are sent."

"Who would send them?" Torvic asked. "Why?"

"Someone who wishes to control us," Audrun aswered flatly, refusing to lie to her children in such perilous circumstances. "Someone who wishes to make me do what he wants. Someone who I will visit as soon as possible." She looked at Meggie again. "Torvic, you said you can hear Meggie's thoughts."

He nodded.

Audrun tamped down desperation. "Does she understand what I've said? Does she know those dreams are lies? Can she not *talk* to me?"

Torvic shook his head. "She won't talk to you."

"These are dreams. *Sent* dreams. They are evil, Torvic. They are purposely sent to us. These are not true dreams!"

Torvic shrugged uncomfortably. "She doesn't believe you. Not after what Lirra did."

Audrun frowned. "Who is Lirra, and what did she do?"

He rubbed a grimy hand across his mouth. "The woman in the forest. She wanted to eat Meggie. She almost did. But Brodhi came and killed her."

It stunned Audrun. She looked at her youngest daughter. "Oh . . . oh Meggie, I'm so sorry. . . . I am so sorry!" But even as she tried to sit up, intending to reach out to her daughter, Torvic shouted at her.

"Don't touch her! Mam, don't touch her." More quietly, he said, "She doesn't want to be touched."

She knew what he left out: Meggie didn't want to be touched by *her*.

"I can't hear her," Ellica said, who sat beside Megritte, "but she doesn't seem right. There's something that's not right."

How could there be anything right about any of them? Audrun thought. *They inhabit Alisanos.*

Audrun looked at Ellica. At Gillan. "Do you see them? The dreams?"

Both shook their heads. "I think we are too old," Gillan said. "Best to hurt you through the youngest."

She knew he was correct. It was far more effective to use the youngest, the smallest, the most vulnerable.

"Mam," Torvic said, "are you going to feed that baby again? Shouldn't we find *our* baby?"

"Yes. Yes, Torvic, we should." She lay back down on the cot and stared up at the stone ceiling, thinking.

"Mam—" Torvic began.

She cut him off. "Gillan, Ellica, take the youngest out. Find Omri. See if he will bring you breakfast." She disliked speaking of Omri as a servant or slave, but nothing here was normal. She had to find the best route through the forest of an unknown culture, its habits and its dangerous inhabitants.

Route. Forest. A road through Alisanos.

For the first time in her life, Audrun swore. For the first time in her life, she wished someone dead.

Karadath.

ILONA OPENED HER eyes. "Oh Mother—there's a task we must do tomorrow. I meant to tell you earlier. I can't believe I forgot!"

His brows arched even as he continued braiding. "Well?"

The wagon rocked in a gust of wind. Lantern light danced and swung crazily. "That woman who lost her child to the draka. Do you remember?"

He nodded. "A heartbreaking thing for the mother. For anyone."

"She came to me for a reading today. She asked me to find where her daughter's remains lie, so they might be brought back for proper rites. During the reading, I found the place. I could take you there." Unexpected tears prickled. "It would bring the woman a little peace."

"Of course. We'll go at first light." He threaded a bead onto several strands of hair. His tone was somber. "There are likely to be more deaths."

She knew it. Helplessness bled into desperation. "Can't you kill it? The draka? You said you'd killed one before."

"No."

"You said you had poisoned a cow, and the draka took it, ate it, and died."

"No," he repeated. "In this world, there's no way a draka may be killed."

It stunned her. For a moment all she could do was stare, mouth opening in astonishment. "You *lied*."

His eyes flicked to hers. "I lied."

But she saw no guilt in him, no regret. As the shock passed, she understood. "To calm the fear rising in everyone. That's why. To provide hope."

He nodded, lids lowered.

"Is there nothing we can do?"

"Stay out of its way." He looked briefly from braid to her eyes. "I don't mean to be facetious. That is the only way to survive."

Now that the thought had arrived in her mind, Ilona could not dismiss it. "What about a Hecari dart? One killed you before. Could it work on a draka?"

He shook his head. "A dart could not pierce the scales."

But certainty, and faith in Rhuan, kindled into flame. "Drakas have eyes, do they not? Eyes don't have scales. Eyes are vulnerable to darts."

Rhuan stopped braiding. He wanted to refuse her, to find another answer that would dissuade her. She could see it in his face, in his eyes.

But he did not speak it. Instead, he said, "I can't swear it's impossible. There is no proof that it is, because no one has attempted to shoot a draka's eye with a dart. But I believe it's impossible."

She nodded, yet continued, picking her way carefully. "You are an expert with knives. Throwing knives. Those." She tilted her head in the direction of the baldric he had shed. "I've seen you use them."

"I *do* miss," he pointed out. "Not often, but I do. Besides, throwing knives aren't terribly precise. They're nothing like blowpipe darts." As the wagon, buffeted, rocked again, Rhuan peered upward. "I suspect we may lose a rib soon."

But Ilona's mind remained fixed elsewhere. "You could learn to use a blowpipe. I suspect it would take you far less time to do so than an ordinary man."

He tilted his head in thought. "Probably."

Hope burned now in concert with regained certainty. "And if you missed the eye—what happens? You try another dart. And you keep trying until you succeed."

"Ilona, I can't exactly approach this draka. It flies. I don't."

She nodded impatient understanding. "But it will return, won't it? There would be more deaths, you said. When it does come back, couldn't you try with your throwing knives *and* a blowpipe?"

"I could try, yes. I could also fail."

"Any attempt of anything could fail." She gazed at him steadily. "Or succeed."

He offered no more argument, merely acknowledged her statements. "Yes."

"Those Hecari," she said. "What about the bodies of the four Hecari who came here with Brodhi? They must have had darts and blowpipes."

He shook his head. "Alisanos took those men, Ilona. Nothing is left of them. Nothing at all."

She drew a breath. "Then we'll have to catch one."

Rhuan stared in astonishment, plaiting forgotten. "Catch a *Hecari*?"

"Of course." Ilona smiled at him. "You can't be killed in our world. You are the perfect person to catch a Hecari, blowpipe or no blowpipe, warclub or no warclub."

"Ilona, I can only die in front of people a specific number of times, remember? *If* I'm Shoia, that is, and nearly everyone believes I am." He paused, then added meaningfully, "As they're supposed to."

She nodded, granting him that. "But you said it yourself: you never tell anyone how many lives you, as a Shoia, have left. How would they know?"

Once again he concentrated on stringing beads into her hair, frowning as he did so. "I'm not so certain I relish the idea of being killed by a Hecari several times."

"That isn't the plan, Rhuan. It's a possible outcome."

"What *is* the plan? Do we have one? Do you? It's my life you're putting at risk."

She hastened to explain. "No, no—Rhuan, if you could truly die, I would never suggest such a thing."

"We can survive being killed by humans. By draka?" He shook his head. "We're of Alisanos, draka and *dioscuri*. Here or there, we die if killed by a draka, and remain so."

All of her certainty drained away. She was indeed putting his life at risk. For a moment, hope had burned within her. But now hopelessness, and helplessness, seeped back. "You're right," she said. "I shouldn't have suggested such a thing. I'm sorry."

Rhuan shrugged. "It's not wrong to consider solutions. This one just seems more dangerous than most."

She nodded. "I understand. There can't be a solution for everything. And there's none for this." Dryly, she ventured, "I don't suppose we could chase it back into Alisanos?"

Dimples flashed. "Unlikely." He was silent a moment. "I suppose it is possible, though."

"What is?"

"Putting a dart into a draka's eye."

She stared at him. "But—you said you believed it was impossible."

"I do. I still do."

After a moment, she asked, "Are you changing your mind?"

"Possibly it's more accurate to say I'm bowing to necessity. The woman you mentioned, the one who lost her child to the draka—we'll collect the remains for her tomorrow. Perhaps I should put that first, rather than the possibility of my own death. How many mothers will lose children? How many husbands will lose wives? How many families will be killed?" He shook his head. "I think I must do something. The attempt may fail, as I said. But it may also succeed, as *you* said."

But now, paradoxically, she feared for him. "Rhuan—"

"Have you a plan to obtain a Hecari blowpipe and darts without actually engaging a Hecari?" he asked.

"Well . . ." No, she didn't. But she thought rapidly; he'd said nothing remained of the three dead warriors given to Alisanos. "Brodhi brought four warriors back with him from Cardatha, and they're all dead, devoured by Alisanos?"

Rhuan nodded.

"Will the warlord let that go?"

"Doubtful."

"But Brodhi will have to tell him, and he might send more warriors here. He probably *will* send more warriors here."

Seeing what she meant, Rhuan shook his head decisively. "We can't allow any of them to come here. Much too dangerous."

"Then . . . there's another way."

Yet again deft fingers stopped moving in her hair. Warily, he asked, "And?"

"You can contact Brodhi, yes? Do a Sending?"

"If necessary."

She drew in a deep breath, let it go. "Send to him. Send to him that we must have blowpipes and darts. Cardatha is teeming with Hecari."

SHE WISHED HIM dead.

It did not shock. It did not stun. It was not chased away by horror that she could possibly think such a terrible thing. Instead, Audrun carefully allowed herself to explore that thought.

Karadath. *Dead.* No more nightmares. No more Meggie terrified of her own mother.

"Oh Mother, oh blessed Mother, forgive me . . ." Her muffled voice died away as she pressed a palm against her mouth. She cut off the plea. No. She neither wanted nor needed forgiveness. The Mother was a Mother. The Mother would understand.

All was clear. It unfolded before her.

Karadath. Dead.

Audrun knew her capabilities. She accepted limitations. She understood that it was a task she could not accomplish alone.

Omri. The failed, faded *dioscuri.* The man who was no longer a man, but a castrate, a slave. He had spoken of tradition, of under-standing, of acceptance. It was the way things were done among his people. The risks that were taken by *dioscuri*.

But if *she* could think of killing a man—if a woman from a cul-ture, from a family, where murder was abhorrent, could think of killing, couldn't he?

The voices of her children drifted in from the open door. A shadow appeared, fled, was banished by the man himself, bringing her a meal.

Audrun elbowed herself upward, set her back once more against the cushion. She accepted the bowl of broth. The aroma stirred hunger—a normal, healthy hunger, the first in days.

She smiled at Omri and gave him her thanks.

He would never, Audrun knew, kill for her.

But possibly, potentially, he might kill *with* her.

Chapter 34

*I*N CARDATHA, SANCORRA'S largest city, the warlord's huge palace squatted in the center of Market Square, dwarfing it. Called a *gher*, it was round and tall with a flat-topped, conical roof. Walls were formed of crisscrossed, lashed-together lattices of stripped saplings covered by hides of many shapes and colors, stitched together by red leather thongs. A large but low square plank platform extended beyond the circular *gher*. It always struck Brodhi as a permanent structure, but the Hecari were nomadic; every part of the *gher* was easily broken down into sections and bundles for transport.

Two years before, on the day before the warlord's arrival (which Brodhi had witnessed) men taken as slaves during the conquest and now watched by warriors, came into the city on blue-painted wagons. In the very center of Market Square, they climbed down and swarmed over the wagons, taking the materials they needed. They lay down the platform planks on risers, set up the lattices, stretched bundled sections, stitched and fastened hide into place. By the time they were done, the *gher* took up much of Market Square. The slaves promptly climbed back into their wagons and drove away, disappearing into crowded streets.

Deprived of their usual spaces, merchants set up wooden stalls in streets and alleyways. The plethora of livestock, often escaping flimsy pens, turned narrow stone-paved streets into treacherous and pungent footing. Wagons could only pass where stalls were not too large. Above the noise of animals and stall-holders' sing-song pitches, one heard cursing and shouting from wagon drivers.

At the mouth of Market Square, as Alorn and Timmon left the party and rode through to the square, Brodhi glanced back briefly. Jorda had pulled aside to let a wagon coming from the opposite direction pass, and another driver had abused that by squeezing in behind. Jorda was effectively blocked. Behind him, on the second supply wagon, the farmsteader looked nearly as grim. Bethid, beside him on the tall seat, clearly was not looking forward to climbing down into the muck.

Horseback, Brodhi held a distinct advantage. He turned back, guided the horse through steadily, and reined in beside the farmsteader's wagon. Bethid transferred her gaze from the fouled street to him, eyebrows rising in inquiry.

Brodhi moved his horse sideways, close against the wagon, with a few taps of his left boot heel. Not one to question good fortune no matter how unexpected, Bethid rose on the seat, swung a leg across the horse's rump, and slid into place behind the saddle, murmuring a word of thanks.

"Not far," Brodhi said, referring to the courier's guildhall, "but you'll see the Guildmaster with your boots relatively clean." And he guided his horse toward the square.

IT WAS NEARLY impossible for Jorda to make any headway through the crowded market stalls. Davyn followed as best he could, since he had no idea where they should go for the supplies Jorda needed. Eventually the karavan-master found a narrow offshoot of a twisting alley, stopped the team, and turned around on his high seat to catch Davyn's eye.

He raised his voice. "We'll leave the wagons and teams here. There's no chance we can put them outside the shops and load directly into them." Jorda climbed down and removed from under the seat two pairs of wooden wheel chocks roped together. "You've a set, too."

And so Davyn mimicked the karavan-master, making certain the wagon would roll neither forward nor backward. He straightened and looked around. The buildings stood very close on either side of the alley, throwing shadows into canyons of dressed stone. He could not help but feel uneasy. They were not so far from a busy lane, but it would nonetheless be a simple matter for someone to slip into the narrow walkway and appropriate the wagons.

And he damned the fact that he thought in such terms now. Once, it would never have crossed his mind that some might be bent on stealing horses and wagons.

Jorda saw the concern. He smiled grimly. "I expect—" He broke off briefly. "Ah, here comes help now."

"Help" consisted of boys somewhere between youth and manhood. They wore soiled clothing nearly outgrown, and were they *his* children, Davyn would have sent them off to wash faces and hands. But they were not his children. His children were in Alisanos.

Blessed Mother, but he ached with pain and grief every time he thought of his family trapped in the deepwood.

"Four of you," Jorda noted, not privy to Davyn's emotions. "Two for each wagon." He removed coin rings from a pocket and tossed one to each boy. "Watch them well, and if everything is as I left it, there will be more coin in it for you."

The boys nodded. Two slipped by to join Jorda, while two remained near Davyn.

Jorda glanced at Davyn. "There will be boys at the markets more than happy to carry things back to the wagon for us."

Nodding, Davyn fell in beside Jorda as he walked out of the narrow alley to the wider lane. The karavan-master wound his way through the crowds, and eventually the lane opened into the square.

Davyn danced aside to avoid a goat bent on escape, trailing a broken rope, and as as he crossed from lane into Market Square, he stopped short. "*Mother of Moons!*"

Jorda heard him. In the lead, he glanced back over his shoulder.

Then he nodded realization, halting. "The *gher*," he said with a weary note in his voice. "That's what they call it, the Hecari. The warlord's palace."

Davyn was struck dumb. Even in dreams he could not have imagined such a structure. Huge, round, and hides of all sizes and shapes stitched together with leather thongs dyed red. It sat atop a low wooden platform on risers, and crimson banners flew from iron crooks, taller than a man, at each platform corner. A massive red banner hung from the flat-topped, conical roof. But it was the huge doorway that caught his attention after the first startled impression. The wooden doorjamb was sheathed in intricate, deep-carved, intertwined designs. And everywhere was the gleam of gold.

Warlord. So close. Just inside. The man who had sent death and chaos into Sancorra, riding with armies of brutal warriors who overwhelmed the province. Rivers of men wielding warclubs, blowpipes, poisoned darts; who built cairns of stripped Sancorran skulls. Thousands had died, women and children as well as those who attempted to defend the province. One man, just one man's appetite for power had caused all.

Davyn noted the warrior-guards ringing the *gher* and posted at platform corners. Oiled skulls were naked save for scalplocks gleaming slick in the sun. Golden ear-spools stretched their lobes. Eyebrows were shaved. The lower halves of their faces were stained a rich indigo.

"Don't stare," Jorda told him sharply. "Never stare at a Hecari. It's viewed as a challenge."

Davyn choked out a blurted sound of disbelief. "What challenge am I? I'm a man who gathered his family and fled."

"A *wise* man," Jorda refuted, "against a race such as this. Now look aside, and we'll go on. You can catch glimpses later, when we've got what we came for."

As instructed, Davyn looked aside. But as he walked once more with Jorda, he shot quick, sidelong glances at the massive *gher*. How could a man not stare at it? It was wholly foreign. Wholly alien. It was, in its own way, more powerful a statement of domination than the piles of skulls scattered across the province.

Davyn raised his voice to the karavan-master, his tone plainly bitter: "Do you know, if I were brought before him, I would ask a question. I would ask him: '*Why?*'"

Jorda grunted. "Because he can."

Davyn thought about that a moment. It struck him as no answer at all. Why would a man conquer provinces just because he could?

He petitioned the Mother. *Help me to understand.*

To understand why one man's orders had stripped from Davyn everything he valued: farmstead and family.

One man's whimsy?

AS GUILDMASTER, AS man, he had always intimidated Bethid. She supposed he intended that, but not necessarily because she was a woman—and the only woman in the guild, at that. She knew other young couriers, male couriers, were as intimidated, though they need not worry that he judged them the same as he did her. Because she was a woman. And it mattered to the Guildmaster.

She stood now in the chamber built of hewn stone, tall iron candle racks in each corner, shedding pale, ochre-tinted illumination. All four walls were tapestry-hung to cut the chill of winter when the stone grew cold. Wooden shelving contained scrolls in cases, end caps carefully marked with a symbol that identified each. On wider shelves, unrolled scrolls were carefully stacked in precise piles.

The Guildmaster was working in a logbook as she entered the chamber and assumed her place before the wide wooden table. Eventually he looked up at her. He waited.

Telling this man about the loss of Churri was the hardest thing Bethid had ever done. Not because her wages would be docked, but because the horse had meant so much to her. Along the way, sharing the wagon seat with the farmsteader, she had forced herself to think about how she might discover from fellow couriers if they would support her idea to draw Sancorrans from Cardatha and gather them at the settlement; about how to broach the topic. And then, about how they might go about implementing the plan.

Again, she thought about Churri. And in the presence of a man who would not understand.

Explanation finished, Bethid resolutely fixed her eyes on the huge map pinned to the tapestry behind the Guildmaster. As always, she marveled at the rich colors inked onto the vellum, the accuracy of detail marking where courier routes, rivers, cities, villages, hamlets, and various destinations lay. She noted, with a twitch of surprise, that the tent settlement and the surrounding deepwood had been drawn onto the map since she had last been in the chamber. Ah. Brodhi, of course.

The Guildmaster sat back in his chair, idly tapping quill against his chin. "A draka," he said.

Bethid met his gray eyes and nodded. "Yes, sir. It would have had me as well, but Brodhi pulled me to safety in time."

His face was tanned and weathered from years of riding under the sun. He wore his usual black with the heavy silver Guildmaster's brooch fastened at his left shoulder. Short-cropped hair was graying. The ice in his eyes did not promise an easy interview. But then, he had opposed admitting her to the guild. He had been newly appointed, and it was his predecessor who had permitted Bethid to enter the trials.

Irony shaded his tone. "Heroic of Brodhi."

Bethid felt warmth rise in her face. She bit back what she wanted to say: *No doubt you'd rather I were taken than Churri.* Which was undoubtedly true, but not something one said to the Guildmaster. She had always been scrupulously polite around him, to give him no reason for dismissing her from service. She knew he would do it more quickly to her than anyone else.

He ran the feather through one hand, studying her. "You grew attached. I see it in your eyes."

Bethid damned her eyes. "I did, sir. Yes."

His faint smile was not kind. "Women and animals. That's weakness, Bethid. It undermines a courier's duty."

"I didn't intend for it to happen—"

He cut her off. "But you're a woman, and it did, and now you're heart-sore."

Bethid kept her tone very carefully under control, offering nothing more than crisp professionalism. "He was a good horse, sir."

He tilted his head slightly. "I allow couriers to settle on specific horses because it aids our rides. When you know a horse well, less time is lost. You know his habits. But attachment, Bethid, can be troublesome. I expect you will now go to his empty stall and cry."

She had anticipated nothing less than the arrogance and mocking tone. But she had done her crying on the road. "No, sir. First I would like to eat. It has been a long journey—" She indicated the map behind him with a motion of her head, to note the added detail. "—and then I will go to the horse-master to select a new mount."

A faint smile, containing less irony, twitched one side of his mouth as he sat forward and put down the quill. "You will need new equipment as well," he observed. "The debt will be a large one."

Bethid clamped the inside of her lower lip between her teeth so he would not see a reaction, and nodded.

"So we are to have you among us for quite some time as you pay this back."

She felt a knot in her belly loosen, as did the stiffness in her shoulders. The Guildmaster had the option of dismissing her for the loss of a valuable horse and his gear. She had, in fact, expected it.

He nodded. "Get something to eat, then see the horse-master."

"Yes, sir. Sir—"

"And try to avoid drakas in the future." He tilted his head toward the door. "You may go."

As she departed, Bethid tried to sort out whether the great relief she felt was as much for leaving his company as it was for retaining her job. She inhaled deeply, then blew out a noisy breath.

And she *did* want to go to Churri's empty stall. But wouldn't.

IT WAS DISCOVERED, as Rhuan and Ilona rode some distance from the settlement, that Alisanos did not form a precise circle. In one area the deepwood fell away on both sides for a short distance, and scattered copses of perfectly ordinary grassland trees offered safety and shelter beneath spreading boughs and leaf canopy. Not far ahead, the untainted land rose into a modest hill crowned with a massive tumble of stones. Not far beyond it, Alisanos once again drew close.

They rode side by side. Rhuan, diverted from the vista by Ilona's presence, watched her in profile, elated that at long last they were partnered. For so long he had loved her, but was reluctant to say so, to show it, because of his journey. No part of the journey forbade him or any *dioscuri* from bedding human women, but to the Alisani these women would never be honored as equal partners. Certainly Brodhi kept himself to Ferize. She could take the seeming of a human woman, as she often did, but she could not truly pass as a human. And that, Rhuan believed, was precisely why Brodhi bedded only a demon. Likely he believed it would soil him, to lie with a human female. Once, Rhuan had asked Darmuth if he had ever taken the seeming of a woman. Darmuth had laughed at him, green gem glinting. Rhuan had got no answer other than that—which wasn't truly an answer—but he expressed neither annoyance nor frustration. Darmuth expected him to ask for clarification, so Rhuan did not.

Now he rode beside the woman he wished to take as his own in the Alisani way, while adhering to Ilona's customs as well. He wanted Ilona recognized as his *dioscara*, so that his people would accept her as she was. Because one day he would take her to the Kiba. She had braided his sidelocks according to his directions in the pattern of marriage braids, ornamented with glass and metal beads. There had been no time to do the rest of his hair, to make and plait together all of the complex multiple braids. Another time. For now, the sidelocks were enough.

"What are you grinning about?" Ilona asked, suspicious.

"Us."

"Ah." She smiled. "Worth the grin, then."

He nodded and began to say something more, but Ilona abruptly reined in. Her face had lost color and her hazel eyes were enormous, blackened by expanded pupils. Her mouth loosened.

Rhuan blurted in sharp concern, " 'Lona—?"

"It's what I read." She pointed straight ahead toward the rise in the land. "Those rocks. The girl's remains are there." She drew in a deep breath, then released it and looked at him. She seemed completely Ilona again. "Can you sense drakas? Do you know if one is nearby?"

Rhuan shook his head. He understood what she was asking. A draka had taken the girl; it might yet be close to the remains. Or it might be hunting elsewhere.

He still didn't like Ilona's color. "If you can describe the area, I'll go and fetch the remains," he said. "You can wait at that tree just ahead."

Ilona looked puzzled. "No, I'll go up into the rocks as well. I can't be sure of the exact place without being present. Why should I stay at the tree?"

"Because you look ill," he said bluntly.

She shook her head. "I feel quite well."

"You don't look well—" But he didn't finish, because once again her eyes widened. What she saw, he realized, was not of the here and now.

Rhuan dismounted swiftly, slipping down between their horses. He reached up, caught an arm, and gently tugged Ilona downward into his arms. Carefully, he lowered her until she stood on her own feet, but he held her shoulders to steady her.

He still had the impression she wasn't truly present. "Ilona!"

She blinked, and her eyes refocused. She seemed surprised to be off her horse. "What happened?"

"I have no idea," Rhuan said, his voice grim, "but we'd best go back to the settlement."

"No! No, Rhuan. We can't. Not without the girl's remains. I promised her mother."

"If you're ill—"

Ilona cut him off. "I don't feel ill. I feel as if I'm reading a hand. Except there's no hand in front of me, just snatches of visions." She shook her head. "It's different, Rhuan. Not an illness. I swear it." She closed her hands around his wrists, pushing slightly so he would release her. "We must find the remains and soon. That poor woman . . . there will be no peace for her, but she will at least know the girl's spirit is with the Mother once the rites are done."

Rhuan still hesitated. "That may be, but I don't want you falling out of the saddle and knocking yourself unconscious." He held up a silencing hand before she could protest. "So, you will ride double with me. And no protest, or we turn around now. I'll lead your horse."

She wanted to refuse. He saw it. But after a moment, mouth twisted, she nodded.

"Good."

Rhuan mounted, then slipped his left foot free of the stirrup and reached down. Ilona put her own foot in the stirrup, caught hold of Rhuan's arm, and scrambled on behind him in a motion made awkward by her skirts. She settled into place and wrapped her arms around him.

"Perhaps this was a good idea," she said with a cheek laid against his shoulder.

Rhuan grinned. "Of course." He took a firmer grip on the reins of Ilona's mount and tapped his horse into motion, leading hers alongside.

But when she spoke again, there was no lilt of humor in her tone. "Mother willing, we'll lose no more to this draka. Or to anything else of Alisanos."

Rhuan might have agreed with her merely to agree. But he couldn't. He knew it was very likely there *would* be more lost to the draka and to other aspects of Alisanos.

AFTER THE THIRD stop to purchase supplies and send them to the wagons via young men willing to carry, Jorda looked at Davyn quizzically as they departed the shop. "From the expression on your face every time we come outside, I'm assuming you've never seen Cardatha before."

Davyn shook his head. "I've never seen a city at all."

"Then it is no wonder your eyes are so large." Jorda laughed at him. "Go on, then. Take time to yourself. We'll stay the night at an inn I know. It's called the Red Deer. Anyone can direct you." He slapped Davyn on the shoulder. "Come back when you're ready."

Davyn watched the karavan-master turn back into the crowds of people moving through the lanes, finding their way to market stalls displaced by the huge *gher*.

He grinned to himself. "Must have resembled Torvic and Meggie, discovering something new." And the grin died. He felt a clenching in his belly: renewed memory of what had been taken from him.

For a moment Davyn stood frozen in place, struggling to keep the grief from showing. They weren't dead. He had been told it plainly. But just as plainly, he knew more was at stake than survival. It was survival of self.

He would walk the lanes later. For now, he wanted spirits. Ale would not do.

THIS TIME, IN her dream, Audrun stood in the very center of the road rather than beside it. Behind her lay the deep-wood; before her, a clearly defined if narrow road. Again she heard sounds of chopping, of trees falling, crashing down to earth—

jarring landings. Again she heard the screaming of predators, and prey.

Upon this road her husband would come. Once more a family, and with baby Sarith as well—Karadath had agreed—they would set forth again for Atalanda. They would leave behind a diminished, desolate province overrun by Hecari. They would be free, all of them, to begin anew, to build a home, to till the fields, to reap what grew in the garden. Davyn had said they would settle closer to a village. It would be easier this time, and less isolated. It was a tunnel, this road. Despite the felling of massive trees and the cutting down of thick grown vegetation, Alisanos still loomed, canopies entangled high overhead. Anyone would travel in fear, despite the promised safety of the road. It was wild here. Too wild.

Something behind her shrieked. Audrun jerked around, terrified. But she saw nothing other than trees. The road ended behind her. In this place, upon the road, she was apart from the deepwood. So long as she kept to the road, nothing of Alisanos would harm her.

Such fragile safety. A way through the deepwood. A road to their future.

But in the meantime, Alisanos worked to alter her children.

Faster. The neuters who built the road must work faster. For her children, she would insist.

BETHID FOUND HERSELF alone in the Guildhall refectory, but solitude didn't last. Corrid, the youngest of them all, came in; not long afterward Hallack and Gathlyn arrived. And after them, a new courier she didn't know at all. She'd heard of the addition. Laric, if she remembered rightly.

She cut herself a piece of ham and laid it atop a fat slice of crusty bread. Carved a sliver from the pale wheel of goat cheese and added it to the ham. Cider was always her drink, and she filled a mug from the keg. Cook would come in soon to prepare supper, but this would do well enough for now.

She slid onto a bench at the long table. The others helped themselves to food and drink as she had. Corrid, Gathlyn, and Hallack all found places at the table, but Laric did not. He leaned against the wooden plank counter and picked at both bread and cheese. He had poured himself a mug of dark, foamy, pungent ale.

Bethid slid a glance at him. Now she looked at all couriers with questions in her mind. What did she know of them? Were they Sancorran patriots? Did they wish to look the other way and keep themselves out of harm's way? Would they possibly be willing to consider forming a confederation of rebels?

Laric was, she judged, in his late twenties. His hair was light brown, his eyes blue, and his face was tanned from days upon the roads, riding from one place to another. He had put off his blue cloak and silver brooch and wore only brown tunic and leggings, his calves wrapped in leather. Stiff riding boots had been exchanged for soft house boots.

Bethid ate her way through bread, cheese, and ham, and emptied her mug. Quietly she rose, returned to the counter, and purposely moved close to Laric. She paused before him, wooden plate in one hand and mug in the other.

"Excuse me," she said. "I would like more."

He was, as all the men, much taller than she. He looked down at her. "Am I to serve you?"

Bethid drew in a breath. "No, but you can move aside so I can serve myself."

Laric smiled. He moved aside. "You're Bethid."

Slicing bread, she said, "I am."

"My sister wanted to become a courier, but my father and mother made certain she understood it was not for her." A different tone could have made that simple statement offensive. But while there was an undertone of amusement, it was not quite meant at her expense. Yet.

"That is too bad," Bethid said lightly. "It's a hard life, but a good one."

"They told her a woman should only think of marriage and children."

Bethid was aware that Gathlyn, Hallack, and Corrid were no longer speaking. Her back was to them, but she knew they were listening intently, waiting to see how she might respond.

She filled her mug, then turned the spigot to stop the flow. "Well, for most women, that is what they want." Bethid turned, looked up and caught his eye. "But not all."

He watched her walk to the table. "Not for you."

She sat down. "No, not for me." She set down plate and mug. "Of course, it will be difficult for the entire guild, now that the Hecari are here. They won't care if we are men or women. In truth, I might be safer than you; Hecari won't pay any attention to a woman courier." She chewed and swallowed cheese, drank cider. Then looked directly at Laric. "Have they troubled you, the Hecari, when you've been upon the roads?"

Laric grimaced. "They trouble all of us. And I suspect it will get worse. You know they will replace us with their own. The warlord suffers us because his warriors are not yet fluent in Sancorran."

Hallack said quietly, "I can't imagine any warrior will desire courier duty. Carrying messages is much tamer than killing people."

"But," Gathlyn put in, "they will do whatever the warlord orders."

Bethid nodded. Then she asked, trying to sound casual, "Do you think we would have any chance against them? For rebellion, I mean?"

Laric laughed curtly. "There *was* a rebellion. It killed many people, including our own prince."

"No," Hallack said. "That was a war to *defend* Sancorra. Any uprising now would be a rebellion. We must be clear on that."

"Why?" Laric asked. "Both mean the same: Sancorrans die."

Couriers always knew more of politics than most through the nature of their business. Bethid nodded, then set her elbows on the table and interlaced her fingers. "Would a rebellion have a better chance, do you think?"

Laric grunted. "We'd probably die more quickly."

Bethid was aware that Hallack and Gathlyn, older men and veteran couriers, were watching her closely. Hallack's eyes were narrowed. Gathlyn had assumed a perfectly blank expression.

She put a touch of irony in her tone. "I realize it's nothing more than words." She shrugged. "But think of it. Couriers ride throughout Sancorra. Perhaps, if we had aided the prince by finding more soldiers among those living distant from Cardatha, we might have withstood the Hecari." She laughed. "But I'm just a woman . . . I don't know how battles are fought."

Hallack said quietly, "That depends on what kind of battle it is."

Gathlyn rubbed a finger just underneath his bottom lip. She saw him exchange a glance with Hallack.

"A battle's a battle," Laric commented, unimpressed. "And we lost. Thousands died. And perhaps thousands more are leaving Sancorra altogether. There's nothing we could have done then—" He crossed his arms, "—and nothing we can do now."

"No," Bethid said, "probably not. We're too beaten down." And she looked over the rim of her mug at Gathlyn and Hallack as she tipped it up to drink.

Gathlyn smiled faintly. Hallack tilted his head briefly, as if to indicate there might just possibly be another answer.

Corrid, so young, rose to replenish his plate. He did so in quiet and returned to his place. "Seems to me a battle needs messengers, if it's to be won."

Bethid blinked. She looked at Corrid to judge if he had any notion of what he'd said, or if it was nothing more than empty words. He had never struck her as particularly clever.

Laric laughed briefly. "What conqueror in his right mind would allow couriers to aid a rebellion?"

Again, Gathlyn smiled, but with his back to Laric it could not be seen.

Hallack stood up, clearly intending to depart. "Laric's right. There's nothing to be done." He paused a moment. "Here. Or now."

Bethid understood. She saw that Gathlyn did as well. Corrid, she couldn't be certain of; but nothing more would be said—or implied—in front of Laric.

Bethid rose and returned her plate and mug to the sideboard. Idly, she said, "I'm off to see the horse-master."

She was aware that Gathlyn and Hallack followed her with their eyes. Bethid nodded to them as she departed the refectory.

No one would count it much of a beginning, but it was begun. She had seen it in Hallack's eyes and in Gathlyn's.

BRODHI STALLED HIS horse at the Guildhall, then walked across Market Square to the warlord's *gher*. He paused before the three steps leading up to the platform, briefly bowed his head in respect to the *gher*, then climbed and walked across the platform to the door. There he waited, head lowered, staring, as he always did, at the gold strips worked into the intricately carved wood of the door-jamb, and at the threshold made of solid gold. In all, thirty warriors ringed the *gher*. He spoke to those closest to the door.

He quietly said that he was to see the warlord, because the warlord would wish it. All of the warriors knew that. All of them knew him. But there were rituals to follow.

The wait was somewhat longer this time, but eventually a warrior returned, carefully stepping over the threshold so as not to profane it with his unworthy self. Brodhi was told the warlord would see him.

He followed the warrior inside, but knew better than to expect an immediate audience. There had been times when he was made to wait half a day. His activities in Cardatha now depended on the warlord's wishes. It mattered not at all what other things a man might need to do.

Escorted by the warrior, Brodhi passed through room after room separated by brilliant tribal tapestries hanging from carved, red-painted rafters. Suspended, too, were countless banners of different shapes, sizes, and colors; prayer flags of every hue; stone animal fetishes dangling from gold wire. Illumination depended on a multitude of hanging candle racks, but also, in good weather, on the large round opening in the top of the palace.

Admitted to the warlord's audience chamber, Brodhi kept his eyes lowered and turned his palms over to show they were empty. As always, beneath his boots lay thick rugs layered atop one another. Cushions were everywhere. But one lone cushion, a rich, deep red, was squarely placed before the chair from where the warlord ruled.

The man in the chair was perhaps forty. Silvering strands threaded the black, braided scalplock that fell forward over one shoulder, decorative gold clasps running the length. As was the custom, his eyebrows were shaved, golden ear-spools stretched his lobes, and the lower half of his face was tattooed in indigo ink. This day he wore green, and multiple fetish necklaces hung against his chest.

At a gesture, Brodhi took his seat upon the red cushion. The warlord's chair was low to the ground, but the high back arched forward, curving over the warlord's head. Carved, polished wood glinted with inset gemstones.

The warlord was, by Sancorran standards, a very wealthy man, rich in conquered provinces as well as gems and precious metals. But he wanted more, and he continued taking what others had held for hundreds of years. Someday, possibly, the world in its entirety would belong to him.

Brodhi wondered what the warlord would have left to do then. But he kept the thought from his face. He simply waited, palms on his thighs, eyes downcast. It was not for him to begin any conversation.

The warlord's Sancorran was accented, but passable. "Speak."

Brodhi raised his head. He appreciated the man's lack of ceremony and diplomacy; he need not concern himself with either, which among ordinary Sancorrans was expected. "Your warriors are dead."

The warlord's eyes narrowed fractionally. "All four?"

"All four."

"What killed them. You?"

"No, lord. Alisanos took them."

The warlord contemplated him a while. A very long while. Brodhi held his silence. He knew quite well the man was weighing whether he had been told the truth. But Brodhi need not dissemble; he had not killed the warriors.

Eventually the warlord asked, "At this place you call the deepwood?"

"Alisanos. Yes, my lord."

"The Alisanos-deepwood took my warriors?"

"Lord, it did." Brodhi had thoroughly explained about Alisanos and its properties on his previous visit to the warlord. It was why four warriors had been dispatched to accompany him, to see Alisanos as well as the settlement.

"How did it take them?"

"They rode too close."

"You warned them?"

"Indeed, lord. I said it this way: 'Devils abide there, and they will behead, dismember, and eat you.'" As a trained courier, he could easily summon any tone, any inflection or accent. "I am not certain they believed me. I'm not Hecari; why would I tell them the truth?"

A quick flash in the warlord's eyes suggested that reaction entirely believable. He studied Brodhi. "But a man can make it through, yes? You have. Other couriers did. Wagons did."

It came to Brodhi as no surprise that the warlord knew about the party from the settlement. "It's not impassible," Brodhi said. "Merely dangerous if one is not careful and rides too close."

"Four rode too close."

"Yes, lord."

A tone of irony entered the warlord's speech, and it was underscored by a hint of threat. "Were they taken simultaneously? All rode too close at the same moment? Because three would have learned from the death of one not to do as he did."

"Lord, I cannot say. I led the way through. They were behind me." He spread his hands. "Perhaps the three attempted to rescue the one, and so all were taken."

The warlord's lips tightened. "My warriors do not do such. If a man is foolish enough to get himself wounded or captured, he is left to die."

Brodhi waited. It was not his place to ask questions of his own, or to broach any subject.

"Twelve," the warlord said. "Twelve warriors, this time. I will see to it they understand the danger of this Alisanos-deepwood. You will take them through safely so they may learn the truth of this place of many *gher*."

Brodhi inclined his head.

"Go." The warlord made a gesture. "Go to your guild-place."

Brodhi rose silently, briefly bowed his head, then turned to follow a warrior out. Another followed him.

Much as Brodhi detested the idea, he would Send to Rhuan so the people would be warned of the large Hecari party. Somehow, this time, they would have to devise a way to kill twelve of the warlord's men.

DAVYN COULD NOT make his eyes behave. His vision was doubled. He concentrated very hard to merge everything into one image. He was successful, but only briefly.

He had consumed more than one mug of spirits. He recalled being served two, but beyond that he couldn't say. He recalled, also, that at one point he had tipped over his stool and landed on the hardpacked earthen floor. Men had laughed at him but also helped him up, righted his stool, and settled him upon it once more. Hands had clapped him on the back in companionship. And, in bitterness, he had told them his wife was gone, his children were gone, because of the Hecari.

That stopped their laughter.

He asked them why. Why had the warlord decided to conquer Sancorra.

No one answered. And no one looked at him anymore.

Davyn drank. But when he finished his drink the pub-master arrived at his table. This time he did not set down a fresh mug.

"Best you go," he said.

Davyn looked up at him blearily. "What?"

It was said more forcefully. "Best you go. I won't have talk of the Hecari in here. A warrior might come through that door any moment; they do that sometimes. Or a man might see his way to coin rings by telling the warlord we were speaking of Hecari. Do you see? Too dangerous. Go home, farmsteader."

"Home is gone," Davyn told him. "Burned. Hecari did it."

The pub-master bent down, shut a hand around Davyn's upper arm, and yanked him up from the stool. He swung Davyn toward the open door. "Go somewhere. Go out of here. I don't care where. But I won't have you in here."

Davyn stumbled forward as the man pushed him toward the door. He nearly fell but regained his balance with effort. He realized then that he was weeping. With as much dignity and steadiness as he could muster, Davyn made his way out of the pub and into the lane.

It was nearing sunset. Clouds blocked much of the sky. People had begun to go in for the evening. Open windows were shuttered. The lane was nearly empty now. Davyn considered trying another pub, but he remembered that he was to ask for the Red Deer.

He wiped tears with the back of his hand. The cobbles were uneven. He nearly fell twice as he staggered onward toward Market Square. And when he reached it at last, he saw the huge *gher* squatting on its platform. The stands at each corner glowed with candlelight. Davyn, at the cusp between lane and Square, did what Jorda had told him never to do. He stared.

And more: he walked slowly toward the platform. It was difficult to maintain perfect balance, as much as it was difficult to maintain clear vision. But he tried to walk, and he tried to see.

He stopped at the bottom of the three steps leading up to the platform. Warriors encircled the round *gher*, were posted at platform corners. They watched him with fierce black eyes.

Two of them moved toward him.

Davyn said, "I just want to know why—"

He felt no pain as the knife cut through his throat. Blood gushed.

Davyn fell to his knees. The last thing he saw in life was the Shoia courier at the top of the steps, frowning down at him. There was neither pity nor surprise in his eyes. Merely contempt.

RHUAN AND ILONA rode his horse double and led hers to the top of the rise crowned with gray-green stones. The deep-wood was just beyond, close enough to make her nervous.

Rhuan seemed to know what she was thinking. "It's not preparing to move," he said. "I don't feel anything. And the draka's not here; it would be in the air already. Now, can you get down, or should I help you?"

"Just give me the stirrup and your arm."

He did. Ilona, gripping the arm, slid down far enough to catch the stirrup with her left foot. As she swung her right leg over the horse's rump, she let herself down. Rhuan dismounted once she was clear.

Tumbled piles of massive boulders surrounded them. Cracks and crevices abounded, small cave-like openings where stones leaned one against another. Thin, sparse grass grew nearly knee-high. Both horses began to graze as Rhuan tied up the reins so a misplaced hoof would not lead to trouble.

Ilona stood still, closed eyes, and gave herself over to the heart of the place. Silence was absolute. No breath of wind. No insect noise. No birdsong. Even in sunlight, Ilona felt cold. She wished she had a wrap.

Rhuan stepped up beside her. Ilona opened her eyes. "Sadness," she said. "Grief."

He looked at her sharply. "Are you seeing that?"

She shook her head. "No. I just feel it." She turned in a full circle, witness to unknown, unremembered deaths. "People died here, Rhuan."

"The girl was dead before the draka brought her here," he told her quietly. "Not so bad a thing, that."

"No, not the girl. People. But a long time ago." Ilona shivered.

"The girl . . ." She closed her eyes and summoned the images she had seen in the mother's hand. She made herself see again details of the boulders, the shapes, the patterns of how they stood like a throw of oracle bones. Then she opened her eyes and began to pick her way slowly through the crown of stones.

It did not take her long to find what she sought. This stone, there. Another, here. And a crevice between them. Blood. Bone. Worse.

Ilona swung around to stare wildly at Rhuan. "Mother, oh Mother—" She pressed both hands against her mouth. Blood and bone, and offal. The carcass of what had been a young girl. The arch of rib cage, the crushed skull, all clad in torn flesh.

She stumbled two steps, took her hands from her mouth, fell to hands and knees and was violently ill.

"Ilona." He was beside her, squatting. "Ah, 'Lona, I'm sorry." He placed a hand on her bent back, but did not attempt to prevent the heaving or to ease her position. He knew enough to let her do as she had to do without interference, even if well-meant. "I'm so sorry."

For the girl? For her? For both? It didn't matter. It was enough that he was present and that he understood.

When Ilona was fairly certain she was done, she caught up a fold of her skirt and wiped her mouth and tears. She rose shakily, and Rhuan steadied her as he stood.

"We'll go to the horses," he said. "I brought canvas for the task, and rope. You can wait there."

For a moment she wasn't sure what he meant, and then she was. "I should be with you," she told him. "With—her."

" 'Lona, I'll do it. Just wait with the horses."

She shook her head and turned. Took the two steps. Looked again upon the remains.

The world turned black. But she didn't fall. She wasn't faint, she wasn't sick, she wasn't on the verge of collapse. She *saw*.

"Ilona?" She was aware of him, but blind to him. She felt him come up behind her. "Ilona!"

She blinked. The world once more came into view. She looked

again at the remains and felt nothing. She was somehow empty of feelings and full of knowledge.

"Ilona—"

She turned and looked straight into his eyes. "I won't come back, this time."

He was clearly baffled. "What?"

"I won't come back this time."

He frowned down at her. " 'Lona—"

Ilona said distinctly, so no mistake could be made, "I am going to die."

BRODHI, ATOP THE *gher* platform, stared down at the body collapsed upon the steps. It lay face down, turned head resting on the middle step. Mouth and eyes were open. Blood flooded polished wood, ran in rivulets to the cobbles. But no more issued from the opened throat.

"Brodhi, Sweet Mother—" It was Jorda, running across the square.

Brodhi moved quickly. He leaped across the body, landed, ran five steps and planted his hands against Jorda's shoulders. He stopped him completely, then shoved him back several off-balance steps.

"No," he said curtly. "Don't go, Jorda. Leave it be. Don't go near the body. They'll kill you."

Jorda's expression was horrified. "I told him—I *did* tell him . . . 'Don't stare,' I said. 'Don't stare at them.' "

Brodhi took his hands from the karavan-master's shoulders. "He stinks of spirits."

"Oh, Mother!" Jorda clasped the top of his head with both hands. "I thought he understood. I told him. I spoke plain. I thought he understood not to stare at them!"

"He probably did," Brodhi said, "*when* you told him. But he was far gone in spirits. They addle a man's wits."

Jorda scrubbed at his hair as if his scalp itched terribly. "I was moving the wagons to the inn . . . there." He gestured briefly toward the wagons. "He was to meet me there after seeing the city. He was fascinated by the *gher*. I thought he might come here. But never this! Never this!" He appealed to Brodhi. "Why?"

"That," Brodhi remarked, "is what the farmsteader said. 'I just want to know why.' He died because he stared and because he dared to ask that question. He died because he was a fool."

Jorda swung around. He walked two paces, still clasping his head, then spun again to face Brodhi. He let his arms drop to his sides. "Will they allow me to claim the body?"

"I'll tend to it." It was not what Brodhi wished to say or do, but he saw no sense in letting Jorda die as well. "Leave one of the wagons for me. Take the other and go back to the inn."

"Blessed Mother," Jorda said, his voice cracking. "I *did* tell him."

Brodhi did not understand why the karavan-master, who barely knew the farmsteader, was so upset. Humans, it appeared, grieved even for strangers.

"He did what you told him not to do," Brodhi said sharply. "There's no blame for you in this."

"He was my responsibility!"

"On the journey, yes. But not here. Not here." Brodhi paused. "Go now. Pray to your Mother to see him safely across the river, as your people say. I'll find a shroud and wrap the body in it, put it in the wagon. Where is the inn?"

Jorda told him.

Brodhi said, "Go."

He watched as Jorda turned away and began to walk toward the wagons. His steps now were more certain, steadier, and his posture spoke of duties recollected. He was a karavan-master. He had seen worse, faced worse, than what had happened here.

Brodhi turned. Two warriors flanked the farmsteader's body. He glanced at them very briefly, then looked at the cobbles where blood had run. "They have rites," he said to the two, trusting that Hecari did as well. "I'll take him back to his people. The body should not be left to profane the warlord's *gher*."

One of the warriors grunted. "Take. Send to its god."

Brodhi was faintly amused. Trust a Hecari to never even consider that the deity was a woman.

The two warriors bent, took up the body by its arms, and flung it, head lolling, from the steps onto the cobbles.

Brodhi looked at what once had been a man. "Fool," he told the body. "What will your woman say when she learns of this?" He shook his head very slightly, mouth compressed. Dead humans, he thought, always looked so empty.

Something fell lightly against his head. And again. Brodhi looked upward into a darkening sky. The Sancorran's Mother of Moons, be she Maiden, Mother, or Grandmother, was not present.

It had begun to rain.

Epilogue

*D*EMON SMILED. SHE sat outside the hut's low door and watched the girl toddle around on unsteady legs. No longer an infant, was she. Demon's memories, clouded as they were, suggested the girl would be accounted two years old, did she live in the human world.

But she did not. She lived in Alisanos, and its magic was in her.

The child's hair remained flaxen, and her eyes, blue. But the pupils within them had changed. No longer round, they were slitted, like a cat's. Like, too, a demon's.

Soft human flesh naked to the world.

The child stretched her arms toward low-hanging boughs and shrieked, mouth stretched wide in a joyous grin. A strip of delicate golden down ran the length of her spine.

She attempted to run toward the water that was, today, a streamlet. But she stumbled over exposed roots and fell hard onto her face.

Demon expected her to scream, to begin crying, and stood to fetch her from the ground and comfort her as was necessary.

But the girl neither cried nor screamed. She sat up, displaying a scrape on her chin, blood upon her mouth, and shouted in childish rage. Then she struck the root with the flat of one small hand.

The root shriveled. Flaked away into dust.

That pleased the child. She looked at Demon in utter delight, and laughed.

Demon laughed back.

Author's Note

When the film version of *Lord of the Rings* hit theaters, my reaction was that of a major portion of the world's population: I waited in line to see it. Three times. And I hadn't even read the books.

I remember very clearly, at my third and final theater visitation, the reaction of two men who sat a row in front of me. At the conclusion they looked at each other, perplexed. As they spoke to one another, it became clear they had no idea that the film was the first in a trilogy. They believed the conclusion of the first movie was the conclusion, period. And they thought it was a really stupid way to end a movie.

With that memory in mind, I say:

This is not a trilogy.

About the Author

JENNIFER ROBERSON has written 25 novels, primarily fantasy, but also historicals, featuring a reinterpretation of the Robin Hood legend with emphasis on Marian and a Scottish historical novel about the Massacre of Glencoe, when the Campbells attempted to wipe out the MacDonalds. Other work includes a novel set in the Highlander TV universe, *Scotland the Brave*; three anthologies as editor; and a short story collection, *Guinevere's Truth and Other Tales*. In a collaboration with Melanie Rawn and Kate Elliott, Roberson wrote the first section of *The Golden Key*, short-listed for the World Fantasy Award. The first of two new Sword-Dancer novels, *Sword-Bound*, will appear in February 2013.

In 2011, Roberson left behind the snows of Flagstaff, Arizona and moved to Tucson, where she breeds and shows Cardigan Welsh Corgis and creates mosaic artwork.